W9-BIQ-940

The Assassin's Dream

The Assassin's Dream

J. D. Townsend

Five Star • Waterville, Maine

First Edition
First Printing: March 2005

Published in 2005 in conjunction with
Tekno Books and Ed Gorman.

Set in 11 pt. Plantin by Minnie B. Raven.

Printed in the United States on permanent paper.

Library of Congress Cataloging-in-Publication Data

Townsend, J. D. (James Denny)
    The assassin's dream / by J.D. Townsend.—1st ed.
        p. cm.
    ISBN 1-59414-282-3 (hc : alk. paper)
    1. Young women—Fiction.   2. Matriarchy—
Fiction.   3. Assassins—Fiction.   I. Title.
PS3620.O9595A94 2005
    813´.6—dc22   2004062490

For Belle

PART I

Chapter 1

Angela had known this moment could come. Still, it jarred her so that she had to clamp her jaw against the dark wave that rose from her gut.

At least she would not spend her last moments in some psychiatric ward being plied with the latest in pharmacological mayhem.

At least there were her children.

At least the work would go on.

The irony of it sat bitterly in the back of her throat. That they would send one of her own genetic masterpieces, one that would soon awaken—might already be awakening.

A honking horn from the street five stories below interrupted her thoughts. No time to waste. She swallowed hard and pushed herself up from the console chair. In the bedroom, she fished in the closet for her favorite suit. While she changed clothes, she mentally composed a message to her son and daughter. Her fingers trembled as she buttoned the blazer, but she willed them to do her bidding.

In the bathroom, she found the bottle of stimulants she occasionally had used during long shifts at the lab. She took four. She would need to be very, very alert.

Back in the living room, she sat before the monitor that occupied much of the wall and stared at the image of waves marching endlessly onto a deserted shore, their last act a gasp before collapsing into formlessness and receding back into the ocean. She barely noticed, remembering instead the distorted image that had appeared there less than an hour ago, and had told her who was coming.

She forced the picture from her mind and thought instead of her children's faces, the strength she often saw there, the promise.

She squeezed her eyelids shut, willing herself to stay in the moment, cleared her throat, and spoke. "Message . . . Parker and Pamela." The seascape disappeared from the screen, replaced with a single word, "Ready."

"Begin," she said.

"Hello Pamela. Hello Parker. I just wanted to say hi, and let you know how much I love you both. It's a beautiful evening here, and I've been remembering some silly stuff from when we all lived together. Missing you, I guess."

"Pause." Angela pushed back the tide of grief rising in her chest. When she regained her composure, she spoke a few trial sentences out loud. When she was sure she had regained the lighthearted tone, she said in a flat voice, "Resume."

"I hope everything is well with you, Pam. Have you decided where to do your residency yet? Even though I've told you I'd like to see you do it at the Weil Center, don't pay any attention to your old mom. You know as well as I do that just because I graduated from there doesn't make it any better than some of the others you've been considering. Just follow your instincts, darling. I know you'll make the right choice.

"And Parker, I saw you last week in the Hemispheric Exhibition games. Wow! You were magnificent! Some of my colleagues even called to tell me they'd seen it. I'm sure the brotherhood was proud of you. I sure was. I wouldn't be surprised to see you go on to the World Games and win the gold."

She forced herself to smile. "Oh, and before I forget,

when you get out to New Phoenix for the regionals, I want you to look up Mother Avalon at the Southwest Council residence hall in Old Town. I've given her something special for you. She'll be expecting you."

Angela paused the recording again, and heaved an exasperated, quivering sigh. How difficult it was to sound casual about something so important. And how futile to try to convey a lifetime of love in a single message. She pinched the bridge of her nose, screwed up her courage, and began again.

"Well, you kids be good. Remember that I love you and that I'm counting on you to do us all proud . . ." She managed another smile. "See you next time you're back in the Plex."

She choked out the final "Stop," and this time the tears came, and she made a sound like a wounded animal, her face contorting in such a way that her own children may not have recognized it. Eventually, she uttered the word "Send," that would forward the messages to the children she would never see again.

She recorded another long message, and afterward spent five minutes setting up the complicated instructions that would replay the message on the wall monitor in her bedroom only after she released the remote trigger, and then expunge it from all records.

By 23:30 everything was ready. She stood up, walked on shaky legs to the bedroom, propped pillows against the bed's headboard, and settled in for the coming visit, her senses tuned to every small noise in the house.

Chapter 2

Through the dimly lit hallway, Kay Black neared the client's door, quietly breathing in the lingering molecular signature from the scent card the Ministry had issued with her orders. She liked the intimacy that scent recognition brought. It deepened her focus, gave her an appreciation of the gifts she had been given and the sacredness of the task at hand. It was in these moments she felt almost as though she were dancing with the client. Or that both were being danced by destiny.

She was tightly focused now. A few moments before she had nearly encountered a woman coming down the stairwell she was climbing. A close call. Being seen in so isolated a setting could have compromised the evening's mission, but Kay ducked into a doorway until the woman passed. She had never failed a mission, nor even had to come back a second time due to some oversight or unforeseen circumstance. She vowed such a thing would not happen, either tonight or in the future. She had trained too long and hard to fall prey to a mistake that could mar her spotless record.

As she neared the client's door, Kay inwardly repeated a passage from The Text:

As the hour of your duty is upon you, give praise, for it is in this moment that you are consecrated unto the Whole Body . . .

She slipped her TeleSlate from the bag, inserted the sensor into the port in its side, and touched it to the lock on the door. Three seconds later, the screen indicated that the electronic locking system had been identified and disabled. Kay replaced the Slate in the bag, and took out a device that to anyone else would have appeared to be a laser pen. It was not. It was a device which released a dart infused with a chemical that instantly paralyzed the heart. The dart would dissolve in seconds, leaving no trace. Death would appear to have been by natural causes.

Inwardly she chanted . . . *Deliverer of death, sustainer of life, shepherd of the sacred balance, sing the Song of Deliverance and be joyful, for now is the Will made manifest and the future assured.*

With her left hand, Kay turned the doorknob so slowly that someone watching it from the inside would scarcely have noticed the movement. When the doorknob would no longer turn, she eased the door inward—a quarter inch, a half inch. No additional mechanical lock barred her entrance. As the edge of the door cleared the jamb, Kay stopped. Light from the apartment poured into the hallway. Not good. It was nearly 03:00. Everyone should have been asleep. It was rare for Kay to encounter anyone awake in these early morning missions.

She focused her attention on hearing, letting the sounds sort themselves out in her mind—the soft whir of appliances, far away traffic noises from the street, the slight hiss of air being circulated through the building's vent systems. Her own blood was audible as it pulsed through her veins, and the ineffable pitch of her own being. Nothing she heard indicated anyone was in the room beyond the door.

There was the scent, though. Angela Potemkin lived here, there was no doubt.

. . . *As the hour of your duty is upon you, give praise* . . .

Kay leaned into the door again, and the crack widened far enough for her to see the edges of several pieces of furniture. Another inch and it was evident the room was unoccupied.

Just then the air in the elevator shaft at the end of the hallway began whistling through the closed doors as its car rose from below. It would not do to be seen if someone were to get out on this floor. With a single swift move, she was inside Potemkin's apartment easing the door shut behind her, simultaneously scanning the room. The lights were on, but either no one was here or they were in some other room, perhaps asleep.

Her eyes fell on a doorway to her right off the small living room. It was partly open, the room beyond brightly lit. Kay knew, though she could not have explained why, that the client was beyond that door, and awake. Her cells resonated with the knowledge, sharpening her state of readiness, stilling her mind. Hyperalert now, she could feel the client now as clearly as she could feel the steady heartbeat in her own chest.

. . . *for now is the Will made manifest and the future assured* . . .

Kay crept on the balls of her feet toward the door, her weapon at ready. When she arrived, her fingertips settled on its smooth surface as gently as an insect alighting on a flower. She increased the pressure ever so gradually until she could feel the door begin to give. No resistance, nothing further to impede her. She inhaled a deep, silent breath and shoved.

She saw the eyes first.

They were sky-blue and wide with fear, riveted on Kay's face. In an instant, everything else registered in Kay's keen senses. Angela Potemkin faced her from the opposite side of the room, atop a bed, propped up against pillows, clothed in an elegant suit. In her right hand, a small, black object.

Time shifted, taking on the curiously slow quality it did on those rare occasions when Kay encountered imminent danger. Her mind registered every detail—the stitching on the red shoulder blazes of Potemkin's suit, the fall of coarse blond hair over the woman's forehead, the beady texture of the bedspread upon which she lay, the bloodless whites of Potemkin's fingernails as she clutched the object in her hand.

But it was the eyes she would remember. There was no surprise in them. Rather, they reached across the chasm between them with a knowing and fierce determination to communicate. Potemkin raised her left hand in Kay's direction, palm out, in the universal gesture of one who wants something that is about to happen to stop, and Kay saw her mouth open to form a word.

By then, though, Kay's training was in full control. The object in Potemkin's other hand could be a weapon, and Kay leveled her own at the woman's heart, her thumb squeezing the trigger. As the perfectly aimed dart whispered out of the barrel, Kay heard the woman's voice drift to her across the room.

"Kay, wait," she said.

But death would not wait. In an instant, Potemkin's hand fell back to the position from which it had come and her head fell forward onto her chest, her body emptied of its animating force like a sail gone slack in doldrums.

Kay stood transfixed, visualizing those two impossible words slowly falling from Angela Potemkin's lips as her slack right hand opened, revealing a device Kay now recognized to be a simple remote.

She could not possibly have heard her name uttered aloud in this place. And yet the wall monitor to her left flashed, and the image of the woman whom Kay had only just seen for the first time began to speak in clear, forceful tones.

"Hello, Kay. Please sit down. I have some things to tell you . . ."

The next words Kay heard made her feel as though she had been seized by a great hand and shaken until her teeth rattled in her head.

Chapter 3

Something different about this one, Aria Helsing thought as she turned the holograph in her hand at different angles and prepared to go under.

There was little in the image to distinguish this woman from the dozen other K-class women she had been assigned to read and report on since coming to the North American Council. It was one of the reasons they presented a special challenge to her. Still, something pulled at her attention like a buried memory.

Natural-borns were far easier to read, Aria thought ruefully, but there were few enough of them anymore. These K-class women rather frightened her. When she turned her inner attention on them and they began to yield their pictures, it was not easy to stay present. It was their lack of emotional depth and feeling that made Aria want to squirm, to let go of the reading state and return to waking consciousness. The last one of these killing machines she'd read had such a pure calculating quality about her, and such a razor-like sense of dedication that it had taken Aria hours to shake off the burning feeling in her chest. And the urgency with which K-class women moved into the killing mode reminded Aria of the heat of sexual passion. Maybe that's what it was, sexual fire in the service of death.

She chided herself inwardly. You're going to talk yourself right out of a job here, Aria. Not a wise idea. It was a privilege, after all, being here. She had jumped at the chance to interview for the position, having no real idea

17

how much it would change her life. It was an arena that few of her sisters had dreamed of.

Having to curtail contacts with her old friends and family was something of a disappointment, but the romance of being one of the elite had tweaked her ambition. Occasionally she missed the easy friendships she had known before coming here, though.

Her biggest shock had come when, after six months, she had been called into a private meeting with Mother Gretel, the council's head for the last nine years, and informed of the existence of the K-class. Mother Gretel had handed her the dossier on one of these women, and Aria remembered how the two top aides in the office had stared at her as Mother Gretel spoke, watching for signs of hesitancy. It had taken effort for Aria to mask her feelings. Later, alone in her quarters, she let down her inner guard and felt like she'd been mugged.

Like most everyone, she was unaware that the North American Council used assassination as a means to maintain its vast power. Governments had always had some shadow elements like this, she knew, secret organizations that carried out operations abroad or at home. Some probably required killing to prevent other, greater problems from happening. But she really had thought that was ancient history, a kind of inevitable byproduct of men being in charge of things, and that hadn't been the case for the better part of a century, not since Acquired Genetic Neurological Syndrome had killed nearly two-thirds of the male population.

It was only natural to think that women would do a better job of running things, Aria thought. And they had. Despite the daunting environmental challenges in the 22nd century—the filoviruses like Ebola and Marburg jumping continents; the climate shifts, the melting of most of the ice caps, and destruction of millions of the oceans' life forms; the rampant bone, blood, and respiratory cancers that long ago had reversed the trend toward longer lifespan—the world was getting better. There were far fewer wars nowadays, all on a small regional scale, and this was undoubtedly due to fewer men being in the world.

There were the doubters, of course, those who thought that humanity was fighting a losing battle with nature. Medical science had done wonders in the field of genetics in the last hundred years, but no sooner than it had conquered one malady, three more would emerge. The world simply was changing, Aria thought, and the Whole Body, the conference of Regional Councils, was doing a pretty good job of protecting the quality of life in the face of such challenges. Most everyone had enough to eat now. Weather manipulation made many of the world's arid places productive. Except for those places in the Third World that clung to tribal customs and economies, the world was more civilized than it had ever been, wasn't it?

So, Aria thought, those who bore the responsibility in the Whole Body had to make hard choices. She supposed the existence and use of the K-class was one of them. She had no idea at whom the council unleashed this whole class of engineered killers. Truthfully, she didn't want to know. Too much responsibility to bear. She was inclined to trust in the motives and intelligence of those in charge to use such power for the benefit of the Whole Body.

Still, having an entire class of women whose sole purpose in life was to carry out assassinations begged some questions, but Aria usually just put them aside.

After all, her life was good here, vastly more interesting than it had been in civilian life. She now had her own private quarters in the council complex, a travel allowance, even Class A access to Sexual Services, something she'd never been able to afford. She had quickly made acquaintances among the sub-council roster, although interaction with them was certainly less free than it had been with her old friends. Early on, she'd understood that her every action was scrutinized by many, and that she must be careful. She wasn't the only one with strong ambitions. Unguarded statements might be used against her by someone who coveted her position.

And she was no fool. Other readers surely were being assigned to read her, maybe even ones from her own sisterhood.

Aria took a sip of her tea, which had grown lukewarm during her musings, and frowned. Time to get to work. She set the cup on the table next to her chair, held the holograph of the young woman close to her face, and said aloud the designation printed under it: "K-1754 . . . a.k.a. Kay Black." Oftentimes the name of the subject had a certain resonance that would help get into the reading. The number designations given the K-class women were often less than useful to her, so she always spoke their public name too. This one evoked a little twinge. Yes, something slightly different here.

Then she took a deep breath, felt her shoulders and face relax, burned the image into her mind, and closed her eyes. She allowed the sound of Kay Black's name and her image to drift down through the strata of her inner being. In these moments, Aria felt as though she enfolded the person she was reading, holding them ever so lightly with her being. Her own thoughts grew distant.

The first image came—the inside of a large auditorium. She was surrounded by young girls whose attention was riveted at the front of the room. Aria felt the pull of their focus, like a field of reeds bending in the same direction beneath a wind. She let herself bend as well, and caught the vague impression of an imposing figure at a podium, a stocky woman who seemed to be speaking, though Aria heard no words. She felt their power, though, and sensed that this was some sort of initiation ceremony, one that left a deep impression on K-1754. Aria's own heart tingled with the adolescent's soaring idealism.

In the manner of a dream, the vision shifted to a large bird of prey circling a lush landscape, in search of living prey below. The scene intermingled with the ceremony, and Aria looked around at the shining faces of young women— plain and bland but for the sparkle of rapt attention the eyes revealed. The hum of sacred devotion was unmistakable. The girls embraced the speaker's words as though they held the essence of life.

A change. A large book lay open before her, and Aria assumed it was The Text. She felt the ardor of the woman reading it, sensed long hours spent poring over it, memorizing its contents, felt the awe the reader held for the book, and her tremendous capacity for retention. A powerful vitality lay in this young woman. Aria sensed rigorous physical and mental training, long hours spent mastering the arts of stealth, and heightened awareness, exhaustion, determination. There was passion—Aria felt it as inner heat— and that swelling in the chest that bespoke righteous pride in work well done.

Faces came then, dozens of them, mostly women but an occasional man, some motionless—as if remembered only as a holograph or seen sleeping—a few animated with surprise or fear. Likely the faces of Kay Black's clients in the moment before darkness fell upon them, Aria realized in an isolated corner of her mind. She carefully nudged herself toward the assassin's emotional ranges, feeling into them like one might test water before immersing oneself. Clearest was the satisfying, visceral tug of devotion, and the nectar-like sweetness of pride. Only vague feelings of warmth or attachment.

Aria held the tension between these experiences and her own identity, aware that she was both the person she was reading and herself. From this latter part of her psyche, she understood that the assassin had no real appreciation of her clients beyond her own projections, little real empathy for them as living beings. They were objects of Kay Black's own faith, Aria sensed, a means to express devotion to the cause to which she was born.

Aria continued to drift through myriad impressions, making mental notes and listening hard for other clues to the assassin's character. From out of the shifting miasma of faces adrift before her inner eye, one suddenly loomed large, filling her field of vision. A middle-aged woman, short blond hair, high cheekbones, haunted, wide-set blue eyes. For an instant, it was animated, beseeching. In the next, it was flat, lifeless. Confusion filled the atmosphere, and Aria felt the solid ground of the assassin's psyche become gelatinous.

Intriguing new ground, Aria thought. She wanted to know more about this event and its effect on the assassin. Her intention manifested instantly as she felt herself falling deeper into the darker substrata of the young woman's being. A sound, a sort of oscillation, began to hum in her inner ear, growing from a faint thrumming until it vibrated in the deep pockets within her being. Like how a massive bell might sound underwater. Fascinating.

And irresistible. Aria floated through a gray mist toward

the sound, and something more—a light less seen than felt. Aria began to feel as though she was expanding at her center, pushing gently but firmly against the outer atmosphere, as the hum grew louder. In her mind's eye, she drifted upward and turned to look down at her body. At its center, she saw the faintest violet glow.

Something new here, seductive and rich. A part of her tried to resist, but it only strengthened the lure, as though a hole had opened somewhere and was sucking up the atmosphere around her. A tiny twinge of panic tickled her stomach.

Her boundaries were going, she realized. One moment she was the reader, the next Kay Black. It was like being spun around while wearing a blindfold. But she could still see, and the images came too fast to analyze. She began feeling bloated, like a balloon filling with air. She wondered momentarily if she would burst. The light at her core became painfully bright, and yet she could not look away. Voices came then, from out of the light—hundreds of them, thousands—men's and women's, speaking simultaneously, urgently. The words were indistinct, but the chorus was insistent, excited, a crowd growing restless, waiting . . . for what or whom she couldn't tell.

Things were happening at such a pace and her emotions whipping so quickly between fear and exhilaration that she couldn't focus. A great sense of portent arose in her. Her skin prickled in anticipation. She felt as though she might scream, join the chorus. Spinning upward in a massive whirlpool, rising . . . spinning . . . faster . . .

A noise sliced the atmosphere and her eyelids flew open. In that split second, the vision collapsed, disappearing as though someone had turned off a light. She slumped back in her chair. She hadn't realized she was sitting at attention.

Her breath came in short gasps, and her body felt like a puzzle scrambling to fit itself together. Again the noise came, and she recognized it as the call tone on the wall monitor. But why was it ringing? She always set the unit to "no ring" before beginning a reading. Then she realized the only call that would bypass it would be a call from the Council Mother's office.

Her heart beating furiously, Aria stood and carefully made her way to the console. She sat down and with her thumb momentarily rubbed the skin between her thick, dark eyebrows, calming herself. When she touched the answer button, the image of Desta Mardrid, one of Mother Gretel's two top aides, appeared on the screen.

"Mother will see you at once in her chambers," the woman said. Her diction was precise and her tone emotionless. "Be prepared to report on your most recent readings."

"Certainly," Aria said, hoping she sounded casual but respectful. "I'll be there momentarily."

She clicked off and sat motionless, though her insides were still spinning. Report to Mother Gretel? The Council Mother had only asked for her twice before, and never for direct reports. She closed her eyes and caught again the fading image of herself expanding, on the verge of . . . what? Later, Aria. No time now.

She realized she was still clutching the holograph of K-1754 between thumb and forefinger. She was reluctant to look at it again. Even thinking about it made her feel like she was being lifted by a swell on an invisible sea.

And what will I say about this one? she wondered.

Chapter 4

Aria paused before entering Council Mother's chambers and smoothed her thick hair. Her fingertips touched the eye-shaped garnet pin that held in place the long tresses that otherwise would fall forward, obscuring the outlines of her prominent cheekbones. The precious stone at the pin's center, weighty and bordered with mother of pearl and ivory, was a gift from her mother and from her mother's mother before her.

One of her mother's many pieces of advice came back to Aria at that moment: "Trust in your inner strengths, my darling, and don't be afraid of fear. You come from a long line of women for whom fear was an aphrodisiac." Aria smiled at the memory. She had been raised in the same sisterhood as her mother, and she knew she had been blessed with fine gifts of vision and intuitive sensitivity, and that these had been honed by the best training in the world. Without the vulnerabilities inherent with her gifts, she would not have the ability to do what she did. But there was strength in that knowledge . . . and power.

In the fifteen-minute walk from her quarters, she had determined a course of action and she was more confident now about her presentation. Her previous audiences with Mother Gretel had always left her feeling as though she should have presented herself better, though. For hours afterwards, she would think of things she might have said, or wonder if Mother had been insinuating something.

She checked the dossiers for the third time to make sure

she had brought them all. They represented the last five women she had read remotely. Kay Black's was at the bottom of the stack. She conjured from her memory the inner sound of flowing water to soothe her, stepped in front of the retinal identifier beside the door, and spoke her name. The door slid open and Aria stepped into the deserted outer chamber, waiting to be called.

A moment later the inner door opened and the unsmiling Desta Mardrid motioned her with a small jerk of her head to come inside. The aide was peculiarly arranged, Aria thought for the hundredth time as she slid past the familiar, angular figure with a nod. Mardrid's square chin, prominent thin nose, and deep-set hazel eyes always gave Aria the impression of a rough-hewn sculpture. She had never seen Mardrid's face express anything beyond suspicion, calculation, or cool anger. She knew the aide had a strong sense of her own importance.

Mother Gretel sat behind a huge teakwood desk, a rarity these days, against the facing wall of the chamber. She was a large woman, broad in the face and shoulders. The dark red robe she wore revealed the outline of her thick upper arms under the drape of its fabric, and her enormous breasts. Her small brown eyes were set close astride a short, sharp nose. Her mouth was thin-lipped and tightly closed, more a gash than a feature. Severe brown braids wound from the back of her head to the front, creating a wreath-like crown that further emphasized the imposing size of her head.

Early on, Aria believed Mother to be in her mid-thirties, but since then she had taken notice of the woman's skin, which seemed stretched too tightly across the broad expanse of her face. At certain angles, it gave her face the appearance of a mask, and Aria now thought Mother could even be in her forties.

On the wall beyond, the six-foot-diameter mandala of the Whole Body framed Mother's figure, unnecessarily announcing her authority. The circle enclosed a perfect square, and at the center of the square, a smaller circle was divided into dark and light halves by a wavy line. Twelve recessed channels radiated from the outside edges of the smaller circle to the border of the square. Something about the design always made Aria feel like snapping to attention.

A second aide, Barena Colter, sat in one of the three chairs against the wall to Mother's right, one leg crossed over the other, reading some papers in her lap. Mardrid moved to Mother's left and stood quietly, surveying Aria.

Mother raised her eyes from the monitor inlaid horizontally in her desk, punched off the desk monitor with a stubby finger, and turned her full attention to Aria.

"You are ready to report on your last five assignments?" Her contralto voice easily filled the room.

"Yes, Mother. Shall I begin?"

Mother ignored the question, continuing to stare at Aria, the fingers of her right hand keeping time on the desk to some inner rhythm. After a long pause she said, "You've been with us for just over a year now. What do you have to say about your experience?"

Less than a minute here, and already Aria felt the urge to squirm under Mother's steady gaze. Unconsciously she shifted her weight to her left foot and grasped the dossiers with both hands so that they covered the front of her hips.

"Well," she began tentatively, "it has been exhilarating, Mother. I am honored to be working for you, and the Whole Body of course, and have learned a great deal since I began."

"Such as?" Mother sounded bored.

"Such as?" Aria repeated, knowing before the words left

her mouth that the repetition sounded foolish.

Mother screwed up the left side of her mouth in irritation and brushed an unseen speck of dust from the monitor beneath her hands. "I want to know specifically what you have experienced, and what you have learned." She spoke as if talking with a slow child. "Proceed . . . please." She folded her blocky hands, resting them on the desk in front of her, and bored down on Aria with her gaze.

Aria realized that she was now clutching her left bicep, her forearm resting protectively across her breasts. It was a defensive posture, a dead giveaway that she was intimidated, but she could not help herself. She frowned in concentration, searching for an appropriate response, then recalled something she had seen in the first month of having arrived at Council Headquarters.

She is walking in the main corridor on her way to her quarters. In a corner of the high-ceilinged hall, she notices Desta Mardrid and a lesser aide whose name she does not know arguing. Their voices are quiet, but Mardrid is gesticulating fiercely, pointing at the woman's chest and scowling. The second woman is clearly under duress, but making an attempt to defend herself.

At the end of the hallway, a large door slides open and Mother's imposing figure fills it, a security detail at her side. The object of Mardrid's venom, who is facing in the direction of Mother's approach, goes slightly pale and drops her hands to her sides. Mardrid catches the change and steals a backward glance over her shoulder. When she sees Mother, she turns, puts on a thin smile, and bows slightly from the waist. The second woman follows suit and Mother stops in front of the pair, looking at them without speaking. Mother turns to Mardrid and says something in a low voice. Mardrid blanches visibly, bows slightly, and then follows in Mother's wake as Mother continues on to wherever she is going. After a dozen steps, Mardrid shoots a withering look over her shoulder, but the woman for whom it is intended has already fled the scene.

If she told this story, Aria knew, she would be treading on dangerous ground. But nothing else came to her. Seconds passed and, reluctantly, she began recounting the event aloud, her knees going rubbery. When she came to the end of the story, a thick silence hung in the room, and Mother leaned back in her chair.

In a conspiratorial tone, Mother said, "And what was it that you learned from this?"

Aria gathered her courage and crossed the invisible line.

"Mother is blessed with strong intuition, and misses little that goes on around her. This talent serves the Whole Body well since she bears responsibility for so many. That she demonstrates this prowess so aptly is a key stabilizing force that underlies the importance and authority of the council." With a quick sidelong glance at Mardrid, she added, "And Mother is hardest on those who are closest to her, holding them to a higher standard than others." Aria knew she had hit just the right balance of diplomacy and truth when Mother's small mouth curled into a smile.

"Yes, vigilance, tedious as it becomes at times, is often Mother's most important role." It was the least harsh tone of voice Aria had ever heard from the woman; she seemed almost tender in that moment. Then Mother's smile dropped away as she shot Mardrid a sour look. Another uncomfortable silence followed.

Aria shifted, felt the weight of the dossiers in her hand, and tried for a diversion. "Would you like to hear my report on these women now, Mother?"

Gretel turned her gaze back to Aria. "Not just yet." There was a mischievous glint in her eye. "I would rather hear your impressions of my two aides here." Her mouth twisted again into a tight, wry smile.

Aria's heart crept into her throat. She opened her mouth to protest, but thought better of it. She stole a look at Barena Colter, who had stopped reading and was looking bemused by the turn of events. From her other side, Aria could feel a wave of anger coming from Mardrid. Aria visualized an inner protective barrier and took another deep breath.

"This would be a very difficult undertaking in these circumstances, Mother," she said, hoping her tone was respectful and that Mother was not completely serious.

Gretel's easy demeanor disappeared, however, replaced with a fishy stare and imperious tone of voice. "It is not a request. Colter first."

Aria swallowed against the sudden dryness in her throat and turned to face the aide on her left. She had had only two brief encounters with this stocky blond woman, the first during the interviews for this position, and the second when Colter had personally handed her the dossiers of the two lower functionaries, telling her to report to Mother the next day. Both meetings had left Aria with a feeling of respect for Colter. The aide had been forthright and taciturn, but there had been no hint of condescension. Aria had long ago decided she liked her.

Aria opened her feelings, closed her eyes and pulled Colter's image inside, silently repeating her name. Warmth began spreading in the middle of her chest, and a feeling she should stand more erect, her shoulders back. In the briefest flash of a vision, she saw Colter holding up a corner of a high ceiling. In the next instant, she saw schedules and calendars, meticulously plotted and orderly. Aria's vision shifted, as though she were now looking through Colter's eyes at Mother, felt a magnetic pull in her being like true north on a compass needle, felt the sense of honor Colter had at being in Mother's service.

Aria drew in a deep breath and willed her mind to be still—she seldom analyzed until she had received a full complement of sensory images. Inwardly she repeated the name—Barena Colter. In an instant she began to feel a deep sadness, a tender wound, and felt herself to be very young . . . a girl . . . hurt by others who seemed to have no ideals, uncomfortable but resigned to making compromises—perhaps many of them—in order to serve the Whole Body. The specifics were buried too deep for such a hasty reading, but from the place where Aria stood apart from the subject she was reading, she felt compassion for Colter.

The face of a young woman appeared briefly, one who bore a resemblance to Colter, and then disappeared, trailed by a feeling of wistfulness. Then Aria caught an acrid odor of sweat, and successive flashes of men's bodies, felt their weight upon her, their brute strength and the delicious sensation of their penetration.

A moment later, Aria stepped back into the part of herself that could put words to her experiences and began speaking in a soft voice, her eyes still closed.

"Balance. Integrity. Devotion. Her respect for Mother is a deep, steady current. She's highly organized and successfully separates the personal from the public, strives to be fair and just in her dealings with others. She is proud of her strength, both physical and mental, proud of her ability to juggle many tasks. Sometimes troubled by others' personal ambition in the face of public responsibility. There's little in her that can identify with such behavior. Among her greater fears is making a mistake that would hurt those for whom she is responsible.

"In the personal arena, her physical mother . . . perhaps it's her grandmother . . . is the prominent role model in her life. I sense a line of public service stretching back for many generations. And she has a daughter . . . her name is from ancient scriptures . . . Sarah, I believe . . . whom she has not heard from in some time, but she maintains a steady concern for her daughter's welfare and choices. She utilizes Sexual Services on occasion, but insists repeatedly on only perhaps three males for whom she feels particular affinity."

Aria opened her eyes and saw Colter fold her hands in front of her and look down, an expression that spoke of modesty and a little embarrassment. When Aria turned again to look at Mother, she saw the ghost of a smile had re-appeared.

"Correct in general, and perhaps many specifics as well," Mother said. She turned to Colter. "And how is Sarah now-adays, Barena?"

"Sarah is fine, I believe," the aide responded. "I haven't heard from her in a while, but I know she's in the Western Region now completing her government studies fellow-ship."

"That's good," Mother Gretel said. "I hope your daughter may someday come to work in this place." Aria felt that she meant it.

Aria breathed easier.

"It seems they have advised me well in the matter of your employment here, Helsing." Mother motioned with her hand, indicating her two aides. "And now Mardrid."

Aria forced herself to look at Mardrid. The aide stood erect, her hands clasped behind her back, her sharp chin jutting slightly forward. Her eyes betrayed nothing. Bolstered by Mother Gretel's comment, Aria inwardly dissolved the imaginary protective barrier she had erected when she felt Mardrid's anger surface, and pulled the woman's image inside of her, again closing her eyes.

For a moment, she was drifting alone in a gray space. Then slowly, faint images began appearing as if from behind a gauzy veil. Aria thought she glimpsed a figure playing in a field. A young Mardrid? There were other figures, boys perhaps, running and jumping. Some sort of athletic play, perhaps, but the image was so indistinct she couldn't be sure.

A clearer vision of a woman Aria had never seen arose next, and then, the image was surrounded by dozens of others, turning and flashing in a way that reminded Aria of the colored shapes inside a kaleidoscope she had owned as a child. Each angle suggested a different aspect of the unknown woman, like holographs taken at moments when the subject was unaware he or she was being observed. Some of the faces bore a look of guilt, the stark vulnerability of having been found out and exposed publicly. Others bore an expression of deep concentration, and still others the bland look of those whose emotions have atrophied from long hours of drudgery. The mandala of the North American Council appeared as it appeared on currency flashed into Aria's mind, and on its heels came the insight that these people had worked under Mardrid's supervision, and dealt with money in some form.

The image slipped away and again Aria found herself floating in dark mist without direction. A small wave of anxiety rippled through her, and she took in a slow breath and exhaled, willing the reappearance of Mardrid's image. What happened next would forever change Aria's sense of her own powers.

First, sharp, pointed teeth flashed across her vision, startling her and causing her breath to catch in her throat. Then in the next instant, as if she were standing before a mirror, Aria was looking at herself. A wavy, liquid-like vertical line began descending from a point above her head, and she could feel her scalp begin to creep as the line touched her there and continued downward, bisecting the image. Something had begun to squeeze the air from her chest. Her eyes fell to the place between the breasts of her mirror image, and she watched in growing horror as a shadowy, worm-like shape took form there, pushing outward and upward in a sinuous, undulating dance toward the face—her face—in the mirror. She tried harder to inhale, but the atmosphere had become so fetid that she nearly gagged. As a result, she lost the remaining air in her lungs and the steady weight on her chest rendered another breath impossible.

She tried to turn away, but her reflection remained perfectly still, hands at sides, eyes fixed straight ahead. The blunt tip of the worm that had sprung from the reflection's chest began sprouting tiny nubs that waved like newborn maggots, stretching toward her face.

Aria struggled for even a single breath as she watched the nubs develop angles and a solid base, and she recognized the growth as a hand—a human hand—black and slimy though it still was. A carved gold band protruded from around the index finger. Claw-like now, the bony horror reached for her face as if it would crumple the features there like so much petropaper. Aria didn't so much see as feel the light leaving, everything becoming dim, falling away . . .

Then it was gone. Just like that. No more pressure, no more hand. It was as if the door on a crypt in which she had been mistakenly buried had just been flung open, and she gasped through her open mouth for the sweet, refreshing air that now felt cool on her moist face. She opened her eyes and saw Mardrid before her, unchanged from the posture and cynical expression she had when Aria went under.

Mother was looking at her too, her large head tilted a little to the side. Aria looked down and was dismayed to see the five dossiers she had been holding lying at her feet. She had no idea when she had dropped them. She felt her face flush and she quickly bent and scooped up the folders.

"I'm sorry, Mother. I . . . I don't quite know what just happened. I'm feeling a little woozy."

Mother's face registered no sympathy and she said nothing, but simply continued to examine Aria as a scientist might examine a life form under a neutron microscope.

Dossiers safely back in hand now, Aria looked again at Mother, trying to breathe evenly.

"Well?" Mother said.

Aria realized Mother expected a report, despite the trauma she had just undergone. Aria pinched her eyebrows between her fingers, now damp with sweat, trying to recall anything from before the moment when she saw her own re-flection. All she could remember was the kaleidoscope cen-tered on the unknown woman, and the vague image of boys in a field.

"Gifted analytically, able to dissect a person's character or a situation on many levels at once. Highly competitive, probably unusually athletic in her youth . . ." she paused, grasping for anything else to say. "I believe she has been in charge of some accounting function here." After another long moment, she knew she couldn't fake this.

"I'm sorry, Mother. I can't ever remember such a fruit-less reading. I . . . perhaps I could try again when I'm feeling a little stronger. May I please sit down?"

To Aria's relief, Mother waved her heavy arm toward a chair on the side of the room where Colter sat. Putting distance between herself and Mardrid felt good.

"It is part of her talent," Mother said.

Lowering herself to the edge of the chair, Aria looked at Mother uncomprehendingly.

"One of the things I value in Mardrid," Mother explained, "is her inscrutability. There are many eyes and ears here at headquarters, and there are times when it doesn't serve the Whole Body for anyone else to know Mother's plans. At those times, Mother can give directions to Mardrid or share with her without worrying about others getting any hint of it. Do you understand?"

Aria stole a look at Mardrid, who at that moment brought her right hand from behind her back and laid it flat against the space between her small breasts. Aria's gaze fell to the index finger on that hand, and she was startled to see there the carved gold band she had seen in the horrific vision moments before.

She understood then. Mardrid had done something no one else in Aria's experience had ever done: shut down Aria's ability to read, blocking her probing mind's eye with fearful images. Aria shuddered inwardly, whether at the implications of Mother's words or her growing fear of Mardrid she was not sure.

"Yes, Mother," she said. "I suppose things here become rather complicated sometimes."

Mother smiled at Aria as if at a child who had said something incredibly naïve. She leaned back in her chair, swiveled it in Mardrid's direction, and gave the aide a long, thoughtful look.

When she turned back, she said to Colter, "Proceed with

the matter we were discussing before this little session, Barena. I'll expect a full report in the morning."

"Yes, Mother." Colter immediately rose, gave a slight bow, and turned to leave the room.

"Leave us now, Helsing," Mother said. "Make your reports to Mardrid today. She will call for you later."

Not words Aria had wanted to hear, but she stood and bowed as Colter had. She wondered if she should say something about the horrific vision she had just endured, but she thought Mother might know already, and she did not want to seem to be complaining.

"Yes, Mother," she said instead. As she turned to leave the chamber, she avoided looking in Mardrid's direction, but from the corner of her eye caught what looked like the shadow of a smile on the aide's lips.

As she passed to the outer chamber, Aria blinked back the tears that threatened to come.

Chapter 5

Kay felt herself coming awake, heard the sigh of the refrigerator in the next room as it cycled off. The warmth of the blanket beckoned her back into sleep. She rolled onto her side, curling into a tight ball, and savored the comfort. Moments later, however, a recollection stole the feeling away— the sound of her own voice, distorted, constricted in the back of her throat, calling out in the night.

The thought brought her fully awake and blinking in the dim light of the sunlight-shielded bedroom. Why had she cried out? Even as she tried to remember, the experience slipped into the shadows of her waking mind. She groaned softly and pushed herself up to a sitting position. Her body protested, like it was still attached to the blanket by the filaments of a spider web. She swung her feet onto the cool floor and stood, pushing away sleep, pushing away last night's experience. All of it.

She stood, stretching toward the beige ceiling, her slender fingers falling an inch short of scratching the nubs from its rough surface. Discipline, she told herself. She would focus on her routine. She'd always been good at that, and it had served her well. The cool air stirring in the room raised goosebumps on her bare skin.

She eyed the Universal in the corner, slipped on the top and bottom of the sweatsuit she had thrown on the floor beside the bed last night, and took a few long strides toward the workout machine. Just as she reached it, she felt her stomach rise into her throat, as though she were falling from a great height. She sucked in a breath and held on to one of the machine's black plastic bars. Something pressed against her throat from inside, a gentle squeeze.

Was she coming down with something? She had been ill only once in her nineteen years, when she was ten. The fever and aches had lasted for three days. The Nurse Mother had told her it was probably an ancient flu virus, something picked up from eating with unclean hands. Had she touched something unclean?

Kay had perfect recall, but she didn't want to go there right now. It felt dangerous. Instead, she clenched her teeth, climbed onto the Universal, and began her workout routine. Forty minutes later, only slightly winded and wet with perspiration, she tested her muscle groups, made the appropriate notes in her log, and stepped into the dry bath. When it shut off, she carefully wiped the remaining absorbent powder from her body's crevices, just as she had done for as long as she could remember, just the way her handlers had instructed her when she was too young to even know her age.

In the bedroom she pulled on a loose-fitting white blouse over her square shoulders, and a pair of drawstring pants. She leaned close to the small mirror and inserted the lenses that transformed the iridescent blue of her irises into the more nondescript brown.

Her stomach rumbled. Good, she thought. Better than that other feeling.

She ordered Meal 1 from the Processing Unit. When it beeped, she removed the tray of steaming cereal and soy patty, and stepped into the SimuTech to eat her breakfast. As she eased into the form-fitting seat, she punched the "Mood" and "Random" buttons on the console and took a bite of the patty. She barely tasted it as the three-dimensional images of lush foliage sprang up on the semi-circular wall in front of her. There were background sounds—rushing water and the songs of long-extinct birds—and the feeling of gentle moisture in the confined atmosphere of the booth, and loamy smells of dark green earth. She far preferred these "Mood" scenes to the movies, which she found annoying for their sensory bombardment and lack of logic.

The scene before her now was not unfamiliar, but not one she usually chose. Her favorite was the aerial view of the mountain village with its snow-covered roofs and smoking chimneys. She liked the clean feeling of stillness it gave her, the sense she was floating, the program's tiny bell-like sounds that tingled in the hollow cavities of her sinuses. The program always reminded her of icicles and the time years ago it had snowed, the fresh feeling it gave her as it had fallen on her childish face.

This program—in the lower right corner Kay saw it was labeled "rainforest"—produced a low, soothing resonance, like the sound from a long wooden flute. She imagined it might be what a lullaby sounded like. She had never actually heard a lullaby, but in school she had read about how mothers used to sing them to lull their children to sleep. Back when everyone had a biological mother.

A moment later, the half-eaten breakfast lay in her lap, and behind closed eyes she drifted on that delicious tone. She savored the moment, walking through the landscape, the warm, porous earth under her bare feet. It was wonderful, familiar. Had she been here before? In her dreams, maybe?

She surrendered to the sounds and smells, her head turning slightly with the inner vision. She was in a clearing now, the canopy of leaves opening to a blue sky above, light touching her face. She spun slowly in a circle, her arms outstretched, an easy smile playing on her lips. She felt very young.

Something in the light changed—or was it a sound? She turned and looked behind her. There, facing away from her stood a small, naked child. Its slender back and bony little shoulders were almost birdlike. It seemed so . . . what was it? . . . vulnerable? Yes, that was it. An unfamiliar urge arose in Kay. She wanted to protect this child, to see its face. She stretched out her hand.

The figure disappeared into the tangle of vines and leaves, taking another portion of light with it. Kay wanted it to come back, wanted to touch the smooth skin of its back. She pushed back the foliage, trying to follow, but it was dense and bit at her bare legs and arms.

The child was gone, and Kay felt stung, alone. And she thought something menacing lay beyond the green wall. Her stomach rose again in her throat. Something dangerous was out there. Despite her foreboding, she put her hands into the dense thicket, pushing it aside, leaning into it . . .

And then, from the other side, the face of Angela Potemkin.

"Kay, wait," it shouted.

Kay reacted instantly, flinging her hands out in front of her defensively, sending the tray in her lap and its food scraps flying onto the floor. Her eyes were wide open now, staring in disbelief at the sylvan scene projected on the screen around her, her heart hammering in her chest.

It had seemed so real.

In a moment, and with effort, she steadied her breathing and heartbeat, but a feeling remained. Kay struggled to name it, to render it powerless. What was it?

A word came to her lips.

"Alone." She said it aloud. She knew the word, of course, but had never felt it quite like this. It had formed somewhere inside her being. Was this what she had felt this morning squeezing her throat? A passage in The Text held that word, she recalled.

There is but one True Master: the Whole Body. In the Whole Body, the servant shall find life and abundance. In the Whole Body is Communion and Salvation. Whosoever forsakes the Whole Body shall wander alone in the wilderness lost to the Embrace and the Light.

Alone. It stung, this word. But why? She hadn't violated any of the Precepts. She'd only allowed her mind to drift. She'd forsaken nothing. Nonetheless, in its two syllables, the word evoked a sort of guilt, defensiveness, but toward what or whom? No one accused her, and yet she knew this daydream was not something she would share with anyone. Such privacy was, if not expressly against the Precepts, not exactly in keeping with the spirit of her training. There had been no secrets in school.

And there were the things Angela Potemkin had said in her message . . .

Kay slammed her open palm on the armrest of the chair, and stood up, a little hiss of air escaping from between her clenched teeth. She grabbed the tray and food from the floor, not bothering to wipe up the cereal that had spilled there. In the kitchen, she loaded everything into the sonic washer.

She stepped to the bedroom mirror, looked into the face she saw there. The few people she'd ever spoken with outside of the Ministry of Termination would have said the face belonged to a young woman named Kay Black. Even at the Ministry, few knew who she really was. But Angela Potemkin had known.

Without thinking, Kay began reciting aloud the pledge she and the other girls had spoken in unison at graduation, words she'd said thousands of times since, a ritual that always before had comforted her.

"I am K-1754, a servant of the Whole Body. I am mother to the Future, sister to the Process, and daughter of the Ideal.

"I am an assassin."

It was the first time she had ever felt the need to remind herself who she was.

It was not who Angela Potemkin had said she was last night.

And Kay was not comforted.

Chapter 6

Parker Potemkin felt the move before he saw it and leaned the upper half of his body slightly to the left just as Michael's foot snapped to the position where Parker's face had been a fraction of a second before. With a precision born of endless hours of practice, Parker tapped his opponent's suspended heel, adding to it just enough to tip Michael's balance. In the same instant, he drove the sole of his right foot into the yielding backside of Michael's supporting leg, and his sparring partner crumbled to the mat, unhurt except for his pride.

"Point," Rayful Edwards shouted from his folding chair just beyond the mat's border. He stood up, waving an arm. "That's it, men. Let's pack it in for the evening."

Michael accepted Parker's hand in pulling himself to a standing position, and with a poorly disguised look of disappointment on his face, bowed formally to Parker and Edwards, his palms flat on his thighs. Both returned the gesture.

"All right?" Parker said, although he knew he'd inflicted no real damage on his teammate during the five-minute sparring match.

Michael nodded, but was silent as he turned to go back to the dorms.

"You're losing friends, Parker," Rayful said under his breath as he watched Michael walk away. Then he winked at the young athlete. "But they'll be happier when you're doing it to someone from another brotherhood."

Parker nodded, unsmiling. He was acutely aware of the distance growing between himself and his teammates, and it was not a source of joy for him. He had always felt like something of an outsider there, but in the five years since he had arrived at the Califas compound, he had managed to stay at least at the periphery of their social cliques. In the last few months, though, his skills had taken on a life of their own. He was now faster, stronger, and had more endurance that any of his teammates of the same age, and was emerging as their natural leader. It was not a role he was comfortable with.

"It's an internal thing," Rayful had told him a few weeks ago. "Right now you are hitting your stride physically. Good! Go for it! Feel your power and don't let up. Sooner or later, the rest will catch up."

"The others, you mean?" Parker had asked.

"No son, the inner part. You can't bring victory all by yourself. In time, you're going to have to learn how to inspire the others, to support them. Right now they only feel the sting of meeting someone who can kick their ass on a regular basis, and they resent you for it. If you show them that we're all on the same team enough times, though, they'll come around."

Right now, though, Parker had no idea how that might happen. He only knew that life with his brothers was becoming more difficult, and this dampened his exuberance over his personal triumphs.

"I'm going to do a run before turning in," he said.

His mentor and elder eyed him with a little surprise. "I think you've had a long enough day. Turn in and we'll work on your forms in the morning."

Parker didn't look Edwards in the eye. "Okay, see you at 07:00 then." He bowed to the man who had been overseeing his progress for nearly two years now.

But Parker didn't return to the dorm he shared with three other young men. Instead, when he was out of sight of Edwards, he turned for the sparsely landscaped trail that circled the fifteen-acre grounds of the Califas compound and broke into an easy gait. Running alone in the dark, he felt the cool of the evening air on his skin and the hum of the biological engine that powered his muscular physique. Lately these runs were about the only thing that brought him peace. He settled into the rhythm, feeling his lungs and heart magically transforming the elements in the atmosphere into raw power, tasting it like others might taste food. Soon he was running at full speed, and though he could not see them in the dark, he was aware of every rock and rise in the trail. He ducked his six foot eight frame beneath the dark silhouette of the tree branch that overhung the western leg of the trail. Wind whistled in his ears. His arms and legs pumped effortlessly at a furious pace, and his feet felt as though they barely touched the dirt beneath them. Eventually, the smile came, and Parker resisted the urge to scream with exhilaration for fear of being heard by others.

The twinkling lights of the compound's dining hall came into view. Parker slowed his pace, the moist air from his nostrils condensing and disappearing behind him in the darkness. Near the end of the trail, he left it and walked the thirty paces to his favorite spot behind a massive boulder and sat down.

As the steam rose from his body, he closed his eyes and began imagining the long series of forms that Edwards would run him through in the morning. Every move in the complicated rituals appeared in sharp relief in his mind's eye, and he accelerated through more than an hour's worth of the exercises in the span of a few minutes. Months ago, he had discovered that such visualization made the actual exercises nearly effortless, and this nightly routine had become a necessary escape from the uneasy atmosphere in the dorm.

Eventually he rose and strolled past the dining hall and into the building that had been his home since he was fourteen. It was 20:15 when he passed through the living room past Will and Thackery, who were running through their nightly sparring routine. The third roommate, Jubal, was out for the evening, having been recruited for temporary work by Sexual Services. Will and Thack paused in their routine long enough to salute Parker with their right hands at shoulder level, fingers straight up and thumb tucked against the palm. Parker acknowledged silently and continued on to the dry bath.

His roommates were in good form tonight, he thought, but even though he was almost a year their junior, he was in *excellent* form. He knew there were things he could do that they couldn't touch. They didn't know it yet, but soon would. If he kept progressing at this rate . . . well, no one could really imagine where he might be in ten years. Probably dead. Most of the great ones seemed to go early. Even the rare man who challenged the odds and went into business or some other field after retiring rarely made it to his fifties. Parker couldn't imagine himself in any other role. He'd only ever wanted to be an athlete, and the best. He hoped he would die before age sapped his vitality and reflexes.

He dropped his bag, which was emblazoned with the electric purple and orange logo that told the world he was a brother with the Califas Order, outside the dry bath. With unselfconscious grace, he stripped out of the two-piece, body-hugging uniform. He pitched the garments toward the open hatch of the cleaning unit ten feet away on the adjacent wall without ever looking directly at it. Though the square opening was only a foot across, the uniform sailed through and into the hopper below without touching any of the sides.

He stepped into the bath, closed it behind him, and slapped the small, square panel embedded in the wall that would send absorbent powder descending from the nozzles above his head. Eyes closed, he rubbed the powder with broad, blunt fingertips through the short brown hair that stood at attention atop his head. As he spread his arms out to the sides, his back splayed up and outward from his waist like the hood of a cobra.

At two hundred seventy-eight pounds, he was heavier than most of the sixty-nine other team members, but not an ounce of it was fat. As he moved, muscles rippled under the skin like strong, unseen currents. He turned in the spray on long, highly-arched feet and tapped the second panel, activating the exhaust vents in the bath's floor and the air jets in the walls. He rotated slowly in the blast, holding his breath, his arms above his head. When the jets stopped whistling, the door popped open, and Parker stepped out to rub off the remaining powder with a towel hanging from nearby rack. With the towel slung over his shoulder, he walked naked into the hallway, past the small, unoccupied rooms of the other three boys into his own.

He tossed the towel on the bed, walked the three steps to the wall desk, picked up the remote, and pressed the power button. In his husky baritone voice, he said, "Messages," and laid the little black unit back down on the desk.

The wall screen lit up, and the words "Message One," rendered in a light blue hue, stretched across the screen. A woman's recorded voice softly repeated what was written on screen. From the closet, Parker pulled on the robe he would wear as he scribbled his resolutions before turning in for the night. Over his shoulder, he heard his mother's voice on the monitor's speaker:

"Hello Pamela. Hello Parker," she began. "I just wanted to say hi, and let you know how much I love you both. It's been a beautiful evening here, and I've been remembering some silly stuff from when we all lived together. Missing you, I guess."

Parker glanced up at her image several times as he continued his routine of turning down the bed and pulling a clean uniform from the wall drawer for the next morning. He had not heard from his mother in many months, but the message seemed breezy and direct, as usual. He noticed the little glitch in the recording that indicated she had paused it after this last sentence.

"I hope everything is well with you, Pam," the message continued. "Have you decided where to do your residency yet? Even though I've told you I'd like to see you do it at the Weil Center, don't pay any attention to your old mom. You know as well as I do that . . ."

Parker stopped, his hand resting on the uniform he was about to set out, and stared at the screen. Something about her tone of voice.

". . . just because I graduated from there doesn't make it any better than some of the others you've been considering. Just follow your instincts, darling. I know you'll make the right choice.

"And Parker, I saw you last week in the Hemispheric Exhibition games. Wow! You were magnificent! Some of my colleagues even called to tell me they'd seen it. I'm sure the brotherhood was proud of you. I sure was. I wouldn't be surprised to see you go on to the World Games and win the gold."

He had heard his mother talk like this often, but something about her tone, or the look on her face, drew him an inch closer to the screen.

"Oh, and before I forget, when you get out to New Phoenix for the regionals, I want you to look up Mother Avalon at the Southwest Council residence hall in Old Town. I've given her something special for you. She'll be expecting you."

"Stop," he said abruptly. "Reverse." A second later he said, "Play," and his mother's voice again filled the room.

". . . I want you to look up Mother Avalon at the Southwest Council residence hall in Old Town. I've given her something special for you. She'll be expecting you."

"Pause." The image of Angela Parker's face froze on the screen as he sank to the edge of the bed, a small wrinkle appearing on the smooth skin between his eyes. Mother Avalon? Who the hell . . . ? He thought back over the last conversations he'd had with her, one about her work at the lab, one about some e-documents pertaining to his birth the Califas headquarters had asked for. He'd never heard the name, he was sure.

He looked at the image of his mother's wide-set blue eyes, so different from his own brown ones, and her thin lips, half open now in mid-sentence. Something odd there? He hadn't thought about his mother in a while, and suddenly he felt as though he hadn't looked at her face, really seen it, maybe in years. She was straining, he thought. A small feeling gnawed at him. There was something on his mother's mind other than what she was saying. He sat for a long while, staring at the screen. Then, as much to dispel his discomfort as to hear her next words, he said, "Play."

"Well, you kids be good," the reanimated image said. "Remember that I love you and that I'm counting on you to do us all proud. See you next time you're back in the Plex." Her face disappeared, replaced with the words, "End of message."

Do us all proud? An odd phrase. He didn't think he'd ever heard her say such a thing. Do who proud? Her associates at the laboratory? He could only recall meeting a few of them in years past. Her and Pamela? He supposed she could mean this, but it still felt off-center. After all, Parker felt only a distant allegiance to his family now. He hadn't lived with his mother since he was conscripted into the Califas Order five years ago, and four years before that Pamela had gone on to further studies. Since then, the order had undertaken all his training and rearing, and when he thought about family at all, his first thoughts were of the Califas elders and brothers.

Still, he looked at his mother's screen image and felt a twinge of regret that he hadn't spoken with her in so many months. Was that urgency in her tone? Perhaps, though it didn't fit her words.

He instructed the unit to save the message. The screen immediately filled with the words, "Message Two," again followed by the soft prerecorded voice, and finally his sister's face.

"Parker, I just got Mom's message. You'll probably think I'm being too sensitive here, but I thought there was something strange about it. I tried to call her back as soon as I got it around 16:00, and she hasn't returned my call. It's 18:15 now. She might be out somewhere, but I feel a little uneasy about it. If it's not too late when you get in, give me a call, please."

Stranger still. He hadn't talked with Pamela in what, a year? He was a little surprised by the maturity he saw in her face. He looked at the timepiece on his bedside: 20:45. Pam's time zone was an hour ahead of his, but there might still be time to call. "Erase," he said aloud, and was about to call up her number on screen when he heard the soft voice say, "Message Three."

On the screen, an unfamiliar, expressionless woman began to speak.

"Hello, Parker. I'm Tanzie Whitman, one of your mother's neighbors. Would you please call me at your earliest convenience? I'll be here throughout the evening." The face disappeared and was replaced with the fourteen-digit number she had left for him.

Parker stared at the number, a gentle pressure building in his stomach and his heart picking up speed. As much out of habit as from conscious thought, he took some deep breaths and sat up straighter, focusing on the point just below his navel that he had been taught was the center of his body since undertaking martial arts training at age ten. His mind raced, but he forced himself to concentrate on his breath, and as soon as he felt his rhythms smooth out again, he spoke to the screen.

"Dial number," he said, and repeated the fourteen digits aloud.

The screen remained beige and blank, save for the small blue flashing dot in the lower right corner that indicated the number was ringing. Parker's eyes fixed on it, but his mind was grappling with the dark feeling that had crept over him. The face of the unfamiliar woman again appeared, now in real time. She stared blankly at him for a few seconds before speaking. "Oh, hello. You must be Parker," she said, almost as a question.

"Yes," Parker replied. He could think of nothing else to say.

"I just talked with your sister a little while ago. It was easier for me to recognize her," the woman said. "She has your mother's eyes."

"Yes." His heartbeat quickened again. This time he did nothing to calm it.

Another pause, and the woman with sharp features opened her mouth as if to speak, then shut it again and looked down. When she looked up again, Parker thought she looked older and tired.

"I've never had to do this before," she said apologetically. "You see, I'm ten years younger than your mother and . . ." Her voice trailed off in mid-sentence.

Parker found his voice again, though it was quieter now. "Do what?"

"Well," the woman said, looking at him with what Parker recognized as resignation in her eyes, "your mother has expired."

Parker said nothing.

"When I came home this afternoon, I knocked on her door to return some clothes I had borrowed. The door was unlocked. I went in to leave her things in her bedroom . . . and I found her sitting up in bed . . . dressed in her best suit."

Still Parker didn't speak.

"I'm sorry. We didn't have any idea she was so close to the end."

Parker could hear in her tone that "sorry" was an overstatement. Her words trailed across his hearing like the vestige of some old formality, some ghost of an earlier age that came by and whispered its scripted lines at the expected moment and then trudged heavily on to its next appointment. He felt heat rising in his chest. He tried to speak, but his throat constricted around the words, giving his breathing a hissing sound. Eventually he managed to say, "Where is she now?" as if his mother might have just stepped into the next room and would soon come on screen to say hello.

"They already came for her. I can give you the number they left for me, if you'd like."

"Yes . . . um . . . okay."

The woman looked down and he heard clicking. Then another number appeared at the bottom of the screen.

"That's it, the number," she said. "I'm sorry. I liked your mother. She was always nice to me and my partner."

The words still sounded flat to his buzzing ears. The woman lapsed into another silence, as if she expected Parker to say something. When he didn't, she pursed her lips and spoke again.

"Well, then. All of her things are still here. I told your sister that when you've had a chance to work things through, she can call me back and we'll make arrangements to get them to her."

Parker managed to thank her and say goodbye, and the woman's face disappeared from the screen, leaving the number she had sent at the bottom. He sat staring at it for a long time, hearing the woman's words echo in his head. Eventually, he leaned forward and shaded his eyes, as if the dim light from the monitor's screen was painful, and wondered what to do next. Call Pamela, he thought, but he stood up and walked aimlessly back and forth in the small space next to his bed.

As an athlete, he had trained for many years to ignore pain, to put it in the back of his mind to deal with later. But this was unlike the pain of strain or injury for which such techniques had been successful. Little had prepared him for the spike he felt now in his chest.

The world shrank to the dimensions of his room. He had no desire to leave it. He could hear Thackery and Will in the final throes of their routine in the main room. They were his two closest brothers, with whom he had shared living quarters and meals and training for years. But this, now, he knew he could not share with them. It was not done.

He sat listening to the bursts of air from his teammates' lungs as they twisted their bodies to meet one another's parrying, envisioning out of habit what stance they were taking. He tried to think about what he had to do tomorrow, what he must be learning for the next competition. But these thoughts kept getting pushed aside by another: Mother is dead.

He stood again and paced the three small steps between the wall screen and the bed. He wrestled with this experience, trying to subdue it like he might have an opponent from another order. This contest, though, in an inner arena he had never before walked, proved to be one he wouldn't win.

In the end, he sat on the edge of the bed and buried his moans into his pillow so the others wouldn't hear.

Chapter 7

"Three days?"

Parker stared at the flight voucher Rayful Edwards had handed him. In the five years he had been living at the Califas compound, he never been away for more than a day.

"You're going to need that much time," Edwards said. "Not everyone does, but it will be good for you."

Parker felt both ashamed for being singled out in this way, and nervous about seeing Pamela again. He wasn't sure he wanted to spend that long with her. Or she with him.

"I don't think . . ." he began.

"No argument, Potemkin." The use of Parker's last name signaled a formal command, but there was warmth in his voice. "Reconnect with your sister, take care of your family business. We're going to be very busy for a long time here. The chance might not come again."

Parker nodded, looked away. He didn't want Edwards to see his embarrassment. "I'll spend a couple of hours on the *katas* every day."

Edwards shook his head. "Not necessary, son. Do a little, but you're in top form. It's not going anywhere. It's good to step back and let things sink in a little. You'll be flying from Philadelphia to New Phoenix two days before the Regionals; there will be time to pick up again there. Right now, the best thing you can do is deal with your mother's passing, get to know your sister again."

He clapped a hand on Parker's shoulder and squeezed.

"Now go," he said. Edwards stood nearly a foot shorter than he and weighed considerably less, but in that moment he seemed larger.

The first evening was awkward. A rather formal politeness colored what little conversation they shared as they combed through the five small containers of their mother's belongings that her neighbor had sent. They resembled survivors of a natural disaster, left with the paltry remains of a lost past, the dearth of their mother's possessions reflected in their empty faces. There were clothes, towels, hundreds of data storage cubes, labeled poorly, if at all. Pamela read them, though, turning them over with deft, white fingers, making a list of the titles she could read. A dozen framed certificates of merit and plaques honored Dr. Angela Potemkin for "outstanding achievement" and "conspicuous contributions to the field of genetic research." Pamela stacked them all next to her, and Parker was glad she was laying claim to them. He would not have known what to do with them.

There were some odd pieces of bric-a-brac—an antique cuckoo clock whose hands had broken off, along with several of the bird figures that had perched on its roof. There was a collection of eight tiny abstract glass sculptures, and a small bust of Madam Curie—a pioneering woman scientist from long ago, Pamela had explained to Parker. They had no idea of what to do with most of it.

Next to them on the floor lay the short, formal message Pamela had received from the Office of Collection stating only the estimated hour of death and the fact that their mother's body had been vaporized the next day, as per the law.

Gradually the items were sorted into piles, the biggest

57

for things that would be thrown away. Pamela's pile was smaller, and Parker's almost non-existent.

They said goodnight early, Parker leaving Pamela's living quarters to stay in a nearby hotel. By the time he got to his room, he felt stiff and deflated. He fell asleep without undressing.

The second day, their relationship, grown almost icy during their long separation, warmed a few degrees. The thaw began when Pamela found an old photo disk amid their mother's things. On it they found several hundred holographs their mother had taken over the years. One of Parker when he was about four years old prompted Pamela to tell the story about the time their daycare sitter had taken ill and gone off to lie down in a bedroom, and their mother came home from work to find Parker tied to a chair, his older sister piling pillows around him, telling him she was going to make of him a burnt offering to the god of the harvest.

It had only been a game, something Pamela had dreamed up after a lesson in ancient history, but their mother had been horrified, and punished them by making them sit for an hour facing opposite walls and not speaking. The story—Parker had only a vague memory of the event—made both laugh. Then Parker reminded her of the time when she dressed him in her own clothes, and herself in their mother's clothes, and the two of them had paraded for their mother, playing out the roles the ill-fitting costumes suggested.

The stories came easier then—the trip they took to Yellowstone Park when Parker was eight. Angela had wanted them to see a bear before the species disappeared completely, but all they had seen was one bear's mangy-looking rump disappearing over a ridge; the time at the Metroplex reservoir when Parker pushed Pam in because she had bragged about having learned how to swim, and how she had to be rescued by the lifeguard, a stern, muscular woman who found no humor in their antics; their mother insisting she teach Parker to dance, and how he'd made them laugh by pretending to be uncoordinated.

Much of that second day went like this, brother and sister reaching for the early and happy memories, unconsciously avoiding the later, more difficult ones when they had begun to find reasons to dislike each other. When the intermittent silences grew uncomfortably long, Pamela said she needed to do some reading for work the next day, and left Parker to his own thoughts.

The final morning Parker awakened to his briefly forgotten misgivings about their mother's demise. He dressed quickly and called Pamela to plan their final day together.

"I can't take any more time from my studies," Pam said. "I'm afraid all I'll be able to do today is have lunch with you."

Parker realized after a moment that he hadn't replied. "Well . . . okay. What time shall I meet you . . . and where?" He hoped his voice hadn't betrayed the disappointment he felt.

Three hours later, Parker stared at the top of his sister's head from across a long table in the Philadelphia Bell Laboratories cafeteria. She was diligently attacking the brightly-colored processed food on her plate. Parker wondered how to bring up his questions.

At the other end of the table, out of earshot, four women kept stealing glances at Parker. From the corner of his eye, he caught the grins and the whispered remarks, the suppressed titters. It happened sometimes when he was out in public, but it still made him uneasy. Men probably didn't come to this facility much, he reasoned. Science was really women's realm now. Most men were doing the relatively few physical labor jobs that remained—construction, driving the huge transports, flying planes.

Or they were athletes. The world had never lost its appetite for physical confrontation and feats of daring. The old team sports like football and baseball had pretty much gone the way of the dinosaurs, though some of the less-developed regions still had competitions. The mostly female population preferred games of endurance and agility, races and confrontations involving high-speed manipulation of machinery and technology. Parker was good at nearly all of them, but hand-to-hand fighting was the sport Parker was becoming famous for, and it was more popular than ever.

It was possible that one of the women recognized him, since most of the events in which he competed nowadays were on InterTV. But it was probably just his size. Even seated, Parker towered over his sister, and the small plastic fork he used to push the food around his plate looked to him as though it were made for a child.

"Do you think she knew she was going to die?" he asked abruptly, looking at the food as if the answer might come from there.

After a long pause, Pam said to her own plateful, "I don't know. You know what bothered me the most?"

Parker waited.

"Why would she put on her best suit? She wasn't going to the lab anymore since the accident, and it's not the type of thing you'd wear around the house, especially at night." She cast a quick sidelong glance at the women at the end of the table. They were leaning close to one another and speaking in low, conspiratorial voices. Parker noticed, not for the first time, his sister's unease about sitting with him in public.

"Maybe she was getting ready to go out," he offered without conviction.

"Maybe, but I don't ever remember her dressing up to go out. It seemed to me more like," Pamela paused, reaching for the right word, "like a statement or something."

"A statement? About what?"

"I don't know, Parker," she said, irritation creeping into her voice. "About dignity or something, about looking her best when she knew someone would find her . . ." Her voice trailed off.

Parker chose to ignore her darkening mood. "But how would she know? I've never heard of anyone knowing they were about to die unless they were really sick. I mean, everyone in their thirties or forties must think about it, but . . ." He let the sentence hang. "What about the message? You said that night that it sounded strange. I thought so too. I couldn't figure out what she meant with that 'doing us all proud' business. I can't remember her ever saying that. It sounds . . . I don't know . . . old-fashioned or something. And then that part about this Mother Avalon having something for me. She never left anything for me with someone else. Did she ever do something like that with you?"

Pamela hesitated, sipping her drink. "Well, not exactly. Once she sent some things I needed to the department chief here. I was out with my group at another laboratory . . . to study how their procedures differed from ours. When I got back, I found a container waiting for me, but I haven't really thought about it since."

"Well, she never did anything like this before with me. I don't really even know how I'm going to get the time or permission to look this Mother Avalon up in New Phoenix."

"It can't be that hard to get away, Parker. After all, you're something of a star nowadays, aren't you?" There was the unmistakable ring of disdain in the way she said it.

"Knock it off, Pam," he said. "I'm really not in the mood for it."

Parker didn't seem to be able to stop the old wounds from opening again. When Pamela had left home at age fifteen to follow her mother's career path, he had showed little interest in her life, barely seeming to take notice that she was leaving. Like most boys his age, he was caught up in the daily rigors of athletic training, and his daily triumphs and disappointments were all he spoke about.

Secretly, though, he was sad to see her go. He had felt strong affection for her, despite the considerable pressure from his schoolmates to be callous in matters where the opposite sex were concerned. When he and Pam were very young, they had shared secrets and made up stories to tell one another. They'd tickled each other until they both cried. When Pam hit her teens, Parker had thought her beautiful, even sneaking peeks at her nakedness when she had carelessly left her bedroom door ajar.

But as time passed, communication grew spotty, and it often seemed discolored by Pamela's jealousy over Parker's achievements, coupled with her embarrassment at having a brother. None of her friends had brothers, and their relationships with men were shallow and mainly sexual. There was little about her and Parker's relationship she could share with them, and after being away from him for a few years, she seemed to have forgotten much of their earlier closeness. The memories they'd dredged up yesterday had been fun, but Parker saw now that she wanted his visit to be over, wanted to get back to her routine.

"Well, maybe it's nothing at all," Pam said. "Are you sure you didn't ask her to send you something? One of your old mementos or something?"

"I'm sure."

The women at the end of the table were laughing again. Parker glanced over at them and saw that two of them were leering at his size eighteen shoes, grinning.

"I told you, I hadn't spoken to her in months," he said. "I didn't even know she was on leave until last week when I tried to reach her at the lab."

They fell silent. Parker tried to remember if his mother had ever taken a vacation from the Central Office for Genetic Research, commonly known as the Ministry of Births, after he left home. He didn't think so, but then he was so caught up in his own life that he wasn't sure. When he had called the lab to tell his mother about the regional games, he had been told simply that Angela Potemkin was not there, and that she was on temporary leave.

He had called her at home, then, knowing she wouldn't answer. She rarely answered a call directly. He never knew why, but she always seemed to prefer communication by recorded message. And so he had left her one, telling her what time the games were being aired, and clicked off. He wished now that she had answered.

"Anyway," Pamela said, "I don't suppose it matters much now. She's gone now and we have our careers to think about."

The women at the end of the table laughed again, and Parker saw Pam's face redden when she realized they were looking at her. Evidently, the women had no idea he was her brother, and probably thought he was from Sexual Services.

"And speaking of that, I have to get back to work," Pamela said. They stood and embraced stiffly, promising to be in touch, but Parker felt the old distance between them, and he doubted they would talk again for a long while.

Three hours later, he gazed out of the window of the supersonic transport as it descended into the New Phoenix airport. The semicircle of the setting sun shone from the edge of the horizon like a fiery coin. Below, the dust glowed orange in the dry air, and the sun's dying light colored the cold spires and domes of the massive building complexes below. Beyond them, their long purple shadows stretched toward the barren desert that seemed to Parker as though it was just waiting to reclaim the land humans had stolen from it.

In the distance, he could make out the familiar oval outline of Sun Stadium where in two days he and the brothers would compete against six other orders in fifteen different events. It was the third time this year Parker's Califas Order had been in this stadium, one of the six arenas in as many areas that formed the axial points in the geography of the most talented exhibition athletes.

Yes, there was the career, Parker thought, recalling Pam's final words over the clatter in the cafeteria. But he realized he was far less focused on the competition than on what would come when he landed. After the regionals, he would try to honor his mother's last request and meet with a woman he'd never heard of, and pick up whatever it was his mother had left for him there.

He would rather have just forgotten about it, but knew he couldn't really do that now.

Chapter 8

The clock in the Beaufort Station read 02:40, and Kay counted only thirteen early-morning commuters in the dim light of the cavernous building. She stood a few feet out from the wall, behind most of the others, mimicking several who were staring dully into the small screens of the TeleSlates they held. In reality, she was acutely aware of every person around her: their clothes, their body language, the faces she glimpsed.

Her tan overcoat and the beige bag that hung from her shoulder did little to distinguish her from the others. Her TeleSlate looked identical to the others being read in the gloomy light, but its versatility and power were light years beyond theirs.

High in the ceiling, artificial sunlight generators emitted a low hum, which Kay had never really noticed before. She was puzzling over this when something else caught her attention. A woman came through the entrance ten feet to Kay's right, and as she passed by, Kay heard yet another sound. At first, she couldn't tell where it was coming from, but with a start she realized that it emanated from the woman.

Actually, "hearing" was not precisely what she experienced. It was more a feeling, she realized, as though she were catching a note played on an instrument out of the range of the human ear. The effect on Kay, however, was not that of music, which often soothed her. Instead, it pulled at her focus, made her uneasy, especially when she began to think she heard more notes coming from others nearby.

She moved farther away, careful to make no quick motions that might draw attention, until the sound was little more than a whisper. She stood just at the edge of what she had been taught was a normal circle of awareness, far enough so that others felt safe, not so far as to arouse suspicion.

A full minute before the Maglev train pulled into the station on its recessed track, Kay felt it coming. The train's nine-ton mass telegraphed its arrival through her feet and legs, despite the fact that electromagnetic pulses suspended its bulk an inch above its rails. She even imagined she could calculate its speed as it approached, slowing from more than a hundred miles per hour to fifteen miles per hour in the space of less than a mile.

She was relieved when it finally pulled into the station and she was able to board. Avoiding eye contact—not difficult since no one else seemed alert or interested in her— Kay found her way to a seat near the rear of the last of seven cars.

At this point on any mission, Kay normally would turn her attention to the client whom she was about to dispatch, but now she only stared out the windows, barely aware of the twinkling lights of the metroplex the Maglev was bisecting. Instead, she saw what she had been trying for two days to erase from her memory. The face of Angela Potemkin, with its expression of grim determination, the lips forming the two words—"Kay, wait"—was wearing away at Kay's ordered world like a chisel on rock.

The other words, the ones that had come later in that awful message, Kay had successfully pushed into a distant corner of her mind. But whenever her mental guard dropped she heard Potemkin's imploring voice. Kay looked down at the TeleSlate in her lap, absently tracing its rounded edges. After a moment, she placed her thumb on the reader pad in the upper right corner. The slate recognized her thumbprint and the screen displayed a single word.

PASS?

Kay raised the slate close to her mouth and whispered the first password. She repeated the process through three levels of security, until the screen displayed a new word.

FILE?

Kay started to say, "Next," which would have automatically opened the file on tonight's client. Instead she sat, the slate poised an inch before her thin lips, her head swaying rhythmically with the motion of the Maglev. The screen blinked FILE? again. Finally Kay spoke: "Potemkin."

The screen filled with the same data she had called up on her way to Potemkin's apartment two nights before. It should not have been there. Standard procedure was always to expunge the records after a successful mission, but Kay had not done so. It was the only time in her life she had violated procedure, and she didn't want to think about why she had done so. Her memory was nearly photographic, but something inside had driven her to break the rules. For two days she had carried the guilt of that; now she intended to do what was right. The word "Delete" was forming on her tongue, but as her eye passed over the characters there, she did not speak. Instead, she scanned the abbreviated information.

Official Business
4.12.2174
Census Accounting Office

Document #T0JSA1334-3759-AB12
Agent: K-1754
#H432L001535N.14573, Angela Potemkin, W.F.C.
—Area 254, Sector 18, 20014 Avenue of the Fathers,
#708.

Avenue of the Fathers. Odd. The name hadn't struck her
when she first had read it, but now she wondered why
streets were named after things that few people living had
ever seen—Great Falls Road and Georgetown Lake and
Pinewood Forest and Eagle's Nest Parkway . . . and fathers.

b2.29.2109
M—1f, Pamela, b6.12.2150; 1m, Parker, b5.15.2155
W—CGR, s18, 50045-A-south Victory Plaza, o#143,
9-15—loa 1.25.2174

Angela Potemkin was born in 2109, was the mother of
two, a daughter, Pamela, now twenty-four, and a son,
Parker, nineteen, Kay's age. Since male births were re-
stricted to one in four, this distinguished Potemkin from
most others. She had been employed in the A building at
the Central Office for Genetic Research in sector 18 for six
hours a day, beginning at nine in the morning. She took a
leave of absence in the first moon this year, no reason
listed.

Kay then did something else out of character. She considered what Angela Potemkin's life might have been like.
Had she called on Sexual Services often? Had she been part
of a large circle of friends? Why had she decided to have a
son? In Potemkin's message to Kay, she had not mentioned
her children. Did they matter to her, or was her life con-
sumed by the work she alluded to in the message? What did

she do that put her on the Termination List?

At the top of the screen was a small icon. Behind it, Kay knew, lay Angela Potemkin's holograph. She didn't want to open it, didn't want to be reminded of this face again. And yet she knew she would.

Setting her jaw, she jabbed the icon and Angela Potemkin's face once again filled the screen. With the scroll bar at the bottom of the screen, Kay rotated the image from left to right and back again, taking in each curve and angle, the length of the eyelashes and color of the hair, the skin tone. She remembered the exact sound of the woman's voice, and the words she had spoken.

"Hello Kay. I was hoping I wouldn't have to meet you this way, but if you're seeing this, it is too late for me to say what I must in person. Please listen carefully, as this will be the only opportunity I will have to tell you some things about yourself that you don't know.

"You are not the person you have always thought you were. You're far more. Your origins are not what you believe. They're not the same as the other sisters in your order. I know this because I am largely responsible for your coming into this world. You probably know that I am a geneticist. My laboratory developed the line of K-class women you are part of. It took thirteen years and nearly a thousand generations of imperfect experiments before we successfully produced you and your sisters. As K-1754, you and the forty or so whose numbers surround yours are probably the pinnacle of our work.

"But this is only part of the truth. You were my special creation. You were given something that none of the other K-class women received. There is no time to give you the details here, but this part of you hails from a far more ancient lineage, a special lineage developed by people who believed that the hope of humanity lay in the refinement, the enhancement, of certain traits that as a race we've only glimpsed in certain individuals in our history.

"You may have heard about how we—the scientific community, I mean—are able to program the genes of certain plant and animal species so that certain characteristics only appear in later stages of their development. Have you begun to notice changes in yourself lately? I cannot tell you exactly how you will experience them, nor exactly when they will begin to occur, only that they will."

Kay closed her eyes and felt again the urge to erase Angela Potemkin's words, to dismiss the woman as deranged, deluded. But one fact made that impossible—Potemkin knew her name and her designation. Kay had always been told that few outside the Census Accounting Office, the bland name for what the elite referred to as the Ministry of Termination, knew of the existence of the K-class, of its origins or mission.

For two days she had held out against the memory of Potemkin's words, but now the dam had burst and she felt them flood over her like dark waters, pushing before them the identity she had always held to. She thought of the dreams she had been having, the strange perceptions, like the sound emanating from the people in the station.

"You have learned from The Text that there is a will to history, and that the Whole Body is now in accord with that will. But there is another way of looking at this that has been suppressed. Most of this information has been expunged from the Record, but parts of it are buried in unrelated studies. I am taking a risk by giving you some of their titles here, but after years of considering your potential and watching your progress, we've decided that you must have access to this material in order to convince you of your own value and move you to action."

Potemkin had then rattled off the titles of a dozen books. "Look at these works, Kay. Find out about who you really are. Act on it.

"I believe your destiny is great, as well as your role in the future of the world. Whether you can fulfill this role is an unanswerable question right now, but I wish you the best. I've given you everything I can. The rest is up to you.

"Goodbye."

Kay opened her eyes and again took in Potemkin's holo. She hated it. She hated the woman's blasphemous words, her sincerity, her admonition. As the anger rose in Kay's throat, she experienced again the feeling that her body was becoming alien to her. This precious body that she had honed and trained and disciplined into a fine instrument. It was a nightmare.

Kay wanted to throw the TeleSlate to the floor and stomp it to pieces. Her face grew hot, and her heart rate raced. She heard a low moan and was momentarily confused, for it sounded like it came from behind and above her. But it hadn't. It came from her own throat.

The realization snapped her back to the present, and she tore her eyes from the screen. In front of her she saw her fellow commuters. No one turned around to look at her. Had she only imagined she was moaning? A drop of sweat threatened to fall from her eyebrow where it had collected, and Kay wiped it away with the back of her hand. She turned the slate face down without looking again at Potemkin's holo.

"I am mother to the Future, sister to the Process, and daughter of the Ideal. I am mother to . . ." she chanted silently over and over until her heart had resumed its natural pace. She was in trouble, she knew, worse trouble than she had ever imagined, and she had no idea where to turn for help.

Chapter 9

Ten minutes later the Maglev pulled into the Burnham station and Kay exited with a half-dozen of the other riders. Moments earlier, she had deleted Angela Potemkin's file, and with a great force of will, examined the data on tonight's client, Marcella Korsos, including the floor plans to her apartment complex the Ministry had provided. She boarded a sleek bus, preferring as usual the more anonymous mode of transport to the cabs that roamed the streets of the metroplex even at this hour.

She got off less than a mile from her destination and walked briskly toward the twenty-five-story building where the client shared living space with three other women. Kay walked around the block on which the building stood, eyeing the various entrances and exits, locating the client's window among the hundreds that stared unlit at the street, checking out the surrounding structures, the few people on the streets at that hour. She passed a filthy male lurking in an alley—a Lost One, as one of her teachers had called them—and he grunted at her but made no move to stop her. She was glad. Once before she had had to put down just such a man, and it had felt off-mission. She needed no more distractions this night.

After a final pass, she decided on the south service entrance to the building. Even from fifteen feet away, she could tell that the building's security system was an old one, probably a two-tiered system that identified only by voice and face recognition. As she approached, she obscured her face with the TeleSlate while calling up the image of one of her client's housemates the Ministry had provided, Theresa Sullivan. Then she retrieved from her waist pack a small laser optical cap. Placing the laser cap over the lens embedded in the wall to the left of the door, she spoke softly to the Slate.

"Identify system."

After a moment, a tiny green ready light blinked on the screen, signaling that the system was identified and further instructions were needed.

"Send voice and image of Theresa Sullivan."

In two seconds, Kay heard the door unlock, and she instructed the computer to temporarily scramble the building's video system, in case there were cameras inside that could recognize her as someone other than Theresa Sullivan. When confirmation came, Kay stepped through the doorway and into a deserted hallway lined with doors. At the end of the hall, she found another that stretched off to another exit, and a stairway. She began her climb to the seventh floor and the apartment of tonight's client.

She climbed swiftly, her specially designed clothing making no sound. At the seventh floor, she reoriented herself with the numbers on the doors, and turned right. As she neared Korsos' door, her mind flicked back to two nights before when she had approached Angela Potemkin's door. With a nearly imperceptible shake of her head, she pushed the memory away. She scratched the scent card.

She disabled the apartment's security lock, entered with her weapon drawn, and was immediately struck with a host of odors—old food, a household cleaner, the outgassing from sleeping bodies, some sort of excrement, the smell of shoes, and the residue of sweating feet. This last smell, she found when her eyes adjusted to the tiny bit of light that filtered in through the closed blinds on the window in the wall opposite her, was from four sets of shoes lined up next to the door. Her sense of smell seemed more acute than ever, and she labored to separate the odors, identify from them the one on the scent card. Toward her right, she located a short hallway and one partly closed door. She crept toward it, and soon heard soft snoring coming from behind it. At glacial speed, she eased the door open.

It was even darker within, but after a moment, Kay could make out two beds lumped with reclining figures beneath covers. She could have used the diffused illumination of a tiny light she carried in her bag to help her identify the target and any obstacles in the way, but she wanted only to be done with this task. She moved through the darkness toward the first figure, a mere shadow in the gloom. Beside the bed, she bent by degrees until her face was but inches from the head of the sleeping figure, her thumb poised over the trigger of the tiny weapon in her hand. She drew a silent breath through her nose, recognized the scent immediately.

Something else, another smell, sent a flash of warning through her brain.

Before she could react, she heard a hiss and something raked across her cheek, tearing the flesh. Kay jerked upright, and a small dark figure below her moved abruptly, streaking from the bed Kay stood poised over to another three feet behind her. Kay knew what had happened, but by then it was too late. The woman in the bed beneath her bolted upright, a surprised "Whaaa?" coming from her lips. Kay fired her weapon into the woman's chest and whirled to see the disappearing silhouette of a cat leap from the second bed, and the woman who had been aroused by its pounce reaching for the light at the bedside.

There was no choice. Kay let loose the second of three

darts the weapon carried and watched in dismay as the figure went limp and fell to bed again, the arm that had been extended toward the light switch flopping noisily on the bedside table.

She nearly flew to the front door of the apartment. As she turned to close it behind her, she caught the faintest gleam from a pair of feline eyes in a corner of the living room.

On her way to the ground floor, she touched the fiery streaks on her face and looked at her fingertips, which were stained red with her own blood . . . and cursed.

"You know, of course, that this will trigger an inquiry?" The woman seated before her was a good thirty pounds heavier than Kay. Her eyes were mere slits and her lips were drawn into a tight pucker. "Not only here, but on the outside. They will find nothing, I'm sure, but two women dying of natural causes at the same moment is bound to be suspicious to some lower authorities."

"Yes, Rinchon," Kay answered. She stood straight and rigid, clasping a wrist behind her back.

"What were you thinking, K-1754? How could you not have checked the area using your light before you struck?"

"I have never encountered an animal in a private quarters before, Rinchon. Because of this, I grew lax in following the procedures I learned in my training. I have come to rely too heavily on scent recognition, my strongest talent. I accept the responsibility and the punishment for failing my duty."

"Of course you do." The woman waved her hand dismissively. "But don't think that you are the first to screw up. You may be good—your marks and your record indicate that you are very good indeed—but you're not infallible."

She stared at Kay for a long moment before speaking again. "Pets are only one of many factors you must take into account in your mission, K-1754, but you know that. Just because there are very few nowadays, that doesn't excuse you from following basic procedure. You will be removed from the assignment roster and required to pass some tests over the next few days. I'm reasonably sure you'll do well on them, and soon be back on-line, the better for your mistake. There will be a report in your file, of course."

The woman, an elder of the I-class, retired after only a few years in the field, tapped an index finger rhythmically against her pursed lips. "Is there anything else about this event that you'd like to tell me? Anything else bothering you?"

Kay felt her breath stop. Was her expression betraying her? She had marshaled all her defenses against this encounter, but now she wondered if she were more transparent than she had imagined. A part of her wanted to blurt out everything—Angela Potemkin, the changes she was feeling—but she knew none of these revelations would be received lightly. It would mean the end of her career.

"No, Rinchon. I simply need to understand my failings and redouble my efforts." It was a phrase one of her early handlers had often used while she was in school.

"Very well, then," the woman said, her eyes never leaving Kay's face. "Report for examination here at 11:00 this morning. That should give you some time to sleep beforehand."

Kay bowed and left the small office, located in an obscure and barely trafficked wing of North American Council Headquarters. She had come directly from the disaster to report, and she felt drained, spent by the voice of the inner critic she had endured all the way to headquarters. Even so, she didn't think she would be able to sleep.

And she was afraid of what dreams might come.

Chapter 10

It had felt like child's play, Kay thought, as she paced the floor of her living quarters. This morning she had finished her final battery of tests, culminating in an interview before a panel of five elders who grilled her on every aspect of her training, posed hypothetical situations and demanded immediate answers, interrupted her answers and changed the scenarios.

At one point during this onslaught, Kay realized from the expression of exasperated incredulity of one of her inquisitors that she had better pretend to be having more difficulty with their questions than she was.

For three days, they had thrown everything they could at her—psychological tests, physical examinations, endurance tests. She had passed it all. When she was dismissed an hour ago, she had been told that they would summon her tomorrow with their decision, but she knew already what it would be. They had no choice. She would be put back online and life would resume as normal.

Only nothing was normal. It was as though she had contracted some dark disease that was eating away at her insides. She could concentrate when the situation demanded it, but when she had nothing to do, when there was nothing external on which to focus, her stomach began tying itself in knots and her mind raced with questions.

She was free until tomorrow, and the prospect filled her with dread. Always before when she had time on her hands, she found comfort in studying The Text, repeating its rhythmic lines and comforting phrases. She had tried this yesterday, however, after the examiners were done with her, and found the words made little sense. She read and reread passages two and three times, realizing each time that she had not really been present. Then she would remember what Angela Potemkin had said, that there were other views of the will of history, and the thought was so distasteful that she felt unclean. Finally she had given up in frustration and taken a sleeping pill one of the doctors had issued her.

Only intense physical exertion had seemed to still her thorny thoughts. So be it, she thought. She would go to the workout sanctuary and push her body until she was exhausted. She stopped pacing and changed into a workout suit. In less than a minute she was out the door.

From her quarters in the north wing, Kay strode through the wide halls toward the atrium at the hub of the sprawling headquarters complex. As always, she paid close attention to those around her, blending in with the mélange of office workers and bureaucrats. No one gave her a second glance.

A quarter-mile later, the familiar stone figures in the center of the atrium came into view. They were larger than the humans they represented: women and men, some frozen in repose, some bent thoughtfully over apparent work, some touching the hem of the robe of the giant figure that Kay knew stood in their midst.

As she passed through the high archway into the expansive room, her eyes were drawn to the high eye-shaped dome. There, rising nearly two hundred feet into the arc, the massive steel and stone form of a sinewy woman reached to the sky above, her palms cupped as if waiting to be filled. Kay's eyes followed the play of light along the silvery web of fiber optic threads that stretched from the solar collectors on the dome's surface to ten thousand tiny passageways into the body of the giant sculpture.

A smile tugged at the corners of Kay's mouth. She loved seeing the tiny, brilliant stars that twinkled at the places overhead where three or more filaments intersected and were fused. She imagined the many miles of these slender threads that shepherded sunlight through the sculpture to the more than five thousand rooms of the Council Headquarters. There, shorn of its harmful ultraviolet rays and carrying with it the twin blessings of the sun's far-off exuberance and the giant figure's peaceful supplication, it illumined the lives of all those living and working there. It was a masterful marriage of technology and symbolism.

As Kay continued briskly toward the south wing where the workout sanctuary was, a small sign at the entrance to one of the corridors that spiked off from the atrium caught her eye. It read, "Hall of Records."

She slowed, staring at the sign, Angela Potemkin's words resonating in her mind.

"There is another way of looking at the will of history that has been suppressed. Most of this information has been expunged from the Record, but parts of it have been buried in unrelated studies."

Kay glanced around her. No one seemed to notice her, though she felt stained somehow, soiled in a way that should be obvious. She pressed at her temples, and for a moment the floor beneath her feet felt as though it undulated. She resumed walking in the direction of the workout sanctuary, longing even more for the release hours of practice and sweat would afford. But the small sign pulled at her again.

"I am taking a risk by giving you some of the titles . . ." Angela's voice returned.

Kay suspected then, though the thought frightened her,

that she was not going to the workout sanctuary after all. She blew out a breath between pursed lips, walked another thirty feet, stopped. Then she turned around and set off toward the Hall of Records, her teeth grinding.

The hall was really more of a labyrinth. Kay stood inside the entrance, taking it in. Always before she had passed by here, noting that it looked deserted. Few people had an interest in history, it seemed. Thirty feet in front of her, seated behind a desk and half turned away, a hawkish-looking woman stared into three monitor screens. She took no notice of Kay. The scale of the dimly lit room dwarfed the woman and her desk. The ceiling was probably seventy feet high, and five levels of mezzanines with railed walkways extended all the way up, circling tables that sat in the center on the ground floor.

From her vantage, Kay could see aisles on each of the floors extending outward like the spokes of a wheel, disappearing between the rows of plastic cabinets that held the library's contents on antiquated electronic storage media. She had heard it said that this room held everything ever written, but found this incomprehensible. Tiny green lights winked on each of the cabinets' drawers, indicating that its contents were accessible and in good condition. In the center of the room, thirty or so monitors sat well apart from each other on long tables arranged in neat rows. A half-dozen women, none of them familiar, worked at the keyboards.

Kay approached the woman at the reception desk, whose slight build and beak-like nose reminded her of a bird. The woman glanced at Kay and motioned to the chair poised at the corner of the desk in front of a hand plate and retinal scanner. Kay took the seat, placed her hand on the plate, and looked into the pinkish light of the scanner. The red light on its base turned green, and the woman turned back to her monitors.

"I'll be here until 14:00. If you have trouble finding what you're looking for, come see me." She resumed studying her screens.

Kay stood and approached one of the empty monitors, scanning the room for signs of surveillance cameras. She saw none, but realized it would be easy to track down whatever she chose to read today. She wondered why the Whole Body went to such trouble and expense to preserve records that so few were interested in. Perhaps no one paid much attention to what people read here.

On the other hand, she decided she would try to make it seem as though she was researching something related to her work, just in case. In her mind she reviewed some of the titles Angela Potemkin had mentioned in her message: *Time Wave Continuum Theory As It Applies to Superspace, Paper 1327; The Collected Poems of Teramina Hoyle Parkinson, 2023–2065; Sociological Repercussions in the Conversion of the African Continent to Unified Market Forces, Chapter 11.*

She sat down at a terminal with a sense of anticipation, and said softly, "Search." The screen lit up and displayed a complicated series of options for searching the vast library. Kay studied it for a moment. In school, she had spent time in the sisterhood's library using a different system and equipment. It only took moments, however, for her to decipher the search parameters on the screen, turn off the verbal recognition function, and key a search on the words, "Text+history+authors."

The result was 40,113 references, a dozen of which Kay opened and pretended to read, stealing quick glances around the room. She keyed another search on "population+control+methods+modern." More results, and she opened a half-dozen of them.

Then she could wait no longer. She keyed, "The Collected Poems of Teramina Hoyle Parkinson, 2023–2065," in the search window. Potemkin hadn't made any reference to a page number, so Kay began scanning the book page by page, reading the titles of the various poems and the first few lines. When she reached one titled *The Rape and Redemption of Psyche*, she stopped. An indefinable urge pulled at her. Her eyes moved over the lines before her:

They sucked the sweet breath of life
From the fragrant mouth of Earth's pure daughter
Covered her sacred body
With broken stones and withered limbs
And circled her tomb
With dogs of war, who with their terrible jaws
Ground to dust the dream of the centuries.

But scattered amidst time's decayed relics
Lay Padeyevsky's pollen and Psyche's golden tresses
Dyed red with the blood of the martyrs
And fed by the root of the Tressaline tree
In whose nascent branches sing
The ancient avian messengers
Of the princesses' promised return.

Sing, oh ye daughters of the promise
Sing 'til the Sun breathes fire
'Neath the potent brew of the Bringers
And on the loins of the Lion,
And sends forth their spawn
To lay waste the unclean city
And silently raise Termalaine's Tower in its midst.

She could make no sense of the poem, but its rhythms and images pulled at her. She had never heard the names it mentioned, and wondered at the poem's other arcane references. Was this really one of the works Angela Potemkin had alluded to in her message? She read it again. Maybe she would come back to it. She instructed the computer to set the book aside into a file she could retrieve later.

She called up another of the titles, *Time Wave Continuum Theory As It Applies to Superspace.* When the screen indicated the file was available to read, she advanced to Paper 1327 and read several uninteresting paragraphs. Then her eyes fell upon a passage:

According to the Padeyevsky Theory of Biogenetics, the key to unlocking the hitherto untapped potential of the human race lies in mastering and influencing the combination of specialized DNA sequences, which he claimed to have discovered during his work on the Human Genome Mapping Project, completed in the year 2000.

Padeyevsky's subsequent pioneering work became the subject of much debate and criticism, most of it centered on his claim that it was not simply the physical manipulation of genetic materials that would produce the result, but the combination of manipulation with intentional mental influence that would produce hitherto impossible combinations of human characteristics.

It is reported that he founded an experimental community in East Africa to test his theories, but funding from sponsoring agencies of the former United States quickly dried up as his views became more widely known. Before his untimely death in

2013 and subsequent and unfortunate destruction of most of his recorded work, Padeyevsky's clinical trials were rumored to have produced significantly enhanced levels of psychoneurological integration in as many as thirty subjects.

Independent observation of such breakthroughs appears to be unreliable or nonexistent. It is generally believed that these controlled experiments were carried out on the consenting adults of the community, who later bore children. It is not known if any of the latter survived to adulthood, or what the ramifications on their physiological or neurological processes might have been. The work of Padeyevsky and others in this time period were significant only in that they formed the foundation for the short-lived Bioplasmic School of thought, later discredited by the occurrence of . . .

The text abruptly stopped and the next paragraph was clearly unrelated to what she had just read. She stared at the screen for several long minutes. She recognized the name Padeyevsky from the poem she had just read. Who was he, and what did he have to do with this? Why would Potemkin have referred her to a geneticist from the last century? The uneasiness came again. She felt as though she was standing at an invisible gateway—like if she passed through this place, she might never be able to turn back.

She looked around her. Nothing had changed. She thought about her life, how fulfilling it had been until now, how hard she had worked, how unquestioning she had been. Her mind stretched out over years of experiences, the training, the sisters, the faces of her many handlers, and the head of her school, Mother Clara. She thought of the feelings of purpose and accomplishment that had been her daily reward. With some resentment, she thought of the gnawing discomfort that had begun just a few weeks ago, the loneliness she had begun to feel, and finally Angela Potemkin's image on the monitor screen saying, "You are far more than you think . . ."

Kay closed her eyes and pressed her fingers gently against the lids. I shouldn't be here, she thought. The words of The Text came floating through the myriad thoughts in her mind:

In single-mindedness toward the will of the Whole Body and the righteous instruction of her Ministers lies the path to Oneness. The path of deviation leads to separation and despair.

She should get up from the chair, walk out of this room, and never think about any of this again.

But then she reread one of the sentences before her: "It is not known if any of the latter survived to adulthood . . ." As though they now belonged to someone else, Kay's fingers moved to the keyboard. She closed the document she had been reading, called up the original search screen, and typed "Padeyevsky."

The screen blanked and then displayed fourteen references, including *The Collected Poems of Teramina Hoyle Parkinson, 2023–2065*. She scanned the list and recognized one of the titles she had seen on Angela Potemkin's message, *Sociological Repercussions in the Conversion of the African Continent to Unified Market Forces*. She opened the document and searched for Chapter 11. She began reading.

Certain ancient peoples believed that 2012 marked what they called the beginning of the Last Cycle. This community began in that auspicious year, operating on the assumption that a new paradigm is emerging in human history, a renaissance in human consciousness that will transcend the boundaries of the time/space reality we have hitherto known, placing us firmly on the path to an uncharted existence.

Thanks to the work of Dr. Theodore Padeyevsky and the other members of our governing council, we have experienced the first intimations of this state of being. Largely because we have used ourselves and our offspring as subjects, we are experiencing vilification both by the scientific community and the neighboring villages. Our attempts to present our results in traditional forums have been blocked, and despite Dr. P's considerable reputation as one of the world's most accomplished geneticists, it appears he may be headed for rough waters professionally.

Amid all this, however, there is little doubt that we are on the verge of a major breakthrough, perhaps many. We have documented among our adult population increased ability to concentrate, to perform selected tasks with radically greater speed and agility, and sporadic episodes of telekinesis, prescience, and ability to diagnose and treat illness. The latter has been accomplished in nearly all cases by means of transference to the ailing subject energies apparently buried within visual images of health and well-being initiated by the treating physician or scientist.

Demonstrable ability to move small objects on occasion without physical contact in a controlled environment has been successful in thirty-four percent of our adults. Foreknowledge of even trivial events is a daily occurrence, and the subject of continual amusement and conversation here.

In the year following the inception of the community, the children are remarkably healthy and demonstrate motor skills and evidence of cognitive functions far beyond average standards. It is too soon to say with any certainty that this is a result of the ongoing work, but that these young Tressalinians—*Kay again recognized the word from the poem*—are significantly more gifted than their parents is unmistakable.

Kay chewed absently on her lip, which was raw from several days of the unconscious activity.

She closed the file and reopened *The Collected Poems of Teramina Hoyle Parkinson, 2023–2065*, and *The Rape and Redemption of Psyche*, and read:

But scattered amidst time's decayed relics
Lay Padeyevsky's pollen and Psyche's golden tresses
Dyed red with the blood of the martyrs
And fed by the root of the Tressaline tree . . .

So Tressaline was the name of a scientific community in the early part of the 21st century working on some sort of genetic project. Who were these people? And why would Angela Potemkin, as her final act in this world, have led her to these passages about a community that existed so many generations ago? Was this what she had she meant when she said: ". . . this part of you hails from a far more ancient lineage?"

Just as the force of realization began to rise in her like an incoming tide, she heard a voice from behind her.

"Well, I'm glad to see someone else here has an interest in poetry."

Kay's reflexes took over. With a flick of her finger, she cancelled the search program on the screen, rose to a full standing position, and whirled around, coming face to face with a shaken Aria Helsing.

Chapter 11

"I . . . I'm sorry," Aria stammered. "I didn't mean to startle you. I was just . . . it's just I haven't found poetry to be very popular here." She felt the blood draining from her face as she stared into the eyes of the very assassin she had read remotely only a few days before.

The woman before her said nothing, but continued her steely gaze.

"I'm Aria Helsing. I'm a Counselor here." Aria hesitated, then extended her hand. The woman did not respond, and Aria withdrew it. It was clear that she had surprised this dangerous woman at an inauspicious moment. She summoned her most unthreatening voice and smile. "I apologize for coming up on you like that. It was inappropriate. I guess I'm still something of a novice in council etiquette."

The tension faded a little from the young woman's face. Aria noticed four painful-looking scratches there, scabbed red lines that ran the breadth of her left cheek.

"That's all right," Kay said, and Aria was surprised by the softness of her voice. The assassin glanced quickly around the room. There were only two others at terminals now, and they paid no attention to the standing women.

"I'm done reading for the day anyway. You can have this terminal, if you like," Kay said, and turned to leave.

"No wait, please," Aria said. "I so seldom get to talk with anyone outside my line of command. Won't you stay for a moment? Maybe we could discuss poets." Then realizing how her voice carried in this mammoth hall, she said softly, "Perhaps we could have a cup of tea or something."

Aria was surprised by her own audacity. Kay Black had not volunteered her own name in response to her introduction. Of course not, Aria chided herself. The woman is an anonymous member of a secret organization. Aria didn't know the extent of the assassins' social lives, but since she had not knowingly encountered any of the others she had been assigned to read, she assumed they stayed to themselves. She knew of no rule against contact, but sensed it was an unstated taboo. By all the signals she was picking up, she had overstepped her bounds.

And yet, there was considerable hesitation in Kay's demeanor. Aria was surprised by the sympathy she felt for her, and even more surprised by her own curiosity. Perhaps it was the unusual experience she had reading the young woman remotely. Something about Kay's presence stirred her.

Kay stopped abruptly and turned. A curious look came over the assassin's face, both thoughtful and sad. "Do you know who I am?"

The forthrightness of the question stunned Aria. She opened her mouth to deny any knowledge of the K-class, but something in the assassin's eyes made her stop. She sensed no threat in the question. She paused and then, screwing up her courage, she took the plunge.

"Yes. Yes I do," she answered in an almost apologetic tone. "As a Counselor, I have access to certain files. I didn't recognize you at first, but you are known as Kay Black, aren't you?"

Aria sensed both surprise and relief in the younger woman. Kay stole another quick look around the room and asked, "What is the role of a Counselor?" To someone less sensitive, Kay's voice would have sounded flat and emotionless, but Aria heard in it the slight lilt of childishness, and behind it a longing, a tendril of hope.

"Well, before I came here . . . to the council, I mean . . . I mostly talked with people who were trying to sort out their feelings in order to make some decision, businesswomen and leaders, people embarking on new careers, that sort of thing. I sometimes have the ability to see life patterns, someone's proclivities, you know? I help uncover the thoughts behind the thoughts and reflect it back to them so they can see things more clearly. Since being here, though, I have been mainly called upon to give Mother Gretel or her aides advice or insight into the character of the people they supervise."

The assassin stared at her in silence for several discomforting moments, and Aria caught flashes of a struggle in her eyes. Clearly she was reticent to communicate, but something in her wanted to come out. Aria had seen it in dozens of people, especially in the world beyond these walls, people whose lives demanded that they present a certain façade to the world. She wanted to say something that would help the younger woman decide, but could think of nothing, so she simply waited.

Then, as if a tiny light had been turned on, Aria saw that the decision was made. "I was just going to the workout sanctuary. We could meet in the heat room," the assassin said.

Aria understood the implication that they should not go there together. She nodded.

"I'll just finish a few things here and then join you. In about ten minutes?" She smiled at the assassin and felt another surge of sympathy as the young woman nodded, turned abruptly on her heel, and strode from the hall.

Aria sat down at the terminal and let all her muscles go limp. "Good Goddess," she swore under her breath. She slipped the bag from her shoulder and let it come to rest next to the chair, and spread her hands on the table. What are you doing? she asked herself silently. This is the kind of thing that could wreck your career.

And yet she couldn't deny that this encounter had a subtle feel about it, a ring of purposefulness, of synchronicity that dimmed her normally strong sense of propriety.

The encounter was nearly as troubling to her as the one with Desta Mardrid. An hour after the meeting with Mother Gretel, Mardrid had summoned her to deliver the reports on the five subjects Aria had thought she would deliver to Mother Gretel. The terrifying images Mardrid had been able to create during Aria's impromptu reading were still lurking in the corners of Aria's mind when the aide had opened the door to her. Aria had steeled herself, putting on an air of official formality. She was relieved when Mardrid said nothing about the earlier debacle.

She reported perfunctorily on four of the readings and was about to begin on K-1754's when Mardrid interrupted. "I am particularly curious about this one. Something odd about her."

For an instant, Aria considered telling Mardrid about the experience she'd had while attempting to read Kay, but something warned her off.

"I did have some trouble getting a solid read on her," she said. "Actually, I was going to request more time to try again and sort things out."

"What things?" Mardrid said, her tone clipped and laced with suspicion.

Did Mardrid have the ability to read her thoughts? After

all, the aide had somehow managed to turn Aria's attempt to fish for impressions in her psyche into a nightmarish experience. Certainly she had a wider range of talents than most people. Aria searched for a plausible answer while maintaining a strong mental image of an impenetrable wall of light around her body.

"Instead of the usual objective impressions I normally get when reading someone, I found myself losing personal objectivity and being swept up in rather disjointed, almost hallucinogenic experiences." It was the truth, but without any of the specifics. "I was unable to make any sense of the reading before you called me to report to Mother."

"Rather like the reading in Mother's office?" Mardrid said, smirking.

Mardrid was testing her, Aria thought. She would not take the bait, but she would let her know that she understood what had happened. "No. There was no conscious attempt by the K-class woman to block my access. It was quite different from that."

Mardrid's hard little eyes betrayed nothing. "Very well. You have another few days to consider the subject. Keep the file until I call for it."

Sitting in the Hall of Records now, about to have a clandestine conversation with a woman who scared her nearly as much as Mardrid, Aria wondered why she hadn't told her superior the whole truth. Odd, she thought, how these unintentional alliances are formed and how at times it seemed she had no control over her life.

She made a pretense of turning on the monitor in front of her and flipping through a few random files, all the while keeping an eye on the timepiece on the opposite wall. Ten minutes passed, and she flicked off the screen, picked up her bag, and headed for the entrance, signing out as she passed the front desk.

The workout sanctuary was nearly deserted. She saw a few women preparing to begin a formal routine in the main room, and a few more were strapped into the electronic workout machines, wires attached to their major muscle groups like so many tentacles. Aria passed through the door of the changing room, placed her bag in one of the empty cubbies, and began stripping off her loose-fitting two-piece suit. Naked, she walked to the table where stacks of towels were laid out, wrapped one around her, and proceeded down the short hallway to the ultrasound and heat rooms.

This could be a monumental mistake, she realized. What if Kay couldn't tolerate someone knowing who she was and simply killed her? Perhaps it was policy to eliminate anyone with such knowledge.

But the assassin had seemed ready to talk about something. Something wanted to come out, and Aria wanted to know what it was. It was risky, but intriguing. Besides, this meeting held the possibility of something more than the superficiality that seemed to define her other relationships at headquarters. Aria was lonely, and this was exciting, she admitted. Was she attracted to Kay?

At the door, Aria pressed the little panel at the side that read "open." The door slid to the side with a quiet whoosh, and the blast of heat made her momentarily close her eyes. When she opened them and stepped into the dimly lit, stifling room, she was disappointed to find it empty. She poked her head into several of the privacy alcoves. No sign of the assassin. Perhaps I waited too long, and Kay changed her mind, she thought. The door closed behind her and she felt the heat sink into her skin. Then again, she thought, maybe she was just waiting to see if I would show up.

She decided to wait in one of the reclining seats for a while. She leaned back against its surprisingly cool surface and closed her eyes against the burning air, soft music coming from somewhere. Just what would she say to the assassin? What would they talk about? Should she try for a reading during the meeting or simply try to be friendly? Was her interest professional or personal?

The heat sank deep into her bones and the tension in her muscles let go. Yes, relax, she told herself. Things would be clearer soon enough. In a few moments her mind was awash in images of swimming beneath the surface of a great pool, the water rushing over her body as she willed herself forward through current. She floated to the surface and took a breath of air that was warmer than the water. She licked her lips and tasted the salty residue of the water. When she realized the water was her own sweat, she opened her eyes.

There, four feet away from her and staring at her with intense brown eyes, sat the assassin.

"Oh, hello," Aria said in a thick voice as she leaned forward and brought her seat to an upright position. "I'm sorry. I didn't hear you come in." She couldn't have had her eyes closed for more than a few moments but she was amazed at how hot she felt. She dabbed at the sweat pouring into her eyes with the corner of the towel and blinked at the figure before her.

Aria couldn't help but marvel at the lithe, muscular limbs of the young woman. The assassin sat upright, alert but relaxed, her posture radiating vitality. A towel hugged her torso, revealing small round breasts and a narrow waist. The close-cropped hair glistened with tiny beads of sweat in the dim light. There was high color in her cheeks and a thin sheen of moisture covered her face, beading on the angry scratches there. The woman was beautiful, but in so subtle a way it could easily be missed, Aria thought.

Kay must have been sitting here silently for some time, Aria realized. How did she get in without me hearing the door? She searched for something to say, but before she could speak, Kay said, "You have been asked about me?"

For the second time that day Aria thought about lying, but decided it would be less complicated and safer to tell the truth, or at least part of it. She would make no reference to Mardrid's special interest in Kay. "I have been asked to read several of the sisters from your . . . order. It appears to be standard operating procedure."

"What did you report?" The question was blunt, but after asking it, Kay looked at the floor between them. No challenge here, Aria knew, but honest curiosity tinged with slight anxiety.

"Well, to be honest, I had a rather difficult time with yours. I sort of lost my bearings while I was trying to read you and wasn't able to report much. It was apparent that you're very devoted to your mission, and that you have strong feelings about the Mother who raised you."

Aria paused, wondering if she should say anything about the strange experience she'd had, the feeling of expansion and the sense that some important event was imminent. "I did get the feeling that something in your recent experience is troubling you, though I didn't report any of that yet."

When the young woman looked up, Aria felt a rush in her chest. There was such a look of despair in Kay's eyes that Aria had to force herself not to look away.

"Can we speak in confidence?" Kay asked. Aria nodded.

"Something . . . unusual . . . is happening to me. I don't understand. I'm having a hard time focusing on my work, and my body seems to be out of balance, inside . . ." She touched the spot between her breasts. "I don't know if you can understand, but I'm having . . . forbidden thoughts . . . feelings about some of my clients . . . well, one in particular . . ." and her voice dropped.

Aria remembered the vision of the face that first dominated her reading of the assassin, and the sickening feeling of vertigo immediately after seeing it.

"Listen . . ." she stopped, realizing she didn't know exactly how to address the younger woman. "May I call you Kay?"

The assassin nodded.

"All right, Kay. Can you tell me how long has this been happening?"

"A few weeks, maybe longer. I don't know what to do to get back on track. I thought I might have gotten some sort of illness, but I don't feel ill. I've slipped out of my disciplines a little. I was headed here to do some training *katas,* but I ended up in the Hall of Records looking up . . . some things. That's what I mean though. I keep getting distracted. And I'm having bad dreams."

Aria remembered feeling as though she had interrupted Kay in the Hall of Records. "What sort of dreams?"

"I don't know." Kay looked almost dejected now, reluctant to go any farther. "There's a child and some danger. I try to reach it, warn it, but I can't speak. Things like that."

"Dreams can be many things," Aria said. "Sometimes I can get inside of people's dreams and some meaning comes clearer. Then again, sometimes they don't appear to mean anything," and here she interjected a lighthearted tone, "or they seem to be the product of a sour meal before bedtime."

Kay looked hopeful. "Could you do that with my dream?" The little girl was back in her voice.

Aria hesitated. Reading Kay the first time had not been

an altogether unpleasant experience. In fact, it had been rather exhilarating. Still, the direction their conversation had taken felt dangerous. Should she continue? On the one hand, she was going to have to report something on Kay to Mardrid within a few days. Direct readings were often more fruitful than remote ones, and the two women were in the most private setting she could hope for.

On the other hand, something about this woman was powerful in a way Aria had never before experienced. Her readings of Kay and Mardrid were the only ones in which she had ever lost control, and she was not eager to repeat that experience. But she might never have another opportunity like this one.

She saw the warring expressions of hope and despair in Kay's features, and was moved. "Well, I can give it a try. Why don't you tell me the dream from the beginning?"

Aria could tell the assassin was also wondering if this was a good idea, but after a long silence, Kay nodded and settled back into her seat, laying one graceful hand atop the other. Aria closed her eyes and cleared her mind. Here we go, she thought.

A moment later, Kay began. "I'm looking out over an ocean, or a big lake. It's very still, so still it doesn't seem possible. It feels like I'm floating. I see a child standing in the water facing away, and over its head are swirling lights, all different colors. They come closer and fall to the surface of the water. I can see now that they are solid, like circles of colored glass. The child begins to pick these up. I feel . . . drawn to the child, and I begin moving over the water toward it. But then I notice something way out on the horizon, a dark cloud or a wall of water. I don't know how, but I know the child is in danger . . ."

Aria followed the sound of Kay's voice, down through its

tonal layers, drifting easily into the images, seeing them distinctly and floating toward the child with the dream's narrator.

Then everything changed.

She was wrenched from the scene into a different setting. She was standing in the middle of a deserted urban street, wondering where all the people had gone. Beneath her feet the earth began to tremble and crack. As she scrambled to get her footing, the tall buildings all around her begin to crumble, sloughing off huge chunks, which fell to the ground and disintegrated into dust.

She was filled with awe. The phrase "end of the world" came to her. Dust rose in huge plumes, dough-like, forming themselves into huge roiling pillars that began moving toward her with the smoothness and inevitability of glaciers. Two columns closest to her were taking on a distinct shape. At their tops they merged and continued growing upward. Aria realized the dust was taking the shape of legs, hips, a human body. Pressure began building in her chest. The heat was becoming unbearable. She tried in vain to catch her breath.

She wanted to turn and flee from the figure, but she couldn't lift her feet. When she looked down at them, she was horrified to find them sinking into the street, dissolving like wax at the base of a candle. She looked up again at the approaching shape, whose massive, doughy head was beginning to form facial features. She tried to scream for help, but all that came out was a sighing, "Oh," before she dissolved into a puddle in the steaming street.

When she opened her eyes again, she didn't know where she was. She blinked at the ceiling and waited for her mind to clear. A moment later she raised her head and looked around. She was on her back on a bench in the room where she originally had disrobed. The towel stretched over her was drenched, whether from her own sweat or from water she could not tell.

How had she gotten here? She propped herself up on one elbow, and felt her stomach churn with a wave of nausea. Immediately she lay back down and took some deep breaths. What had happened? Where was Kay? How long had she been here, out of the heat room? How did she get here?

Again she attempted to sit up, swallowing hard as she came to a sitting position. She rested her elbows on her knees and her head in her hands until the room stopped spinning. Must've gotten too hot. Then she remembered Kay beginning to relate her dream, and she knew that it was not just the heat. Kay's dream images flashed in her mind, and the feeling of the earth trembling beneath her feet.

It had happened again. She'd lost it, only this time it was worse.

She groaned. Something extraordinary was going on here. Something much bigger, more dangerous than she had imagined.

What she didn't know was what she was going to do about it.

Chapter 12

Parker wiped the stinging sweat from his eyes and looked again into the face of his opponent, Stanislav Breckner. It was at least ninety-five degrees in the Sun Stadium, despite the fact that the officials had called an hour-long delay in the games in late morning while the dome was raised and cooler air was circulated below it.

Breckner was older than Parker by a year and easily as big, with fists the size of cantaloupes and small gray eyes set deep above high cheekbones. He was ranked second in the Northern Hemisphere League. Parker was considered the underdog here, and the way this last match of the day was going, he deserved the title.

When the two had squared off against each other for the eight-minute one-on-one round, the right side of Breckner's wide mouth had twisted into a mocking half smile, a look of contempt. Parker had instantly disliked him. The feeling had not been enough, however, to save him from several minutes of punishing blows. He'd miscalculated each of a half-dozen of Breckner's attacks, which came early and hard. Four had caused Parker considerable pain and had momentarily shaken his confidence, particularly the stinging kick he'd taken to the right side of his head. With that one, Parker had stepped back two paces, his left heel treading outside the diameter of the eight-foot circle the athletes occupied. It had cost him a full point.

Severe contact was frowned upon in these matches, and the judges subtracted half a point for each infraction. Athletes like Breckner, and their overseers, however, considered the psychological impact of causing pain worth the initial demerits.

The break in the action gave Parker a moment to take a breath and re-center himself. In that moment, he visualized how Breckner had dropped his right shoulder too far in recovering his two-footed stance. Parker's anger, which had flared momentarily with the pain, vanished with the realization, and he had moved back inside the circle with the intention of drawing Breckner into repeating the move.

Parker feigned a punch with his right hand, repeating the move that had gotten him into trouble a few moves back. When Breckner responded with the anticipated kick, Parker gave a tap to the oncoming foot, turning Breckner just enough so that the back of his head was exposed. Then he delivered a perfectly executed glancing kick to Breckner's head, just enough to put his opponent off-balance. Breckner's shoulder dropped again as he tried to regain his stance, and Parker threw two perfect cheek jabs with his right hand—like butterfly kisses—and a harder one to the rib cage with his left. When Breckner staggered backward, surprised, Parker swept the man's supporting foot with his left leg, and felt a great surge of satisfaction as Breckner's huge frame headed for the ground, face first.

The crowd roared its approval. The take-down was worth five points, putting Parker only two points behind. Breckner bounced back upright, his face red with embarrassment and anger. In contrast, Parker felt his body cool, and his concentration drop into that deeper level he was becoming familiar with. The noises of the crowd faded away, and he experienced something like omniscience, as though he could perfectly anticipate Breckner's slightest move. From this place, he let Breckner make all the aggressive moves, batting away each of the man's attempts to do harm. The more angry and frustrated Breckner became, the more focused Parker became, until, in the final seconds of the match, Parker took him down again, this time with Breckner's whole torso outside the circle.

Thousands in the stands jumped to their feet, cheering and stamping. He left the arena with the knowledge that he had led his team to the most wins of the day, acknowledging the cheers with a wave of his hand. What he felt, however, was not the hubris of the victor, but something more like peace. The experience stayed with him for hours, until he left for the appointment with the woman whose name his mother had left with him.

"I am here to see Mother Avalon," he said to the featureless door. "My name is Parker Potemkin."

It was nearly nightfall and the shadows fell sharply across the face of the odd old building, an anachronism amidst the sleek contours of offices and dwellings built in more recent decades. Its three stories sat squat and comparatively narrow on this street in an outlying area of New Phoenix. Parker looked up from the doorway to the single rows of windows that ran from corner to corner across the building's tan face. Several lit squares indicated that there were occupied rooms above. The day's earlier heat still radiated from the rough surface of the building.

He was a little surprised at how readily his request for a solo outing this evening was honored. He had always thought the order was stricter with this sort of thing. Maybe there were privileges for people who brought success to the team. The thought brought a twinge of guilt. In all the years of training, the order had always emphasized one-for-all, and all-for-one. One wasn't supposed to get special treatment. Maybe he'd been naïve.

He hadn't much experience on the outside, seldom finding reason to leave the various Califas compounds around North America where the brothers lived and trained. The others had long ago given up on trying to convince him to join them on their field trips.

He was content to fill his days and nights with training and study. This, among his other oddities, cast him apart from his brethren. Though they respected him for his skills and achievements, socially they found him to be unnerving, and Parker knew it.

Two weeks after he'd received his mother's message, the feelings of sadness and suspicion lingered. He had spoken of these to no one, save Pamela, but they gnawed at him. Sometimes at night he would lie awake wondering why he wasn't able to shrug them off.

Tonight's task, meeting this woman whom his mother had foisted on him, annoyed him. He didn't want to be here. Even flush with the day's victories, when he had called Mother Avalon to make the appointment, he had felt awkward and self-conscious.

Things outside of the arena that he couldn't control often set him on edge. Inside the arena, uncertainties and an opponent's unexpected moves were different. For these he trained vigorously, testing his limits of physical knowledge, challenging himself to react more quickly, to learn more. Breaking his routine like this, however, and being in an unfamiliar part of this city, these were not things he would ever do on his own. He resented his mother a little for asking him to do this.

Mother Avalon had been cordial, though, and on the telescreen her smile had been welcoming. She had suggested he come at 17:00. The taxi had deposited him at the door five minutes early and sped away. Over his shoulder, other taxis buzzed past on the relatively unpopulated street like desperate insects in some barren field. He shifted his weight to the other foot and squeezed his left wrist behind his back. They were taking a long time to answer, and he considered simply turning away and returning to the compound. Then, from a speaker somewhere above the arched door a woman's voice sounded.

"Come in, Parker. I'll meet you in the foyer."

He heard the door click, but it didn't slide to open. He realized it must be an old one, and he reached out tentatively and gave it a little push. It opened into a tiny, well-lit entryway, and he stepped in, stooping to avoid striking his head on the frame. With a little difficulty in the cramped space, he managed to get himself on the other side of the door and close it. When he tried to straighten up again, his hair brushed the ceiling. The inner door had a low, round window in it, and as he bent down to get a look inside he could see the floor of a foyer and the base of a curved stairway with a polished wooden handrail.

To the right stood a set of wooden doors, deep brown in color and ornately carved with a forest scene, trees that appeared to be bending low, offering their leaves to the upturned mouths of deer walking among them. To the left of the entranceway hung a large portrait of a stately-looking woman dressed in black, her gaze unapologetic and her hands, with very long and delicate fingers, resting in her lap. Parker was wondering who she might be, and if this were an exclusive residence for Southwest Council members, when he saw a foot appear on the stairs.

It was tiny, shod in a simple moccasin-like slipper of black. When the second foot appeared, he saw above it the hem of a robe in official blue, hinting that this would be a formal meeting. He was glad he had decided to wear his dress uniform.

As the figure came into view, Parker saw a diminutive woman, no taller than five feet, with very wide hips and narrow shoulders, above which appeared a face unlike any he had ever seen. The chin was quite small and narrow, the mouth so tiny it seemed unlikely any food could pass there. Wide cheekbones were set apart by a long, thin nose, and even wider-set, dark eyes looked out from beneath a broad, creased forehead. Her eyes were so far apart that Parker repressed a smile when it occurred to him that she might be able to see to the side without turning her head.

Parker was surprised by one other feature he had not noticed earlier on the low-resolution telescreen—tiny crow's feet at the corners of her eyes. It struck him that Mother Avalon might be the oldest woman he had ever met.

She reached out to touch an unseen button, and the inner door swung open.

"Hello, Parker. Please come in, won't you?" Her voice was full, like a public speaker, Parker thought. She brought her right hand up to her shoulder in a formal salute.

"Thank you, Mother Avalon," he said stiffly, returning the gesture.

"Did the games go well today?"

"Yes, very well. Did you watch?"

"I'm afraid I have little interest in sports," she said. "I manage to keep quite busy without that sort of diversion."

Such comments sometimes struck Parker as demeaning. People often said such things in a dismissive way, tweaking a deep place of insecurity in him. He was confident enough of his abilities on the field, but even though athletes were objects of much attention, adulation even, they were generally not taken very seriously as citizens. Something in the way Mother Avalon had said it, though, made the comment less a slight than a statement of fact, a choice based on a sense of priority rather than a judgment.

She turned toward the carved doors and gestured gracefully in their direction with her left hand. "Shall we go into the study? It's larger and far more comfortable than my quarters."

Parker nodded and Mother Avalon padded noiselessly to the doors and twisted a small glass knob at its center. The door was large, but it yielded, and she stepped inside, waiting. Parker again ducked his head to avoid the low frame. When he straightened up, he stood wide-eyed and silent. The room was lush and elegant. Beneath his feet a thick, old carpet was festooned with elaborate red swirls and patterns, a knotted fringe at its edges. Huge, plush chairs upholstered with fine fabric sat in each corner. In the middle of the room an ancient sofa with spindly, curved legs and a high, curved back squared off in front of a small, low table. His eyes lingered on the table's gleaming surface and the rhythmic striations of wood from which it was made. Its warm, deep color was echoed by the wood visible atop the sofa's back, which was carved into symmetrical sworls suggestive of waves.

But what struck him most was what lined the entire wall behind the furniture: row upon row of books, standing at attention like soldiers in formation, at least forty feet high. He'd only ever seen a few and only actually held one in his hands, and here were hundreds, perhaps a thousand, in all sizes. Long before Parker came into this world, the use of wood to make paper had become too costly, and electronic media had otherwise rendered the form obsolete. He scanned the spines at eye level, trying to read the titles from where he stood. Most were barely visible, perhaps worn away by countless handlings.

Mother Avalon turned, saw the look on Parker's face, and smiled. "There is not another collection like this in the world." She waved her small hand in the direction of the shelves. "Would you like to take a closer look?"

Parker tore his eyes from the shelves long enough to nod. "Where did they all come from? I didn't think they still existed."

"This has been the project of the Nestercine Sisterhood, the order in which I was raised. You saw the portrait on the wall outside? It is of Mother Theophilus, our founder."

She nodded toward the books. "It was her vision. For seven of our generations these were brought from all corners of the world, carried by hand and bought at great price . . ." she paused and shot him a look ". . . and some at great personal sacrifice."

Parker wondered what exactly the look was meant to convey. Without further comment, though, Mother Avalon turned and walked toward the shelves, and reached for the nearest book. She held it delicately in her left hand, touched its cover with the fingers of the right, as one might caress a child. Then she opened the cover, gazed at the title, turned the book around, and held it out to Parker. He came forward, his eyes moving from her face to the opened book, and read silently: *The End of Freedom: Sociobiological Tyranny in the Post-Apocalyptic World*, by Marcel Irvington.

"May I?" he asked, reaching tentatively for it.

"Of course." Mother Avalon relinquished the book.

Parker carefully turned the pages, scanning the information in the front, including the date of publication: 2027. Leafing further, he paused at some of the charts and old two-dimensional photographs of people he didn't recognize. He looked at the slightly bemused face of Mother Avalon.

"It's pretty old." It was an inane comment, he knew, but he could think of nothing else to say.

"Yes it is," she replied, gently taking the book from him and replacing it on the shelf. She gestured toward the sofa. "Shall we?"

Parker looked at the ancient piece of furniture, doubtful that it would support his large frame.

"It's quite all right," Mother Avalon said, sensing his question. "It's a fine, sturdy place to sit."

Parker eased onto one end of the sofa, resting his right arm on the carved wood along the back. When she settled on the other end, he began abruptly. "As I said when we spoke earlier, my mother sent me a message shortly before she passed away that you had something for me."

Her mouth turned slightly upward, as though his words reminded her of something pleasant. "Your mother was a brilliant, brave woman."

Parker looked down at his hand spread wide across his thigh. He squirmed a little, avoiding her gaze. He didn't know what to say, and the moment grew long. His cheeks felt warm.

After a while she spoke again, but her words did little to dispel the tension. "Parker, do you know anything about your mother's work?"

"Well, a little. She was a genetic Designer with the Ministry of Births. I know she worked very hard. When I was little she used to come home and fall asleep in a chair sometimes." He remembered the commendations he and Pamela found in her effects. "She must've been very good at what she did."

The little smile reappeared on Mother Avalon's face. "Yes, quite good, far better than even the Ministry knew."

Again, a long silence followed and she seemed to be

thinking deeply about her last statement, her small fingers
passing idly back and forth over the embroidered fabric of
the sofa. At last, she spoke again. "How do you like being
an exhibition athlete?"

"Like it? I . . . I like it fine." No one had ever asked him
such a question.

"What exactly do you like about it?" she asked, her eyes
holding his.

He thought for a moment. "I guess I like having a big
challenge and rising to meet it. I like centering my mind
and concentrating on a goal and working hard to reach it. I
like bringing honor to the Califas Order."

These last words rang a little hollow even to him, like a
child's lesson learned by rote. Mother Avalon said nothing,
but Parker knew she was waiting for a deeper answer.

"And I like the feeling that comes from knowing I am
doing my very best, or when I discover I am better at something than I imagined." He paused, remembering that day's
match with Breckner, "Or than someone else thought."

Her smile broadened at this last remark. "What else?"

Parker warmed to her question. He thought again of the
last moments of that final match. "It's like I'm the fine edge
of a knife, and I'm slicing through a thin, filmy cloth.
Things get . . . shiny, as if they're lit from inside, and my
body feels light. It's like I know my opponent's intentions,
what he's going to do next."

He felt her gaze on him like heat, similar to what he had
felt radiating from the building's façade earlier. What he
said next surprised him, as though someone else were
speaking. "It's pure thought, like there's no difference between thinking something and making it happen. And even
though it's me doing it, it's as though something bigger is
moving me."

"Yes," Mother Avalon said, clapping her hands once. "You've described it very well. The colonists called it 'the field.' "

"The colonists?" He had no idea what she was talking about. His head buzzed a little.

Mother Avalon didn't answer, but sat unmoving and upright at the other end of the sofa, her hands now folded in her lap, her gaze intense. Parker squirmed again and looked away.

"Do you sometimes feel you are different from your brothers, the others in the order?" Mother Avalon finally asked.

"Different?" He heard himself echo another of her questions and wondered why he sounded so stupid. He imagined she was sparring with him, only in another arena entirely. "How do you mean?"

"How do you think I mean?"

Parker clasped and unclasped his hands, then crossed his arms in front of his chest. "Mother Avalon, I don't wish to be disrespectful. I appreciate you seeing me on such short notice, but I really came to . . ."

"I know why you came, son," she interrupted, reaching out to touch the part of his hand not concealed by the broad bicep, "but our time together is short and I have wanted to meet you for a very long time. Do you think you might indulge me for a while longer?"

"Well . . . sure, I guess," he said, suddenly ashamed by his impatience in the face of her interest. There was something about her he liked, something welcoming in her attention. He felt different, somehow, in her presence. "Forgive my ignorance, Mother, but I don't remember ever having heard your name before my mother's last message, and yet you seem to know a lot about me. I'm a little surprised, I guess."

She looked at the folds in her robe, smoothed them, studied the pattern they made. "It will not be the last surprise, Parker," she said finally. "I will tell you more about this, but I'd like to ask a little more about how you see the world, how you feel about things."

She looked directly into his eyes, held his gaze, and Parker felt a rush in his chest, like a space had just opened under his feet. "So do you sometimes feel different?"

It was a very personal question, and not one that would have been thinkable at the brotherhood. He was about to say so, but when he opened his mouth to speak, he was seized with a memory so vivid he froze.

It's the week after his fourteenth birthday, a week after his acceptance into the Califas Brotherhood. He's walking back to the training camp after a ten-kilometer run with the eleven other boys who make up the Blue Team, to which he had been assigned at the beginning of that first week. The camp is set at the outskirts of the Philadelphia megalopolis, and when he first arrived, he was thrilled at the playing fields strewn across the expansive grounds, and the running paths that curved over rolling acres crowded with trees and shrubs and ferns. In the metroplex where he had lived with his mother and Pam, there had been many small squares with carefully laid out trees and flowerbeds. Most of the buildings in which they had lived had extensive atria and even basement gardens that grew lush under sunlight piped in from collectors on the roofs. Parker had loved the moist and fresh smell of these places, but compared to the Califas grounds, they seemed puny. In the first few days there, he had heard and seen things he'd never seen growing up—richly colored birds, a fox, and glimpses of small furry creatures that he didn't recognize.

On this day, as the boys walk and joke with each other, a small, emaciated wild dog wanders into a clearing in front of them and stops, eying them warily. Suddenly, the eldest boy—Alfeo, taller by inches than the others and scarred by a peculiar purple birthmark on his right cheek—lets out a whoop and leaps off in pursuit of the hapless creature. The dog flees into the meager stand of trees nearby. In an instant, the other boys take up the chase, leaving Parker trailing behind.

"Wait," he shouts, but no one pays attention.

When he finally catches up to them, they are surrounding the growling, cowering creature. Parker knows what will happen next, and he wants to stop it, but can't get the words out. Alfeo springs forward and delivers a kick to the dog's head that snaps its neck and sends it spinning end over end until it comes to rest limply against the base of a struggling sapling a dozen feet away. The other boys shriek in a way that makes the hair on Parker's neck stand up, and for the next few minutes they stomp the limp body into an unrecognizable bloody mass. He stands by fighting waves of nausea, wanting to turn away but afraid of being ridiculed by the others.

Parker realized he had been sitting staring into Mother Avalon's eyes, saying nothing, as this memory fired in his mind. He closed his mouth and swallowed, his throat having gone dry.

"Well, there was this once . . ." In a quiet voice, he began the tale. He was ashamed, but he didn't want to stop.

Mother Avalon listened intently, nodding and, on occasion, closing her eyes as if feeling the contours of Parker's dark memory. When Parker finished, she reached across and lightly tapped the back of his hand with her fingertips.

With a note of sadness in her voice, she said, "Yes, boys can sometimes be quite cruel. I understand."

Parker looked down at the small table and let out a long breath, surprised by the relief he felt.

"And what of your experiences with women?" Mother Avalon said, raising one thin eyebrow. "Have you explored your sexuality?"

Again her frankness startled him. This was a topic he wasn't going to explore with her. He'd never really spoken to anyone about such things. "I don't really . . ." he began, and trailed off. Her eyes held him fast. Something passed through him again and again, a subtle wave that pushed gently against some inner boundary of his being.

Mother Avalon's hand came to rest on his. "It's all right, you can tell me."

And he believed her. "There was one woman," he began.

It's early in his sixteenth year. He's finally enrolled at Sexual Services. His reluctance has been the cause both of good-natured kidding and not-so-benevolent ridicule from the other boys in the order. He's the last of the Blue Team to sign up. He hasn't been able to articulate the reasons for his reluctance even to himself. It isn't as though he hasn't fantasized about women when he is alone in his bed. But the thought of being with one in the flesh fills him with foreboding.

Peer pressure and surging hormones are finally having their way with him, though. His hand trembles a little as he signs the SS roster, and the next morning he finds himself in the Head Master's office, Rayful Edwards handing him a note containing the woman's name, directions to her home, the expected time of his arrival. Edwards gives him a small SS identification pin (a circle with a phallic obelisk jutting upwards from the circle's base). When passed over a client's scanner, Edwards explains, the pin would reveal a code by which its owner could be requested again, if desired. Edwards delivers a brief obligatory speech on upholding the reputation and honor of the brotherhood, a sly smile, and a pat on the back as Parker leaves the office.

He arrives on time, and is met at the door by an attractive brunette he guesses to be in her early twenties.

"Marta Sylvan?" he asks.

When she sees the SS pin on the breast of his form-fitting jumpsuit, she smiles broadly and looks him over from head to toe, obviously surprised and delighted. She crooks her finger at him, turns, and leads him by the hand through the living room past three of her housemates lounging there, toward the open door of a bedroom.

"Oooh, Marta," one of them teases, "look what's for dinner tonight—a big hunk!" Nervous laughter fills the room. "Robbed the cradle, she did," the woman says. A second woman hoots, "Woo hoo, check out those feet. You woman enough, Marta?" More laughter.

Parker tries to force a little smile in their direction, but the look on the face of the silent third woman instantly chills the effort. Parker feels her jealousy like an icy finger in his chest.

"She's gonna be walking funny tomorrow," the first woman says.

"Shut up, Fay," the pinched-face third woman snaps.

Parker feels like apologizing to her as the bedroom door closes behind him.

Marta is tall and athletic-looking, with broad shoulders, slender hips, and a fluid walk. She makes no attempt at con- versation, but walks around Parker, gently running her palms over his shoulders, his back, his buttocks, his broad chest and flat stomach. When she touches his rising manhood through his jumpsuit, she takes in a breath through her *pursed lips and says, "Oh my!"*

Parker stands like a statue, awash with physical sensations. When Marta begins pulling her silken blouse over her head, he feels his heart pounding in his ears.

"Well," she says as she slips out of her dark blue tights, "am I going to have to undress you, too?" Her voice is teasing, raspy.

When he is out of his jumpsuit, Marta comes to him like a cat, all slow grace, eyeing him up and down, a sly smile on her lips. She twirls the soft, curled hair on his chest with a finger, brushes the smooth skin of her stomach against him, and stretches her slender arms to encircle his neck. When her torso comes into full contact with his, Parker feels as though his body will crack open and spill its contents onto the floor. A light seems to be flashing in the room, and he hears sounds like water rushing through pipes. He groans under the sensory onslaught.

"Yes," he hears her whisper, and she runs her warm tongue slowly over his left nipple. Parker shudders. She loosens her grip around his neck, slides down to a kneeling position, and takes as much of him as she can in her mouth. Parker's legs tremble like he is hoisting a great weight.

A few moments later she stands, licks her lips, and brushes them against Parker's. He smells his own musk on her breath. She takes his hand again, pulls him to the bed. She turns him around and pushes on his chest until he is forced to sit down, keeps pushing until he is lying flat. She stands looking at him, his erect manhood and flushed skin, as though he is a table of delicious food. She parts and moistened her lips again with her tongue, and with her eyes closed halfway, begins slowly stroking herself, her breath loud in her throat.

Parker's mouth is dry. He starts to sit up, but she pushes him back down and straddles his supine form, the soft hair between her legs sending small charges through his body as it brushes the taut skin of his manhood. She stares into his face, licking her lips, cupping her breasts like offerings and squeezes their reddened, puffy tips. Small moans of pleasure escape her throat. She wets a finger with her juices and puts it to his lips.

"Taste me." He can even before she forces the finger into his mouth. And smell her. The room seems filled with the dark odor of her armpits, her crotch. Her skin glows and hair between her legs glistens, slick with moisture.

With her free hand, she traces the contours of his pectorals. He winces as she rakes a fingernail across his nipple, and his abdomen quivers as she brings the nails lower. She threads her fingers into the lush hair that frames his cock and tugs at it. His erection bounces against her and she gasps.

Finally, she reaches between her legs and squeezes him. Parker feels his back arch. With a long, low sigh, Marta lowers herself onto him.

It's like melting into her. At one moment he feels himself lying on his back on the bed, and in the next he is on top looking down at his body. And in the next all of him is inside of her, tumbling in sweet, warm blackness. In the next he is her engorged nipples crying out to be squeezed. He feels her hand pressing on his chest now, but then feels his (her?) hips opening wider and the delicious, almost unbearable sensation of being filled. He hears gasps, but can no longer tell from which of them they come. The bed begins to spin and rock, and static crackles in his ears. His (her?) skin feels like it is peeling away as they climb upward in a dizzying spiral.

Something is giving way, thinning. He (she?) rushes toward something, the atmosphere around them groaning, snapping. Beneath his closed eyelids, Parker sees both of their bodies become wispy fog, like the Milky Way looks on clear summer nights. He watches as if from a distance as they swirl into one another's space, melding and exchanging subtle hues, watery rainbows swaying and intertwining in rhythmic patterns, passing through them. In this instant, Parker lives this woman's lifetime, knows her bruises and fantasies, sees the faces of her mother and sister and shadowy images of others in her lineage, the letters of her name and its significance. He knows her emotional struggles, her studies, her insecurities, experiences each of her many other lovers, feels her involuntary pelvic contractions as his own . . . and in the distance he hears a terrified scream.

Startled, he opens his eyes. Marta is backing into a far corner of the room, her face a mask of terror and confusion. When she reaches the adjoining walls, she slides down into a crouch and flutters her hands before her like little flags in a stiff wind.

Parker manages to find his voice. "What's wrong? Are you all right?"

"Get out! Go away!" she screams.

The scratchy sound of her voice makes him flinch. He scrambles from the bed and reaches for his jumpsuit lying flaccid at the foot of the bed. Before he can cover himself, the door flies open and the housemates rush in, their eyes wide and faces white. Seeing Marta cowering against the wall crying, one rushes to her side and tries to grab Marta's flailing hands.

"He's in me. He's in me! Get him out!" Marta screams. She claws at her arms and breasts, raising fiery welts.

The second housemate backs away from Parker, her eyes full of fear. She is stopped by a small table behind her, and the lamp on it falls to the floor with a crash. She picks it up and swings it around in front of her in a pathetic gesture of defense. The pinched-face woman stands in the doorway and screams, "You bastard! You filthy pig! What did you do to her?"

"Nothing," Parker stammers. "I don't know what's wrong with her."

"Oh God. He's in me!" Marta wails from the corner.

His very cells ache. His insides feel torn, bleeding.

He wants to help Marta somehow, but the cowering, panicked women keep yelling at him. He manages to dress and leave the apartment in a matter of seconds, but the struggle to regain his composure takes hours. When he finally returns to the Califas compound, no amount of prodding from his brothers can pry the story from him. Eventually they give up, and ever after consider Parker even more of a freak. Sexual Services never again calls. If they had, Parker would have refused. The SS pin still lies at the bottom of a drawer in his quarters.

From out of the swirl of horrific memory, Mother Avalon's face appeared to him. "It was quite painful for you." It was not a question. "And you never tried again?"

Parker shook his head.

"No, I don't suppose you could have. I will venture a guess as to what happened. She wasn't able to meet your power, even then. It is not something to be ashamed of. It was devastating for you, yes. If you opened to her, and it seems you did, you crossed her psyche's defenses. In a sense, you became her. This is what often happens during such intimate moments, though most of the time, most people are unconscious to the process. You inducted her into it, however, and she was quite unprepared."

She patted his hand. "Do you know what happened to her?"

"I . . . I never saw her again, but one of the elders took me aside a week or so later and told me she had been institutionalized. He said she must have been an unstable person, that it wasn't my fault. He encouraged me to sign up for SS again, but I can't . . ."

"No, that would not do," Mother Avalon said. "I wouldn't feel too badly, Parker. She probably will be all right someday, if she's not already. She got more than she bargained for. I expect that someday you will meet someone who . . . well, things have a way of working out over time. It is important that you understand that it could not have been otherwise. You are, shall we say, special."

Parker gave her a wary look. "We're trained not to think like that. One of us may excel at something, but it is because we all work and train together. We say group intention and focus create opportunities to overcome opposition."

"Of course, that's true, son, but if you look deeply enough inside without such dogma, I think you will find something more profound than that. We are each made from the same material, and at one level we have the ability to meld together and create something that is more than the sum of the parts. But there are deeper levels at which, paradoxically, we are both distinct and part of something even grander. At such levels, if we can remain conscious to them, it is said we can do remarkable things.

"There are those who have taught that at such levels we are the essence of The Creator and can manipulate matter and time, heal or harm, or participate in the miracle of creation."

She looked at him, waiting for him to comprehend what she was saying. "For instance, why do you suppose your memories, so long forgotten, are suddenly available to you again here in this room?"

Parker considered it, and realized what he had been feeling since they had begun talking. There was something almost magnetic about Mother Avalon, something invisible gently pulling at his inner being. "Are you . . . doing something to me?"

"No," she said, "not to you. To us. Or more exactly, to this space and this moment. I'm simply creating an energetic container, a safe place in which we might have a look at what lies hidden under the surface of our everyday thoughts and habits. It is one of my talents. One of the things the Nestercines train for. We help uncover things.

"You have much buried within you, son. Don't you think it would be better to let it out?"

Her words were like a hand at his back, urging him to walk forward, to look into the deep pool of his being. Something else began surfacing from there, coming up from the depths. He was powerless to stop it.

He's halfway through his first year at the Califas training compound, running alone across the compound. He rounds a corner of a building, and nearly collides with a knot of other boys. He recognizes some of them from the Orange Team, with which Parker's Blue Team has an inevitable rivalry. Two newcomers are in the midst of the boys, who are circled around them. They're being roughed up by their older teammates. The boys' eyes are dark with fear. The Califas Order has extensive initiatory rites that involve endurance and pain for its newcomers, but these are always administered under controlled circumstances by the elders of the order. Parker has undergone such a ritual, but this one is clearly not sanctioned. The newcomers are being shoved first in one direction and then the next. Each time they come into contact with the circle, they get an elbow in the ear, a knee in the groin, a fist in a kidney. One of them is bleeding from his nose. The other is making little squeals of pain every time he is shoved. Parker again sees Alfeo, the eldest, taking the greatest delight in the sport, delivering the cruelest blows while displaying the broadest smile.

As Parker grasps what is happening, something stirs within him. Almost without willing it, he pushes himself into the circle. The boys are moving, shouting all around him, but it's as though each moment is distinct from the next, frozen bits of time that can each be held and studied like reflections in a tiled mirror. The group is bathed in a clear, bright light. Parker hears each boy's breath, and beneath the taunting shouts, each of their pounding hearts. And still beneath this, a sound that is part hiss and part high-pitched tone. It seems to emanate from everywhere at once. The blood flowing from the newcomer's nose is not just a red liquid, but a living creature, moving and pulsating . . . like everything else around him.

Just then, the second newcomer is spun around and shoved hard toward Alfeo who stands at the opposite arc of the circle. Parker sees Alfeo raise his forearm in anticipation of the contact it will make with the off-balance newcomer's face and knows that the blow will be fatal. He sees the twisted glee on Alfeo's face, the naked desire to do harm, sees deep into his ugly nature. Parker feels no judgment toward Alfeo, only that he is someone not needed in the world at this moment.

Something within him reaches out. Not his hand, or even his own will, but something deadly, an invisible force that hums with dark intent. Parker feels no emotion, no anger, not even what might be called enthusiasm, but a deep sense of purpose, like duty. He feels this power penetrate Alfeo's ribs and breastbone and contract around the malleable heart muscle there. Parker can feel the tissues, the life force pumping through them, as though the heart were in his own hand. Alfeo gasps once, pales, and crumples to the ground. The boy who had been flung toward him stumbles over Alfeo's feet and falls on top of his limp body. A loud whoosh of air explodes from both of their lungs. At first stunned, but then seeing his chance for escape, the boy scrambles to his feet and begins running from his tormentors.

As if a switch has been thrown, the other boys stop the hazing. They rush to Alfeo's aid, kneel beside his lifeless body, scared, all their bravado gone, desperately trying to revive him. Several of the boys press the emergency signal button on their wrist units at the same moment, and soon others from the order are on the scene. Parker stands there, his hands at his sides, stunned by what he has done. Only when Alfeo is being carried off toward the training camp's headquarters by the strong arms of four of his brothers, does he realize that no one is paying him the slightest attention.

Has no one seen? Has he only imagined his role in Alfeo's demise? No one gives a hint that he has seen anything other than an unusual and inexplicable heart failure of a very healthy boy. Parker stumbles away, back to his dorm room, alone. Within a few days, he has pushed the event so far away that he barely remembers Alfeo's name.

"Your memories are deep," he heard Mother Avalon say. Her voice startled him, and he opened his eyes. He didn't remember closing them. Mother Avalon's own eyes were staring into his, radiant with compassion. He felt a deep welling within him. He started to speak, but instead of words, what emerged from his throat was an anguished sob, which he choked back with considerable effort.

Mother Avalon gently laid her hand on his and looked

deep into his eyes. "You're not alone, Parker," she said quietly. "It is time."

Her clear voice seemed to reverberate in his bones, and his pride and stamina drained away like blood from the gash he felt in his heart. He was in that moment very small and weak, and, all shame flown, he buried his face in the blue folds on Mother Avalon's lap and wept for unnameable sorrows, his shoulders shuddering convulsively with each new breath, shrugging off the weight of experiences for which he had never had an explanation, nor a friend to confide in. He felt her hand alight on the back of his head and, like a drowning man in a maelstrom, he clutched at it and longed for the experience to end.

A long time later, calm descended on him, and with it a twinge of self-consciousness. He pushed himself upright, wiped his face with his hands, and looked sheepishly at Mother Avalon.

"I'm sorry . . ." he began, but she raised her hand to silence him.

"Don't do that, Parker." Her voice was soft but firm. "Don't push it away. Savor this moment. It's an important turning point. Just close your eyes again. Breathe. Feel your body. Let the feelings move you and move through you."

Beyond reason, Parker trusted her, this woman whom he had barely known an hour, and he allowed himself to follow her words. He closed his eyes and in a moment felt himself floating in a vast, perhaps even limitless, space. He sensed neither dark nor light, but felt he was not alone there, that if he but reached out he would touch the essence, the lives of thousands of others.

But the word "touch" could not approach his experience, or the words "seeing" or "hearing." It was an intimacy, a contact at which senses could only hint. A great peaceful hum animated the atmosphere, penetrating and thrilling him to his core. He had felt something like this before in times of great challenge, but never so clearly. He drifted in this state, buoyed and entranced, letting the energies play through his being, surrendering to them. He felt he could become huge or very small in the space of a single thought. He felt as though he could simply turn his attention to any part or cell in his body and dive into it, like into a pool of clear water. A sound like tiny sparks came from his cells, and he could follow the tracks of energy aligning along neural passages in his limbs and organs.

After what seemed like years, he heard Mother Avalon's gentle voice again.

"Come back now, son. We have work to do."

Chapter 13

"The first thing you must know is that your mother did not die of natural causes," Mother Avalon said.

Parker stared at her. Fifteen minutes after coming out of the unfamiliar experience of trusting himself to Mother Avalon's invisible ministrations, his insides still buzzed. The delicate teacup she had given him a few moments before stopped on its way to his lips. He lowered it to the saucer and cleared his throat. "What do you mean?"

"Years before you were born, your mother was introduced to some people who have certain ideas about where we must go as a race of people, ideas that are not acceptable to the councils. She found these ideas compelling, and quietly turned her talents to the task of realizing some of them."

She took a sip from her teacup, holding Parker's gaze. "She did this at great risk to her own well-being, and eventually paid the price for her courage."

Parker felt his misgivings about his mother's death rising like a dark wave. "She was killed? But who . . ."

She cut him off. "It doesn't matter who did it, Parker. Someone, or perhaps several someones, who are responsible for maintaining the present direction of society ordered it. Your mother knew the risks, but she carried on anyway."

"What kind of work are you talking about? When she died, she was on leave of absence from the Ministry of Genetics. She wasn't even working anymore."

"Because she'd been found out," Mother Avalon said.

"There was a shakeup at the lab, some meddling with their budget, and ostensibly she had been placed on leave until the ramifications could be determined. She suspected that somehow her work had come to light, but there was nothing anyone could do. So she simply waited at home until it became clear."

She looked down at her fingertips, lost in thought. "Before she was killed, your mother was told it would happen. She knew someone was coming to end her life."

Her words commingled with Parker's memory of the urgency he had sensed in his mother's message and the odd sound in her voice. "But why?" he asked, his anger rising. "What work was she doing that was so wrong?"

"Wrong is a matter of perspective, Parker. She didn't believe what she was doing was wrong, only that it was not approved by the council. In fact, she knew it was not only right, but essential for the future. If there were time today, I'm certain that I could make you understand, too. In due time, I am confident that it will become clear to you."

Parker leaned forward and put his elbows on his knees, clasping his hands. "Well, I don't know. I mean this is all kind of unbelievable." He shook his head. "You say that she was doing this . . . work . . . since before I was born?"

Mother Avalon stood up and began walking away, her hands behind her back. "Do you know where you were born?"

"My mother told me I was born in Bethesda Hospital." He realized he was not sure of anything at the moment.

"And that you were a natural birth?"

"Yes, she once told me it had made her happy to bring me into the world that way."

"Have you ever considered how she became pregnant?"

Mother Avalon had stopped walking now and was again looking directly at him.

Parker flushed. He had, in his studies at school, learned about the mechanics of laboratory insemination. And he knew that natural insemination had long since ceased to be practiced by nearly everyone in the developed world. But the whole area was shrouded in mystery, and he realized how little thought he'd ever given to how he was conceived. He shook his head.

"Your mother was one of the most highly talented Designers in the Ministry. She had access to the most advanced research in the world. In fact, she was part of the team responsible for the development of several strains of humans that are now an integral part of the management of the Whole Body. Had you ever heard that?"

"She never really talked about her work when we were young."

"No, I don't imagine she would have. How is Pamela, by the way?"

He was a little surprised she knew his sister's name. "She's fine, I guess. I saw her earlier this week. She's studying in Philadelphia. I think she's planning a residency at the Weil Center."

Mother Avalon nodded. "She's undoubtedly going to be a very talented scientist. How could she not be, given her lineage?"

"You mean because of my mother?"

"Of course, and her father, too."

He wasn't sure he'd heard her correctly. "Father?"

"Yes," Mother Avalon said, drawing the word out almost playfully. "Does the word shock you?"

She turned back toward him. Her hands were still behind her back and Parker noticed that she was nearly flat-chested.

"You must know that it was not always like this. Natural insemination didn't disappear from our society's practices all that long ago. Maybe fifty or sixty years ago. But when it did, so too did much of the concept of a personality associated with the masculine lineage. Now the male gene is simply extracted from among samples categorized by propensities for various physical or mental attributes. Few people ever speak of character anymore, or of fathers as 'who.' Haven't you thought about this?"

In fact, he hadn't. He scarcely knew how to think of the word "father." He forced himself to ask. "You know who Pam's father was?"

Mother Avalon turned to the long rows of bookshelves and her gaze lingered over one of the titles. "Your mother was given access to special information, historic information. The records are there, but they are buried rather deeply. It is a matter of policy, you see. It doesn't serve the purposes of the Whole Body for the general populace to know the things your mother knew. Most of the people at the Ministry don't know either, but as I said, there are records."

Parker began to see where this was going. "Do I have a . . . father? I mean, did she know who my father was?"

She turned now and looked at him. "Yes, Parker. She chose him very carefully."

Parker heard his own voice come almost in a whisper. "Do you know who he was?"

Mother Avalon reached into the pocket of her robe and produced a small key. "I thought you'd never ask," she said, smiling, and walked to a section in the bookcase and touched the spine of one of the books with her index finger. A group of five books suddenly swung outward with a soft mechanical whir, and Parker saw a small wooden cabinet door in the space they had vacated. Mother Avalon inserted the key into an ancient-looking lock on the left side of the cabinet and opened the door. Parker watched her careful, deliberate motions, feeling his impatience acutely now.

Mother Avalon replaced the key in her pocket, reached into the cabinet, and produced a book from its depths. It was smaller than the ones on the shelves, and Parker saw it was worn, with slightly irregular pages, as if it might have been bound by hand. She closed the cabinet door, swung the façade of books back in place, and came back to sit next to Parker.

"This is what your mother sent you to me for." She held the book out to him. "I was to put it in your hands if anything happened to her before she had a chance to share it with you herself."

Chapter 14

Diary of Dr. Augustus Termalaine
The Tressaline Project at Dar es Salaam, 2012–2014

Parker looked up from the simple title page, the question in his eyes.

"It will make sense very soon," Mother Avalon said. "I'm going to leave you alone for a while. It is not necessary to read every word right now, but I suggest you read the first fifteen or so pages and the last four. When I come back, we'll talk. Then you must get back to the brotherhood."

She shut the ornate door quietly behind her. Parker stared at it, Mother Avalon's small frame lingering in his vision. How long had he been in this room? A lifetime, it seemed, as if he had been someone else, someone much younger, before he met this oddly familiar woman. How much more could he take in? He gazed at the tattered book that was nearly engulfed by his left hand.

Now there was this. Part of him didn't want to open it. What did he care who his father was, or what happened more than a century ago in some distant city? Nonetheless, it was impossible to not open this dark little cover and read what was inside. Before today, he hadn't realized that he had questions about so many things. Now he knew that the questions had been with him all along. There had just been no one to ask.

Before he had been a young man with little to think

about other than the next competition. Now he could almost see that part of himself walking away, shrinking with each step, being swallowed by a vast expanse that stretched toward an invisible horizon. He grieved a little for that young man.

He blew out the air in his lungs and hefted the book, feeling both how light it was and how heavy its portent. He leafed through a few yellowed pages, fascinated with the primitive, ornate lettering. The jagged type looked almost encrusted, nothing like what he'd always seen on screen. The pages on the left were handwritten, or rather copies of a hasty scribble, and the pages on the right were transcriptions set in type. Parts of the handwritten pages were smeared, the writing indecipherable, and large spaces between many of the paragraphs on the right reflected the missing words.

He turned back to the first page and began reading:

Inception of the Tressaline Project.
2/14/2012

The last of the team, Dr. Helga Katzmueller, arrived last night, and we all met this morning for a long breakfast and opening session. I must say I've never been so excited about a project. The array of talent Dr. Padeyevsky has assembled here is impressive indeed. Can't help but comparing it to what the U.S. did last century with the Manhattan Project to develop the A-bomb. This one, though, is privately funded. Thirty-two scientists on the roster, some single, some accompanied by wives or husbands. Probably a dozen boys and girls, ranging in age from about five to fourteen. Particularly pleased to see Dr. Barnard Selby, with whom I worked on the Damoscene Project in 2005. A brilliant man, and a jolly fellow to boot.

Raina had some misgivings before we came, but they seem for the moment to have disappeared. She's a patient wife. I'm probably undeserving of her. Good there are several other women here she knows and likes—she'll have someone to talk with other than her workaholic hubby.

At least six of the team members I've not heard of, undoubtedly because they have distinguished themselves in the "soft" sciences, and I'm woefully behind in my reading. That Padeyevsky has the vision and charisma to bring together such disparate disciplines is rather impressive.

Main points of Padeyevsky's intro talk this morning:

* An intense, fully-funded project to bring about and introduce into the planet's lifestream a stronger, smarter, healthier strain of humanity.

* A live-in community in which the participants have agreed to use their own bodies as proving grounds for their science.

* Initial three-year commitment by all to the research. After that, it depends on additional funding sources and how well the community is getting along.

These were the main things that drew me and Raina to the community in the first place, but new to me, and particularly exciting, was the introduction of the "Silasian element," the namesake discovery of Dr. Erica Silas, whom Padeyevsky succeeded in recruiting to Tressaline. Dr. Silas' breakthrough studies on the cathartic effects of directed thought (she calls it focused bioplasmic energy) on the successful combining of DNA caused quite a stir last year. Padeyevsky thinks that with Silas' techniques we can significantly increase the pace of the project. Introduced myself to her after breakfast.

Quite nice, if rather serious, and completely nonplussed with the special attention she received. Nice change from the norm.

3/28/2012

This is the most intense, sustained pace I've ever tried to keep on a project. More than a month since my last entry. Should be quite exhausted, I suppose, but it's been so exhilarating working with people of this caliber that I often find myself disappointed to have to sleep.

Raina, contrary to my earlier fears, finding much to occupy herself in my long absences. When we do get time together, I can barely get a word in edgewise but for her excitement over organizing the library and communication protocols. Padeyevsky's reach is far beyond the boundaries of our little community here. He's involving colleagues from diverse places through dialogues and teleconferences, relating the progress of some of our experiments, soliciting their input. Raina is thrilled to be facilitating all this on the Supernet. It's probably given her a better overview than mine.

Dr. Silas immediately initiated training with a dozen or so of us from the various subteams, those who were willing to lay aside skepticism and learn her techniques for directing subatomic matter and affecting magnetic (or energy) fields. I had the advantage of having been a meditator for many years, so some of her techniques were familiar. Several of the scientists have shown a proclivity in the experiments on organic matter, accelerating growth cycles and such. Next week, Silas says she will introduce some of us to the experimental drugs that were instrumental in her successes last year.

Before we began working with her, I assumed that she

was a likely candidate for the Gates in a few years (already a Nobel laureate). Now it occurs to me that, if she is as successful with us on the Tressaline Project, we could all be candidates.

4/16/12

A few months ago, I would not have believed what I've seen this week with my own eyes. Dr. Silas has led us through a training program, using a concoction of consciousness-enhancing drugs (tailored to each subject's body chemistry), that's enabled us to increase the surface temperature of remote objects, influence magnetic fields, even disrupt (bend) laser beams. Seems only to be possible after arduous hours of focused exercises in the lab. Even then, the state of mind is tenuous and intermittent. Sometimes a minor distraction will scotch an experiment. Silas is pleased with our progress, though. The goal is to begin working with genetic materials next month.

Dr. P heads evening conferences in which the reps from each of the disciplines report progress . . . brilliant at this. His work on the Genome Mapping Project has given him a hell of an overview, and he takes pains to make sure the various specialists get the larger picture. He prods with exacting questions and asks for comments on what's being reported. It's a rare conference that doesn't end with more enthusiasm and energy than it began with, quite an accomplishment considering our long hours and furious pace.

5/22/12

Unbelievably, we have already duplicated Dr. Silas' celebrated results from last year, essentially fusing two strands of DNA that nature never saw fit to join. This is so improbable an occurrence that for at least thirty years, university labs have used this same experiment's failure to demonstrate the imperviousness of nature to some of our human meddling. That we accomplished this is mind-boggling, and, I must admit, a little disturbing.

It throws into question myriad assumptions we've made about our limits in genetics, and at least in my mind raises legions of ethical questions. Silas maintains (somewhat on faith, it seems to several of us) that the universe is simply revealing new layers, and that it is impossible to go beyond the universe's ability to accommodate new permutations and life forms. In other words, if we can create it, it must be okay. This kind of reasoning bothers me, but our momentum is so strong that I scarcely have time to stop and consider the ramifications.

According to Dr. P's projections, we're to begin the masterwork within a few weeks. Seems optimistic, but the man has an uncanny ability to marshal energies, dispel doubts, and get things done.

I really must get a few more hours of sleep tonight.

Parker paused in his reading and realized that his heart was beating faster than normal. He was fascinated by what he was reading. He'd never known a man to speak like this before, or one who was even involved in the sciences. It seemed incredible to him. History suddenly felt alive, as though he was there with these people. Termalaine's excitement seemed to be coming right off the pages.

He skipped a few pages and read on:

8/3/12

Dr. Alswain's trajectory proved to be a dead end. He

was none too happy to announce it at tonight's conference, but the lessons learned will greatly assist the rest of us.

Remarkably, I have seen almost none of the parochialism and backbiting that has characterized some of the past projects I've been on. Everyone seems to share in each other's successes and disappointments. We've become a close-knit family. Certainly there is competitiveness evident in our banter. Indeed, it seems a key strategy in the way Dr. P has organized the project. But when someone announces a success during an evening conference and the room breaks out in cheers, it is the most . . ."

Here was one of those places where the handwritten notes were unintelligible. Sad that the words were probably lost forever. The notes were so personal, and even though Parker had no idea who these people Termalaine was talking about were, he could almost visualize them.

He read on:

. . . seven initial thrusts have become five as we discovered the common elements of two of them. Dr. Chang posed a hypothesis last week—our seven tracks would eventually boil down to one or two. Since her track record for circumventing the normal laws of probability are by now legendary, I wouldn't be at all surprised if she's right. She illustrated the idea with a wall chart that starts wide at the base and narrows with each combination. She dubbed the result "Termalaine's Tower" and it instantly found its place in the team's vernacular. Meanwhile, Dr. Pedersen's team announced the . . .

. . . Tower is on the fifth tier now. The Delta and Epsilon thrusts today became one. Because it makes the chart look lopsided, Raina suggested we rename it "Pisa." Ever the humorist, my wife . . .

. . . agreed the Padeyevskys would be the first to bring forth a child. It came as no surprise that The Lion, as we've come to call him, and Pasha (Mrs. P) should take the risk. He's always shown a willingness to put everything—his reputation, his contacts, the funding—on the line for Tressaline. I've only met Mrs. P socially, but Raina admires her greatly, says the Padeyevskys chose to remain childless until the Tressaline colony could be realized. I'm moved by his foresight and determination. Undoubtedly, the prospect of his progeny being the first of a generation of new humans would have been a powerful motivator for him. It is for me.

So, nine months or so from now we shall begin to see how successful we have been. In the meantime, Raina is scheduled to begin carrying in June.

Again Parker paused. They had begun conceiving children, these colonists, and Parker realized that it might have even been the beginning of the kind of controlled genetics that were now common in the world. He wondered how they must have felt, beginning a bold new work like this. He began skimming quickly through the pages.

. . . Chang's fourteen-year-old son seems to be doing particularly well. Only two weeks after implantation, he began demonstrating notably stronger powers of concentration and retention. Six weeks out, he was scoring thirteen points higher on the AMV test. Dr. Inskeep reports that three of the six adolescents who came here with their parents are taking . . .

. . . revived both mice thirteen minutes after death was induced by suffocation. She reported first feeling "a humming" at the base of her spine and a sensation "like static electricity" around her hands. She never touched . . .

. . . not surprised (few are anymore) to find the vital functions could likewise be interrupted. Dr. Joliet reported discovering that his eight-year-old daughter, Marbella, mentally terminated the family dog after discovering it suffering from a broken pelvis and punctured lung from being hit by a car outside the compound. Until that moment, Marbella had shown no effects from the implant. Joliet surmised that perhaps emotional trauma (or extreme empathy) served as a catalyst to awaken . . .

Parker's experience with Alfeo was fresh in his memory: the humming, the strange slowing of time. His face, he realized, was getting warm. It seemed to him they were describing something he knew about.

. . . taken on faith. She does, however, demonstrate an undeniable ability to retain information. Once she has seen, read, or heard something, she can recall it to the smallest detail. Dr. Ramakrishna is performing at similar levels only two months after implantation. At this point, it is impossible to separate out causal factors from the whole environment. This will make for endless . . .

. . . suggests such quantum leaps are the result of the "bioplasmic stew" (his term) that we're brewing at Tressaline—the drugs, the intense interaction with each other, the hormonal changes especially in the women, the focus. Keeping a sound scientific record is becoming a major challenge amidst the euphoria that . . .

. . . in strictly statistical terms. A thirty-six percent increase in accuracy alone is remarkable enough, but when you add the factor of increased distance, it becomes clear that we have in thousands of years of natural evolution barely tapped our potential for eye and hand coordination. Safe to say that our concepts of sport and athletic achievement are in for some serious revision.

Parker thought about this morning's match with Stanislav Brechner, how everything had become clear. He'd been able to anticipate every one of Brechner's moves, delivered each blow with such speed and accuracy that nearby observers had gasped audibly. What had Mother Avalon said? "The colonists called it 'the field.' " He glanced at the bottom of the page and saw that he'd already gone past where Mother Avalon had suggested he read. He flipped hurriedly through the little book until he came to the last four pages.

. . . regrettably isolated from current events. We only heard about the Madagascar Conference last week, and by then it was too late. Apparently, most, if not all of Asia has acceded to Chinese demands and the announcement of a new confederation is expected within days. Unbelievable that this has happened so quickly. Even the unflappable Dr. P said last night that there is some cause for concern, given our location and the unstable nature of our international funding agencies. But he doesn't think we will be noticed for a while. The U.S. is apparently in free fall . . .

The change in tone jarred Parker. What had happened to

turn this ebullience with which Termalaine had written so quickly dark?

. . . contingency from the New African States Council was a grim bunch. Dr. P spent three days with them explaining the nature (and importance) of our work here. He said they seemed placated by the time they left (if not terribly enthused), but the general consensus seems to be we are in for some rocky times. The timing couldn't be worse, as we are only thirteen days away from the final phase and tensions are high enough without the outside trouble. Everyone is . . .

. . . unbelievable that we have come this far only to be swept away by political currents. What we have accomplished here is far more revolutionary than another round of coups and geopolitical musical chairs. That we have the key to unlocking human potential at our fingertips absolutely dwarfs considerations of territory and authority. But then, I never have given much truck to governments. There is even talk about our lives being in danger. In the midst of this, we're still trying to stay on track. Raina is due to give birth this month. God, I hope things stabilize before then.

. . . will fly to the Seychelles in Dr. P's private plane. Raina has friends there who can hide us temporarily and help us find our way back to North America, providing the upheaval there isn't as great as it is in Africa. The depth of my sadness is unfathomable. To have come to this. The horror is tempered somewhat by the birth of our daughter Leona (named in honor of "The Lion" Padeyevsky), but it also complicates matters. For one, it makes it more difficult for us to travel incognito. With a last monumental effort, we all have done our best to successfully preserve the research records by dividing, encoding, and sending them both electronically and by courier to secret locations. The precious culminating strains are safe, I believe, with friends and colleagues. Last night, like a bunch of monks at the beginning of the Dark Ages, we dubbed ourselves "The Bringers" and took an oath to protect the work and bring it to fruition, though few of us now believe that will happen soon. Goddamn politicians.

2/8/14

The Lion is dead—Chang received word last night.

Parker stopped reading, stunned. He looked at the handwriting on the left page. It was lighter and more cramped than it had been on previous pages. He thought he could feel the writer's grief in the script, the dull confusion that sets in when something incomprehensible happens. In just a few short pages, he had developed a feeling for Dr. Termalaine and the others, and absorbed their respect for their leader, this Dr. Padeyevsky, the one they called the Lion.

More slowly now, he read on:

Typically, he stayed on at the compound too long attending to details and making sure others were away safe. No word on Pasha or their infant son. We heard others were apprehended, but no names. There are no words to express my sadness and rage over this. Padeyevsky was perhaps the greatest scientist and truly gifted man I have ever known. It seems impossible that such a light is gone out of this world. It is beyond comprehension that such an act of ignorance and brutality came from this new council of women.

En route to Saskatchewan. Less upheaval there, they say, and it may afford us some time to determine the next step. Still in touch with Selby, Chang, and Ramakrishna through Raina's knowledge of clandestine Supernet pathways. Thank God they're safe. We've all taken assumed names and have had help obtaining passports and other ID, but it's unlikely we'll go undiscovered for long. We have friends, however, many of whom will carry on should we meet with trouble.

It may take some time, but I don't believe the unborn beings who stand poised at the pinnacle of Termalaine's Tower will be denied their time in the world. Safe environment for their upbringing must be secured. One scenario: programming the genes in such a way that their full potential remains dormant until they mature enough to establish themselves within whatever system emerges after this chaos. It's clear they'll be endowed with the most significant evolutionary advances since the advent of Homo Sapiens on Earth. How they'll use these gifts can't be foreseen. If they . . .

Parker's hands were trembling now. Deep inside, pieces of a puzzle were falling into place. Only one page remained.

I've thought long and hard on this question during these tumultuous months, and have concluded that I believe there is evidence of some unseen hand guiding this race throughout the millennia. I believe it has demonstrated benevolence over the long run. He, She, or It has always afforded us the tools to shape our world. Many of us have proven shortsighted in the application of these tools. But if we think of ourselves as a work in progress, I believe . . .

The text ended, and Parker turned to the final page. There he saw an unsigned italic note:

Dr. Augustus Termalaine and his wife, Raina, and their infant daughter, Leona, died in an airplane accident on February 14, 2014, while en route to Saskatchewan, Canada. Others known to be on the flight included Dr. Uta Chang, Dr. Barnard Selby and his wife, Sonja, and Dr. Herman Inskeep.

May the fruit of the Tree fall to earth in the warmth of a new day.

As Parker stared at these last words, goosebumps rising on his arms, he heard the door open. Mother Avalon stood in the doorway, with sad and serious eyes. After a long pause, she spoke:

"So you see, Parker, many have died that you may live. Your responsibility is great, indeed."

Chapter 15

"Only twelve strains were saved from the Tressaline Colony." Mother Avalon sat next to him on the sofa, looking into his face, the vertical lines between her brows deeper, her hand atop his. Parker's own eyes stayed fixed on the floor, as if the patterns in the carpet might hold the key to unlocking the mystery that his life had become since entering this room.

"Each was based on the DNA from the participants, who as you have likely gathered, were some of the finest scientists of their time. But by virtue of the techniques the colonists brought to bear on them, the eventual permutations were quantum leaps ahead of their original donors.

"Most of the colony's research records were confiscated and presumably destroyed in ensuing years. It was only due to the dedication of some of the colony's friends, and Raina Termalaine's skills in Supernet encoding technology, that we now know something of the strains' origins . . . and that you were born."

"How did you get this diary?" Parker asked. "Wasn't it with Dr. Termalaine on the plane when it crashed?"

"When you first came in I told you that the Nestercines have collected works such as these for many generations. This is a treasured part of our mission, preserving the record of forgotten and suppressed history, and we have paid dearly to obtain and keep them. I won't tell you exactly how this came into our possession, but I can tell you it is genuine."

"What happened to them, the colony?"

"The record of their work was swallowed by history. In 2011, the governing bodies of the world began to fall apart, almost as if there was an invisible change of seasons and the old systems were leaves falling from the trees. New regional governments took shape with incredible speed, fell apart, formed again. This I'm reasonably sure they taught you about this in school."

"The Great Consolidation," Parker said. "In 2025."

"Yes, but it began before then, on the heels of the AGNS contagion. You know about this?"

"Acquired Genetic Neurological Syndrome. It killed most of the world's men."

"Yes, this is the period when women moved into positions of power. Dr. Termalaine refers to the Madagascar Conference in his diary. You read that?"

Parker nodded.

"That was when the New African States Council was formed," she continued. "It was a very unstable time, and the council got wind of this radical community that was working on revolutionary genetic research. Padeyevsky had not been secretive about the work. He thought the world should know what they were doing, and he used his considerable charisma and fame to make sure it did.

"It was his undoing. A woman by the name of Dubangi took control of the East African Council. She hated and mistrusted both the Europeans and the Americans. Padeyevsky was born in Germany, and many of the scientists were living here, on this continent, when it was still the United States. Dubangi was a psychopath and a tyrant. She incited fear and old superstitions among the council members about the colony's work, and the colony was destroyed, most of its members killed. However, as I said, the colonists were able to secret away some of the strains that they developed. Only twelve were ultimately saved."

She looked at him gravely. "Very few people in the world know about this, Parker. Now you are one. Do you understand why I have told you about it?"

Silent, he took in her words, his eyes still held by the patterns in the carpet. "I'm connected to them, aren't I? I'm descended from one of the strains."

The corners of Mother Avalon's mouth rose in a gentle smile. "Of course, Parker, of course."

Unbelievable, he thought, but a wave of excitement passed through him. "You hinted before that you knew who my father was."

"Yes, I did," she replied, withdrawing her hand from his. She rose and walked again to the rows of books and, reaching high above her head, removed one of the thicker ones from its place on the shelf. She walked slowly back to the sofa, opening the book to the last page. She turned the book around so that it was facing him.

Parker took it and gazed at the old two-dimensional photograph. The unsmiling man staring back at him had intense brown eyes and a full head of wavy black hair that had grayed at the temples. The hair was combed straight back, but looked as though the battle for control over which direction it would take was still undecided. The forehead was very broad and deeply lined, both horizontally across its full width and vertically between the hoary eyebrows. These latter lines, Parker thought, looked like he had long strained to see something at a great distance. The strong jaw line was emphasized by a tangled beard, trimmed close and shot through with streaks of gray. The broad nose, set off by protruding cheekbones, was as indelicate as the rest of the features. The man really did resemble a lion.

Beneath the photograph was a single paragraph:

Dr. Theodore Padeyevsky was born in Stuttgart, Germany in 1952. He received his doctorate in Applied Genetics at Berlin University, graduating Summa Cum Laude, in 1980. He was awarded the Nobel Peace Prize in Science in 2006 for his pioneering work in the field of Genetic Research. Dr. Padeyevsky, his wife, Pasha, and their dog, a high-spirited setter named Rudolph, presently divide their time between homes in Dar es Salaam and Portsmouth, New Hampshire.

Parker touched the faded portrait with his fingertips. He imagined what the face would have looked like had it been animated with life force. He imagined its owner's voice booming across a roomful of people gathered to hear him speak, or the hearty laugh that surely would have emanated from the generous mouth. In the piercing eyes, Parker thought he saw passion and wisdom, and a hint of mischief.

Gently, he closed the book and looked at the title on its cover. *Genetics and the Social Imperative; Man's Responsibility on the Eve of Evolutionary Self-Determination*, by Dr. Theodore Padeyevsky.

"He was one of the greats of his time," Mother Avalon said.

Parker placed the book on the table in front of him, his hand lingering a moment before releasing it. "Are you sure about this? There's no mistake?"

Mother Avalon shook her head. "We've known about you since before you were born."

"What about others, from the other strains?"

"Yes, now you must understand something very important. In order to protect you, and the others, no one person knows the exact details of the whereabouts or status of others. This was done so that if any one with knowledge was detained and forced to reveal what she knew, it would be more difficult to find them."

"But why?"

"Think about what you've read, Parker. No one really knows the potential of the Tressaline offspring. Nearly all records of the experiments and their outcomes were lost. All we have are allusions to remarkable breakthroughs and increased capacities for thought and action gleaned from rare and sketchy writings such as Dr. Termalaine's diary. And the strains themselves. Your very existence, should your origins be discovered, poses a threat to the Whole Body."

"But that's ridiculous." Parker stood and began to pace. "I'm no threat to the councils. I'm just an athlete . . . and a man. There are no men in positions of any authority anywhere that I've heard of!"

Mother Avalon heard the bitterness in his voice and stood too. "For more than fifty years now, the Whole Body has been intensely working to control all aspects of society, right down to the gender and characteristics of newborns. Your mother was one of their best. She and her colleagues were directly responsible for successfully engineering limited life spans, and introducing several new strains into the culture, lines that, incidentally, have helped consolidate and focus the power of the councils.

"But your mother, like many of us, came to believe that we needed to break out of the lockstep direction the councils were going, that it's a scientist's responsibility to bring into the world humans who by their genius and innate talent have the potential to lead us into a new phase. Once she was introduced to the work of the Tressaline colonists, there was no turning back. Don't you think that the presence of someone who may possess greater capabilities than the best of the councils' creations would represent a threat?"

"But I've threatened no one!" Parker nearly yelled. "I'm not even aware of these 'greater capabilities' you're talking about. I'm not even sure . . ."

"Parker!" The knifelike sound of Mother Avalon's voice cut through to a deep layer within him, and suddenly every sense was keen as he whirled to face her. He heard the air whistle in his ears with his movement, heard the fabric of his uniform whisper across his back as his body shifted, smelled the musty odor of the old books that lined the opposite wall.

Shimmering patterns danced around Mother Avalon's body, like the lines that iron filings make around a magnet. Through the faint hum he felt in his bones, Parker heard her next words resonate inside his chest: "Be still! There has never been a moment in our long and sordid history like this one. You carry the gift of ages within you. Never, never deny it or treat it with disrespect. It is blasphemy. Too many have paid with their lives to bring you into this world. Would you deny their cries?"

Even as she spoke, Parker heard the murmur of countless voices as if from afar, pieces of conversation, whispered hopes, a cacophony of rustlings and stirrings of people purposely at work, the footsteps of generations stretching back to infinity. He stood utterly still, caught in this stream of timelessness that rushed over him like warm water, his bones resonating with the onslaught.

"You see," Mother Avalon's voice came again, softer this time, "the maturation process is well underway. There is no time for you to falter, Parker."

Slowly he felt the presence around him evaporate. He eased himself to the floor, overwhelmed by everything that was happening to him.

"These things were programmed in your cells to emerge in early adulthood. We don't know how long it will take for them to come to full flower, but certainly the process has begun, and you must now be extremely vigilant. Forces apparently are gathering to prevent you from achieving your full potential. It was inevitable. All systems work toward stasis. They fight change at every turn. Your mother was discovered. It is only a matter of time before you fall under suspicion . . . and danger."

Parker felt the truth of her words deep inside. He didn't want to change, and yet change was happening. He'd felt it even this morning in the competitions. He thought about some of the things he'd read in Termalaine's diary—

". . . revived both mice thirteen minutes after death . . . terminated the family dog after discovering it suffering . . . barely tapped our potential for eye and hand coordination . . ."

He remembered Alfeo, and understood that he'd known even then that he was different. He was becoming something . . . but what? "What am I supposed to do?"

"I'm afraid that's not a question anyone but you can answer. We simply don't know enough about what traits the colonists were aiming for, other than those you've just read about. We are hoping you will educate us."

Parker gave a little snort.

"That may not set well with you," Mother Avalon said, "but would you take an old woman's advice?"

Parker looked at her without answering.

"Search deeply inside of yourself to find out what matters to you, what you think is right and good and just, and then allow yourself to follow it. You have been gifted with fine tools, not a map."

She reached for his hand and squeezed it. "I have lived longer than most, and have been fortunate enough to have grown up surrounded with learned and wise people. Whatever I can share with you in the time that I have left, I shall, if you are willing. Perhaps, by conversations like this one, things will become clearer to you—to both of us."

Another hour passed in animated and intense conversation. Eventually Parker looked at the timepiece on his wrist. "I've got to get back." He looked toward the small table and the two books that now lay there.

"It would be unwise to take them with you," she replied, intuiting his thoughts. "The less you have that can confirm any brewing suspicions, the better."

Parker nodded, rubbing his empty hands together, then looked once again into Mother Avalon's wrinkled face. "Can I come again . . . sometime?"

"I would be very disappointed if you didn't," she said, smiling. "But make it sooner rather than later. I have no illusions about my time here. I don't know how much longer my position will afford me protection. Someone may make the connection between your mother and me. There is little that can be done about it."

Before Parker could ask another question, Mother Avalon stood and carried the books back to the bookcase. "There is one more thing." She opened the hidden compartment; when she withdrew her hand, it held something about a foot long, wrapped in a soft cloth. She crossed the room and handed it to him. "Open it."

Parker unwrapped the cloth. His eyes grew a little wider.

"It's an African ceremonial knife that belonged to your father."

Both the unpolished blade and wooden handle were deeply etched with curved lines and symbols, and at the end of the handle was the depiction of a male lion, its mane luxurious and its gaze fierce and proud. Parker had never seen anything like it.

"He would have wanted you to have it." Mother Avalon took it gently from his hands. "I will ship it to you at the brotherhood. It's not the kind of thing you'll want to carry around the streets or on airplanes."

She turned and walked to the door of the study, pausing before she opened it. "I am happy I could finally meet you, Parker. I think your father would be quite proud of you if he were here. Goodbye, young man."

With a reassuring smile, she turned and left him to find his own way out.

Chapter 16

"Is your report on K-1754 ready?" From the monitor, Desta Mardrid's eyes appeared flat, unreadable.

Aria pinched and rolled the fabric of her slacks between her thumb and finger, out of the aide's line of sight. "Yes, as ready as it probably is going to get. It remains a most difficult reading."

"My office in five minutes." Mardrid's face disappeared from the screen, replaced by the ubiquitous mandala of the council.

Aria leaned back in the chair and chewed at her bottom lip. She had been dreading this moment since awakening yesterday in the locker room of the workout sanctuary. Every time she thought of Kay she felt the simultaneous pull of empathy and a desire to get as far away from the assassin as possible.

The woman was carrying a charge that Aria felt wholly inadequate to deal with. And yet she must. It was her job. Asking for more time would only increase her problems with Mardrid, something she wanted to avoid. The woman could ruin her, destroy any chance of her rising to prominence, either in the council or the outside world. Aria found her formal robe and slipped it on over her suit. As she did, she realized it would be unwise to tell Mardrid everything. She would relate nothing of the incident in the workout sanctuary. Such information could only raise questions about Aria's judgment. The clandestine meeting itself could even cast Aria and the assassin in a conspiratorial light.

It would be difficult, but she was going to reveal only as much as would get her through the report, and hope that Mardrid was too busy or distracted to delve any deeper. Obfuscation was not going to be easy. The aide was clearly interested in this reading.

In the living room Aria reached for the file on K-1754 she'd been reluctant to open since yesterday. She paused, her fingers hovering an inch above it. Then she opened its cover and looked at the holograph at the top of the first page.

"I don't know who or what you are," she said to the face of the assassin, "but I hope you are not going to get me in any trouble."

She closed the folder and left for Mardrid's office, her stride confident. Inside, however, she felt anything but.

"You mean you were unable to read her?" Mardrid's expression was hard and her tone accusatory.

"No, I mean I am not clear on the interpretation," Aria answered, quelling the anger she felt welling up inside. "I read her very well, perhaps too well. Sometimes it happens that a subject resonates so strongly that it disturbs one's analytical faculties."

Mardrid's look was laced with equal parts suspicion and disgust. "Are you . . . attracted to this fiver?" It was a disparaging reference to the months required for gestation in the laboratory of special strains, such as the K-class.

Aria felt a slight blush creep into her cheeks. "Not at all." But the question felt more challenging than it should have. She was attracted, but Aria had told herself that it was professional curiosity. "Most people's psyches present themselves in what my sisterhood calls 'tones,' like chords with dominant notes or harmonies that soften one another and allow the reader to play with the harmonic resonances these evoke. That play is what gives one the time or space or nuance necessary to form some coherent thoughts about the person.

"Occasionally, however, a subject, for whatever reason, presents less of a chord than a single strong note. That note can resonate more strongly with one particular reader than with another. In such cases, it hinders that reader's ability to form solid conclusions."

"Don't condescend to me," Mardrid warned, fixing Aria with a fishy stare.

Aria swallowed hard. In her anger, she momentarily had forgotten whom she was dealing with. "I'm . . . sorry, Rinchon," Aria said, using the formal title she'd been taught as a child to employ when addressing one's superior. "I was only trying to explain . . ."

"You were trying to excuse your own failure to provide Mother with what she asked for," Mardrid spat. "Do you think me a fool?"

"No, of course not, Rinchon. I was going to suggest that a different reader may have more success at interpretation."

"Perhaps, but you're the second who's come up short."

That was a surprise. Aria had assumed she was the only reader assigned to the assassin, but quickly realized how naïve the idea was. Of course, Mother Gretel would seek as much information as possible on those around her. She wouldn't rely on one person's opinion, regardless of how talented they might be.

"I see. May I ask who the other reader was?" She felt a glimmer of hope that it might be someone from her sisterhood. "Perhaps we could confer on this reading."

"She's . . . no longer with us," Mardrid said, a smile pulling at the corners of her mouth.

Aria felt a chill. Had she just been threatened? Was her predecessor's failure to provide the required information the reason for her "departure?" Aria could only guess. She was unable to read the woman.

"Well then, let's just lay aside your interpretation of the reading for the moment," Mardrid said, her voice laced with sarcasm. "Tell me exactly what your experience was when you attempted to read her . . . and failed."

Aria silently sighed with relief. It was what she had prepared for as she walked to this meeting. Already she had erected a mental image of a wall around the workout sanctuary experience. She would not reveal it unless somehow Mardrid managed to penetrate her defenses. Instead, she began relating the experience of her initial remote reading of Kay, of the soaring idealism in the young girl's heart, the intense devotion to her order and to the study of The Text. She told Mardrid of Kay's unexpected distress over a recent execution, and the image of a face, presumably of the deceased, that had momentarily flashed into Aria's vision during the reading.

Mardrid interrupted. "Could you identify that face if you saw it again?"

"It's unlikely. It's mostly the energetic pattern I sense, not the details of the face. There are certain genetic traits that might be . . ."

"Go on, then," Mardrid said, impatient now.

Aria related as much detail as she could remember, hoping that in doing so she would avoid having to reveal her second meeting with Kay. She explained how in the first reading she had fallen into a sort of ecstatic vision, about looking down at her body and seeing the light growing at its center, about hearing countless voices and the sense of expectation in the air.

"Expectation of what?" Mardrid demanded.

"I don't know. It just seemed like many people were very excited or agitated." Like they were anticipating some cataclysmic change, Aria thought, but didn't say.

Mardrid appeared bored, but Aria knew she was listening keenly. "What else?" Mardrid barked.

"That's everything I can access."

One eyebrow raised slightly. "Everything?"

For the briefest instant, Aria thought she had somehow failed to cloak the second meeting well enough. But something on a subtle level inside rallied, pulling her instinctively away from feelings of guilt or fear. "Is there something more you were expecting to hear?"

Mardrid looked surprised by the forthrightness of Aria's response, and stared hard at her for any sign of challenge. Apparently finding none, she said, "You have proven reasonably good at what you do, Helsing, with the exception of this case. Colter sometimes has a good eye for talent."

Aria sensed two things simultaneously, the first that she was being paid a compliment. Had it come from anyone but Mardrid, she would have accepted it at face value. But beneath it, Aria felt Mardrid probing for a response concerning Barena Colter. Colter had been the one most directly responsible for Aria's presence at Council Headquarters, conducting the preliminary interviews and making her recommendation to Mother Gretel. Aria suspected Mardrid might be trying to identify Aria's loyalties.

"Thank you, Rinchon," she responded after a moment's hesitation. "I only hope to be of service to Mother and the Whole Body." She invested the formal and superficial response with enthusiastic sincerity.

It seemed to be enough. Mardrid looked bored again, and gestured dismissively toward the entrance. "Mother will likely call for you again before next week's meeting of the Grand Council. In the meantime, there are seven more reading assignments on my secretary's desk. Be ready to report anytime after tomorrow."

The aide turned her back and began studying the horizontal monitor on the desk there. Aria wasted no time leaving the room, holding her breath until the door closed behind her.

Chapter 17

When the door slid shut, Mardrid swiveled around in her chair and rested her elbows on the desk, her index fingers absently pinching her thin lower lip. This was a tricky one, she thought.

Clearly the assassin was trouble. The last reader who had attempted to delve into Kay Black's psyche had never recovered. They had found her in her room, staring at the wall, unable to speak, the assassin's file clutched in her hand. She was still in confinement in a little-used wing at Council Headquarters, but there was little hope of her being of any use. At least Helsing had come away with something.

The business about voices raised in expectation had a familiar ring to it, Mardrid thought, like the Asiatican conspiracy of thirty years ago, which she'd studied before becoming Mother Gretel's aide. In that case, a reader had been assigned to report on one of the security people close to the Council Mother. She had reported seeing a group seated around a table, and a feeling of dark purpose emanating from them. Subsequently, she identified one of the faces she saw there, a high-ranking member of the Security Detail.

Follow-up uncovered an assassination plot and a plan to install a more progressive leader. All of the suspected conspirators were arrested in the course of one night, and the Asiatica Council maintained status quo for another twelve years. Mardrid thought it would have been better if the conspiracy had succeeded because the council steadily lost power and prestige in the Whole Body. Even today, eighteen years after that Council Mother died of natural causes, Asiatica was still struggling to recover.

That would not happen here, she thought. If this was a conspiracy, it could be controlled, co-opted, and used to force Mother Gretel from office. Gretel had held the office for so long and with such authority that the other council members were long since cowed into laziness. Everyone knew that Mardrid and Colter were more powerful than any of the elected members. When it came to choosing Mother Gretel's successor, the Council Mother job was almost certain to fall to one of them.

Mardrid rested her chin in her hand and stared into space. If there was a conspiracy afoot, it would have to be crushed at precisely the right moment, and those behind it would have to be stopped before they could do any real damage to the council's grip on power. She needed to understand more, and soon.

She turned back to her monitor and pulled up the file she had begun compiling after the first botched reading of Kay Black, the event that had initiated her suspicions. Conspiracies were not uncommon. Eight in North America alone had been unearthed and squelched over the past fifty years, both through dumb luck and the kind of diligence Mardrid was now undertaking.

Without Mother Gretel's or Colter's knowledge, she had begun tracing the assassin's origins through the Ministry of Births back to the main laboratories of Genetic Research, back to Angela Potemkin, one of the leading scientists responsible for the K-strains. This was where things got interesting. Despite the quiet efforts of several trusted auditors from Mardrid's days in Expenditures, records of the assassin's birth and genetic background were missing or incomplete.

Then came the revelation that Angela Potemkin had worked briefly with a scientist who later was implicated in suspicious activities in Africa. Twelve years ago, the West African Council had routed a group who it suspected was planning to seed the African gene pools with unauthorized strains. The council had moved swiftly and ruthlessly on the suspect labs, but the bodies of two women, including that of the scientist Potemkin had worked with, had not been recovered after the raid.

Evidence was found that pointed to involvement by the Nestercine Order. The Nestercines had been trouble since the order's inception nearly a hundred years ago. Their founder had been brilliant and clever, and early on the order had managed to secure positions for many of their members on councils throughout the world. Despite the fact that their fingerprints were on any number of questionable activities over the years, with their strong base of power on the councils they always managed to thwart any attempt to banish the order.

Of course, the Nestercines had denied all knowledge of the African plot, and well-placed members had managed to head off or deny funds for subsequent investigations.

Mardrid knew in her soul that there was a connection between Angela Potemkin and the Nestercines, and she believed that Kay Black was part of it. She just didn't know what those connections were or how to prove them. It had occurred to her that if she was to place some pressure in the right places, something would pop out that would make things more evident.

And so she did. She had pulled several well-placed strings and managed to divert a huge block of funds meant for the Ministry of Births to other priority programs, creating a personnel crisis. Some thirty positions had to be pared until more funds could be found. It had then been a simple task to place some quiet pressure on the ministry's lead administrator to make Potemkin one of those put on leave of absence. If Potemkin was up to something, Mardrid figured the forced leave might rattle her enough to cause her to slip up. Then she put the scientist on twenty-four-hour surveillance.

A few weeks later, her hunch was confirmed: Potemkin had been seen passing something to a woman who sat next to her on a bench in the small square near Potemkin's building. The two had pretended not to know each other, but surveillance clearly saw Potemkin clumsily leave a tiny electronic storage cube on the bench when she stood up to leave. Moments later, the other woman casually covered it with her bag, and when she left, the cube was gone.

Mardrid's people apprehended the accomplice minutes after the drop, retrieving the cube and shipping the accomplice off for interrogation. The information on the device turned out to be records of genetic coding, but so far no one had been able to decipher its significance. The accomplice was, of course, not who her ID indicated. Unfortunately she died under the rather severe interrogation administered by the freelance "professionals" Mardrid had been forced to employ. Because it was all off the record, Mardrid couldn't even have them demoted.

It had stumped and angered her, but then Cartene Resnick, her oldest and most loyal associate from her days in Expenditures—and one of the few people she confided in—made a suggestion. Resnick had since become a high-level manager in the Census Accounting Office, the blandly named center that actually controlled the council's assassination assignments. Resnick told Mardrid that, despite the supposed safeguards in place, it was possible—for a price, of course—to get Angela Potemkin's name added to the termination list.

Mardrid had jumped at the suggestion. If the geneticist were eliminated, others in the conspiracy might feel the heat and, again, slip up. It had been a remarkable bit of irony, Mardrid thought, that Kay Black had been assigned to the task. Since Resnick had no influence over who was assigned to carry out the orders, it had to be coincidence, but a damned odd one.

What made no sense, though, was that the assassination came off without a hitch. If Kay Black knew Potemkin or was involved in something nefarious with her, it hadn't stopped her from ending the scientist's life. On further reflection, Mardrid realized that the chances the assassin had ever come into contact with Potemkin after being born in the laboratory were slim. Black had been raised in isolation, and her life at Council Headquarters was reclusive. Her record was spotless, her discipline exemplary. She was one of the very best the labs had produced.

What had Helsing said about the assassin's reading? That she had seen a face, and that the assassin might be experiencing unexpected distress over a recent execution? Was it Potemkin's face? Some sort of genetic memory imprint? The most talented readers, like Helsing, could sometimes uncover ancestral patterns over many generations.

If, indeed, there proved to be an assassination plot, the trick was to let it meet with just enough success to either do away with Mother Gretel, or discredit her enough to cause her removal from office. A Council Mother who was unable to sniff out conspiracies was not fit for office.

Mother's iron grip and spectacular successes had angered many and fomented a lot of jealousy, particularly among those on the South American and Baltic Councils. Those were the likely sources for conspiracy, Mardrid figured, though the Asiaticans would benefit immensely by a North American fumble.

If she was extremely vigilant, Mardrid told herself, she stood a good chance of letting someone else do the heavy lifting. Inserting herself in Gretel's place afterward wouldn't be easy, but she relished just such a challenge. She was ready to take the reins. She had skill and the will. Had she not risen faster and farther in the council's power structure than anyone in recent history? Only a few years ago she had been in charge of Expenditures, literally and figuratively in the basement of North American Council Headquarters. Uncovering her predecessors "irregularities" in numerous accounting schemes had brought her the attention and accolades she needed to climb up the ladder.

And climb she had, all the way to the top. She would be Council Mother one day. It was her fate, but she was not above giving fate a little shove.

Had she missed anything? She had quietly assigned one investigator to do further research on the late Angela Potemkin, her children, and associates, and another to ferret out more information on Kay Black. DNA samples had been retrieved and were being analyzed, but trying to trace her origins or characteristics through billions of possible cross-references and permutations was slow, painstaking work. Yesterday afternoon she had assigned an operative to watch and report on anything unusual in Black's activities.

No, there was little more she could do right now. What was it The Text said?

The servant of the Whole Body is patient, as the Whole Body

166

Itself is patient with the slow unfolding of the Will of History.

She would be patient. She had things more or less in control. The matter was under observation. Sooner or later it would become clear.

She turned back to her monitor and more immediate concerns.

Chapter 18

"This may not go over well in the main office," the woman said. "Why do you need this extra time, again?"

Kay looked her supervisor straight in the eye and lied. "I feel my performance would benefit from a few more days of study and training. I could begin taking assignments again right away, if the CAO feels it is necessary, but I want to be certain that I am prepared for whatever I might encounter in the field. I've doubled my workout schedule and am told I can schedule some time in the reaction simulators in the next few days. I would like to be in the best possible form. No more mistakes."

The supervisor looked Kay up and down, then at the reports in her hands. "All the testers say you're in perfect shape. You've recovered from this mishap completely, it would appear. Why should we consider this request?"

Kay could feel the woman's eyes boring into hers, but she knew she was the best agent they had, and that they would think twice about turning down the request. "I have no desire to cause any more problems, Rinchon. I simply want to make sure I've done my utmost to reinforce their confidence in me."

The woman laid the reports on her desk. "Very well. I'll contact you when I get an answer."

Kay turned on her heel and walked briskly the quarter mile to her room. Once there, she went directly to the SimuTech and punched up her favorite program—white snow clinging to uplifted pine boughs, the tiny village below with its smoking chimneys and snow-rounded roofs, the pristine sparkle of crystalline flakes falling through clean air. She sought its comfort, consciously relaxing her shoulders, slowing her breathing, letting the picture and the sound wash over her.

She had told part of the truth. She was not ready to go back to work. The experience with Aria Helsing the day before had unsettled her almost more than the encounter with Angela Potemkin. Watching the counselor drop into unconsciousness and begin twitching and moaning in the midst of listening to her dream, Kay had felt darkness close in on her. She had sat nearly paralyzed, looking at the limp body of the woman with whom she had taken a chance.

The experience confirmed Kay's worst fears. Something inside of her was wrong, so wrong that it had overwhelmed this woman who had reached out to her. Kay had gone on automatic then, checking outside the heat room to see if anyone was nearby. When she found the area deserted, she lifted the reader's limp body, carried her into the outer locker room, laid her on the bench there, covering her with a towel.

Kay had dressed hastily and left, employing all the tricks she knew to avoid being noticed.

She needed time to pull herself together, and to find out more. The voice of Angela Potemkin almost never shut up now. "You are not the person you have always thought you were," it said again and again.

". . . we have decided that you must have access to this material in order to convince you of your own value and move you to action."

What action? What was expected of her, and who expected it?

"Your origins are not what you believe. They are not the

169

same as others in your order . . ."

Kay flashed on the faces of the many sisters she had grown up with. To strangers, they might have looked so alike as to be nearly indistinguishable from one another. The only blatant difference had been Kay's blue eyes. Several others had them, but they too wore brown lenses. Kay knew each sister distinctly, though. She remembered experiences and conversation they had shared, bruises they had inflicted upon one another in training, beds in which they had chastely slept side by side for years. Yet now it was as though these things had all happened to someone else, and these once-familiar faces were strange, imperceptibly altered. She was losing her past.

She gazed over the SimuTech screen again, letting the tension go, pushing Potemkin's voice away, letting her thoughts drift idly, like the smoke lifting gently into the bright gray sky on the screen. Something inside softened, and for a moment she reached a sort of stasis, a peaceful lull that felt almost like floating.

By the time she noticed the first tear run down her cheek, it was too late to stop. Like an untended flame rising from the core of her being, it grew, pulling at and loosening the grip of frozen emotions around her heart, the encrustations of a hundred laboratory-born generations. Despite the engineers' best efforts, and the stultifying hand of the Whole Body apparatus, it came. For the first time since she had sucked in gulps of air as a newborn fiver in a sterile room of the Ministry of Births, Kay wept. It came in waves, shuddering through her lungs, making her throat ache, filling her with a sense of such deep longing and loneliness that she wanted to die.

With her face buried in her hands, she felt like the little child she had seen in her dream, standing at the edge of some terrible danger, unable to move.

But she must move. With great effort, she stood and went to the water recycler where she moistened a towel, wiped her eyes with it, and held it on her flushed face. She took some deep breaths and looked at her face in the mirror as if for the first time. It seemed naked, somehow, like it had been stripped of invisible layers.

My face, she thought. Not a face that belonged to the Whole Body or to her sisterhood. *Her* face, a thing of wonder. Me. And who is that? Suddenly she understood that no one else was going to come forward with that information.

She was alone in this, and must do what she could to answer the questions. She ran a hand through her prickly hair, took a deep breath, set her wrist angel to vibrate when her supervisor called, and walked out the door.

At the Hall of Records, Kay signed in as before. Only two other women were in the room now, one studying something in her lap, and the other turned so that Kay could see her profile in the dim light of the monitor.

"Search," Kay said softly as she sat down at the table where she could see both women and the entrance. She would not be surprised again by a voice at her back. When the search template appeared on the screen, she typed the title of another of the works Potemkin had named in her message.

The title screen for *Sociological Repercussions in the Conversion of the African Continent to Unified Market Forces* appeared immediately. Kay typed in "Chapter 11" in the search window in the corner of the screen. What appeared next was not text, as she had expected, but a two-dimensional photograph of a woman's face. Oval in shape, it had a sharp, well-defined nose, a wide, thin-lipped mouth, and strong chin. The hair was long, held on top of the head in a fashion Kay had not seen before.

The eyes were brilliant blue, brimming with life, and the same shape as her own, wide-set and slightly turned down at the corners. There was subtle wisdom in them, and not a little sadness. Tiny wrinkles graced their corners. Someone had once told her they were called laugh lines, and she had wondered then if they numbered the times that their owner had laughed. Kay could only recall laughing a few times in her life, and she counted the lines on the woman's face. Apparently she had laughed at least a dozen times.

Then it hit her. The woman looked like her, like the face she had seen earlier in her own mirror. Not exactly, but enough that someone else might notice.

She pressed the scroll button on the keyboard. What followed was a letter:

My Dear and Faithful Family,

My heart is filled with gratitude for the sacrifices you have continued to make for the sake of our common goal. Those of us who have escaped the mindless machinations of the councils have surely been enriched by our struggles, inasmuch as experience breeds wisdom and struggle against tyranny breeds love of freedom. We at Abingdon are aware of your travails, and the councils' recent destruction of the Augustine community and its laboratories, having received word from the three surviving members.

We were greatly relieved and uplifted to learn of your own escape, and the subsequent progress you have made with the Triune project. We were moved by the example of your determination and resourcefulness. Our own experiments are showing great promise, and we expect to be able to report success within months, if not weeks. Preparations for seeding are well underway, and we have made new friends in high places who are trustworthy, courageous, and utterly dedicated to helping us at the time of sowing.

Time is our greatest enemy, it seems, in that the longer it takes to implement our plans, the more complicated and dangerous the situation becomes. But I have a deep and abiding sense that history will be our friend. Though we now frequently imagine immediate obstacles to be insurmountable and interminable, future generations will see our saga as a brief and ultimately victorious battle against the forces of stagnation and regression. I am not alone, I know, in this vision. Many of us have the gift of sight, and have foreseen the moment when the confluence of our consistent efforts and the will of history will bring the new dawn.

Know this like you know the feeling of blood rushing through your veins: We will accomplish the work. It is as inevitable as the rising of the sun. When that hour is upon us, the leaves of the Tressaline Tree will turn to the Sun, and the loam beneath its roots will groan with joy and give up its sweet sustenance to her fragrant blossoms and tender fruit, while an ancient chorus of hidden stars reverberates in her branches with songs of celebration.

Until that moment, carry on with the assurance that together we manifest collective forces stronger than those of the dying civilization that seeks to destroy us, along with our important work. The world beyond awaits the birth of our precious charges. As long as the spark animates my body, I will remain faithful to that responsibility, and to you.

I send you a radiance of love, and all thoughts for the success.

Yours in the work,
Leona
2.28.2042

It was blasphemy, of course. Kay had never read anything that was so blatantly anti-council. She felt almost soiled having read it. Even though it was written nearly a century ago, Kay could feel its power and eloquence. These people had died for their beliefs, and the letter described the councils that destroyed them as ruthless. She had never thought of the councils as anything but benevolent, collective parents that carried out the will of the Whole Body, the guardians of harmonious order, an engine running smoothly. All her life Kay had revered The Text, and the Mothers, and the Councils. Dissent seemed outrageous to Kay, and this letter an ugly, dispiriting vision. These were dangerous words, like some cyber virus that might gnaw at the foundations of her mind until it collapsed.

She scrolled back to the photograph of the woman, Leona. The similarity to her own face was unsettling. It was not the individual features that set the face apart, but their effect as a whole. They seemed more like a map of some territory beneath its surface, a diaphanous world of sensations and intentions, formless yet imbued with shifting patterns.

In her peripheral vision Kay saw movement in the Hall's entrance, and she glanced up to see a tall, lanky, angular woman signing in at the front desk. The woman never glanced in her direction, but something about her held Kay's attention, set off a silent alarm. Kay could think of no reason why. She closed the file on the screen and watched the woman covertly until she passed out of her line of sight. Behind her Kay heard the scrape of a chair, heard the woman ease her weight into it and begin typing.

Kay shrugged off the feeling and returned to her thoughts. Who was this Leona? How could she find out? She began executing various searches, using words in the woman's letter—"Abingdon," "Triune Project," but after nearly an hour of following the resulting references to a dead end, she stopped.

She thought back to what she had read earlier about the children of the Tressaline community: "It is not known if any of the latter survived to adulthood . . ." Was Leona one of the survivors? It was apparent she was some sort of leader. Again Kay remembered Angela Potemkin's words ". . . your origins are not the same as others in your sisterhood."

The angel vibrated on her wrist. Kay looked around for a private place to take the call, and spied a nearby door marked "Listening booth." When the door shut behind her, she answered.

"You are cleared for two more days before assignment," the supervisor's voice said. "Use them well."

"Yes, Rinchon, I will," Kay answered, and disconnected. She returned to the reading station and clicked on again. She had only a moderate amount of experience in cyberspace, but as she sat quietly staring at the screen, ideas began to form in her mind.

She placed her fingers on the keys and began typing commands, tentatively at first. Within moments, however, her fingers were flying over the keys. It was a strange feeling as one screen of coded text after another appeared, disappeared. One part of her was rather astounded that she knew how to do this, but there was no denying that something in her was learning about the internal workings of the system at a remarkable speed. It was exhilarating. One more surprise for the day, she thought.

Twenty minutes later, confident she had erased all traces of her activities, she clicked off, rose from the chair, and headed for the exit. As she neared the portico, something pulled at her attention—like a peculiar smell but not one that came through her nose. Instinctively, she turned to look over her shoulder. The tall woman who had arrived late averted her eyes.

Something wrong here. Kay burned the woman into her memory and made her way to the workout sanctuary.

Chapter 19

Margaret Michaels stood at rigid attention, her hands sweaty at her sides, before Desta Mardrid's desk.

Michaels was twenty-five years old, a bony woman with stringy brown hair and pasty skin. In the year since coming to work at Council Headquarters, she had never before been asked to personally report on any of her investigations. In fact, she had never even seen the woman who sat before her. She knew who Mardrid was, of course. Even in the dim little offices where Michaels and a dozen other clerks conducted their investigations at the behest of various council members, mention of Desta Mardrid caused a quickening of the pulse.

In some ways, the women in Michaels' office held Mardrid in high esteem. After all, this high-ranking aide had once been a clerk herself, albeit in the Expenditures Division. But she had blazed a trail to the top echelon of the council's hierarchy, and that was an accomplishment none of Michaels' cohorts could fail to appreciate. Mardrid was also known, however, to be ruthless, and someone who could end one's career with a change of mood.

It was only one of the reasons Michaels was nervous about her report. The assignment itself was one she felt pretty shaky about, since nearly all of her past assignments had been routine background checks on women being considered for recruitment to council positions. This one, though, had stretched her skills thin. She had little experience accessing some of the required records, and though she had worked on this project exclusively and nearly without sleep for the last two days, she was not at all confident she was adequately prepared.

Mardrid had glanced at her only briefly when handed the files that now lay on the desk before her, but it had been a chilling look, malicious and slightly disgusted. After a few uncomfortable moments in which Mardrid studied the holograph of Pamela Potemkin and the first several pages of the report, the aide broke the silence.

"Proceed," she said, not bothering to look up again.

Michaels cleared her throat and began speaking, self-consciously aware of the nasal quality of her own voice. "The subject is presently following a course of study at Olin University that likely will lead to her recruitment by the Ministry of Births, apparently following in her mother's footsteps. She is an above-average student, though she shows few signs of being as gifted as her mother. She is due to graduate next year. She has applied to the Weil Center for graduate studies."

"Background?"

"She's twenty-four, a natural-born, lived with her mother and brother Parker until age fourteen, when she was accepted into the Graciane Sisterhood and left for Philadelphia. Subsequent training was standard, no incidents of note since then. Communication with her mother during those years was slightly more frequent than the average, but she seems to have adjusted to her new environment and was encouraged to pursue studies in genetic medicine. When she entered university, she lived in the local residence of the sisterhood. She then followed the typical course and moved into the graduates' dormitory, where she still resides."

"I'm unfamiliar with the Graciane Sisterhood. What can you tell me about it?"

Michaels shifted her feet and her mouth twitched a little as Mardrid turned her eyes upon her. "Uh, I'm afraid nothing, Rinchon." She cleared her throat again. "I have little experience in the genealogy of the sisterhoods."

Mardrid released the woman from her gaze and made a small note on the pad next to her. Michaels wondered if it was a bad mark against her or simply a note to investigate further.

"Any travel or unusual contacts?" Mardrid asked.

"Just three trips, all with classmates to associated research facilities. In all aspects, the subject appears to be a model citizen. She's quiet, obedient, dedicated to her studies. She received a visit from her brother last moon, three days after their mother died. The visit lasted only three days. Since the mother's effects were sent to the sister's residence upon her passing, it can be assumed the visit was occasioned by that event."

Mardrid again focused her reptilian gaze on Michaels. "At headquarters, we cannot afford to assume anything."

The menacing tone had its desired effect.

"Yes . . . I mean no, Rinchon," Michaels stammered. "Of course. That is correct. I was only . . ."

Mardrid cut the woman off with an impatient wave of her hand. "And what of the brother?"

"He's also a natural born, nineteen years of age, the top-ranking athlete of the Califas Order, which he joined at the standard age of fourteen. Since then, he's proven himself extremely gifted. He's rumored to have the potential to become the best exhibition athlete in the world."

Michaels paused. "One odd bit of information," she said, hoping to redeem herself with the only thing she had found that was out of the ordinary. "He had only one experience with Sexual Services, when he was sixteen. He has never been called again."

"Trouble?" Mardrid asked, raising one thin eyebrow.

"The woman to whom he was sent was severely traumatized. Nothing physical, apparently, but she became nearly catatonic for the next few weeks, unable to speak or eat. She has had ongoing and extensive therapy since. An unstable type, perhaps."

"Mmm," Mardrid grunted, flipping through the pages of the report before her. "Genetic background?"

"The son?"

Mardrid fixed her with another stare. Michaels flushed and continued. "Nothing unusual that I was able to uncover. Angela Parker was inseminated with a son in the eighth moon of 2154. She herself came from stock gifted in the hard sciences. Her grandmother was one of the founders of the Monterey Institute, from which was later recruited a number of the scientists to found the Ministry of Births. The sperm for both of her children appears to be from a standard cache, although the Ministry records are not totally accessible even to us."

Mardrid held up a hand to stop her. Michaels stared at the bony hand with the single band around the forefinger and held her breath. Mardrid was staring at something in the report, but Michaels couldn't tell what. The silence grew so long that when the aide spoke again, Michaels was startled by the sound of her voice.

"Movements?" Mardrid barked.

The investigator cleared her throat again. "Quite extensive, as you can see from the notes on the following pages," she said, nodding to the small stack of papers beneath Parker's holograph. "His schedule is rigorous. He travels at least seventy times a year to major competitions, four times a year to the Califas' New Templar camp in the high desert of the Southwest, and twice to their seaside camp, called

Santos, on the Baja peninsula. In the twelfth moon, the entire order goes . . ."

"Yes, yes," Mardrid cut the woman's monologue short. "Any *unusual* movements in the last year?"

Michaels swallowed. "I could find only two trips unrelated to training, competition, or performance. The first was to the medical facility at Olin . . . where his sister is." Michaels felt foolish after adding this last part, not knowing whether she sounded redundant.

"And the second?" Mardrid asked, looking up now into Michaels' gray eyes.

"Six hours spent away from the brotherhood in New Phoenix, following a successful competition at Sun Stadium there. I have not yet been able to determine the purpose."

"A victory party, perhaps?" Mardrid asked.

"Unlikely," Michaels answered, looking straight ahead to avoid Mardrid's malefic gaze. "He is known for not participating in such activities. He is extremely strict and disciplined, both in his training and his social life. According to the headmaster I interviewed, others in the order are somewhat put off by his high standards and unwillingness to engage in extracurricular activities. He tends to keep to himself."

"So where did he go?"

"Well, according to the taxi records I found, he went to an address in the old part of the city. I checked on it and it appears to be the residence of several Southwest Council members, a Mother Avalon being the ranking member. I did a background review of each of the residents. They are all from an order I've not heard of before, called the Nestercine Sisterhood."

Mardrid sat up straighter in her chair. "The Nestercines? Are you sure?"

"Well, yes, Rinchon," Michaels said, surprised by the aide's sudden reaction. Her mind raced over the information she'd gathered, and she wished she had been more clear-headed over these last two days and had more time. Perhaps she would have discovered more about this sisterhood. She hadn't thought the information very important.

"I want an immediate background check on this Mother Avalon," Mardrid said, rising to her feet. "And I mean a complete one. Have it to me this afternoon."

Michaels' face fell, and she wrung her hands. "Uh, may I give it to one of the other investigators, Rinchon? I've been up for several days already working on . . ."

"No!" Mardrid nearly shouted, her voice slicing through the fog Michaels felt in her head. "I want no one else involved and no one else to know about this. I told you this when we began. Did you not understand?"

"Yes, Rinchon." Michaels backed toward the door. "I'll take care of it right away." She turned and hurried out, her face pinched and pale.

"Damn," Mardrid spat aloud after Michaels had gone. She rose from her desk and walked aimlessly around her spacious office. This was not good. What the hell was going on here? Angela Potemkin's contacts with the Nestercines were one thing, but now her son turns up in one of their lairs. Her very talented son. What were they cooking up?

If the Nestercines were involved in some move against the North American Council, she thought, they probably would be working on several plans at once. All along she had suspected K-1754 was involved. But why would they be dealing with Parker Potemkin? He was an athlete with no access to Mother Gretel, or any council doings. His sister, Pamela, on the other hand, was on a track to become involved with the Ministry of Births, one of the key agencies in the council power structure. A few short years and she might well be close enough to do some harm.

It didn't make a whole lot of sense to Mardrid, but she was not willing to leave it up to chance. It was easier to eliminate one potential problem now than to wait until there were three or four in her lap.

She returned to her desk and pressed the icon on the screen that activated her videophone. "Cartene Resnick." In a moment, the face of Mardrid's accomplice in the CAO appeared on screen.

"In need of yet another favor, Desta?" There was a hint of avarice in her voice. "This one will cost you."

Chapter 20

The roar from the crowd was deafening. From the pedestal in the center of Lisbon Stadium that elevated him above the other brothers from his team, Parker felt every cell in his body resonate with the chorus. At moments, he thought he could distinctly hear each of the more than a hundred thousand voices. Outwardly, the colorful throng appeared to Parker like a shimmering, undulating reflection on the surface of a large body of water. With his inner vision, however, it was like staring into the vibrating throats of a primeval, multi-headed beast, its triumphal cries rising into the clear blue heavens above the open-air arena.

He had just led his team to the most stunning victory the Califas Order had ever known, taking first place in every single event in the final World Game trials. Only once, nearly twenty years ago, had an order risen to such prominence, and the number of today's wins dwarfed that achievement by eight. In a week, the Califas athletes would enter the giant arena at Dar es Salaam, the site of this year's World Games, as the most famous team in the Games' history.

Parker's teammates were smiling and waving, flushed with pride and awash in the crowd's praise. Parker, however, felt the same inner calm that had been with him since the Games began that morning. He was recalling the extraordinary moments of the various individual and team events that had led, like an inexorable force, to this moment. From the outset, Parker had clearly anticipated ev-

184

eryone's moves; it was as though some sort of time-space continuum had opened in his mind, a moving blueprint that reacted to some deeper will within his being.

He had felt his teammates' weaknesses and strengths, and reached out to them internally, surrounding and holding them in an appreciation of their wholeness, embracing them with clarity and warmth, augmenting their mental states with his own. He could hear the essence of each, like notes in a chord, which under the focus of his attention had resolved itself from dissonance to harmony, and grown in power and volume.

In the midst of intense competition, he had seen each of his opponents' beauty and grace, and been moved by his determination. None had been able to match Parker's speed or facility, and many had gone down to defeat in befuddlement, anger, or even gratitude for having been engaged so fully.

Through it all, Parker's underlying feeling had been akin to a sense of responsibility. He knew he was experiencing "the field," as Mother Avalon had called it the day he first met her, but in the few short weeks since he had heard the term, the feeling had transmogrified from one of euphoria to something deeper, more mature. It was as though he had aged years in that short span of time. His brothers now seemed more like sons, someone he could and must protect and nurture.

As the crowd cheered, Parker wondered what would become of him now. In the midst of this powerful victory, he had a premonition that athletics would not offer the ultimate test. He sensed a greater challenge that lay before him, approaching from the shadowy future like a phantom.

His team climbed down, and Parker walked with his arms around his brothers toward the gaping hole in the south end of the arena that led to the dressing rooms. The brothers talked excitedly with one another, slapped each other on the back, and waved to the crowd, but Parker looked straight ahead at his mentor Rayful Edwards. Edwards was not smiling. He stood next to the exit, a piece of paper in his right hand.

Parker knew the paper was intended for him, knew that when the team passed out of the arena, Edwards would call him aside. Before Edwards could motion to him, Parker disentangled himself from his teammates and strode to where Edwards waited.

"You were remarkable out there today, Parker," Edwards said, the awe evident in his voice. "I am truly honored to have been here for your performance."

Parker felt his words deeply, and knew that he had surpassed even his most ardent supporter's expectations. "Thank you." He bowed slightly and moved his gaze from Edwards' face to the paper. "For me?"

Edwards followed Parker's eyes to his right hand. Reluctantly he held it out to Parker, his usually blank face betraying sadness. "This came for you an hour ago."

Parker took the note and turned to follow the others into the bowels of the arena. Behind him the cheers of the crowd came again to him. He turned to face the stadium, and stood momentarily, a mute witness to the adoration being heaped upon him. He bowed to the assemblage as he had his elder moments before, and was flooded with a feeling of compassion for each of them.

"Let the feelings move you and move through you," he heard the voice of Mother Avalon say. A wave of grief welled up in his chest, and he knew with a thudding finality that neither the spectacle before him nor the thrill of being the best would ever touch him as it once had. He was in uncharted waters now, heading toward an unwritten destiny.

Slowly turning his back on the scene, he walked down the steep ramp, crumpling the paper in his hand.

When he reached the end, instead of turning in the direction where he would find his ebullient teammates, he found a dimly lit corner removed from the shouts and hurrying athletes, managers, and media. He turned to lean against the wall, slid down onto his haunches, and grasped the edges of the wrinkled paper, pulling it taut to render the words printed there legible.

To: Califas Order
From: Office of Collections, Area 4, Sector 15
Attn: Parker Potemkin
This office was enlisted at 14:00 this afternoon to remove the remains of your sister Pamela from her quarters at the Graciane residential hall at Olin University. Please contact the University Housing Office if you wish to retrieve any of her personal effects.

Officer 298

The words blurred through the tears collecting in his eyes. His lower lip trembled, but he made no sound. He might have appeared to those who passed by as a man silently struggling to rise above the fiery pain of an injury. Then, crumpling the paper again, he slowly stood, squinted as if at a faraway horizon, and headed toward the locker room.

At 17:15 the next evening, Parker stepped from the shuttle that carried him within a mile of the Southwest Council residential quarters and Mother Avalon. In the pocket of the casual khaki-colored pants he had bought at the airport was the approval slip for a two-day leave he had received from the order to retrieve Pamela's effects. The loose-fitting, charcoal gray shirt and the translucent sun visor he had bought at the same time served to somewhat obscure his now-famous identity.

After putting on the new clothes and stuffing the old ones in his travel bag, he had changed his booking from Philadelphia to New Phoenix. He would have to answer to the elders later for this, but just now he didn't care. He needed to talk with someone. Mother Avalon was the only one to whom he could turn.

Minutes before his scheduled departure, he had stopped in a videophone booth to call her and tell her he was coming. He was about to speak her name and address into the voicedialer when he felt the unmistakable sensation of someone's attention on him. He paused, focused his attention on the feeling, and turned to look behind him.

There, amid the hundreds of travelers intent on their destinations, a woman stood against a far wall peering at him from beneath a row of monitors that announced scheduled arrival and departure times. She immediately had tried to look away, but Parker held her gaze fast as he strode toward where she stood rooted like a tree before a hurricane. With each oncoming step, the woman's chest rose and fell in faster, shallower breaths, and she appeared profoundly confused.

Finally, her will to remain standing left her altogether, and she slid down the wall and looked blankly at her outstretched feet, her mouth slack and her eyes as unfocused as a newborn's. Busy travelers stepped around her, shooting her looks of annoyance. No one stopped to offer assistance. If they had, they would not have received a coherent reply.

Parker passed her by as well, only slightly surprised at what had transpired, what he had done to her. When he had begun walking toward her he had no plan, only the deeply felt desire not to be followed. But the changes that had begun in him since his first visit with Mother Avalon were becoming so pronounced that he wondered if he would ever again feel surprise.

Actually, he was grateful for discovering he was being followed for it had made him realize what a mistake it would be to call Mother Avalon. Someone was paying far too much attention for him to risk putting her in danger. A black thought: Had his visit to Pamela after their mother's death been the catalyst for his sister's demise?

Now, as he walked the mile down the New Phoenix street to the Southwest Council residence hall, he wondered too if he had done enough to keep from endangering the woman who had revealed to him the truth of his origins. He was acutely aware of standing a full head above the people on the street around him, and felt the old embarrassment stirring in him. He saw only a dozen other men out in the open, and for an instant, he wanted to have been born a woman, to have been blessed with the normalcy and anonymity most seemed to enjoy. He wished his emerging abilities included rendering himself invisible. He allowed himself the fantasy, and for a moment thought that people were paying less attention to him. He was reasonably certain no one had followed him from the airport.

He wished he had another confidant besides Mother Avalon, but he could trust no one else, not even Rayful Edwards. Mother Avalon would accept his decision to visit, he knew, even though it might put her in peril. The knowledge did little to make him feel better.

When he reached the door of the hall, the sun had settled below the horizon, rouging the old building's face the color of blood.

"Parker, come in!" he heard Mother Avalon say after he announced himself. He stooped to enter the alcove when the outer door opened. The sound of her voice brought a smile to his lips.

"Come in, come in, dear boy!" she said when the inner door opened at her touch. "How wonderful to see you again so soon." She took his hand in both of hers. "I thought you would still be in Lisbon celebrating your victory."

"You watched the trials?" He was surprised.

"Yes," she said, a twinkle in her eye. "I've recently taken interest in a certain young athlete's progress. Magnificent. I actually found myself enjoying it!" She gave his hand a little squeeze and looked up into his smiling face. Her expression turned serious as she released his hand. "What is it, Parker? What has happened?"

Parker started to speak, but she held up her hand to silence him. Turning, she gestured for him to follow, and walked to the door of the study. Once inside, she led him to the small sofa and they sat facing one another. Mother Avalon closed her eyes for the briefest of moments, as though she was listening to some inner voice, then opened them again.

"Tell me," she said.

"They've killed Pamela," he said. "Yesterday."

Mother Avalon's face fell. "Oh, Parker." She took his hand again. Parker felt the wave of grief pass through him, and was grateful for her touch. "And so it begins. I'm sorry, son. It's sooner than we expected."

"You told me that I might be in some danger, but you never said anything about Pamela. Why would someone do that? Couldn't you have warned her, or me?"

"I didn't anticipate this, especially so soon. And I don't know why they would have targeted Pamela. Perhaps because she is a scientist following in your mother's footsteps, I don't know. Someone feels threatened and is being extremely zealous." Her face grew more grave. "Have you sensed any threat to you?"

"A woman was following me at the airport. I . . . stopped her," Parker said.

"Stopped her?"

Parker described what had happened, and Mother Avalon listened intently, nodding. When he finished, she stood and paced the room, immersed in thought. "Tell me about Lisbon, what you felt and what you think is happening to you."

Parker described how he anticipated the moves of his opponents, how he rallied his teammates, how he felt simultaneously present and distant from everything as it happened, and how he thought the intensity of competition had triggered his experience of "the field."

"It is there almost all the time now, just under the surface," he said.

Mother Avalon continued wandering as he spoke, her head slightly bowed, her hands pressed together, fingertips at her lips. When Parker was done, she came to sit beside him. "It may be possible for me to find out where the order for Pamela's termination came from. If I can, then we will determine a course of action from there." She looked worried. "Parker, I can't offer you any protection yet. We have been working on plans for a retreat, a place for you and others like you to go as things became dangerous, but we've had complications. I'll have to contact several people and see what can be done. This will, of necessity, take time, something I fear we are running short of."

191

She bounced a knuckle on her tightly pursed lips. Almost to herself, she said, "So, what's to be done in the meantime?" She looked at him again. "You can see now—from what you accomplished in Lisbon, and from your description of the airport encounter—the potential of your awakening. We have not known what form it would take, nor have we known exactly what talents would emerge, but it is most remarkable, don't you agree?"

Parker felt a curious dichotomy. On the one hand he felt like a small boy, needy and confused, wanting Mother Avalon to tell him that everything was going to be all right. On the other, he sensed something growing within in him, like an engine of immense power humming beneath the surface of his consciousness. Its dark outlines both fascinated and frightened him. He wanted to turn away from it, and he wanted to turn away from what he sensed Mother Avalon was going to say next.

"I'm sorry to have to say this, Parker, but until something can be arranged to provide more safety, it seems that you yourself might hold the best key to your own survival."

Parker felt his face growing hot. He stood now and turned his back, walking toward the shelves of ancient books. He began to speak, his voice rising with each new syllable: "That's it? That's all you can say? My life is falling apart, people following me . . . I'm becoming . . . what, a . . . a freak . . . and that's what you offer me: 'I hold the key?' "

His fingers curled into fists. "I never asked for this. Who do you people think you are, anyway? What gave you the right to put my family in this situation, or to bring me into this world for that matter? Why couldn't you have left whatever made me . . . ."

"Parker . . ." Mother Avalon said in a thin, strained

voice. Her hand was at her chest, grasping the fabric of her robe between her small breasts.

". . . in some test tube somewhere? I want my life back." He slammed the base of his fist against the spines of the books in front of him. "A few weeks ago I was happy to get up in the morning and . . ."

"Parker . . ." Mother Avalon said, a mere whisper this time. Her face was wet with perspiration. Her hand reached toward his back as she leaned forward on the sofa.

". . . train all day. Now I'm . . ." Parker spun around at the moment the Nestercine, pale and stricken, pitched toward the floor.

It took only a second for him to comprehend what he saw, and in a single, smooth motion he was across the room scooping the woman up in his arms.

"Mother Avalon!" he cried, holding her small frame to his chest and cradling her head against him. "No. No. No," he said quietly, rocking back and forth. The anger was gone, replaced with remorse and then a feeling of love that poured out of him in waves. Mother Avalon's eyes fluttered briefly and she groaned, raising her hand to the side of her face.

"I'm sorry! I'm sorry!" He stroked her hair, tears welling in his eyes. She gasped for air, and he laid her gently on the sofa. "Are you all right? Can you hear me?"

She drew quick breaths. "Must be careful," she whispered. "Growing so fast . . . very strong."

Parker pulled her close, ashamed for what he had nearly done, grieving for his own loss of innocence. His very emotions had become weapons, and he didn't know if he could control all the aspects of himself that might pose a threat to those around him. He wanted to curse the lineage that had given him the cells in his body, but knew that he couldn't even do that.

Color returned to Mother Avalon's cheeks, and she stared at him with soft eyes, and with a thumb wiped away the tears on his cheeks. "It's all right, son, it's all right," she rasped. "You're just . . . growing up."

Parker could feel his energy encircling her, but he could also feel her slipping into the rooms of his being, like wisps of smoke through an open window. He wondered if there was anything he could hide from her, if there was a tiny corner of one of those inner rooms that remained private. He didn't know if he could survive such vulnerability.

After a while, Mother Avalon was able again to speak in a normal voice. "Believe it or not, Parker, it is this way for each of us. We never know what the world has in store for us, but then our destinies call to us from long ago, through the hopes and dreams of people dead sometimes for many centuries. They envisioned what might be and lived their lives for that promise. It falls upon us to take their gifts and play them out, to build on what they've left for us, and add to it our own vision of what the world might be. Maybe we don't have a choice at all.

"Our responsibility, yours, is great. But remember—you're a good man, and what comes forth from you will be good. Be brave, and very, very alert. Trust in your best impulses, and be on guard against that which would carry you to destruction."

For the next hour they talked, Parker of his experiences at the competition, Mother Avalon of what she knew of the Tressaline Colony and the other progeny. Parker felt his control return.

Mother Avalon sensed this and took his hand. "Now you must leave. We have no more time to waste. Take the shuttle to the airport and go see to your sister's things. Then return to the brotherhood and your schedule. If you're asked about your trip here, tell them it was unfinished business about your mother, that I asked you to come. I'll back that up.

"Be vigilant, son. I will contact you when I have found out anything to help you. If you haven't heard from me by the time you go to the World Games next week in Dar es Salaam, call this number."

She spoke a fourteen-digit number and told him to repeat it. When she was sure he had memorized it, she said, "I won't answer, but whoever does will know my whereabouts, and can safely reach me without endangering others."

She squeezed his hand. "Goodbye, son. I have every faith in you. Be brave and of good cheer. You often feel like you're alone, but know there are forces at work on your behalf."

She showed him to the outer door and before he left, hugged him. For a moment, Parker was transported back to his childhood and the arms of his deceased mother.

"Go now," she said. "Go. It will be all right."

She turned back toward the study as he left. In her heart, she hoped she could believe her own words.

Chapter 21

"She what?" Mardrid said into the speaker.

"She was found sitting on the floor at the airport. She doesn't recognize anyone, and she hasn't spoken a complete sentence since we brought her in," the voice on the other end said.

"What happened to her?" Mardrid demanded.

"We don't know, Rinchon. We're running a second series of labs on her now. So far we've found nothing."

"Well, what kind of weapon could do that to her?"

"We've tested for the agents that might have done something similar, but found no trace. Most of the ones we have are meant to induce this type of state only temporarily. This seems to be a profound scrambling of the woman's thought patterns, and it has lingered for three days now. I'm not sure I can tell you anything else right now."

"Why wasn't I told about this sooner?" Her voice settled into an even, menacing tone.

"As I said, Rinchon, we only found her yesterday. Airport security had no idea who she was and she carried no identification. It took us a while to locate her."

"What about the boy?"

"We've traced the subject's movements. He apparently changed his plans at the last minute, diverting from Philadelphia where his sister's effects were to New Phoenix."

"The Nestercine's building?" Mardrid's dark eyebrows arched.

"We don't know. If that's where he went, it was by

public transport or foot. And he was not there long. By evening he was on his way to Philadelphia."

Mardrid drummed her fingers on her desk. She should have had someone watching that building. And what had happened at the airport? Without a doubt Potemkin had used a sophisticated weapon on the woman assigned to follow him. It meant that whoever she was dealing with was better equipped and perhaps more dangerous than she had imagined.

"Get back to me the minute you learn more."

"Of course, Rinchon." The line went dead.

Mardrid swore under her breath. For the first time she was having doubts about her ability to control this coup, or assassination, or whatever the hell it was. In the beginning, it had seemed like it was going to be a simple thing. She had rather enjoyed the game of it, the feeling that she was pulling strings and watching for this figure or that figure in the distance to move.

Had she been naïve? It was, after all, her first real opportunity to play this manipulation game in such a large arena. Perhaps she had miscalculated. It was easy to think of the people around her as incompetent, beneath her talents and burning ambition. To realize she was not as much in control as she once had believed angered her.

Maybe it was time to be more aggressive, to stop toying with these people, whoever they were. Obviously, this athlete had something to hide or he wouldn't have done whatever he had to Mardrid's agent. If anyone was naïve, it was this boy. Did he really think his trip to New Phoenix, and this taking out of the woman following him, would go unnoticed?

She considered what Margaret Michaels' research on Mother Avalon had turned up. The woman was old, in her sixties, a member of the Southwest Council, but supposedly serving in a rather minor functionary role. The problem with the Nestercines though, was that the hierarchy in the sisterhood was secret. None of the damned investigations—and there had been too few of them—had been able to ascertain the real extent of any sister's power. Those investigations, that is, that hadn't been sabotaged by the Nestercines who sat on the councils. Avalon must be better connected than her role on the Southwest Council suggested.

Connected well enough to manipulate the termination lists? Perhaps, but Mardrid doubted it. Maybe it was time to get Avalon put on the list. If the Potemkin boy were on the list, it might raise some suspicions, but unless Mardrid eliminated him now, there was no telling what she might be faced with later. It was risky, but if he was allowed to get further in whatever plan was brewing, Mardrid's tampering might be uncovered. Supposedly, a limited number of agencies had the privilege of adding to the lists—the Office of Social Responsibility, the Medical Security Agency, the Homeland Security Task Force, and of course, the head of the North American Council. No one but the Census Accounting Office knew for sure how many people were officially terminated every year. Mardrid guessed it was in the thousands—the destitute, the diseased, those whose aberrant behavior threatened the stability of the Whole Body, illegal aliens, anarchists.

Still, if it came down to a serious investigation of CAO records, there was a chance she could be found out. She saw herself trying to explain to Mother Gretel or the rest of the council how or why she had Angela Potemkin assassinated in the first place. It was a chilling prospect. And yet, she realized, she had better be prepared for the worst if this all came crashing down. She would have to show that there was good reason for it.

Meanwhile, there was no time to waste. She once again dialed Cartene Resnick's private number at the CAO.

Chapter 22

Maureen Hong heard the beep of the videophone as she walked into her office. Closing the door behind her, she hurried to her desk, her thick, shoulder-length black hair swaying heavily with each step. It had already been a fifteen-hour day, and the Assistant Director of the Census Accounting Office was tempted to ignore the call and simply go home to bed.

Her round, flat face hinted at her Oriental lineage, though many of her ancestors had chosen to be inseminated with European sperm. Her sister looked more Caucasian, as did her sister's two daughters. Hong, however, had chosen not to carry on the lineage. Her top-secret job and its many demands left no time for the experience of motherhood.

She sat erect in front of the monitor and saw from the small blinking red light in its corner that she was receiving a secure call. She sighed, and then said, "Receive." The face of Mother Avalon appeared instantly on screen. Worry was evident there.

"Did you know P-2's sister has been terminated?" Mother Avalon said without so much as a hello.

Maureen Hong blanched. Avalon used the code name for Parker Potemkin, even though the secure line made it unnecessary. "When?"

"Day before yesterday. How'd this slip through, Maureen?"

Hong sagged in her chair. "I've explained to you before, I have no real control over the termination lists. Selections are approved in a different section and there are simply too many safeguards involved for me to make any clandestine arrangements. I have the ability to influence assassin assignments, as I did with P-2's mother, but the lists are way beyond my reach."

"I'm not blaming you, Maureen, but someone there has tampered with the lists and they specifically targeted both the mother and daughter," Mother Avalon said. "You and I know neither fit any of the profiles for termination eligibility, so someone there has access. Can you find who it is, or for whom they are working?"

Hong rubbed her eyes with the flats of her palms, feeling more tired than she had in many years. "The list controls are strict. There has never been a known breach of the ministry policies, and the penalties for violating them are severe. But if you really think someone has been tampering, yes, I think I could stir up an investigation over the matter."

"Don't you think someone has gotten outside access? Doesn't it seem obvious?"

It did, but Hong didn't relish the prospect of bringing it up to Internal Affairs. "I suppose so. But truthfully this is quite risky for me. If IA looks too closely into this, there's a chance they'll find out I was the one who got K-1754 assigned to the subject's mother. It's not a firing offense, but it certainly isn't supposed to happen."

"I'm sorry to have to ask, Maureen, but things are moving very quickly and I have little choice," Mother Avalon said. "P-2 discovered he is being followed. I don't believe it was an assassin, as there was no attempt on his life, but I can't rule it out, either. We must find out immediately if he's on the list, and if not, who is ordering the surveillance. Are you still confident this channel of communication is secure?"

"Yes, of course, but . . ."

"Then please call me right away when you find out anything. I'll be in council meetings all day tomorrow, so I may not be able to return the page immediately, but I will within minutes. Have you any idea how long this will take?"

"This probably is not the answer you want to hear, but it could take weeks, or we could get lucky. I can probably find out if P-2 is on the list by morning. The rest will take longer." Hong realized that the prospect of seeing her bed was fading rapidly. "Remember, though, once someone is on the list it is virtually impossible to have him or her removed. I am still only able to influence the designation of the assassin."

"I understand," Mother Avalon said. "You must hurry, though. Any forewarning could mean the difference between failure and success."

Hong knew there had never been a case of someone on the list escaping his or her fate. Nevertheless, Mother Avalon was not a woman to be denied. Besides, Hong liked the Nestercine. She'd known that after their very first meeting years ago at a government function. As their friendship grew, Avalon began to reveal bits and pieces of a vision for the world—heretical ideas, really—that Maureen found compelling. Mother Avalon had always been very secretive about specific plans or actions being undertaken to realize this vision, but she had hooked her with her quiet passion and enthusiasm.

Until now, Mother Avalon had asked only one favor—the assignment of K-1754 to the Angela Potemkin job. At the time, Hong had worried that it might lead to further risk on her part, but she did it anyway. Now she couldn't remember why.

"Look," she said to the face on the screen, "this is more

than you've ever asked for. And it's dangerous. My ass is on the line here." She rubbed her forehead. "Frankly, I'm not sure it's worth it."

Mother Avalon said nothing, and after an uncomfortable silence Hong broke the tension.

"Perhaps if I better understood the scope of this project of yours, and why it is so important to you . . ." This Potemkin family, and K-1754, figured prominently in whatever the Nestercine was up to. But Mother Avalon had never really said what it was.

Mother Avalon stared at her for a long time, her face occasionally betraying signs of an inner struggle. Finally, she spoke. "All right, Maureen. I'll tell you this much. It has taken many decades of planning and work to bring P-2 into this world. You can't begin to imagine how difficult it has been, how many have sacrificed in order to make this happen. Why? Because he and others like him hold the key to a world we have only been able to dream of. If we were to lose him, it would be an unspeakable tragedy."

She paused here, momentarily looking off-screen as if searching for her next words. When she looked back at Hong, her eyes were dark. "His life is worth a hundred of mine. I would give mine in a second if I thought I could protect him. He is the future of our race."

Hong blinked. Had Mother Avalon just implied that she was involved with gene pool tampering? That was dangerous indeed, a capital crime. And yet Hong could feel the old admiration she held for this woman. Avalon had not really told her anything, she realized, at least not in words. As always, it was the ineffable way she said things that tugged at her resolve.

"Okay. I hear you," Hong said, her lips compressing into a tight line. "I'll go to Internal Affairs from here. I'll call as soon as I know something."

"Thank you," Mother Avalon said. Her smile was warm, if brief, before her face disappeared from the screen.

Damn the woman, Hong thought. I hope she knows what she's doing.

Six hours later, Maureen Hong sat before her monitor and felt numbness pressing down on her. She could not remember having to make such a difficult call. Her eyes passed over her spare surroundings as if the right words might spring forth from the bare walls. Finally, in a thick voice she said, "Secure dial." The sound of the tone filled the room, and she spoke Mother Avalon's number. When a recorded voice said, "Leave a message," she began speaking.

"IA informed, investigation underway. List tampering strongly suspected. Search is narrowing for person responsible. Latest list reviewed . . ." She paused and cleared her throat. She couldn't tell Mother Avalon the information she'd learned in such an impersonal way.

"You'd better call me right away. End."

She leaned back in the chair, wishing not for the first time that she had chosen to have children or some other career path.

Thirty minutes later, Mother Avalon's face again filled Hong's screen. Hong saw her own tiredness reflected in Mother Avalon's face. But she also could see the set of the Nestercine's jaw, and the resolute look in her eye.

"What is it, Maureen?"

"It's the current list." Hong swallowed once, took a deep breath, and found her voice again. "P-2 is near the top . . . and so are you. I'm sorry."

Mother Avalon said nothing, but stared back at her, nodding slowly, over and over again, her lips pulled into what might at another time have been a smile. At long last, she spoke. "Thank you for your information, Maureen, and for being such a help in these last few months. Your contributions have been vital."

Hong wanted desperately to say something more, but words suddenly seemed almost trivial. Finally, she said them anyway. "I wish . . . is there anything more I can do for you now?"

The Nestercine's eyes closed as she thought. "Yes, there is. I have two last favors to ask. I'd like you to get K-1754 assigned to P-2. Can you do that?"

Hong thought she could, and nodded.

"And I need to get a message to her before she leaves for the assignment. Do you think you can manage it?"

Hong hesitated and then nodded. "I believe so. Will you send the message to me here?"

Mother Avalon shook her head. "She probably has no means to deal with the encryption I would need to use if I were sending it to you online. I will have it delivered to you in a format she can read. Can you arrange to be met in a public place?"

"Yes. I can be at the Macky Transport station, say at Track 12." She looked at the timepiece on the wall. "Is an hour enough time?"

"Yes. I will send someone. I'll have her approach you and ask if this is Track 15. At 07:00 then?"

"Make it 07:10," Hong replied.

"That's fine. Again, I am most grateful."

"I wish I could do more. I really do."

"Thank you, Maureen. Your words are comforting, but it is my time. I've been preparing for a long while. I think I am ready. There are others to carry on."

"I didn't hear that," Hong said.

"Yes, of course." Mother Avalon brought her hand up to her shoulder in a formal salute. "You'll not be sorry for what you've done for us, believe me. Goodbye, Maureen."

And she was gone from the screen.

At 07:28, Hong handed the small package that Mother Avalon's messenger had given her at the Transporter station to another courier, with instructions to deliver it to K-1754 at her quarters at North American Council Headquarters. Just as the courier closed the door to her office, Internal Affairs called.

"We have one of the list managers, a Cartene Resnick, in interrogation," the woman on the screen said. "There is evidence to suggest she is the source of the tampering we discussed. You're welcome to observe the procedure, if you care to."

Hong sighed. She had found the one other interrogation she had witnessed to be highly distasteful, but she told them she would be there in a few minutes.

She stood, opened her desk drawer, and found the small bottle of stimulants she kept there. She tapped one of the small white pills into her palm, popped it under her tongue, let out a long, slow breath.

It was going to be a long morning.

Chapter 23

Standing in still, knee-deep water, looking at the naked back of a child. Beyond the child a wall of gray-green water rising on the horizon. Ominous. Moving this way. Danger! Reach for the child, press it to me, hold it tight, safe.

I am the child, strong arms wrapped around me. Can see through the wave. There are shapes there—masses of people. Armies?—suspended in the emerald green water. Wave so big, like a mountain, looming overhead, roaring, but not moving . . .

Kay awakened with a start at 05:15 and for a moment felt like she was in two worlds, one filled with the growl of the ocean and one with the incessant high-pitched whine of her pager. She raised herself on one elbow, swiped her free hand across her forehead to clear it from the grips of the dream, and got out of bed to silence the pager.

"Call Zero One," the recorded voice said when she pressed the retrieve button. Sleepily, she made the call, and the face of K-89, the eldest of the assassins stationed at headquarters, filled the screen. "Report to the office in fifteen minutes for a new assignment," she said, and signed off.

Kay dressed quickly, flashes of the dream tumbling through her mind. What was this about? She was rarely reassigned. She made her way to the business wing of the building.

When she arrived, K-89 was seated behind a small desk. "You have special orders. The assignments you received yesterday will revert to others. You are to proceed to Africa, today, Dar es Salaam. That's part of the East African Council. Your transport leaves in an hour and forty-five minutes. A driver is waiting to take you to the airport. Are you prepared?"

"Not quite, sister," Kay said, keeping the surprise in her voice to a minimum. "This is unexpected. How long is the flight?"

"A little more than seven hours."

Kay had never been assigned outside the North American continent. She hadn't known such assignments happened. Didn't other councils do their own wet work? "I will need about half an hour, I guess."

"Very well." The woman pushed a TeleSlate across the desk toward her, along with a sealed packet. "Your instructions, your client's file, and some other things you'll need. There is a major public event where the client is appearing. Termination is to take place afterward. We will expect you back on the first available flight when the mission is accomplished."

"Of course, sister," Kay said, reaching for the small pile of objects. She felt a small rush of anticipation as she touched it, and paused before picking it up. The elder sister noticed, gave her a curious look.

Kay recovered quickly and said, "Will that be all?" tucking the items under her arm.

The elder woman folded her hands and leaned back in her chair. "You're to be congratulated. This is an important assignment. Apparently someone at the Ministry is acknowledging your talents, showing a lot of confidence in you, despite your last fiasco."

Kay felt wetness in her armpits. "Yes. I understand. Thank you, sister." She gave a formal salute. "I'll go prepare now," she said, turning to leave. Then she stopped. "Do we often go to foreign regions, sister?"

"Almost never. Like I said, this must be important."

As she strode down the nearly deserted hallway toward her quarters—few people were up at this hour—Kay pulled out the Slate and thumbed it on. There was a closed file and an icon for the client's holograph. She touched the latter, and when the broad face of a young man appeared, she stopped. That this was a man gave her no pause. She had dispatched three in the last twelve months and had thought little of it. But there was something about this man's face. She opened the text file:

Parker Potemkin, W.F.C. #H729B00236F.11536—
Area 42, Sector 12, Califas Compound, Bldg. 6,
Unit 4.

Then came the feeling, the same as it had on the shuttle that had carried her to Sector 18 and her fateful meeting with Angela Potemkin, like she was falling sideways into a world just beyond the visible one around her. The Slate slipped from her hand and smacked to the hard floor of the corridor.

Aria Helsing had arisen earlier than usual again this morning. She was on her way to the workout sanctuary, hoping that exercise would help dispel the uneasiness that had disturbed her sleep patterns ever since her blackout experience with the assassin. She was tired, and the long, dim corridor offered little to sharpen her dulled senses. The sharp noise behind her, however, jarred her into alertness.

She turned to look over her shoulder.

She recognized the young woman bending down to retrieve a TeleSlate from the shiny marble floor. Without a second thought, she abandoned her plans, turned, and walked quickly to where Kay stood.

Kay looked at her with the eyes of a hunted animal—and not the brown eyes Aria had seen in their other encounters, but blue ones, as pale and striking as a late summer sky.

"Kay," she said, "what's wrong?"

Kay glanced behind her at the deserted corridor. She turned and opened her mouth to speak, but closed it again and looked down at the Slate.

Aria's heartbeat quickened, and a small rivulet of sweat crept out from her hairline. She looked around her and saw a nearby door marked "Utility." On impulse, she covered the space in four steps and tried the handle. It was unlocked, and the small room behind the door was occupied by only a bank of humming panels and numbered conduit pipes. There was a narrow space where two people could stand.

"Come. We can talk in here," she said, beckoning with her hand.

After a moment's hesitation, Kay followed her, glancing in both directions before entering.

"You're in some trouble," Aria said, closing the door. "Can you tell me about it?"

Kay looked from Aria's face to the Slate in her hand, and back again. Deep in her body, the assassin felt an odd compulsion, an urge to throw herself against the frame of the counselor and cling to her like a fly in a windstorm. Aria took a step backward, her forehead now shiny with perspiration, though the small room was no warmer than the corridor.

"Kay," she said, "wait."

The assassin looked at her with horror, Angela Potemkin's last two words echoing in her head.

Aria held her hand up, as if to shield herself. "Please, I'm here for you, but you've got to try to relax." She was breathing hard, as if she'd been running, and her ears buzzed. "You're very strong. Please, I'm having trouble staying with you. I want to help, but I need your help if you want me to be here with you."

Kay understood that she was affecting the counselor again as she had in the heat room, and so she wrestled with the anxiety that threatened to engulf her, took some deep breaths, and inwardly recited a passage from The Text:

Peace is the fruit of the highest purpose. The servant who undertakes the highest purpose reaps the reward of righteous labor, the reward of peace.

Her calm returned.

Aria wiped her forehead with the back of her hand. "Okay. Better now." Damn, this woman was strong, Aria thought. She gathered her courage and nodded toward the Slate in the assassin's hand. "What's in there that has you so upset?"

For just a moment, Kay thought she had made a terrible mistake coming into this room with a woman she barely knew, a woman not part of Kay's sisterhood, a foreigner, really, to her world. But there was genuine concern in Aria's demeanor, and Kay desperately wanted to talk with someone. She heard her words come tentatively at first, then faster, telling the counselor of the assassination of Angela Potemkin.

Finally she said, "I don't know how, but the woman knew who I was. She said my name just before she died— 'Kay, wait,' like you did just a moment ago. Then a message came on the wall monitor. She'd recorded it for me. She said . . . things. About me. She said I was different than my sisters. She named books and passages in them that I looked up. They were all about people who lived a long time ago, people who were persecuted . . . killed . . . for trying to introduce a new kind of human into the world."

She looked at the floor. "She said I was one of them. I didn't want to believe it, but . . ." She stopped speaking, her face contorted as though she might cry.

Without thinking, Aria reached out toward Kay to comfort her, but saw that her own hand had begun to tremble. "I think I'm beginning to understand," she said, reluctantly withdrawing her hand. "I knew you were special from the moment I first tried to read you, but I had no idea why."

She nodded at the Slate Kay clutched to her chest. "Is this her file?"

Kay shook her head. "Her son's. I've been assigned to terminate him."

Aria's stomach was quaking now. What she really wanted to do was run from this room before she had a complete breakdown. Instead, she forced herself to speak. "May I see it?"

"It's forbidden," Kay said, though she heard little conviction in her voice. To allow an outsider to view the contents of a termination file, she knew, was a capital crime.

"Yes," Aria said, nodding once. Then carefully, "But I think we've gone beyond that now, don't you? You trust me, I believe."

Aria watched Kay's eyes as this truth sank in, and the look of loneliness there gave way to tentative hopefulness. Kay slowly opened Parker's holograph again and held out the Slate. Aria recognized the significance of the offering, acknowledging it with a little bow. Then with her trembling hand she turned the Slate the right direction, and blinked at the face of Parker Potemkin.

"Are you sure this is the woman's son?"

"The next text file confirms it."

Silently, Aria focused on Parker's broad features and felt for that part of her that swam in her subjects' inner waters. The holograph blurred for a moment, then, as if it had sprung from the screen and slammed into her face, it filled the entire field of her vision. Tears began to roll down her cheeks, and her lower lip trembled. She was too surprised, too immersed in her feelings to name them, or even to move. She remembered something similar happening to her at age twelve when she first met her principal teacher—feelings of awe, reverence, and, yes, fear.

And something else—a deep sadness, a sense of the tragic, like labored hands reaching for her, tugging at her heart.

She felt Kay's eyes on her, and yet she could neither look away from the holograph nor stop the flow of tears. A full minute later, with a great act of will, she closed her eyes and withdrew from the intensity of the experience. She swallowed once, took a breath. "Can you refuse this assignment?" It came out softer than she had intended.

"No. Such a thing is never done." A flat voice.

"There is great danger here, Kay. This is no ordinary man. I don't think you ought to do this."

"I have no choice. This is what I do. I'm born to this."

"But why must this young man die? What has he done?"

Kay looked at the floor. "I don't know." A passage from The Text came to her . . . *and the willingness to sacrifice even that which is most dear.* An assassin didn't question the Ministry's choices, even those that tore at the fabric of her convictions, leaving holes that yawned and emitted whispers from the emptiness beyond.

Aria nearly protested, then realized the futility of it. Disobeying an order might even be dangerous psychologically for Kay. The young woman was likely not capable of it. Her entire being was focused on this service. To tamper with that could place an untenable burden on her. She laid the Slate on a nearby bench and gazed at it for a long time.

Then she drew her lips into a tight line, stood to her full height, moved closer to Kay, and before she could think anymore about what she was doing, put her arms around her. She felt Kay stiffen, and felt her own conflicting emotions—fear of this deadly woman, compassion for her, attraction and repulsion—swimming through her like tiny fish fleeing a predator.

There was an excruciating moment in which she thought she had made a mistake, had penetrated a boundary so sensitive that it would result in catastrophe. Then she felt Kay's lithe arms tentatively encircle her torso and cling. It was like diving into a pool of cold water. Aria gasped and shivered, and fought the feeling of drowning by holding onto Kay more tightly. Her heart felt as though it would explode.

In that moment of intense sweetness, she knew she would do anything in her power to help Kay.

Eventually she found her voice again. "Do what you must, then, but use every skill, every bit of awareness and wisdom you have. This is a critical moment. I don't know why this has come about, but something very important is happening, and you must enlist all the resources you've known up until this moment. And maybe some that you don't know about."

She stepped back, put her hands on Kay's shoulders, and looked into her face. "I don't know what else to tell you. I'm sorry."

And she was. Never before had she wanted so badly to advise someone, to give comfort, and yet felt so impotent.

The two women looked into each other's eyes. Through a teary mist, Aria saw something magnificent in Kay, something both utterly vulnerable and powerful beyond belief. Then, almost as if a veil descended behind the assassin's eyes, the look faded away, replaced by resolve.

Kay shrugged off the counselor's hold on her shoulders, took a step backward, picked up the Slate, and carefully opened the door. When she saw no one in the corridor, she half-turned back to Aria and shot her a brief, haunted look. "Thank you . . . goodbye," she said. And was gone.

Aria stood still, one hand over her trembling mouth, staring at the closed door. Finally, she wiped her cheeks with her fingertips, straightened her clothes, and set her jaw. "Goddammit," she said aloud. "Goddammit." Then she made a decision.

Once outside the door, she headed directly for Barena Colter's office.

Chapter 24

"I have a communiqué for K-1754 from the Assistant Director."

The woman from the CAO flashed her credentials at K-89, who was seated behind the desk in the unmarked office.

The elder assassin masked her surprise behind a brusque reply. "K-1754 is on assignment. You may leave the message with me."

"It is urgent and confidential. I have been instructed to personally deliver it to her this morning."

"Not possible. She left more than an hour ago for the airport. She'll be airborne by now."

Without speaking, the woman spun on her heel and went back into the hallway. Out of earshot, she pressed a button on her wrist angel. When she heard the answering voice of Maureen Hong in her earpiece, she said, "The subject is unavailable. She's airborne on an assignment. How shall I proceed?"

Maureen Hong spat into the phone. "Shit. How long ago did she leave?"

"She went to the airport nearly an hour ago."

"Damn. All right," Hong said. "Come back here. Who's in charge there? I'll phone directly."

"Just a moment." The woman went back to the office, flashed her credentials, and asked the woman behind the desk for her designation. She relayed the information to Hong and left.

★ ★ ★ ★ ★

Hong clicked off and called up the number for the assassins' Council Headquarters office on the screen. "Dial." She tapped her fingers on the desk as the number rang.

"Hello."

"This is Assistant Director Hong. Visual please."

K-89 clicked the number at the bottom of her screen to confirm the call was coming from the CAO. Then she sat up straighter, touched the activation point on the screen, and the face of Maureen Hong appeared.

"Where is K-1754's assignment today?"

"Dar es Salaam," K-89 answered. "As per orders from your department, we reassigned her local clients to others so she could make the trip."

"Which client?" Hong asked.

K-89 hesitated. No one from the Ministry had ever inquired about the names of assignees before. She thought it particularly odd, since these names originated in their office. "One moment." She pulled a file on screen that partially covered the image of the Assistant Director. "Parker Potemkin. He is an athlete competing at the World Games there."

Hong made a hissing noise, which K-89 found unsettling. "Is something wrong?" she ventured.

Hong ignored the question. "What's the scheduled arrival time?"

"At 14:47 at Kala International Airport on North American Flight 1099." She wondered why an assistant director didn't know where the target was located. Was the bureaucracy really this disjointed?

"Page K-1754 and inform her a courier will meet her at the arrival gate with a communiqué, a woman in a blue vest."

"Of course," K-89 said. "May I ask what this is about?"

"You may not," Hong said flatly. "Call me if there is a problem. Otherwise, forget we had this conversation."

Five minutes later, Mother Avalon's face appeared again on Hong's monitor. "K-1754 left for Dar es Salaam more than an hour ago," Hong said, "assigned to P-2. I didn't realize they would assign her backlog to someone else, and I didn't know her target was out of country." Nor had she realized Parker was competing in the World Games the next day. Someone was risking drawing a lot of attention to themselves by going after an athlete at an event that was going to be seen around the world.

"I am going to take the chance of sending your message electronically to a courier there. She'll deliver it as she arrives. And I am having K-1754 paged to tell her to meet the courier. It's the best I can do."

"Can you be sure that the message will be read by no one else?" Mother Avalon asked.

"Reasonably sure. There are reliable services outside the normal channels."

"Then please put me in touch with one. I want to get a message to P-2, as well."

Gravity pulled at Kay as the supersonic transport climbed to cruising altitude, and she thought about how different flying was than she had once imagined. Her mind drifted back to the day when she sat amongst the girls she had thought of as her sisters—was she ever really of the same stock?—listening to Mother Clara speak in ringing tones about their responsibility to the future, watching the bird of prey circling behind Mother Clara on the giant SimuTech screen at the initiation ceremony.

How glorious it had all seemed then, how full of purpose and righteousness. How weightless the bird seemed to have been, floating above the world. Not like this force that now pushed her down into the seat. Not like the weight in her heart.

Mother Clara's image, big-hipped and upright behind the podium, stood frozen in Kay's mind.

On this day, you become the mothers to the Future, ensuring that our race will live on in perpetuity . . .

Had Mother Clara believed her own words? Did she know that one day one of her charges would be assigned to carry out questionable terminations? Would there be others like this? Parker Potemkin's face drifted across her inner vision. So young—her own age, in fact. Why would the Whole Body require such a sacrifice? Could an athlete really pose any risk to the Whole Body? Was he diseased somehow? Unlikely. A spy for another council? But she knew athletes led very disciplined and mostly isolated lives. What access could he possibly have to foreign powers?

You become sisters to the Process, maintaining by your loyal service the harmony and order of the Whole Body . . .

Didn't such a killing violate the Precepts? Or was she simply too young or too shortsighted to grasp the larger picture? Was there some great purpose beyond her understanding, or was this some test of her loyalty? Everything about this mission felt wrong. Would they test her on an innocent citizen?

The Whole Body is mighty and magnificent, and yet as fragile as our will to sacrifice. It provides generously for all, but demands our unerring loyalty and the willingness to sacrifice even that which is most dear.

Kay had no choice, really. Some actions in life are bound to be difficult. Whatever, or whoever, had made the assignment had done so for a reason. Even if Kay didn't understand that reason, even if her insides screamed in protest.

For this purpose were you brought into this world, and in its grand design you shall find your destiny and fulfillment. So shall it be.

Angela Potemkin's words also echoed in Kay's mind: ". . . that your origins are not the same as others in your sisterhood . . . historical cusp that depends on your decision." What could she decide? She was simply a servant. Decisions were made elsewhere by others, people higher than she. How could she be responsible for something over which she had no control?

The pale blue sky beyond the window offered no succor. She had to shut down this gnawing doubt or she would botch this mission, and she couldn't afford that again. I will do my job, she said to herself. I will do what is before me and do it well, even if I can make no sense of it.

Methodically, then, she pushed away the warring voices in her head, concentrated on the task at hand. She pulled out the packet K-89 had handed her a few hours ago and broke the seal. Inside was an entrance pass to the World Games and two small bundles, one of African currency, one of North American.

She thumbed on the TeleSlate and read the instructions. Termination was to take place at the massive Kala Arena, which had been built twenty-five years before when the African Council received approval from the Whole Body to host their first World Games. Tomorrow's games were the second in Dar es Salaam. Her client was the leader of the Califas team, one of the top contenders for the coveted cup.

Even if the client and his team were to have a poor showing at the games, she thought, the challenge was to get near enough to carry out her mission. If they won, the adulation likely to be heaped on them would make it even more difficult.

She opened the file that held the stadium plans and scanned them. There were numerous entrances, both to the outside and to the inner arena. She had never attended a sports event, but she had seen enough of them on InterTV to know that the athletes entered and exited the inner arena by way of large porticos around the inner ring of the arena. These would be a likely place for a fatal encounter, if she could position herself in the right portico. How would she find it?

Her timepiece read 09:27. According to background information, the games began the next morning at 09:00. In the seat pouch she found a reference sheet for time zones. Ten hours difference. That would put her into Dar es Salaam the evening before the games. That would allow her time to scout the area and find a hotel where she could get a few hours' sleep, and to arrive early enough at the stadium to make her plans.

And what of the language? She scrolled to the briefing document. "Official language: Swahili. English spoken throughout the city."

Kay glanced at the digital angel on her wrist. She had turned the pager function off, as per airline regulations. Headquarters had never paged her while she was out on assignment anyway, she thought, so it was unlikely she had missed anything. Nonetheless, the realization headquarters could not reach her was a spiky reminder of how far away from home she was.

She squirmed in her seat, feeling restless and stiff. She wanted to get up and feel the floor beneath her feet. There was a waste station, she knew, some twenty rows back. She touched the button that released the shoulder harness, stood, and turned toward the rear of the airplane. As she did, she caught sight of a familiar face a dozen rows behind her on the opposite side of the aisle. It was the same woman she had seen in the Hall of Records on her second visit there.

The woman glanced up for a fraction of a second, saw Kay coming toward her, and looked away, trying to appear bored. Kay read the lie, though, and understood not only that the woman knew her, but that she was following her.

Her first thought was that someone had discovered what she had been reading in the Hall. Was she under some sort of suspicion? Or had the Ministry sent someone to see if she was going to be faithful to this mission? Whatever the answer, something was wrong here.

Her thoughts raced as she drew nearer. The woman was now shifting her legs and attempting to obscure her face with a TeleSlate. Kay sensed a deep vibration in her body, an audible hum, which began to transform into feeling ranges—hollow, dark, suspicion tinged with fear. She smelled again the unpleasant odor she had first noticed when she left the Hall of Records that night.

Something inside shifted to defensive mode. The humming took on a shape, like an invisible bubble, and Kay could almost see it begin to expand from the contours of her body, reaching toward the woman. She wondered if others could hear the growing hum. She was alongside the woman now, and the light streaming in from the little light above the woman's head seemed to darken and distort, as if Kay were looking through a sheet of murky water. From the corner of her vision she saw the woman's head loll forward on her chest, jaw slack and eyes closed.

In the waste station, Kay wet a small towel and dabbed at her face. She tried to wrap her mind around what had just happened. It was as though she had always known how to do this thing. She knew that the woman was not dead, but merely unconscious, but how? Kay felt no shame or regret—clearly it had been necessary—but now what? She squeezed her temples. This was all too complicated. The assignment was difficult enough, but now someone was tracking her. Why? And who?

Despair shot through her when she realized she had no one to talk to about this, no one she could trust. She remembered the reader, Aria Helsing, the cramped utility room at headquarters, the momentary comfort her arms provided, the sweet smell of the woman's sweat. So far away.

For now, there was the assignment. Kay set her jaw, pitched the towel away, and opened the door. On the way back to her seat, she scanned the other occupants for potential threat, found none. As she passed the unconscious woman, she noticed a spreading stain in the woman's lap, the drip from her slack lips. The woman sitting next to her was ignoring it.

Three hours later, the transport touched down in Dar es Salaam. Kay stood and took one glance behind her before making her way to the exit. Several people were trying unsuccessfully to awaken the incapacitated passenger. Kay made herself small, blended with the departing passengers, and headed into the Kala Terminal.

She never thought to reactivate her pager, and the courier who was waiting at the gate to deliver Mother Avalon's message never even caught a glimpse of her.

Chapter 25

Deep in the bowels of Kala Stadium, Parker slowly pulled on the one-piece uniform that had been made especially for today's World Games. In the new design, the Califas insignia retained its place high on the left breast, but now it lay on a blaze of orange that shot across the purple field from the left shoulder diagonally across his broad chest to below the knee of his right leg. The air crackled with energy and excitement. His teammates suited up, talking and joking nervously, mostly about the opponents and teams they were about to square off against.

Parker joined in none of it. He was silent and, his teammates thought, grim. He'd been this way since before the World Game Pre-Trials, and the brothers, well aware of his responsibility to lead the team, gave him a wide berth. One or two tried to engage him in conversation now and then, but when they looked into his eyes, something there made them fall silent. It was superstition, though they would not have admitted to it. Whatever had happened to Parker in recent months that had made it possible for them to accomplish what they had, they dared not interfere. Each had developed a deferential attitude toward Parker, one that bordered on reverence.

Amidst the hubbub, the door at the far end of the room opened and Rayful Edwards pushed into the mass of bodies. Parker looked up from fastening his shoes and caught his eye. Edwards motioned Parker to come outside.

"This just came for you," he said when the door closed

behind them. The small envelope in his hand was stamped with Parker's name and the words: "Urgent" and "Personal and Confidential."

"I hope it's good news this time," Edwards said, forcing a smile. He put the envelope into Parker's outstretched hand, but made no move to leave. Parker pulled at the sealed flap at one end and shook out the contents, a small silver square inside a plastic case.

"There's a spill-over media room down the hall on the left," Edwards said. "You can play it there. Only twenty minutes before opening ceremony. Do you want me to hold it for you until the end of the day?" It was clear he thought this would be the wise thing to do.

"No," Parker replied. "I'll just be a minute."

He strode down the hall, aware of the elder's eyes on his back. He found the door marked "Media," and stepped inside, closing it behind him. The room was empty, save a row of a dozen monitors at a table along the far wall. Parker crossed to the closest one, opened the case, and inserted the square into the carriage beneath the screen. Without sitting down, he said, "Play" and heard the machine whir into action.

A mechanical voice said, "This encrypted message is intended only for its recipient and is protected with voice-recognition programming. Please state your name clearly."

"Parker Potemkin." The machine whirred through its permutations of decoding, and in another instant, Mother Avalon's face appeared on the screen.

"Hello, Parker. I hope this has found you before the beginning of the Games. I'm sorry to have to bring you serious news at such a moment in your life, but I'm afraid it is inevitable.

"We have discovered the person responsible for ordering

the assassination of your mother and sister. Her name is Desta Mardrid, and she is a top aide to Mother Gretel of the North American Council. We don't as yet know why she did this, but we know how, and steps have been taken that will prevent her from ever ordering such a thing again. Nor do we know if she did this with the approval of the council, but at this moment it seems unlikely.

"I'm afraid I also have some bad news."

She looked as though she would rather not continue. "Unfortunately, we were not quick enough. I learned yesterday that this woman set in motion assassination orders for two more people: you and me. I can't explain why right now, Parker, but these orders cannot be rescinded. They're beyond my reach. The sad truth is I can do nothing further to protect you, save giving you this message.

"As for me, by the time you see this, I am likely no longer among the living. You have a better chance of survival. The person who is to make this attempt on your life is coming all the way from North America, so there is some time for you to prepare. We know who she is. Please take a close look at this holograph."

Her words were numbing. He could scarcely believe he had heard her correctly. The screen filled with the three-dimensional image of a young woman with close-cropped hair.

"She's known as Kay Black. She's a highly trained killer, Parker. Most of the time, her victims never know she's near. Most never see her before they die. The only hope you have of surviving is to use all your senses, everything. Do you understand? I have learned that her instructions are to carry out her attack after the Games. This should work in your favor, because from what you told me about your experience at the World Game Pre-Trials, your senses are greatly sharpened by competition.

"There is something else you should know about her: she also is descended from the Tressaline Colonists, in fact from Leona Termalaine, the daughter of the scientist whose diary you read in my study. She may or may not be aware of this. We attempted to convey this information to her, but we have no confirmation it was received or embraced. Nor do we know how developed she is. In physical and mental acumen, she may be your match, but whether she has awakened to the other abilities you are discovering, we have no idea.

"When I found out you were on the list, I was able to arrange to have this woman assigned to this mission, a last favor from an old friend. I did this on some slight intuition, or wishful thinking, or perhaps just out of desperation. I arranged it because I thought that since she too is gifted, you may somehow be able to communicate with her on a level that will interfere with her sense of mission.

"We've attempted to get her a message today, too, but again at this moment I don't know if we were successful. Even if she did get it, I can't know how she will respond. It may be that you have to kill her, if you can, but my deepest hope is that neither of you will be lost. I can't tell you how sorry I am it's come to this.

"If you should make it through this, Parker, remember the number I gave you before. It is good for a day or two. After that . . ."

Parker stared at image on the screen, a hollow thumping in his chest.

Mother Avalon sat silent, her eyes closed. When she opened them again, they were soft and warm. "And so this is goodbye, son. I am grateful we had the chance to meet as we did. I think you can understand now how very much it meant to me. You are the culmination of my life's purpose, everything your mother and I had hoped you'd be: beautiful, strong, deep . . . So much depends on your life. Live, Parker. Survive this terrible turn of events and grow, and embody the greatness that is your sacred heritage . . . and remember me, this old woman who loved you."

She gave a last, long look into the camera, and then reached forward to shut off the recording. When the screen went blank, Parker tried to replay the message, but it had erased itself. It didn't matter. The assassin's face, and the face and voice of Mother Avalon, would forever be etched in his mind.

He remained motionless, lost in a deep sense of loneliness.

Soon Rayful Edwards opened the door behind him. "It's time."

Parker took a slow, deep breath and exhaled, drawing his lips together tightly, his face a mask of determination, his hands balled into fists. When he turned toward Edwards, the elder brother looked at him, his eyes growing round.

"Is everything all right?" he asked, unnerved by what he saw.

Parker pushed by him without answering and strode into the hallway that was echoing with the opening fanfare of the World Games.

Chapter 26

Kay arrived at the stadium in the early dawn, raw fingers of sleep still pulling at her. A mere four hours before, she had checked into a hotel. It had been difficult to get to sleep, and when she did, she had vague, troubling dreams that fled each time she awoke.

She was glad now, however, that she arrived early, as she managed to secure a spot fairly near the front of the lines. Several hundred people must have been waiting all night to get in, but when the gates opened, the line moved quickly. She roamed the length of the arena for the better part of the morning, piecing together a plan.

Security was surprisingly lax. Kay was undeterred in all of her explorations. First, she discovered a passageway to the inner arena through a maintenance area. It was locked, but the TeleSlate fixed that. The area was dimly lit and cluttered with stationary pumps and equipment for moving materials around in the arena, but otherwise deserted. On the far side of the room, she found a door that opened to the arena. It was situated no more than fifty feet from a giant portico. Later, when the Games commenced, she watched with satisfaction when the brightly-arrayed athletes poured like wasps from a hive onto the inner field through that very archway.

Three times Kay made her way from her assigned seat on the aisle and near the railing that surrounded the field, down the wide ramp, right at the bottom for approximately two hundred and ten feet to the maintenance area, and through to the door that opened to the inner field. If she walked at a steady pace, it took just under three minutes. As the stadium filled up and she had the additional factor of a crowd to deal with, she mentally added another minute and a half to the time. If she were able to run, it would take her even less time, but that would make her more conspicuous.

It was enough. When the Califas team made its final exit at the close of the Games, she would be standing near the mouth of the portico, waiting. One brief, close-range sighting of her client, and it would be over. Her weapon was only accurate at a mere twenty-five feet, but she was confident she could maneuver herself into a clear line of sight. She would disappear in the ensuing chaos, making her way to the street.

High poles at the edges of the arena were crowned with giant screens on which she followed the Califas team's progress through the morning. They were taking nearly every major event, setting new records and bringing the crowd to its feet again and again. As each hour passed, Kay's mind grew fuzzier around the edges. She had heard the term "jet lag" and assumed that she was experiencing it. She did everything she could to counteract it: breathing techniques, rhythmic tightening and loosening of various muscle groups, walking the length and breadth of the stadium at the fastest pace possible given the density of the crowd.

By noon, she had taken five stimulant tabs, three more than she had ever taken in a single day. The constant movement of the crowd and the loud cheers became increasingly irritating.

Shortly after 16:00, as the brilliant sun settled in behind the steep walls of the stadium, she watched Parker defeat another young man in a spectacular final match. It was an impressive performance. She, like nearly every other person there, stood staring at the screens, fascinated by Parker's fluid movements, the almost eerie sense of calm amid chaos he projected, as though the lightning-fast punches and parries were all choreographed, the outcome known beforehand. At least in her mind, there was never any doubt as to who was in command.

When the cameras showed Parker in close up, her eyes followed the strong line of his jaw, the bulk of his shoulders and the tapered waist, the terrifying speed and grace with which he outmaneuvered his opponent. She realized with a start that she thought him beautiful. She admired his mastery, the spirit that animated him. On the heels of this realization crept a sense of melancholy, the sadness that had first broken the surface of her consciousness when she gazed at the holograph of Parker's mother. She felt it even more strongly now, knowing that in a very short time she would put an end to this young man's brilliant career, close the door on his future.

Weariness tugged at her. With every roar from the crowd, the dark inner shadows seemed to grow. She closed her eyes and tried to shut out everything, grasping for but not finding the flat sense of normalcy that had always been her anchor. She tried to recall some passage in The Text, something to help her through this. What came was:

Herein lies a mystery: The performance of duty generates the vital force that animates the Whole Body, and she who dedicates herself to the fulfillment of that responsibility creates a channel through which the Whole Body pours its unrestricted vitality back to her.

Why, then, do I feel so drained? she thought. Guilt surged through her as she realized she still held doubts about her orders. Was she questioning The Text, as well?

The crowd roared again, and Kay felt the stadium floor beneath her undulate. She grasped a nearby rail for stability. Suddenly the crowd surged around her, and she was pushed forward into the railing. The entire Califas Order was passing by, not seventy feet away, on its triumphal march around the field. Two men in the front of the team giddily waved the Califas banners at the crowd. Parker was near the front, surrounded on both sides by brothers whose faces shone with equal parts of pride and astonishment.

Had she known this procession was coming, she could have been on the field and within range. One tiny dart and Parker would have collapsed, and his death might have been attributed to overexertion.

The moment passed. To draw her weapon would have been foolish. The team completed its circumnavigation of the arena and headed toward the pyramid of pedestals that stood at the center. She watched Parker on the overhead screens as he climbed to the highest point and stood like a living monument to humanity's grace and power. She lowered her eyes to the tiny figures on the field, and thought that the close-up shots lent a false importance to this man. When one looked with the unaided eye, he was just another human being, insignificant really, in the realm of the Whole Body.

Again a wave of fatigue. She felt like she had been rooted in this spot for hours, watching this ritual of hero worship. The pain in her bladder reminded her that she had not been to a waste station in hours. She longed with all her heart to be done with this business and headed home.

Home. How hollow the word sounded. She thought of her small room with its bed, the SimuTech, the food-processing unit, the thudding familiarity of it all. She imagined herself wandering the curved corridors of the North

American Council building, seeing its muted lighting, its many doors and offices, the huge sculpture in the atrium. With the images came the dull realization that it was not a place to which she felt any attachment.

She had always thought life was about doing, performing her duties to the satisfaction of her superiors. Place never had mattered. Now she felt emptiness when she thought about being back in her room. When had this feeling come? Where else was there to be?

Movement on the field, a fanfare blared over the loud-speakers. Her eyes snapped to the pedestal in the center of the field. Vacant. A look at the screens told her that the athletes were on the move. She turned toward the exit, but a flood of spectators again rushed toward where she stood at the railing. Her frustration went up a notch. How could she have been so inept to have not realized that the crowd would want to get close to the young men who had just made history?

She dove into the crowd, dodging, shoving, and fighting her way against its current. Finally she broke free at the bottom of the long ramp. She turned right and walked as fast as she could, following the curve of the wall toward the maintenance room. As the door came into view, she stopped.

A guard now stood there, feet planted, hands behind his back. She realized her mistake: until now, there had been no urgent need for a guard. At the climactic end to the Games was when they might expect trouble.

The guard was tall, stocky, possibly a former athlete. The look on his face told Kay he was annoyed at having to be this far away from the action. She fingered the faceplate on her ring, beneath which was a tiny needle coated with poison. She could put him down, but it surely would draw unwanted attention, further restricting her ability to get into the inner arena. How to get past him, then? A distraction, but what?

Create a need.

Kay felt a twinge from her full bladder and flashed on an idea. Remembering her experience with the woman on the transport, she reached out mentally and let the feeling of discomfort in her body expand. She felt it balloon across the gulf that separated her from the guard, at first nudging and then enfolding him. His expression grew anxious and he began shifting his weight from side to side, a parody of a small child unable to hold his water. He jammed his right hand into the pocket of his uniform, and Kay could see him squeezing himself against the possibility of soiling himself. Finally, he looked furtively in both directions and scurried away in search of the nearest waste station.

Kay sprang to the door the moment his back was turned, used the TeleSlate to disable the lock, stepped through the doorway, and pulled the door shut behind her. Precious minutes had been lost, but there might still be time. She ran at full tilt, dodging and leaping over the maze of pumps, pipes, housed motors, and loose machinery that lay between her and the door to the inner arena. As she ran, she pulled the pen-like weapon from her pocket and positioned it for deployment in her right hand. When she reached the unmarked door, she eased it open and slid into the melee.

A crush of athletes, officials, guards, and InterTV crews were pouring into the portico from the inner arena. A few yards to her left, a woman stood three feet taller than anyone else, apparently atop something. Kay worked her way in that direction, squeezing through the tangle of arms and elbows. She saw that the woman had climbed onto an aluminum air vent protruding from the arena's floor. There was scarcely room for one person to perch there, but Kay leapt up, grabbed onto the woman's shirt, and balanced with one foot on the corner of the vent. She ignored the woman's protest and scanned the scene for purple and orange Califas uniforms. None were in sight.

She peered down into the dimmer light of the ramp to her left. She could just make out the last of the team turning the corner at the bottom. She had missed them! She disabled and pocketed the tiny weapon, fearful of a misfire in the jostling crowd, and leapt into the river of humanity now flowing down the ramp.

She made steady progress, slipping between the hundreds of people between her and her client. Over the heads of those in front of her, she caught brief glimpses of the Califas colors, and knew she was getting closer. But when she came around the next corner, she saw the tops of buses wobbling with the weight of boarding passengers and knew it would soon be too late. The first bus was already pulling out of the large garage entrance.

Kay pushed forward until she was within fifty feet of the last vehicle. From there she could see the backs of the athletes still boarding. With some difficulty she managed to squeeze another few feet forward, but was still out of effective range.

Then she saw him. Parker climbed the steps of the last bus and turned to face the crowd, raising his hand to wave. Hands all around Kay came up to wave back, and she briefly lost sight of him. Then she got a good look and was struck by his expression. Though he was now the most celebrated athlete in the world, he wore no smile. Even at this distance, Kay could see his eyes, intent and peering out over the crowd like search beacons, sweeping left to right. They were the eyes of a hunter, intense and cold.

Kay's stomach rose in her throat, and she ducked behind a taller woman. For a moment, she didn't know why she hid. Then it struck her.

He knew.

Her client knew he was a target. There was precious little empirical evidence to support such a conclusion, but in her gut, she was nearly certain. Even more unsettling: he was neither hiding nor afraid, reactions that would have made sense. No, it felt as though he was seeking her out, defiantly, aggressively. For an instant she felt exposed, naked, as if he were reaching out for her with invisible tentacles. She ducked down further. Had he found out? How? This changed everything. The element of surprise probably was lost.

Keeping her head low, she pushed her way toward him, peeking over shoulders every few seconds to confirm he was still at the entrance to the bus. She was nearly in range now—forty feet . . . thirty. Then Parker turned and disappeared into the dark mouth of the bus. Kay's eyes darted quickly to the windows to see if she could see where he would sit, but they were all tinted nearly black.

The bus began to pull away and Kay broke free of the shouting crowd and sprinted to the street outside. The bus had already turned onto the main thoroughfare outside the stadium when she reached a stand of taxis and yanked open the back door of the first one.

"Follow those buses ahead," she yelled to one driver. "No Englash," the dark-skinned man replied, holding both palms as if to ward off misfortune. Kay remembered the translator function in her TeleSlate, but there was no time to lose. She slammed the door and ran to the next cab.

"English?" she asked the driver through his open window.

"Oh yes, Miss. Pretty good I am told."

Before he could finish the sentence, Kay had pulled open the door behind him and dove into the back seat. "Follow that bus." She pointed out the front window.

"Oh yes. Those men are pretty," the driver said, laying on the horn and nosing the little vehicle aggressively into the snarled traffic of the boulevard. "No, I mean they are pretty good," the driver corrected his English, chuckling and shaking his head at his mistake. "Me . . . my Inglash sometimes broke." He gestured at the bus ahead. "They strong."

Kay had no idea really what he was talking about, and didn't much care. She leaned back in the seat, positioning herself so he couldn't see her face in the rearview mirror.

"Yes, I saw . . . no, I heard some Games. Very exciting, no? InterTV, you?"

"No," Kay grunted, "not a reporter."

"Ah. Want to touch athletes then?" he asked, his grin widening in the rearview mirror.

"No." She was hardly a fan in search of contact.

"No?" the cabbie said in a mocking tone over his shoulder. "I hear pretty big, they," he said, and his shoulder began moving up and down. Alarmed, Kay leaned forward far enough to peer over the driver's shoulder into his lap. The man had grabbed his crotch and was moving his hand up and down in a suggestive way. The gesture surprised and offended her momentarily. Then she understood that the driver was alluding to the reputed size of athletes' genitals.

She leaned back in the seat without responding and looked at the dark skin on the back of the man's neck, and his tightly curled hair. All day long she had been exposed to black people, something new in her experience. Most blacks had disappeared from North America, along with Hispanics, during the Reordering more than fifty years ago. In this confined space she smelled how different he smelled than the people she shared space with in North America. And there seemed to be many more males here than back home. For a moment, she was distracted. Then the anger over missing her opportunity at the arena came back. "The buses are getting too far away. Can't you go faster?"

"Oh, no worry. I know where going."

"You do?"

"Yes. Almost all stay at hotel same. Purple and orange, they stay there. I see last night."

The Califas colors. "Can you get there first? Before the buses?"

"Maybe," he said. "I know short way."

"Do it," she ordered.

Chapter 27

The cabbie made a half-dozen lurching turns onto narrow streets and up alleys crowded with trash containers and dirty children at play. In a few minutes, his little taxi buzzed out onto a major thoroughfare and into a district dominated by tall buildings. Turning onto a street, he pointed through the windshield at a forty-story tower at the end, the tallest building in the cityscape. At the top of the building was emblazoned the name, "Africa Softiel."

"That one," he said. "Behind . . . back side, eh?"

"Yes."

They pulled up to the service entrance, and Kay jumped out of the cab, threw some of the bills the Ministry had provided into the driver's lap—too many from the expression on his face—and slipped into the entrance. She hurried through a few foul-smelling hallways, past rooms and small, empty offices, until she saw an elevator. She ducked into a doorway just as two uniformed men came out of one of the offices, talking loudly and gesturing at a clipboard one held. They turned and disappeared up the hall.

Above the elevator, the floor indicator lights began from the left with P, B, L, M, 2-39, and PH. It seemed likely that the elevator was a product of North America and the letters referred to words in English. B would stand for basement, L for lobby. The lobby seemed the most likely place for her to get close to her client. She started to punch the upward-pointing arrow on the panel next to the elevator door, but heard the elevator car descending behind the closed doors, and voices from within.

Instinctively, she looked around for a hiding place. At the end of a short adjacent hallway was a door propped open by a yellow plastic bottle. She sprinted toward it, slid the bottle inside, and pulled the door nearly shut just as she heard the elevator door slide open. She held her breath against the strong odor of chemicals. The lilting voices of two women speaking rapidly in an incomprehensible tongue drifted into the small room. When their conversation grew faint, Kay slipped out and released her breath, her heart pumping hard for oxygen.

She scanned the area for a stairway on which she likely would encounter fewer people. Finding none, she again went to the elevators, touched the up arrow. The door opened immediately and she stepped into the empty car, pressed the L button, and again palmed her tiny weapon.

The car jolted to a stop, and when the door slid open, she was facing nearly a dozen people who barely noticed her as they began crowding into the elevator. As the doors began to close again, Kay managed to slip by them into the midst of lobby's pandemonium. It was full to capacity with people, each of whom seemed to urgently need to get to somewhere besides where they were. With some effort, Kay waded into the undulating sea of bodies, searching for the Califas colors.

Above her to the right, she glimpsed InterTV crews on a mezzanine hastily setting up cameras. One woman wearing a headset was pointing to an area out of Kay's range of vision and speaking into the mouthpiece. Kay knew it was where she needed to be. Even if she managed to push her way through the crowd, on this level there was too much risk of being seen or recorded to carry out the kill.

She skirted the edges of the crowd, searching for a stairwell. Near the south end of the lobby she found one and took the stairs three at a time to the mezzanine. It was crowded too, but she deftly slid past the knot of preoccupied media people toward the InterTV crews. Over the low wall that afforded a view of the lobby, she spotted the still points in the eddy of the crowd. One of the Califas athletes stood at the center of each, surrounded by reporters. Parker was not among them. Perhaps he had already made his way through the crush.

She thought again about how his eyes had seemed to be searching her out at the stadium. A flash of Angela Potemkin's face came: her words, "Kay, wait," her knowing look. Who would have warned this young man and his mother, and why? With Angela, it had not made much difference in Kay's ability to carry out the mission, but if Parker was expecting her, she was in danger.

Still, somehow she must find a place where she would come into contact with him, a place with fewer people to witness the act. He would be staying here in the hotel with the rest of the team. They would probably be housed together, and undoubtedly under heavy security. If she could find out which wing or floor the order was staying on, perhaps, a plan would emerge.

She inched her way toward where the nearest InterTV crew was working. One of the women was bent over a case, unpacking a camera.

"Quite a scene," Kay yelled to her over the din of the crowd. The woman looked up and nodded.

"No kidding. You would think the director could have foreseen this mess. I mean after the Califas showing at the Pre-Trials last week, it was obvious they were going to be mobbed. Damn well should've been better prepared."

"How about up on the floor where they're staying?" Kay asked.

"No way," the woman said. "Can't get us near there. Guess I can't blame them. I'd want some privacy somewhere. They're not going to get much of it for a long time."

"I was just up on thirty," Kay said. "Weren't any guards there."

"Thirty? No, they're on thirty-seven, and I guarantee we aren't going to get within two floors on either side. Califas and Potemkin made history today. Thirty's probably one of the other team's floors. Not many interested in talking to the losers today."

The woman slammed the camera case and stood up. "Whose crew are you with anyway?"

Kay pointed behind the woman over the railing to a corner of the lobby. "Hey, there's one."

The woman turned in the direction Kay was pointing, instinctively searching for something to capture through a lens. When she turned back, Kay had disappeared.

In the stairwell again, Kay bounded upward. Fewer people there than in the elevators. Just as she started to round the last corner to thirty-seven, she saw the pant legs of a guard's uniform above her. She turned back before being seen and opened the door marked 36. A few women were wandering in and out of rooms, but no athletes.

Kay assumed the demeanor of one who belonged there, strode to the bank of elevators, and touched the up button. A moment later, the door opened and she stepped into the car with six other women. She reached for the button marked 37, but before she could touch it, the woman beside her said, "Can't get off there tonight unless you have clearance. You can only get off on thirty-nine or the penthouse. Too bad. I could spend a night on that floor with all those gorgeous hunks."

The others snickered and began chattering about the

men they'd seen in the hotel.

Kay nodded without making eye contact, and withdrew her finger when she saw that the light marked "PH" was already lit. When the doors opened, the incoming air was redolent with the smell of heavily spiced food. It was not a penthouse at all, but the foyer of a restaurant. She sidestepped another group of women waiting to board, and moved into the plushly appointed room. As the elevator doors closed, muting the annoying sound of the women's voices, Kay spotted a waste station to the right of the restaurant entrance. She covered the distance in six steps, pushed open the door, and was relieved to find she was alone. She went into one of the stalls, shut the door, and sat down.

How was she going to gain access to the thirty-seventh floor? The media was barred and the entrances were guarded. If she appeared on the floor, she likely would be the only woman, making it impossible to move undetected. She heard the waste station door swing open and footsteps on the tile floor. The smell of food made her stomach growl. She hadn't eaten since that morning, but her hunger gave her the glimmer of an idea. The athletes had to eat, and they probably would not be allowed out in the teeming crowds.

Someone, then, had to bring them food. Probably from this very restaurant. When the unseen woman left the station, Kay stood up, slipped back to into the foyer, and stood by the elevators as if waiting.

"Finally," she heard over her shoulder. She recognized the voice of one of the women she had ridden with in the elevator.

"Hell, Maxine, it's not worse than the Ashcroft back home on a Friday night. Quit bitching," another voice said.

Kay cast a glance in the direction of the little group as they were being led into the dining room by one of the hostesses. She slid in unnoticed behind them, past the woman at the receiving desk who was poring over a seating chart and fending off inquiries from other impatient diners.

As the group turned a corner into one of the smaller dining rooms, Kay spied an entrance to the kitchen and peeled away from the group with a brisk air of purposefulness. Just in front of her, a stocky black waitress carrying a tray full of dishes hurried through the double-hinged swinging door into the kitchen, pushing it open with her free hand. Kay fell in behind her and followed the woman into the clamor of shouting chefs and clanking dishes. A glance to her right revealed an area with benches and lockers where a white woman was removing one of the garish green and orange smocks that Kay had seen on the other waitresses. She found her way to the woman's side.

"Hello," she said. The woman was turned away from her, retrieving a small bag from one of the lockers.

The woman gave Kay a puzzled look over her shoulder. "You speak English?"

"Yes. You too?" Kay answered.

"Sure. I guess they ran out of natives. If they keep working us this hard, they're gonna run out of transplants, too. This was my first day, and I've been here since 06:00. My feet are killing me. You night shift?"

"Yes," Kay lied. "But I'm new. Do you know where to find a smock?"

"Goddess, you'd think they would have prepared better for these stupid World Games. They need twice as many wait staff. It's really been a mess." She jabbed a stubby index finger toward a small door behind the lockers. "If they got any clean ones left, they're over there in that closet. The one I just threw in the bin has curry stains on it or you could use it. May have to anyway."

"Thanks," Kay said. She went to the closet. There were two smocks inside, one clearly too small. She pulled the second one from its hanger and held it up to her shoulders. It was just long enough to cover her to mid-thigh, and she quickly slipped it on.

"Who do I see about what to do next?" she asked the woman, who had begun walking away with a large cloth satchel thrown over one shoulder.

The woman pointed. "See the woman over there in the dark blue? She's the coordinator. She'll get you going." She turned and wagged her fingers at Kay over her shoulder as she headed toward the door. "Good luck, honey. You're gonna need it."

Kay remained next to the lockers and tried to decipher how the kitchen worked. She had seen few such places in North America, where she thought people ate more often from their processing units than in public. A larger percentage of women working here than she would have expected. Back home, more men waited tables. In the section nearest to where she stood, plates were being filled with food and organized on trays, which were then snatched up by waiters and waitresses and carried into the dining room through the door by which she had entered.

She shifted her position and peered farther into the kitchen's recesses. Just beyond where the coordinator stood barking orders to those around her stood a row of shiny carts. She watched one of the chefs lift the bulky lid of the nearest one and place a half-dozen dishes loaded with steaming food and replace the lid. He laid a square of paper on top of the cart, then shoved the cart through an open door behind him. This must be the means of delivering food to the various hotel rooms. Kay slid toward the open door where the cart had disappeared.

Near the door, she saw the back of a man seated at a desk behind a monitor, wearing headphones and typing. Kay drew closer, and could hear his thick accent.

"Yes, that iss numbah twelve on you menu. Yes, approximately fifteen minutes. Room 2832. You are welcome, suh."

He typed something on the keyboard and Kay stared at the screen over his shoulder. She saw the number 12 appear next to the room number 2832. Then her eyes widened as she looked to the left of where the numbers appeared and saw the names of the room's occupants.

Just then another smock-clad waitress appeared and began wheeling the cart down a hallway to the right of the desk. Kay came all the way into the room and watched the waitress head toward the doors of a service elevator at the end of the hall. The man behind the desk tore off a square of petropaper that appeared from the top of the printer next to the monitor, and laid it on the base of a small window within arm's reach to his left.

Through the small opening in the wall, Kay could see the bustling kitchen. A dark hand appeared in the window, snatched up the paper, and a loud voice called out something unintelligible. Kay guessed it was the number for the order.

The man at the desk, oblivious to Kay's presence, pressed a button on a console next to him. "Room service. May I help you?"

No one was looking in Kay's direction. She took two steps to where the man was sitting. As she moved, she slid the face from the small ring she wore on her left hand, revealing the tiny needle. She pressed it into the side of the man's neck and he slumped in the chair. She stood behind him to shield the limp figure from wandering eyes, and bent over to peer at the monitor's screen. She found the proper button on the keyboard and scrolled through the floor listings until she came to thirty-seven, and then scanned the names that appeared next to the numbers.

There it was. Room 3716. Parker Potemkin. No other names were listed with it. He had his own room.

Calm and focused now, Kay turned just as two more carts were rolled up to the entrance of the small room. She grabbed the first and began wheeling it down the hall toward the service elevator. A black woman stepped out of it pushing an empty cart, gave Kay a sideways glance as they passed, but said nothing. Kay pushed the cart into the elevator and punched 37. A small square of paper had been laid atop the cart. It indicated that the delivery was for someone in room 1642. Kay put it in the pocket of the smock.

When the elevator door opened at 37, a tired-looking stocky young man in a security uniform gave her an annoyed look. "More food? Who for this time?"

"Potemkin in 3716," Kay said in a bland voice as she eyed the laser stun gun strapped to his belt.

"Oh, the man of the hour," the guard said. "What's he eating?"

He lifted the cover. "Shit, don't look much better than what the rest of us get. I woulda thought they'd give him something special after that ass-kicking he handed out today." There was an undertone of sarcasm in his voice.

"I wouldn't know anything about that," she said, avoiding his eyes, "but it's getting cold."

"Yeah, yeah, go ahead. The star mustn't be kept waiting."

Kay turned to her right and started down the hall when she heard the guard's voice again.

"Wait a minute, sister."

In an instant, she had slid the face off the ring for the second time that day and turned to face the guard, ready to pounce.

"Wrong way. 3716's this way."

"Oh. Sorry. I'm new here today."

The guard squinted at her. "Aren't we all? I flew all the way from Sector twenty-five last night for this job—that's in the Euro States. You live here?"

She turned the cart around and wheeled it by him without answering.

"I get off in an hour," he said to her back, "in case you need anything."

She understood what it was he thought she might need. "I'm working late tonight," she said without turning around. "Maybe another time."

"Not likely. Whole floor'll be empty by 09:00 tomorrow. Everyone's flying back home."

"Well then, have a pleasant journey," she said, hoping that was what people in the Euro States said to one another, and hurried on down the hall.

She passed descending numbers on the doors: 3740, 3738, 3736. When she reached the end of the hall, the last number read 3718. To her right, the hall continued at a right angle, and she realized 3716 must be in that direction. She looked back to where the security guard stood talking with a young man who was dressed in the orange and purple jumpsuit of the Califas Order. Neither of them saw her turn the corner. She marveled at her good fortune. The next door she came to was 3716, and the hall was empty.

She took a deep breath, slipped the TeleSlate from

around her shoulder and placed it onto the cart's lower shelf, pulled the small weapon from her pocket, and raised her other hand to knock on the door.

Chapter 28

Parker lay on the bed, his hands behind his head and his feet extending far beyond the end of the bed.

His face showed no emotion, save for the bulge of his jaw muscles as he clenched his teeth. He was grateful that for once the brotherhood had seen fit to give him his own room. Later, he would thank Rayful for the extraordinary measures he had taken to allow Parker this privacy. The elder brother had told him that he thought he needed time alone to deal with the news of his sister's death.

What he could not know was that Parker could no more have joined his proud and jubilant teammates than he could turn off the signals that were now charging his very cells.

Nor could he know about the assassin.

The thought of facing the media made Parker recoil inwardly. He had nothing for them, no self-congratulatory twaddle or smiling face. He could not act the part of the hero, nor could he tell them the truth—that he was a fraud. Not one who guzzled illegal gene cocktails like others he knew of, who, when discovered, simply confessed, repented, and took whatever punishment was meted out, then went on with their lives, mildly disgraced but able to carry on. For him, no such reconciliation was possible.

What could he say? That he had worked hard to become a champion? He had, but he couldn't say that what really had put him at the top was the fact that he was a freak. The product of mutations created nearly a century ago by a group of scientific zealots. The test tube son of a megalo-

250

maniac who believed he was ushering in a golden age.

Alone and away from the eyes of the world, he let the dark feelings have their rein. He thought bitterly of the colonists, and his mother, and Mother Avalon. Had they not thought about the outcome of their work? Could they not have thought it through? You give an athlete the greatest tools ever known to work with, and yet steal the very soul of the matter, the joy of competition, of accomplishment? They'd provided too well for him. They were dazzled by their own idealism, blind to the shadow it cast.

Today had been the great anticlimax of his life. The roars of approval from the spectators still rang hollow in his ears. He had passed through every event like the only man awake in a bunk hall, his sense of joy, of accomplishment, evaporating with each victory. In its place lay a vast, barren plain, stretching behind and before, endless and gray. Inwardly, he roamed it, searching for something to hold his interest, some place to stand. But the only points of interest he could find were the times when he built and held the invisible field of energy that supported his brothers, and those offered little comfort. The past seemed to him now counterfeit, his former joy naïve, childish.

For this empty Eden his mother and sister and Mother Avalon had been killed? He heard again Mother Avalon's voice: "Live, Parker. Survive this terrible turn of events and grow . . ."

He sat up, rested his elbows on his knees, and clasped his hands together, his fingers white from the grip. Grow into what? Why? For what? Everyone he now knew he cared about most was gone. There was no greater challenge than the World Games. Could he simply go on training and repeat the same charade in three years at the Oslo World Games?

His mind turned to the woman, this K-1754, who was somewhere in Dar es Salaam seeking his death. At one point after the Games, he was certain he had felt her presence, but she hadn't appeared. It seemed appropriate that she had come on this day. Someone was here to end his life and he could think of no reason to go on living.

He looked around the room, empty save for him, a few scraps of furniture, his bag in the corner. It struck him that it was a fitting place to die. If he were to get up, walk out into the hallway, and join with the first group of brothers he encountered, he might temporarily add color to the bleakness he felt. But then again, it seemed pointless. Why avoid the truth? Why turn from the inevitable? His life was over in any sort of meaningful sense. Why not have it be over in reality?

He lay down again, closed his eyes, and cast himself adrift in a sea of feeling and thought. He drifted across time and space to Mother Avalon's study, sat across from her, looked at the wrinkles around her eyes, heard the soothing tones of her voice. Gone.

He heard his mother's voice. "Remember that I love you and that I'm counting on you to do us all proud."

Had he done that today? Was that what she had wanted, to validate the work of some bizarre scientific colony? What did they imagine a few mutants were going to do to change the world? What they had done in actuality, he thought, was create a human being who no longer belonged in the world, an alien with no idea of how to live among others. The anger twisted in his gut. He saw the faces of his mother and Mother Avalon, and wanted to hate them for their part in putting him in this absurd scenario.

Then a surge of grief shot through him, and he knew he missed them dearly. Only they knew of his condition. They were the only ones to whom he could have talked about any of it. And they were gone, caught in someone's trap.

"Stupid. Pointless." They were gone now, and for what? Pam, his poor sister, who'd never had a clue as to what was going on, no plan other than to get through her studies and take her position in the Whole Body. The assassin, whose holograph he had seen only this morning. Just such a woman had killed them all, he thought, turned off their lives as coldly and casually as one might turn off a light. The evil and senselessness of it gnawed at him.

An acrid taste rose in his throat. His teeth clamped down and this time stayed there. His fingers curled into fists. He remembered the feeling he had once in Mother Avalon's study, like he was a toy, a marionette whose strings stretched across time, attached only to twitching, disembodied hands that caused him to whirl and dance to music no one could hear, a perfect puppet of an absent master. Part of him wanted to rise up and smash everything and everyone around him.

Then came a knock at the door.

Chapter 29

"What?"

The voice from behind the door was deep and resonant, and angry.

"Room service," she said, mimicking the accent of some of the waitresses she had heard in the kitchen. She pressed gently down on the door's lever. It was locked.

"I didn't order anything."

"I have a special meal here for Parker Potemkin, courtesy of the hotel."

"I don't want anything now."

"Sir, if you'll just let me wheel the cart in, I can say I delivered it and won't get in any trouble." She paused and tried to sound plaintive. "Please?"

For a moment, there was no response. Then, "All right. Just a moment."

She heard the soft click of the door lock.

"Bring it in."

One glimpse of him, and this whole business would be over. She could make her way to the airport and sleep all the way back to North America. She reached for the lever. This time it gave under the pressure of her hand. She quickly pushed open the door, the weapon extended slightly before her.

The next instant, she saw a blur from her right, and felt a sharp pain in her wrist. Her weapon arced across the room, and before she could turn to get a glimpse of her attacker, a large hand fell squarely in the middle of her back and shoved. She tried to take a step to brace against the forward momentum, but something blocked the front of her shins and she sprawled headfirst toward the floor. There was a flash of brightly colored bedspread and the beige of the carpet fibers rushing toward her face.

Her reactions were quick, though, and before she hit the floor she had begun to twist in the direction the blow had come from, her knees curling and feet preparing to kick upward.

Too late. The next thing she saw was a huge shoe swinging toward her face. She turned her head just in time to avoid the full force of the kick, but it caught her on the left cheek. She heard the ratcheting sound of her neck bones popping. The pain was blinding. Instead of landing on her back as she had planned when she began her roll, she crashed to the floor on her right shoulder, spun by the force of the blow. Her right cheek ground into the carpet fibers with a fiery friction.

Even in the midst of the pain, she remembered her ring, and she tried to thumb the panel from its face. But just as she touched it, a massive weight fell upon her back and pinned her right arm and hand beneath her torso.

Never once since she had begun her mission at the Ministry had Kay come into physical contact with a client. She was unprepared for the pain of it. Her skills were skewed toward stealth and speed. But the sisterhood had put each of the girls through several years of rigorous martial arts training, and those ingrained lessons took over now. When she felt the smallest shift in her attacker's weight on her back, she drew her unpinned legs up under her and pushed upward with her knees, swinging her free left arm in a wide arc to increase her leverage.

It was just enough to free her right arm, and now she did

thumb the ring open. In the split second it took to expose the tiny needle within, Kay twisted her hips and shoulders and fought to turn her face toward her attacker. She saw only the silhouette of his head in her peripheral vision and felt his weight come down again on her full force. But her right hand was almost free, and she swung it with all her might toward what she thought must've been his leg on her back.

Instead of the gratifying contact she had expected, however, her hand met only air.

Then something viselike was around her wrist, pulling, and something beneath her lifting. She felt like a tiny, spineless doll being tossed by malicious child. Suddenly in her vision arose what seemed like the wave from her dream. But it was no wave, it was a wall, and it was rushing toward her. Reflexively she put her hands out to stop its progress, but she was rolling in the air and her back was turning toward it.

It was like falling backward from a great height. She heard the sound of the impact before she felt it, and as her consciousness slipped away on a rush of pain, she saw Parker Potemkin springing up from the floor, his face calm and focused, his smoldering eyes burrowing into hers.

At first, there was only a sensation of soaking wetness on her chest. Then Kay felt a pain that shot from the back of her head to the middle of her back. It quickened her senses, and in a moment she realized the moisture was coming from her own lips, which felt rubbery and slack and were dripping because her chin was resting on her chest. She closed her mouth and sucked on her bottom lip, and tried to raise her head. The effort sent spears of heat down her spine, and she moaned aloud.

She grimaced and managed to pull her head upright and pry open her heavy eyelids. At first what she saw meant nothing. It was the outline of someone in front of her, then the bed the person was sitting on, then the room beyond.

Then, she remembered.

Her body reacted instantly, every muscle springing into action. But nothing happened. For a moment she couldn't understand, and continued to struggle. Then she looked down again and saw her body swaddled in something white. It appeared to be a sheet, wrapped tightly around her from her neck to her feet, like the windings of an ancient mummy. It held her fast to the chair in which she was sitting.

And Parker Potemkin sat directly opposite her, his stare steady and deadly, on the edge of the stripped bed.

Kay realized the futility of her struggle and stopped, turning her eyes from Parker's gaze. One of her cheeks throbbed where he had kicked her, and the other was on fire from the carpet. Her head felt like it was balanced precariously atop her neck by the slenderest of props, that if she tilted her head too far in any one direction, it would break off and roll across the floor. No one had ever inflicted such pain on her before, and she felt a momentary anger at the violation. When she realized she was about to die, however, the anger dissolved in a rush of regret and resignation, and finally a sense of calm.

Parker got up from the bed. As he walked slowly to the other side of the room, Kay stole a glance at the mass of his shoulders, the muscles rippling under the form-fitting jumpsuit, the sheer bulk of the man, his fluid movement. No wonder she had been unable to fight off his attack. Even if she had been rested and on more familiar ground, it might have ended like this. A fleeting thought: this was

257

probably how Parker's mother had felt in the second before Kay's dart took her life. She looked away again, and the pain it caused made her wish momentarily that Parker had snapped her head completely off, and ended it.

Why hadn't he? Her stomach muscles tightened at her next thought. Perhaps he had something slower, more painful in mind.

He turned toward her now and she saw that he held her weapon. Though it looked tiny in his big hand, the contrast made it seem even more deadly. Her eyes moved to his face, and she could see beneath its broad exterior signs of an inward struggle, emotions passing like some underground river, subtly shifting his finely honed features. His eyes fixed on hers and she felt something press against her chest, as if he had reached across the room and placed one of his hands there, forcing the air from her lungs.

"Why?" The word emerged from his throat like a slow, hot wind. The pressure on her chest increased, her face grew hotter. Drops of sweat popped out on her forehead. One began a descent to her eyebrow.

"Why?" he said again, this time louder, and she swallowed hard against what felt like a rough egg moving up her esophagus. She felt its outline and then its essence—rage. Parker's rage. Hot and spiked, jagged, expanding, pressing against the tender organs and tissues in her torso. She was powerless, she knew, to stop it. It would rip her apart from the inside. Something would give out, collapse under the assault. She hoped it would happen quickly.

Her mind recoiled from the pain, and she saw herself as a child, running with the other girls, always in the front of the pack. Mother Clara's broad face appeared, praising her in front of the others for always setting high standards. Endless hours of training and study Kay had endured condensed into seconds, parading before her eyes. She relived her graduation, her placement at the North American Council Headquarters. She reread the name Angela Potemkin on the assignment sheet from the ministry, saw the body of Parker's mother slump on her bed, her message to Kay play on the wall monitor.

She saw Parker's name on the termination order, saw Aria Helsing taking her aside into the tiny utility room the day before, saying, "There is great danger here, Kay. This is no ordinary man. I don't think you ought to do this."

She heard herself telling the counselor that she had no choice. This last she would have explained to Parker, right here, right now, in this moment before she would cease to exist. She would have said she didn't know how to answer his question, and that she hadn't really wanted to kill him, but had not known what else to do.

This and more she might have said, but somehow she couldn't remember how to make her tongue move and vocal chords vibrate, couldn't swallow against the odious egg now in her throat. Couldn't even draw a breath.

Parker's face was shimmering now, its outline watery, as if heat were rising from sun-baked ground between them. Watery, yes, like waves in her dream, the tide pulling at her legs, drawing her out to be swallowed by the oncoming wall of sea. She felt the longing to release, to simply float away and lose herself in the liquid darkness rushing up to envelop her. So easy. Just let go. One brief instant and it would be over. The air vacating her lungs whispered like a receding wave on the shore. Floating . . . floating.

From somewhere far distant, a faint sound, nearly imperceptible. At first it blended with the quiet hiss that suffused her. But it was insistent. Dreamily she cocked her inner ear in to catch the intonation. A plea? Louder now, taking on the quality of a voice, the plaintive voice of a child, a child in trouble. An annoying, inarticulate sound, but clarion, irresistible. It pulled at her, at odds with her willingness to ignore it and simply fade away. It was needful . . . warning . . . calling to her.

NO! DON'T! NO!

Suddenly, Kay wanted more than anything to breathe. Against the feeling that her ribs had collapsed all the way back to her spine, she struggled to fill her lungs. Her body shook with the effort, and she swallowed hard against the monstrous egg in her throat. A tingling began in her skin, and a deep humming arose from the base of her spine, building like the silent fury beneath layers of the earth's crust. It glowed and expanded, rumbling and rising, cracking through another layer and yet another. An oddly familiar feeling.

The light began to return to her perception. She saw again the bed before her. Beyond stood the looming monster—Parker Potemkin, she remembered—halfway across the room, his face distorted with anger and hurt. She focused on that face, laser-like, and felt a great gate within silently slide open. A roiling flame of fury surged from her core, its pressure throwing open her throat, her mouth, and lips, melting the orb lodged there.

The sound that came out of her was like the twisting of solid metal, the screech of a billion molecules being crushed and warped into a hideous shape. Like a living being, it arose from her and filled the room, flooded the furniture. The light from the lamp on the bedside table took on a pinkish hue and its base rattled against the smooth surface.

And it all came to bear on Parker Potemkin, whose face at first showed surprise, then fear, then nothing at all . . . because it had disappeared behind the bed when he collapsed.

Chapter 30

"Parker, what's going on in there?" one of the voices said. "Hey, Parker! Are you all right? Parker?"

Years had passed, it seemed, before Kay found another breath. When it came, she heard something pounding and the voice. Over the cusp of the bed whose covers had been stripped and thrown on the floor, she saw the top of Parker's head bob up, then sink, then appear again, followed by his face. It was paler than she remembered, and bore a look of astonishment. He eyed her warily, then turned his face slightly toward the closed door of the hotel room, his eyes still fixed on her. She saw his mouth move, and through the hissing and popping noises in her head, heard him speak.

"Yes, I'm fine. Nothing's going on. I . . . have a guest in here, that's all. Just need some privacy." His lips seemed to Kay slightly out of sync with the words.

Her body felt like it was vibrating, almost singing. Everything in the room—the furniture, Parker—appeared to be lit from within. She was aware still of the pain in her neck and cheeks, but it was like someone else's pain. As the voices behind the door grew fainter, Parker rose slowly to his full height and put his fingers to the side of his head, rubbing lightly and still watching her.

"Go on now," he said to the door. "I'm okay. See you in the morning."

She heard what she thought was laughter, more mumbling, then the voices faded. Parker hesitated, then stepped cautiously in Kay's direction. He eased around the bed and sat down, as if worried that sudden movement might re-awaken whatever he had just encountered, whatever had just defeated him. Directly in front of Kay now, he looked into her face, ever so slightly avoiding full eye contact. He opened his mouth, as if to speak, but closed it again. Gradually, his features softened and his gaze seemed to turn inward in thought.

A few minutes later, he leaned slightly forward and put his elbows on his knees. Then he slowly closed his eyes and tentatively extended his big right hand until his fingers rested on the top of her thigh.

Kay watched with almost a distant curiosity. The sound that had come from her was like a lightning bolt that had charged and cleansed the atmosphere, rearranged the molecules. But as Parker's hand descended toward her thigh, she felt her skin rise up to meet his touch. Simultaneously, the raw edge of her pain began to blunt and soften. Her taut muscles slowly unwound and she felt as though a gentle rain was slipping over her skin. At first, she didn't know what was happening, only that she felt a great relief. Then, she knew it was Parker doing something to her. A soft presence enveloped her, then a sensation like hundreds of fingers gently probing the soft tissues of her body, emitting something like sound or light, but which was neither.

Whatever it was, she understood that it was repairing torn muscle, releasing endorphins, mending ligaments. Tears of relief welled and spilled over her cheeks, dripping from her chin onto the front of her already damp chest. Her eyes remained riveted on Parker, and she thought she saw something pass between them, something wispy and bright with tiny points of light. Subtle layers, like gauzy veils, seemed to peel away, and with each his features grew more distinct, until it became nearly unbearable for her to look at him.

The breath caught in her throat and her eyelids blinked rapidly, both beyond her control. Her eyes rolled back in her head. Amidst this cascade of sensations, something new began to take shape deep in her being. She felt its outline like a blind person might feel a face, reaching for understanding, a sense of its character. Then, in a rush of recognition, it came: she knew this man. Perhaps more than she had known even Mother Clara or any of her sisters. She knew his essence, the infinite strings of numbers that spelled out his being, that knitted his bones and muscles together and colored his flesh. The contours of his being were as familiar to her as her own face in the mirror.

For an instant she experienced a split within herself. One part, with its logic and reason, vainly sought to grasp the meaning of this knowledge, the other simply embraced it. The first knew its purpose was to kill this man, the second celebrated the vitality of his being. These two parts danced around each other like leaves in a whirlwind, at times touching and then moving farther apart. Soon she sensed a third part, a silent self, observing the dance, removed from the passions and peregrinations of the others, and the awareness carried with it a deep sense of peace. There were other selves too, hundreds perhaps, waiting silently for what would happen next.

Parker's eyes opened now, and Kay felt some part of her float, weightless, into their depth, no longer confined by the sheet that encased her. Simultaneously, she felt her body, each vein swelling with the pulse of her heart, and heard the movement of blood-like waves against a steep shoreline. It was like dreaming, she thought, but dreaming that she was awake, more awake than she'd ever been. With her eyes, she

263

saw that she sat opposite him, separated by a short distance. But in the recesses of her mind she saw them as two points of consciousness surrounded by vast space, dark but far from empty, not filled with things, but a thing unto itself, vibrant and present.

After a long while, the experience faded, and the sharp edges of the room came back into focus. Kay sat utterly still, awed, hanging wistfully onto the sensations as if they were the sweet strains of a passing orchestra. Finally, she licked her lips and tentatively tried her voice.

"Who are you?" Her voice cracked. The question sounded strange even to her. Despite knowing his name and all the things she had read about him, and the strange experience of intimacy she had just had with him, it was clear he was a mystery.

It was a long moment before he answered. "I'm not really sure, but I think I'm beginning to find out."

Silence again stretched between them, the words hanging in the air like ghosts. Finally, Parker spoke again. "I knew you were coming."

Kay nodded.

More silence.

"How?" she asked.

"I had a friend."

Kay heard the sorrow in his voice, rich and poignant, and was surprised by the depth of the unfamiliar feeling.

"A good friend. She warned me."

Kay took in a deep breath, letting it out slowly, and rolled her head slightly, amazed at the ease with which it moved. "How . . . did you do that . . . take the pain away?"

A little shrug. "Can't say, exactly. It's one of the things about myself I've only lately discovered." He cocked an eyebrow at her. "How did you make that . . . sound?"

264

Kay thought she saw a flash of bemusement pass over his face.

"I don't know." She felt a smile tug tentatively at the corners of her mouth. "It was like something coming through me." How odd her voice sounded to her, how at ease, she thought, how liquid. "What else do you know?" she asked, faintly embarrassed by the odd feeling of levity rising within her.

"My friend told me your name, what you're called. I've seen your holograph."

He stood now, put his hands in the pockets of his jumpsuit, and began walking away from her. At the other side of the bed, he turned and Kay saw a renewed seriousness in his eyes. She could feel him struggling to decide if he should say something. Then he did.

"I know that your orders to kill me came from a woman named Desta Mardrid."

She stared at him. It was shocking to hear this name, here in this room halfway around the world. She tried to understand what she had just heard. Orders didn't come from someone at headquarters. They came from the Ministry of Termination, the CAO.

"Your friend said Mardrid gave the orders? That's . . ." She was going to say that it was not possible, that there was strict policy about who was placed on the lists. But that was only what she had always believed, she realized, and much of what she had believed seemed questionable now.

"I report to her at North American Council Headquarters," she blurted, aware of her sudden candor. "But she's not supposed to have any say in who . . ." She stopped short. Civilians did not know of the existence of the K-class. How could she explain? Instead, there was something else she wanted to know. "Who is your friend?

How could she know this?"

"She is dead now. She knew . . . many things. I got a message from her this morning telling me about you and this Mardrid woman. She told me both she and I were targeted, but she didn't know why. She also told me that Mardrid ordered the deaths of my mother and sister."

Kay felt a sinking sensation in her stomach and fought the urge to turn her eyes away, fearful of what he might see there. She didn't want to speak, didn't want to say the words that she knew would act like a sharp knife on this tendril of communication between them. At any moment he might ask if it was she who had slain his mother, and the weight of her knowledge bore down on her. Instead, he said something that shocked her even more.

"I also know that you're descended from the work of same group of people I am."

Kay blanched, her mouth open slightly, her eyes wide.

"The Tressaline community," Parker said. "Do you know about the Tressaline project?"

In a flash, Kay saw herself sitting in front of a terminal at the Hall of Records, reading an obscure poem:

But scattered amidst time's decayed relics
Lay Padeyevsky's pollen and Psyche's golden tresses
Dyed red with the blood of the martyrs
And fed by the root of the Tressaline tree . . .

"My friend showed me a book," he continued, "a diary written by one of the members of that community during their time together. His name was Augustus Termalaine."

And raise Termalaine's Tower at its cancerous center . . .

"What is Termalaine's Tower?" she asked.

Now it was Parker's turn to look surprised, though whether by the question or her eagerness to know Kay couldn't tell. "It was what someone named the chart that tracked Termalaine's project, his team's progress toward a breakthrough strain of genes. They were working on developing a human with accelerated sensitivities and talents and abilities."

He came back around to her side of the bed and sat down. "How did you hear about this?"

"Someone . . ." she tried to banish the image of Parker's mother in her mind ". . . told me about some writings. I looked them up and found references to this tower . . . in a poem . . . and others about the Tressaline community." The words began to tumble from her faster. Before she could stop, she had told him about everything she had found in the Hall of Records.

When she finished, Parker leaned back on his elbows and stared at her. "Do you understand, then? We are the product of something that was conceived a century ago. We're freaks."

There was bitterness in his voice.

"My mother gave birth to me, but my father's been dead for many generations. He was the founder of the Tressaline community. My friend told me that you were the descendant of Leona Termalaine, the daughter of the man whose diary I read."

Kay recalled Leona Termalaine's holograph and letter, and the feeling that had come over her at seeing the woman's face. "Are we . . . ? Is this why . . . ?" She stopped to gather her thoughts. She felt like she was tangled in underbrush. Too many secrets. Too many unstated assumptions. Inside she felt a growing urge to speak, to reveal herself to this man, to rip open the heavy doors behind which her voice was trapped.

But how far could she go? She had never shared anything of her life and origins with anyone other than the sisters and that once with Aria Helsing. She had never spoken other than superficially to a man. But the voice clamored. It would not be denied. It was going to come out and she didn't think there was anything she could do to stop it.

And so she began: "I was born into a sisterhood, conceived in the laboratory. The only mother I ever knew was Mother Clara, who raised my class. We are known as K-class. Our mission is to serve the will of the Whole Body." She paused and took a breath. "We . . . eliminate those who would destroy the balance of the Whole Body."

The words began to tumble out, Kay revealing the sacred secrets that had lain safe in her heart for her entire life. They were all going to come out now, she knew. She couldn't stop them. Parker watched her silently, barely moving, receiving her torrent of words like the ocean swallowing a river. Kay lost sense of time, even of what she was saying, all the while her sense of relief growing so great that she felt as though she might float to the ceiling.

Finally, inevitably, she came to the point in her story when she was assigned to assassinate Angela Potemkin. For a mere breath of a moment she hesitated. Then, knowing that the words might be the last she ever spoke, she told Parker everything—her brief glimpse of his mother, her death and recorded message, the sensitivity she'd begun to feel, the abilities that had emerged that enabled her to render the woman who followed her here unconscious, transmitting counterfeit physical sensations to the guard at the arena—everything.

When there were no more words, Kay closed her eyes

and rejoiced in the sense of relief washing over her, as palpable as the sweat standing on her brow and upper lip. Even though she was still fettered in the sheet with which Parker had bound her to the chair, she felt the greatest sense of freedom she had ever known.

At that moment, she truly felt like the bird that she had first witnessed on the giant SimuTech screen at her graduation, soaring on sweet winds, the pull of earth a mere whisper below her.

Parker would kill her now for what she had done. It was only natural. No matter. This delicious instant of surrender rendered death almost a triviality. In a moment, her life would end, but in this moment, she knew serenity.

A long time passed before she heard him stir from his position on the bed before her. With her eyes still closed, she heard the bed hiss to fill the space where he had been, felt his powerful presence moving toward her, smelled the musky scent of sweat that permeated the fabric of his jumpsuit, heard the quiet whistle of breath in his nostrils, his measured steps as he moved behind her. She felt the tiny hairs on her neck rise and wave in the direction of his movements, like grass bending in a breeze.

A tingling sensation began in the soft tissue where her body's weight met the chair's seat and rose sun-like through her torso, filling the dark spaces there, relaxing every muscle. She let her head fall forward, her chin again brushing her breastbone, offering her neck to the coming blow or violent wrenching that would end her short life. And now to sleep forever, she thought, and it comforted her.

She felt a tug, a tightening of the linen cocoon that encased her.

Now. Now it would come. In her vision, the graceful

rising and falling of the landscape, the gentle lifting of warm air beneath the wings that stretched to each horizon, the caress of warm air over the sleek body that carried her higher, higher . . .

Then the pressure around her torso fell away. She opened her eyes, saw the sheet spilling off her lap onto the floor, and was confused. Parker moved from behind the chair and stood in front of her, presenting his broad back. The small weapon he had earlier taken from her lay beside him on the bed.

"Kill me, if it is what you must do," he said. "It doesn't really matter now."

Kay heard the layers of emotions in his voice, resignation and anger, but also thought she heard hope. She looked again at the sheet, then, dreamlike, pushed herself to a standing position, her leg muscles straining with the effort. Parker stood close enough to touch, his hands clasped behind his back. Kay imagined herself picking up her weapon and finishing what she had come to do. She envisioned herself reporting on a successful mission to her superiors and to Mardrid, imagined the quiet commendation she would receive, saw herself resuming a daily routine, going back to her room in the North American Council Headquarters, back to the endless stream of assassinations . . .

She watched her own hand, the slender fingers trembling, reach out. But it was not the weapon they sought. They alighted like a butterfly on Parker's brawny shoulder, and she heard him let out a breath. Like a statue come to life, then, he turned to reveal a face so utterly radiant that her eyes closed involuntarily.

Inside, from between her legs to the crown of her head, she hummed like the plucked strings of a harp . . .

Chapter 31

There was only one.

Despite the mismatched clothes strewn about the bed, despite the disparity in size and obvious differences of anatomy between the two bodies, or the differences of pitch and timbre in the two voices that rose and fell in monosyllabic cries of ecstasy, for a tick of eternity, only one being existed in room 3716.

With its many hands and fingers, it explored its new parameters, dipping and sliding into the tangled, dark places and across slippery new terrain. It anointed itself with the blood and semen and saliva flowing from its willing wounds. Splayed and stretched to the edges of physical limits, it groaned as again and again fiery eruptions melted away into a velvety silence.

The fecund, sweet scent of earth wafted through the room, rich with the eternal transmutation of decay into life, pulling at its senses like thirsty roots that beckon water. And there in that darkness something new, a confluence, woven from the etheric strands of ancient memory, charged with life force and set on its course in the three-dimensional world.

Kay and Parker drifted into sleep, spent but buoyed on the subtle energies that played in each other's fields, into vague dreams filled with laughter and music, the playful press of bodies. When they slowly awoke, it was to a feeling of fulfillment and wonder at the touch of interlaced limbs, of soft breath in dry mouths. For a long while they lay there, neither speaking but in silent communion nonetheless, the knowledge seeping deep into them that their lives had changed irrevocably.

Kay could scarcely recall how it had happened. One moment they were face to face and her breath had caught in her throat at Parker's beauty. Then a force like nothing she had ever known had swept through her and they were tumbling through space, tearing at clothes, licking and biting as if they might devour each other. She remembered flashes—the musk of his hair, a mouth on her nipples, the feel of his manhood in her hand, a brief, searing pain as Parker entered her—but the rest felt like it had happened in some other dimension.

Kay blinked at the ceiling as if it were the horizon behind which the sun would soon rise. She reveled in the softness, the utter vulnerability of her damp skin, the sweet throbbing she felt between her legs. Eventually, she licked her lips and found her voice. It was deep and sounded odd to her ears.

"Unbelievable."

"Yes," was Parker's only response.

She rolled toward him, moved her hand across the expanse of his bare chest, her fingers tingling with each curled hair they encountered. She watched her hand as if it belonged to someone else. It moved downward, gently pushing away the sheet that lay across his stomach, as if it was sure of its destination but was in no hurry to get there.

When it did arrive, Parker sucked in his breath, and Kay marveled at how something could feel hard and soft at the same time. She lifted her head and rubbed her face against the skin on his chest and stomach, savoring the fragrance there. She grasped that mysterious part of him and pointed it toward the ceiling, wondering how it was possible that something so large had fit so perfectly inside her.

She moved so that she could feel its softness against her cheek, rubbing her face ever so gently against it, passing its length over her lips, her eyelids, following it down until her nose was buried in the tangle of hair at its base. She inhaled his essence. Parker groaned and the sound of his voice filled her with hunger. She wanted to taste him, to swallow him. She wet her lips and pressed the tip of his manhood to them, slowly opening her mouth. Parker moaned louder now, and she could feel the pulse of his heart between her lips.

In seconds, she was awash again in surprising sensations. She wanted to be filled in every part by this being, wanted him to melt into every orifice and hidden place within her. She felt his hands in her hair and his hips writhing beneath her. He pulled her from him now, and she felt a hand slide down her back and one beneath her hips. He lifted and turned her, and she felt his face, deliciously rough with stubble, pressing against her breasts and her stomach and between her legs. She felt the voice arising in her again, but this time there was no terror or rage or fear, only the joyous sound of life announcing itself to the world through her.

They lay quietly, Kay tracing the outlines of muscles on Parker's abdomen.

"What are we going to do?" she asked.

Parker took a long, deep breath and let it out again. "We can't stay here."

"I can't . . ."

"No, I can't go back either," he said, finishing her sentence. Parker gently untangled himself from her embrace and sat up, leaning against the headboard. He stared at the wall for a long time before he spoke again. "There may be a place."

He told her about Mother Avalon's final message and the number she had given him, and glanced dolefully at the Interphone monitor on the nightstand. "We can't call from here. Too easily traceable."

Kay slid her hand from his chest, cupping the side of his face in her palm, and brought her open mouth to his lips. Their tongues danced wetly together and receded, and when their lips parted, Kay placed hers alongside his ear and whispered, "Then we must go."

They remained silent and still for a full minute more, listening to the sounds of their breathing and the chorus of thoughts reverberating within, the echoes of the life they had lived until this moment. Then, with no outward acknowledgment of their intention, they rose from the bed, found their scattered clothes, and dressed. Parker put the few items he had unpacked in his small bag and looked at the timepiece on the nightstand: 02:15.

Kay found her weapon on the floor and pocketed it. "I left some things at my hotel that could be useful."

Parker nodded. "We'll go there first."

He lifted his bag, went to the door, and pressed his ear to it. No sounds from the hall. He cracked the door open, listened again, then opened it wider and looked up and down the dimly lit corridor. He turned back to Kay, his eyes full of tenderness and intent.

She reached out and found his hand.

They slid out the door, stepping around the room service cart Kay had earlier abandoned. Kay retrieved the TeleSlate and moved in front of him. Parker followed her to the end of the hall. Kay edged up to the corner and stole a quick glance toward the guard station by the elevator she had passed earlier. A new guard had replaced the one she encountered earlier, and with his chin resting on his chest, he nodded rhythmically with each breath.

Without speaking, they both knew what must be done. Sending the guard into an even deeper sleep was an easy task. As they approached his station in front of the elevator, they watched him slump over onto the small desk before him. They took the stairway to the basement. Through the deserted service area by which Kay had entered the hotel, they picked their way through the reeking bags of garbage awaiting disposal, into the cool morning air behind the building. A few yellow street lights cast soft shadows as they made their way for several blocks, eventually turning left toward the main boulevard and the occasional blur of passing vehicles.

When they reached the boulevard, Parker ducked into a dark doorway and Kay stood at the curb awaiting the next taxi. She looked to where Parker was silhouetted in the refracted light of the street lamps, and her heart swelled against her ribs. Even if her life were to end tomorrow, at least for this night she had truly lived. She regretted nothing. With the back of her hand, she wiped away the unfamiliar tears that had turned the reflected pinpoints of light on the storefront glass into four-pointed stars dancing around Parker.

The whine of an engine caught her ear and she turned to see an approaching cab. She held out her arm and the small green vehicle pulled to the curb just beyond her. She ran to it and yanked open the back door, the sound of drum-rich music spilling into the street from within. Parker ran crouched from the doorway and ducked into the back seat. Kay slammed the door and got in the front seat next to the driver.

"Ha ha! You get one! I knew you fib." The driver was grinning, a mouthful of big teeth.

Kay recognized him at once as the man who had taken her only a few hours ago . . . or was it years? . . . to the hotel. The streetlights glistened on his teeth.

"A big one, he too!" he said, craning his neck backward over the seat. "Where we go?"

Parker gave Kay a questioning look. "He brought me to the hotel," she said.

Parker nodded. "We need to make a call." His legs sprawled sideways across the back seat and his head touched the roof. "Can you take us to a call station?"

"Oh yes," the driver said, turning to look over his shoulder for oncoming traffic while slapping his leg to the rhythm of the music.

"We can't use our cards," Parker said. "Do you have a call card?"

"Sure, yes."

"We'll pay cash if you'll make the call for us."

"Oh yes, I help. Mothusi always help lovers. A good tonight is a good tonight. You watch." The force of his acceleration into the traffic lane pressed them back into the seats.

"We go," he said. The music blared.

Ten minutes of rocking turns and g-force accelerations later, the little cab pulled up at a service booth that housed InterPhones and monetary exchange machines. Parker peered out the window at the street, relieved to see it was deserted.

"Good," Parker said to the cabbie's back.

"Yes," the driver said, "Mothusi knows."

Parker and Kay's eyes met; a silent understanding passed between them that the driver was relishing his role as a co-conspirator. Kay handed Parker a wad of bills from what the Ministry had provided for her.

"Come," Parker said, and opened the door nearest the booth. The cabbie followed.

At the phones, Parker peeled off five bills. "I'll tell you a number to dial for me," he told the driver, and pointed at the call button. Mothusi looked pleased and surprised by the number of bills in his hand.

The cabbie pressed the button and inserted his small plastic card into the ID slot. When the speaker emitted a low tone, Parker softly spoke the number into his ear, and the cabbie repeated the number into the microphone under the small video screen. In a moment, the screen sprang to life, casting a faint glow on his face. A small icon appeared in the center indicating the person answering had no desire to be viewed by the caller.

"Yes?" a voice said.

Parker motioned the cabbie out of earshot and took his place in front of the screen. "I was given this number by Mother Avalon of the Southwest Council of America. Can you help me?"

"Who is this?" a woman's voice asked, noncommittally.

Parker hesitated, wondering if revealing his name was inviting disaster. "I am a friend of Mother Avalon's. She said to call this number if I needed help. I need help." He hoped the urgency in his voice was getting across.

There was a pause. "Your name, please," the voice said calmly.

He turned toward the cab and saw Kay's face behind the passenger window, pale in the artificial light. Mothusi had retreated and now stood near the driver's side door, bouncing idly from one foot to the other. Parker decided he had no choice.

"Parker Potemkin," he said quietly. If they had any sophisticated equipment in this country, they could voiceprint him anyway, he thought.

A long pause followed, and Parker heard some rustling at the other end of the line. After what seemed like minutes, the screen flickered and the heart-shaped face of an olive-skinned woman appeared.

"Where are you?" Her thick eyebrows nearly met at a crease above her long nose.

"At a service booth somewhere in Dar es Salaam. I have a cab waiting . . . and a companion."

"Who?" the woman asked, one of her long eyebrows arching ever so slightly.

"One who was sent to kill me." The woman's face remained expressionless, and she said nothing, as if waiting for something further. "It's too much to explain right now," Parker said, "but we both need to disappear."

"I see." The woman nodded slightly. For a moment her face became so still that Parker wondered if their connection had been botched and he was looking at an image frozen in time. "Wait," she said, and her face was replaced by an animated advertisement for communication devices.

Parker turned again. Mothusi had gotten back into the driver's seat. Kay's eyes held Parker in a gaze he could feel. A taxi whizzed by in the opposite direction. Feeling utterly removed from anything familiar, Parker suddenly recalled Mother Avalon's image and voice on her last message to him.

"So much depends on your life. Live, Parker."

Only a few hours ago he didn't care if he lived. Now he vowed he would find a way. He peered into the fog that was his future, seeing only dim shapes moving there. Something. His life would mean something. If not now, soon. He would find a way to use this thing lodged deep in his cells, this . . . gift. He smiled at the word. Until now, he had felt it more a curse than a gift. He looked at the cab and Kay's face behind the glass, and saw something more than the plain, perfect features there . . . something . . .

His thoughts were cut short by the screen flickering back to life.

"I'm sorry," the woman said. "There is nothing we can do for you."

The screen went black.

Parker stared at it, incredulous. His stomach felt hollow. He slammed his open hand into the phone, shaking the whole booth. He turned back to see concern on the driver's face. Parker motioned him to come back to the booth.

"Dial again," he said, and the driver reinserted his card and spoke the number into the receiver, giving Parker a wary sideways glance.

When the screen lit up again, a message scrolled from right to left in Swahili and English, a woman's voice repeating the written sentence. "The party you are trying to reach is offline. Please try again later."

Parker groaned aloud. He rubbed his temples.

"Okay everything?" Mothusi asked quietly.

Parker ignored his question and walked to the cab's window where Kay's face indicated she knew the news was not good. As the window slid down, Parker squatted next to it. "They hung up on me. Something's wrong. Maybe it's gotten too risky for them to help us any further."

Kay nodded, looking over Parker's shoulder to where the driver stood waiting by the booth. "All right. We need to find somewhere to sleep for a few hours. I'm not thinking very clearly. Maybe something will occur after some rest."

Parker felt the weariness in his own body and knew she

was right. He stood slowly and gestured to the driver to return to the cab.

"We go?" he asked as he climbed back into the driver's seat.

"We go," Parker said without enthusiasm. "We need to stop at your hotel," he reminded Kay.

As Kay told the cabbie where she was staying, Parker tried to imagine where they would go next.

Chapter 32

In the waning hours of darkness, they pulled up to Kay's hotel. Parker watched from the back seat as Kay disappeared with cat-like grace through the front door. Mothusi drummed his fingers on the steering wheel in time with the music, and they didn't speak until Kay returned minutes later, a small pack slung over one shoulder.

When they were underway again, Kay explained to Mothusi that they needed to find a place to sleep where they wouldn't be recognized. Parker was famous, she told him, and his absence would be news in a very short while. They wanted to spend some time together before he returned to his team. She thought Mothusi might rally more easily to their cause if she played into his apparent enthusiasm for lovers.

The cabbie appeared thoughtful. "Okay, I can do," and sped away. After a while he turned down the music so that he could more easily be heard. "I am Mothusi, you know, but sometimes too hard to remind—no, remember—right? So I am M, just M, to friends. You call me M, okay?"

"Okay," Kay said. The proper thing would be to now tell the cabbie their names. She looked at Parker and saw that he understood and nodded. "I'm Kay."

"K?" the driver asked. "I am M and you are K? That is good!" He laughed heartily, and it sounded so merry it made Kay want to laugh too.

Was everyone in the world this friendly, she wondered? Apart from trusting Aria Helsing that once, Kay had never allowed herself to consider trusting others. This man, however, seemed to inspire such feelings. "And he is Parker," she said, nodding her head toward the back seat.

"Parker? Parker Potemkin?" His eyes grew wide.

"Yes," Parker said from the back seat. "You've heard of me?"

"Yesterday I watched." He pointed to the small dark screen imbedded in the dashboard of the cab. "I didn't, uh, remind you. No, I didn't see you that I know . . ." He waved a free hand in frustration at his lack of English.

"You didn't recognize me?" Parker offered.

"Yes, yes. That's it," M said, laughing again. Then to Kay, "You catch really big one, I think."

Kay felt her cheeks grow warm, and a smile come unbidden to her face. She relaxed a little into the seat, and the weariness she had been holding at bay since beginning the hunt for Parker pulled at her muscles. She leaned her head against the headrest, her mind scrabbling for purchase on the possible scenarios for the future as rhythm filled the little cab.

"You like the drum?" M asked. His seemingly permanent grin was turned again on Kay.

The question seemed oddly compelling, cutting through the noise in her head. "Yes, I think I do." Conversation was easy with this man. She listened more intently to the music, and could not remember ever hearing anything quite like it. She recognized the sounds of many of the instruments—a flute, guitars, some other sort of wind instrument, many drums of different pitches—but she had never heard these played together with such vitality.

M's knees moved up and down in time to the music, his dark and wrinkled fingers tapping his thigh, and Kay could visualize people moving to this music—dancing, it was called of course, though Kay had neither experienced it or actually seen it done anywhere but on InterTV—and she could imagine the musicians wearing the same smile that now spread across M's face. They seemed to be more than just happy, almost as if they *were* the music, music that found its visible counterpart in their movement.

"You will hear nowhere else," M said, waving his hand to indicate the rest of the world. "Special music, special lover music." He chuckled to himself, glancing sideways again at Kay. She found herself vaguely embarrassed by his frankness about the intimacy she and Parker had experienced. Were such matters so openly discussed?

"From North America, yes?" M said, quick nods in both Kay's and Parker's direction. Kay nodded without speaking, as the music vibrated her bones.

"Especially in North America," M said. It took Kay a moment to realize he was talking about the music. "White people lose much. Black people too, but some find again."

Kay shifted in her seat. M's words hung pregnant in the air.

"Meaning?" she asked.

"Roots," he said, and held up his right hand, his fingers pointing at the floor and wiggling like worms. Kay looked at his hand and suddenly recalled something she had seen in her early schooling, a jerky time-lapse movie of the roots of a tree growing downward into soil rendered translucent by some sort of penetrating light. The air in the cab seemed to grow still, and Kay looked from the cabbie's fingers into his brown eyes, which held her gaze.

Kay felt something shift inside, as if some dark space had expanded beneath her. M's eyes seemed at once unfathomable and comprehending of things far beyond the confines of the small cab. An ancient image flashed into Kay's mind, something she remembered seeing somewhere in her past, of an unblinking eye atop a pyramid. When she realized she was holding her breath, she broke their visual connection and quickly glanced at Parker in the back seat.

Parker's expression confirmed what she was feeling: something extraordinary was going on here, something odd, perhaps special, about this man, though she still sensed no danger. She searched for the right words to move the conversation along, but before they came, he chuckled again and spoke.

"After the Reordering . . . you know about . . . ?" M asked her, though he spoke loud enough for Parker to hear.

Kay nodded, remembering from school about how after the great councils had been formed a worldwide movement of deconstructionists had managed to convince key council members that centuries of intermixing of the races had proved a bad idea. Nearly six decades ago in North America, people of recent African and Hispanic descent—somehow the Asians were not subject to the same rationale—were offered strong incentives, both negative and positive, to return to the regions from which their ancestors had come.

The more highly educated and powerful of those races saw opportunity in the reordering, while others wanted simply to live without having to deal with the racial hostilities that had been unleashed when the old systems collapsed. The various councils collaborated, treaties were written, arrangements made. Within a little more than a decade a global shift of humanity took place unlike anything in modern times. The movement was so successful that Kay had seldom seen a human being with skin as black as M's in the North American Council region. Nearer the border between the hegemony of the South American and North

American councils, skin tones were supposedly more diverse, but Kay had never been there. In the colder climes, no more than two percent of the population were darker than Kay.

M continued, "In those days, most peoples come here to live just on top."

She had no idea what he meant.

"On top, yes?" he said, this time turning that strange-looking hand horizontal and indicating a flat surface. "Some others, a few, find way down in." He wriggled his fingers at the floor again, and once again Kay experienced the hollow sensation of the air becoming still.

"Roots." The word resonated deep in his chest. "M thinks maybe you understand." Though his smile remained, his eyes were beseeching, serious.

Suddenly she felt the barriers of race, language, and all external differences fall away, replaced with a feeling of kinship with this man that was as surprising as it was comforting. Her mouth dropped open, and she broke eye contact with him long enough to look at Parker in the back seat.

Clearly he had felt it too.

Kay wasn't sure if the cabbie had meant these people had found their way into the earth, or down into some deeper place in their being. Perhaps he meant both. She was intrigued.

When M spoke again, all the frivolity had gone from his tone. "You have trouble, no?"

Silence. For a dozen heartbeats the odd trio bounced along in the speeding taxi, processing what had just transpired.

"M thinks you have trouble big. M thinks maybe we can help."

It was Parker who spoke next, and the urgency was clear in his voice. "Pull over somewhere. I think we need to talk."

For more than an hour they sat inside the little cab on a quiet side street and listened as M wove a tale about women and men around the African continent who had begun to experience unusual perceptions and abilities. As these powers grew, he told them, the society around them had become increasingly hostile toward them. Some were even killed, accused of sorcery, a belief that had never quite died out in Africa. And so, one by one, these people had fled their communities and families. Some had become wanderers, some moved to the larger cities and labored in anonymity. As they discovered others who shared their abilities, a network began to develop, and many had been led by dreams and rumors to come to Dar es Salaam.

For a dozen years now, these had been building a clandestine colony there, and practicing a way of life that M spoke of with equal parts reverence and endearment. M told them he was not one of the original people, but had given a woman a ride when she first arrived in Dar es Salaam. He described how he had felt the woman's power when she stepped into his cab, similar to what he felt when Kay and Parker got into his cab, and how he had immediately fallen in love with the woman.

She had soon found others there with The Sense, as M now called it, and begun establishing the community they called The People, taking M as a lover. Some of the colonists were like him, M told them, not born with The Sense, but having it bestowed in degrees by apprenticing themselves to the founding members, being inducted into their energies, or as M put it, "their spirit world."

Parker occasionally interrupted him to ask questions.

Had he heard of the Tressaline colony? Was he aware of the Nestercine Sisterhood and their work? M had not, which surprised Parker, but then he realized that other efforts might have sprung from his father's work, or even independently.

M told them that despite their remarkable abilities, The People were aware they were as yet not strong enough to live openly in the world. Instead, they built their community underground, literally, fending off intrusions by means of the mental powers of Guardians, community members who developed specialized abilities in this area. M's lover was one of these, he said proudly. Her home was a portal, he told them, and he would take them there if they were willing to undergo her testing.

It took Kay and Parker only moments to agree, to realize the improbable synchronicity of this meeting and its implications for their future, and the utter lack of options. After making a call from a service booth, M drove them to a neighborhood on the outskirts of the city, to a dull-white building.

The light from the breaking dawn illuminated the round arch atop the front door, the only feature that distinguished it from others on the block. The three of them sat silently looking at the door, a sense of destiny thick in the air.

"Go now. M sees you again soon, but now you go. They wait."

Kay looked into his eyes and again felt her insides quicken.

Parker stared at the door, suddenly ambivalent. The resolution he felt back in the hotel room to leave the life he knew had waned. Kay, this strange woman whose life seemed to be about death and obedience, and who lived amid those who ordered the deaths of people like his mother and sister, peered at him from the front seat, the question in her eyes. Insane, to walk through that door with her, he thought. And yet, as his mind flew over the landscape of alternatives, he saw none.

Something Mother Avalon said came back to him: "There are moments in life when, though you may feel you have no choice, you have. The choice lies not in what you must do, but how you greet the situation, and it is the most important one."

A smile found its way to his mouth, and he silently thanked the old Nestercine.

He put his hand on M's shoulder, feeling the density of the man's muscle and bone, and the vital energy that ran through him. Parker let the feeling of gratitude flow through his cells and out his fingertips. "Thank you, M."

M said nothing, only nodded. But his eyes were rimmed with tears. When he looked over at Kay, the cabbie's face beamed. "Something big for you, M can feel."

She didn't touch him as Parker had done, but something passed between them nonetheless, and she felt the portent in his words. She reached for the door handle. "Goodbye." They stepped from the cab into the soft morning light.

As the cab sped away, Parker and Kay saw they were alone on the street. They walked to the door and Parker rapped on its rough surface. An instant later, they both experienced a sensation not unlike being prodded all over by invisible fingers. It mingled with the warmth of the rising sun as it spread across their shoulders, and they turned to look into one another's eyes. Was this the test that M spoke of?

A moment later, the door opened and a striking, tall, dark-skinned woman in her mid-twenties stood facing them. Her hair fell about slender, bare shoulders in thin braids, each tipped with blue and red beads. Her colorful dress brushed the tops of her bare feet and was bisected by an orange cloth belt pulled tight to a tiny waist. But most striking were her large eyes, the pupils dilated so far that only the color black was discernable. Parker and Kay felt caught by them, pulled into their depth like divers into a pool of dark water.

"Welcome, Pilgrims," the woman said after a moment's hesitation, a broad smile spreading across her face. Later Kay would tell Parker that she wasn't sure whether she had actually heard the words, but there was no doubt she had felt them.

PART 2

Chapter 33

Outside the oval window, the night sky was so black it seemed to pull at the little light above Aria's head like a vacuum, sucking it out into the darkness beyond. Her faceless silhouette reflected in the glass was the perfect symbol, she thought, for who she had become—a woman without an identity.

She switched off the light, closed her eyes, and let her mind drift. Moments later, she had a vague auditory impression of a bustling crowd. Then came a dreamy image of a primitive marketplace, and a large-boned, dark-skinned woman faced Aria from within a rickety stall, holding strangely shaped yellow vegetables in each hand.

The vision disappeared at the sound of muttering at Aria's shoulder. She opened her eyes to look at the occupant of the seat next to her. The woman's head was lolling to one side, her mouth working, her eyes closed and eyelids fluttering. She uttered another unintelligible noise. A dream, Aria thought. She too has her visions.

Aria adjusted the dull brown blanket she had wrapped tightly around her legs against the chilly, lifeless air of the transport's cabin and tried to recapture the market scene. A fantasy? Prescience? She sighed. She couldn't tell. Lately, many of her inner images had felt alien, unfocused. Ever since she realized she was going to seek out the missing assassin.

For nearly seven moons, she had been haunted by her last encounter with Kay, the brief embrace they shared, the glimpse of something magnificent beneath Kay's cold blue eyes, the image of her turning to go. Kay's last, lonely look over her shoulder.

After that encounter, Aria had requested an audience with Barena Colter. Colter had received her, counter to protocol, and Aria related what she knew about Kay and the Potemkin assassinations. Colter appeared intensely interested, and told her she would look into it. But over the following days and weeks, Aria's further requests for an audience had been refused. Finally, twenty-five days after Kay disappeared, Aria was again admitted to the aide's office.

"I appreciate your having come forward, Helsing, but you are to have no further role. The entire matter is under investigation, and appropriate actions are underway. As I told you, you are to speak about this with no one. Dismiss the entire affair from your mind and make no further inquiries about it. I do not wish to see you in my office any more. Do I make myself clear?"

Aria had nodded. "I understand. I'll put the matter aside. Thank you for your time."

Even as the door had closed behind her, Aria knew she wouldn't obey. She wondered if it was obvious to Colter.

It had taken all this time to devise a course of action. It had not been easy. After several false starts, she had found the help she needed in Carola Binski, one of the sisters from her order who, since graduating, had used her talents to carve out a niche in the travel industry. Binski's clients were, for the most part, wealthy North Americans who entertained a desire to visit some of the last forest and game preserves on earth. Since most of these were in Africa, Aria knew Binski stood a better chance of securing travel arrangements to Dar es Salaam than she did.

Her friend had received her enthusiastically, wanting to hear all about Aria's life at Council Headquarters, her work, and such. When Aria told her where she wanted to go, Binski had been a little surprised but told her that it could be arranged, especially since the recent World Games had helped establish new routes to that city. But when Aria told her that she needed to travel incognito and that no one must know where she had gone, Binski's friendliness disappeared. It had taken all of Aria's persuasive powers, reminders of past favors and promises of future ones, to get her old friend to even consider how such a trip could be accomplished.

Binski had come through eventually, involving other friends and even relishing the conspiratorial adventure. Through the manipulation of names in flight databases, the record would show that Aria flew only to New York. After landing there, ostensibly to visit her mother, she would become someone else and fly to Egypt, where she would take on yet another identity and continue on to Dar es Salaam. Since terrorism had been crushed in the mid 21st century, airport security was not as stringent as it once had been— no voice print identification or fingerprints. All she needed was a scannable passport with a holograph, some savvy technological friends to erase her tracks, and she could disappear. Simple. She had sworn Binski to secrecy, but considering her friend's fear about being implicated in such subterfuge, the oath had been unnecessary.

Aria's mother had been less of a problem than anticipated. Most everyone was cowed by Portia Helsing's strong presence and skills at psychologically outmaneuvering those around her. Where Aria was concerned, however, she had always remained remarkably acquiescent. When Aria had told her that she would not be coming for a vacation as she had promised, and that in fact she was going somewhere neither her mother nor anyone else must know about, her mother had pressed her for details. Aria stood her ground, though, and as Aria knew she would, her mother ultimately agreed to cover as best she could if anyone came looking. For a while at least, Aria didn't think they would.

Finding Kay would be more difficult. Aria adjusted the pillow behind her head and stared again into the darkness. It seemed like a very long time since she had decided on this course. In fact, it was only three moons ago, a gray afternoon in which Aria had submitted her reading of the woman who now performed the duties and occupied the quarters Kay once had. The reading had stirred things up again, strong and suddenly. One moment Aria had been alone, and the next it was as though Kay was in the room with her. Aria felt, rather than saw her, and knew instantly something was very different about her. She let her consciousness be drawn into the presence, and then allowed it to wander around the body where it would. It settled into a hum and glow just below the waist and lingered there. It reminded her of the first reading she had done on Kay, when she had seen the violet light at the same place and felt herself expanding like a balloon.

With a start, Aria's eyes had snapped open. Impossible, she thought immediately. K-class women were genetically incapable of pregnancy, weren't they? But then Kay Black seemed anything but typical of that strain. With some difficulty, Aria calmed herself and drifted back into the experience. An hour later, she had little doubt. Somehow, Kay had become pregnant.

Even more surprising was Aria's conviction that she was to play a further part in this remarkable turn of events. She could not have explained how she knew this, only that it called to her. Thinking of Kay as being with child filled Aria with a sense of purpose she had not felt since she interviewed for her job at the council.

Now, thirty thousand feet over the continent of Africa, she smiled at the seeming absurdity of this conviction. What would she do once she found the assassin? She knew only that she must. Kay had no training or life experience to prepare her for childbirth, and Aria doubted that wherever Kay had ended up, there was any support for this anomalous pregnancy. Kay was hiding somewhere in a foreign land, and almost certainly being sought by her sisterhood and probably others. Somehow Aria must help.

It was absurd, of course. Aria had neither carried nor birthed a child, yet against all reason she believed it would come naturally to her. Through the Hall of Records, she had found manuals on childbirth and even some old texts on midwifery. She had studied them, a thrill rising as she pored over the illustrations and holographs. Eventually she had come to accept the twisted logic of her feelings, or rather the lack of it. Since her first remote encounter with the assassin, it was as if something had been planted deep within her psyche, and now it was almost as if Aria herself had been impregnated, not with a child but with the compulsion to insert herself into Kay's life.

She had made some half-hearted attempts to resist this impulse. Twice since Kay's disappearance she had tried to banish all thoughts and internal images of the assassin, practicing cleansing rituals taught by her sisterhood. After the second time, when she had experienced such a sense of grief that she wept, she surrendered.

For this trip, Aria had given herself an out. If in twelve days she had failed to locate Kay, she would return to her work at the council and think of a new plan. But if she somehow found her, Aria was prepared to leave everything behind. In the bag under her seat was a palm computer that held all her financial records and the codes she would need to withdraw the remainder of her savings. Binski had instructed her how to manage such transactions so that the discovery of where the transactions had originated would at least be delayed. Underneath Aria's clothing, strapped to her waist, a belt contained a substantial amount of North American currency. Though most transactions on the North American continent were done electronically now, currency was still accepted in many other regions. Once in Dar es Salaam she would find an exchange office and then . . . what? Her mind went blank, as usual.

She reminded herself of the times when, lost in cities during youthful travel, she simply sat down, went inside of herself, and followed the urges that would come forward—take this street, ride this bus, turn left here. They had never failed her, she reassured herself. She had never been to Africa, but she had spent nearly a year on the road with a trinity of her sisters, seeing parts of the Southern Continent, Europa, the Mediterranean and the states of Asiatica. The sisterhood had encouraged and supported such exploration, knowing that the experience would sharpen the girls' senses and resourcefulness. Now Aria felt gratitude for her elders' unwitting training for her defection.

In less than an hour they would be landing. She settled back into the seat and closed her eyes. Relax, she told herself, willing the adrenaline rushing through her veins to dissolve. Something will come forward to guide you.

She found a small hotel. She wanted to bathe and take a nap, but the dry bath at the end of her hall was not working.

Neither was the air conditioning, and it was warmer than she had imagined. Even though she felt exhausted, a nap in the stifling room was out of the question. On the street at least a breeze might cool her. Several hours of daylight remained, so after organizing the few things she brought, she consulted a map and located Kala Stadium.

Less than a kilometer from the hotel, it was the only place she knew Kay would have come on her assignment. Aria walked the distance through what might have passed for a modern city in North America in the last century. Some buildings looked new, probably built in anticipation of the economic upsurge the World Games usually brought in their wake. But some seemed deserted, and there were far fewer vehicles in the potholed streets than she was used to seeing in North America.

In the alleyways she passed mounds of rotting garbage and an occasional glimpse of a man or woman who seemed to have nothing to do or nowhere to go. She recalled other sights like this when she had traveled in her youth. She had thought Dar es Salaam would be better off, but this whole continent had always been resistant to the relentless striving after progress that motivated the rest of the world.

At the stadium, she found the gates locked and the grounds littered with debris. A few disinterested-looking men and women shuffled around behind the fence that surrounded the perimeter now, maintenance workers she presumed. There was nothing to suggest that several hundred thousand people had been there to witness the games less than a year ago.

What it had been like? She pictured Kay, anonymous among the throng of people, intent on killing Parker. Aria had watched the Games on InterTV, saw the triumphant young Parker and the Califas brothers on their victory march around the arena. For days afterward she had expected to hear news of his death, but it never came. Was he alive? Aria had seen no interviews with the champion after the team's stunning victory. His teammates had been on the news in subsequent days, and they frequently praised his leadership, but as far as Aria could tell, no one had seen Parker's face since it appeared on screen, bigger than life and unsmiling, at the close of that day's competition. After a few weeks of the media haranguing the Califas Brotherhood about his whereabouts, the story faded away.

And where had Kay gone? Aria leaned against the fence and closed her eyes, willing some vision of Kay, some trace of her presence here, to come forth in her mind. It didn't. Instead, she felt the heat and the strain of the long flight, and reluctantly decided to go back to the hotel to rest. She would need to begin fresh. Tomorrow would be a better day.

It wasn't. She roamed the northern sectors of the old city, through litter-strewn, noisy streets, a white stranger among throngs of mostly dark-skinned people. The hotel breakfast was wreaking havoc on her digestive system, and locating public waste stations had proved a challenge. Midday she found a transport station and sat for a long while on one of the ancient benches, watching the comings and goings of hundreds, but catching no hints of what she was looking for.

Being inconspicuous was nearly impossible, given her western clothes and fair skin, and she was surprised at the presence of uniformed police in so many places. Many times she ducked into shops or open doorways to avoid confronting one of them as she walked. She had prepared a cover story that she was doing research for an upcoming trip by younger sisters from her order. She carried a portable translator for the occasion, should it arise, but she hoped it wouldn't. Explaining her presence here to an official might not be easy.

When night began to fall after a long, fruitless day, Aria caught a taxi back to her hotel. She was not yet confident enough to be alone at night on the streets. That night she felt more dispirited than she wanted to admit.

By afternoon of the third day, she felt she had made a mistake. She had walked until her feet were blistered and her bones tired. She had taken taxis to nearly every corner of the city without feeling the slightest twinge of intuition. It was nearly 15:00 when she stumbled onto a ramshackle marketplace in the southern quadrant of the city desperate for a waste station and something—a mild bread, perhaps— to soothe her system.

Stalls with brilliant flowers or earthenwares stood next to displays of hand-held navigation devices and InterTV monitors. Portable water detectors took their place next to graven images of ancient nature spirits. Aria had seen similar markets on the Southern Continent years ago, and she was fascinated by the variety of wares, the cacophony of voices, and the smells of overripe fruit and meats cooking in the open air.

The place was vivifying, and she inhaled the heady scents as if she hadn't taken a deep breath since arriving. Gratefully, she found a waste station and then a relatively untrafficked place next to a stall where a woman was selling dried meats and herbs. Aria sat on the ground with a sigh, closed her eyes, and let the smells and sounds of the marketplace wash over her.

Drifting, drifting. Images of tropical trees and scenes

from bygone cultures floating through her awareness like clouds. Then, without warning, Kay's face. She opened her eyes, startled. Black people, a few whites, milling this way and that, stopping before stalls. No Kay, but Aria's pulse quickened. She closed her eyes again. Which way had the image of Kay been facing?

To the right. Aria stood and eased herself back into the shuffling crowd, turning right, her senses keen. A few minutes and another right turn later, she stopped. There, a little ways before her was a vegetable stand with a crowd of people around it, jockeying for their chance to buy something. Between the bobbing heads she caught a glimpse of the face of a woman who was speaking rapidly, collecting money and filling customers' baskets.

Aria smiled. Yes, it might just be the face she had seen in her reverie while looking out the window of the transport.

She worked her way into the dozen or so people waiting to buy and looked closer. The woman was tall, with long, slender limbs. Her almond-shaped eyes were suffused with humor and a dark glint of knowledge, and set aside a large, flat nose. A dozen strands of beads and seeds hung around her neck, over an earth-colored blouse and prodigious breasts. She was talking rapid-fire in Swahili to a prospective buyer. Varieties of fruit and vegetables were displayed waist-high before her.

Aria waited at a distance until the crowd thinned to a single customer. As the customer turned to leave, Aria hurried to the stall.

By the time she arrived, the woman was facing away, bent over nearly empty boxes of vegetables on the ground at the rear of the stall, gathering replacements for what she had sold. When she turned around, the scene appeared to Aria almost exactly as she had it from the window of the

SST—the woman facing her, standing tall, square-footed, both hands full. When she saw Aria standing there, a smile lit up her face, revealing large white teeth, perfect but for the brown line that ran horizontally across the two in front. Vegetable stains? Tobacco? But when the woman looked into Aria's eyes, the smile faded a bit and her own eyes became subtly veiled. Aria looked down at the unfamiliar fruits in the tray, tentatively touched a few.

"Do you speak English?" she asked without looking up.

"No," the woman replied, "no Angleesh."

She was lying. Aria could sense it. She quickly sought and found the woman's eyes again. "I have a friend." She put her hand to her heart, which she noticed was pounding insistently against her breastbone. "A friend who needs my help."

The woman waved a hand dismissively and spoke a few words, her tone harsh over the sonorous syllables of her native tongue. Aria reached into her bag and found one of the holographs of Kay she had copied surreptitiously from the council's classified files. She tried to hand it to the woman but the woman took a step backward, shaking her head, muttering protests. Aria pulled back the extended holo and simply looked at the woman, who was growing more unhappy and nervous by the minute.

Aria knew she was creating a delicate situation here, but she had not come this far to be timid. She fished in her bag for a laser writer, and turning the holograph over, wrote on the back, "I am here. I've come to help."

Then, recalling the dream Kay had shared with her so long ago in the heat room, she added, "The wave still hovers on the horizon." She signed it, "Aria."

Then she laid the photo on top of the mounds of fruit.

"Please," she said to the woman. "Please."

J. D. Townsend

The woman waved the back of her hand at the holo as if brushing away one of the flies that delighted in the bounty of the marketplace. Her other hand fell into what Aria guessed was some ancient gesture to ward off evil, her long thumb thrust between index and second fingers. Aria ignored her protestations, found a large denomination bill in her bag, and laid it on top of the holo.

"Please. I'm a friend." She touched the place between her breasts with her hand. "Friend." Then, reluctantly, she turned and strode away. "I'll be back in the morning," she said over her shoulder to the fading sounds of the woman's protests.

That night, Aria barely slept. At 07:00 she awoke, dressed, and went to the café in the lobby. She forced herself to order and eat a generous breakfast of unusually large eggs, fruit, and some rich, rough-textured bread, aware that she might not get another chance to eat. A cab driver had no trouble finding the market she described to him, and she made her way back to the woman's stall. As she approached, the woman caught her eye but gave no sign of recognition.

Aria stepped up to the display and made a show of examining a few samples. The woman seemed pleased by this charade and picked up a guava in each hand, making a seesaw motion with them and speaking again in Swahili. Aria played along, holding up two fingers. The woman shook her head, a constant stream of patter flowing from her lips, and held up three fingers. Aria shrugged, nodded, and pulled three bills from her bag. As she did, from the corner of her eye she caught the woman's nearly imperceptible nod to someone beyond Aria's shoulder. She resisted the urge to look. The woman took Aria's bills, handed her the fruits, and with a quick smile that belied the consterna-

304

tion in her eyes, turned away.

Aria slipped the fruits into the bag she carried and spun on her heel, hoping to glimpse whomever the woman might have been signaling. No one paid special attention to her. She looked back to the stall, but the woman had begun an animated conversation with a heavy woman in the next stall.

Aria began walking very slowly back the way she had come, her eyes scanning the faces swimming before her for a clue. Nothing. Had she misread the entire situation? Were there no leads here at all, only a misunderstood transaction between two women from different worlds? She continued her casual pace, her bag remarkably heavier now with its additions.

Then, at the edge of the market she felt the presence of someone just behind her. A hand circled her arm. She turned to see the face of a young black woman who didn't return her gaze but who steered her gently but firmly toward a small nondescript vehicle parked among others at the curb. When they reached the car, the woman bent down, opened the door to the back seat, and gestured for Aria to get in, still averting her eyes.

Either my search has paid off or I'm being kidnapped, Aria thought. She decided to risk it, and slid into the seat. Immediately the front door opened and a tall, bony young man with light brown skin and head completely shorn of hair moved in behind the steering wheel. Before closing Aria's door, the woman's hand appeared holding a small scrap of paper. Aria took it and the door closed as the driver gunned the vehicle. On the note, Aria read an address: 3160 Mombasso Avenue.

She clutched the note as the silent driver sped furiously through traffic, taking a dozen turns that made Aria reach for the door handle to keep from toppling sideways in the seat. Eventually the driver slowed, pulled over beside a green street marker atop a square brick pedestal, and turned to face her. With his right hand, he indicated she should get out.

Aria shrugged, holding the note out to him. He shook his head and pointed out the window toward the street marker, and impatiently repeated the gesture for her to leave. Reluctantly, she stepped out of the car and watched the car buzz away almost before she could close the door. In the bright afternoon sunlight, she read the address on the note again and looked at the street marker. Mombasso. She was on the right street at least. She looked to the building behind her and saw 2100 outlined above the doorway in bright green tiles.

Her heart hammering in her chest, she started down the street, counting the numbers as they rose, until she came to a small brick building with an antique door, a graceful arch at its top. Above the door stood the number 3160.

This was not a busy street compared with what she had seen over the last three days. Nonetheless a dozen or more people walked purposely within her sight, and a stream of vehicles whirred by in the street. If this place was being watched, or she was followed, she neither saw nor felt evidence of it. She put the slip of paper in her bag, climbed the three stairs to the door, and took a deep breath. No intercom or bell. She knocked softly. In a moment, the sound of footsteps inside.

A small panel at eye level slid to one side, and Aria felt invisible eyes examining her from the darkness behind the door. It was an odd sensation, as though she was being observed from all sides at once. The panel slid shut and she heard the soft clink of a latch as the door opened to reveal in the interior shadows a small, doughy black man who stepped aside and with a quick movement of his hand, urged her to come inside.

Stepping out of the relentless sunlight and into the cooler air beyond the door, Aria had the impression that she had been transported back in time. The foyer was flanked by two large tropical plants, which began thinly, fanned luxuriously, and rose to the wood-tile ceiling five feet above her head. Arched doorways defined by ornate ceramic tiles opened to two rooms on either side of the foyer, and a wrought-iron spiral staircase stood at the rear of the room in the center.

The little man shut the door behind her and silently took her proffered hand in both of his, his slight bow revealing a bald spot that gleamed in the subdued light. Without a word, he walked toward the staircase, then slipped behind it, turning to give her an imploring look.

Aria followed him and discovered a narrow doorway nestled behind the staircase. Beyond it, a set of stairs descended into dimmer light. The man turned and began leading the way down. At the bottom, they passed through another arch into a long hallway that smelled of earth and mold.

At the end of the hall, yet another doorway led to another set of descending stairs and the walls became rough, as if hewn from the very bedrock beneath the old building. But they couldn't still be under that building. How far had they walked? Half a kilometer? More? She resisted the urge to bolt, or to ask the little man where he was taking her. She could barely see into the darkness ahead, and she couldn't tell where the scarce light that did guide them was coming from.

Finally the man stopped at a T-shaped intersection and

before what appeared to be a solid stone wall, and turned to face her. He bowed again and made a little circle in the air with his finger. He was asking her to turn around, she realized. The thought of turning her back on him in this place where she had not seen another living soul gave her only brief pause.

She felt a soft fabric brush her forehead and descend to cover her eyes. Trust, Aria, she repeated to herself silently. She felt the fabric tighten as the man tied it in the back. He turned her around a few times so that she could no longer tell which direction she faced. They walked for another twenty or so steps and stopped.

She was startled by the loud, groaning sound of something heavy—stone?—grating against another surface. Almost imperceptibly beneath it, she identified the whir of a motor. She felt a rush of warm, moist air on her face, and smelled the unmistakable, nearly-intoxicating fresh scent of growing things. Some sort of door, she realized, and in a moment, she felt the man's hand on her upper arm, carefully guiding her into the humid air.

The door scraped shut behind them. Again they walked, Aria holding her right hand out in front of her, afraid that she would run into something. Soon, however, her body realized she could trust the man's guidance. Another few turns and she heard faint voices ahead. What was this place? The voices grew louder, and she heard the lilt of purposefulness in their tones. People at work, she thought, but here?

The delicious humidity seeped into her skin and clothes, and she smelled the rich, dark odors of soil, of intermingled decay and growth. Another few minutes and turns later, they halted. The man fumbled with the knotted scarf, and Aria opened her eyes as it fell away.

Her first fleeting thought was that she had been led into a giant SimuTech, programmed for a jungle scene. But this was no simulation, these were actual plants. All along the walls of this cavernous room, giant trees reached nearly to the high ceiling, which was aglow with bright but diffused light. Clustered beneath their broad leaves, Aria could see the rich colors and rounded shapes of fruit. The center of the room was filled with a pyramid-like, tiered structure that held bed after bed of leafy growth. Amidst this stunning proliferation of greenery, men and women busily tended to the plants from pathways invisible to Aria from this angle. Birds called unseen. She heard muffled conversations, and the clank and rustle of machinery, though she saw none.

Her guide turned to her and spoke in nearly accentless English. "Please wait here," he said, and was gone, treading off on the narrow curved path that led beneath the canopy of outer trees.

Aria stood transfixed by the enormity of this project. She opened inwardly, and felt a great sense of peace in this room, feelings of contentedness and enterprise mingling like the smells in the oxygen-heavy air. Clearly this was a growing station, like ones she had read about. Never, though, had she heard of one far below the earth's surface. How many people was this providing for? And who? Did they all live here?

The ceiling high overhead glowed evenly like a thinly clouded sky. Even the outer walls seemed lit from within, and Aria thought she was probably seeing sunlight carried from the surface high above them through fiber optic filaments, like in the rooms of the North American Council Headquarters.

She stared down the empty path in the direction the

little man had disappeared. How long would he be gone? Her curiosity nudged her forward. After a few meters, she noticed an opening in both the pyramidal structure in the center and the outer wall, and a small track that crossed the path. As she approached it, two women emerged from the opening in the inner structure, their clothes mostly covered by thin white coats, pushing a cart nearly twice their height along a track.

Aria stopped and watched as they easily rolled it into an outer room, seemingly oblivious to her presence. She ventured up to the doorway and peered after them. A dozen or so people were at work around the room, unloading enormous fruits and vegetables from several carts similar to the one just rolled in, dividing them into various areas, giving them a cursory inspection, and loading them into what appeared to be processing machinery. In the far right corner, one woman was intently staring into a monitor screen across which moved various patterns of undecipherable figures. Scientific instruments were scattered about this part of the room, and Aria deduced that the woman must be analyzing the nutritional or genetic content of the food.

Without warning, the woman turned and looked directly at her. Instantly Aria was self-conscious and wondered how she was going to explain her presence here. The moment their eyes locked, Aria had a fleeting sensation of weightlessness, as though the space between the molecules of her body had expanded, allowing something to pass through.

Then the woman simply gave her a warm smile and turned back to her work. Aria felt briefly that she knew the woman, but suppressed the urge to approach her. She retraced her steps, arriving in time to see the guide returning with another man at his side.

The second man was taller, black, and wore a multicolored tunic over white pants and white shoes. As the two approached, Aria again sensed the loosening of her body, and thought it must be some kind of probe, that she was being invisibly examined at some deep level. The feeling passed and the little guide again took her hand in both of his, bowed slightly, then turned and departed. Her new companion flashed a neutral smile, turned, and began walking away. Aria followed.

They passed through several more doorways and halls. People they passed gave the pair only casual glances. Even in those brief moments, though, Aria felt an intensity that told her these were not average people. A minute later, her young guide halted before a closed door, and stepping aside wordlessly, gestured for Aria to step toward it.

Aria saw no handle, but when she approached the door, it slid noiselessly to one side, revealing a well-lit room, sparsely decorated with a few chairs and tables, a small kitchen area in one corner and a bed in another. She stepped inside and the door slid shut behind her, leaving her alone. She walked around the room, touching the few utilitarian objects on the tables, searching for clues as to who lived here. Given some time, she thought, she could go into a trance state and find out more, but she had no idea how long she would have to wait before someone came for her.

She put her bag on the floor and eased herself onto one of the chairs. It was surprisingly comfortable, made from a dark material, almost like wood but with no grain apparent. There was little else in the room to draw her attention, so she closed her eyes and took some deep breaths, reached out for some sense of the place. A moment later, she knew someone was in the room with her.

She opened her eyes and saw a woman with hair considerably longer than when she had last seen it, and whose once angular shape had given way underneath a loose-fitting gray tunic to the bow-like curves of pregnancy.

"Hello, Aria. I thought you might come."

The eyes were still a brilliant blue, and Aria felt a powerful presence behind them, felt the hair on her arms begin to rise.

"Hello, Kay," were the only words she could manage to squeeze from her throat, where her heart seemed suddenly to have lodged.

Chapter 34

The assassin retrieved one of the chairs from the other side of the room, placed it across from Aria at a slight angle, and sat down, resting one hand casually atop her swollen belly.

Aria watched each movement with a growing sense of awe. Gone were the furtive, almost calculating attributes of someone whose modus operandi was to move swiftly and anonymously among others. Instead, Kay now moved with an almost regal poise. In each nearly imperceptible rise and fall of the foot, each arc of the arm and turn of the head, there was such grace and power that it nearly took Aria's breath away.

Qualities Aria had only glimpsed before seemed to have been honed and magnified. She felt, to her surprise, something like a child around a towering grownup.

"Does anyone know you're in Dar es Salaam?" Kay asked. Her voice, too, was richer, fuller than Aria remembered.

With some difficulty, Aria found her own voice. "I took as many precautions as I could. Eventually, someone will discover that I am not in New York with my mother. A friend was able to get me onto the flights to Egypt and here under assumed names."

"Why have you come?" There was no recrimination in her tone.

Aria started to answer, but suddenly found the question too large to grasp. Until this moment, she had imagined reasons that now seemed absurd. What had they been—that

Kay was in need of help? That she was stranded here? Betrayed and hunted by her former overseers? That she needed a midwife? All of these paled in the light of the woman Aria now saw before her.

"I'm afraid I don't know," she finally replied, "only that I had to come. I . . ." she fumbled for words, ". . . I am *supposed* to be here, to be with you. Everything else in my life slowly lost its vitality when you disappeared. I tried to continue as if nothing had happened, but my focus became blurry. I was having more and more difficulty with my readings. I knew that if I didn't do something . . ."

With some effort, she looked away from Kay's radiant face. "It was as though I didn't really have a choice." She had never spoken the words out loud before, but the truth of it resonated deep within her.

Kay nodded. "Perhaps not. I know the feeling." She smiled, and Aria realized that their roles were now reversed. Kay was the one confident in her environment, and Aria was tormented by some inner calling whose ends were unclear. "Nonetheless, your presence presents some difficulties."

Aria felt her spirit sag. Would Kay send her away? Had she come all this way for nothing? She was surprised by the depth of her reaction. She barely knew this woman, even less now for what she had become. And yet she felt the unmistakable pull, the gravity of Kay's being. I'm like a comet passing too close to the sun, she thought. She wondered if she would be incinerated, and how long it might take.

"What is this place?" Aria asked, hoping to change the direction of the conversation.

Kay's eyes settled upon her face, and Aria again felt as though the spaces between the atoms in her body were expanding, a feeling she was beginning to enjoy. "A community of men and women who found themselves without a world in which to live. And so we've created our own."

"But how do you manage?" The thought of living so deep beneath the earth gave her a slight chill, even though she had seen little of Kay's new world. "And how long do you think it will be before you are discovered? I can't imagine that the councils would allow this to go on."

"We produce everything we need here," Kay said. "Food, clothes, oxygen, even much of our own light. For what we can't generate here, we've hidden solar collectors on the surface, which help nourish our gardens. Some of that we convert to electricity for machinery, but we have perfected other generating capabilities, and technologies that the councils have not yet dreamed of. We rarely venture to the surface."

"Are there many here?"

"A little more than two hundred, mostly Africans, and every moon a few more arrive." She ran her hand over her swollen belly. "Soon there'll be children, too. I'm not alone in this."

"There are genetics labs here, too?" The idea seemed too fantastic.

"No," Kay said, looking now at Aria as if to see how she would react to her next sentence. "We're reproducing naturally."

Aria was stunned. Natural conception had all but disappeared in North America at least fifty years ago. With all the advances in genetic science and birth control, engineering of humans had become so commonplace that few considered using the old methods, even among those who were poor or lived in outlying regions. The risks were too great, as was the demand for people with advanced skills and high resistance to disease. "But why?" she asked.

"Aren't you afraid of . . . problems?"

Kay leaned slightly forward and focused intently on Aria. "Not all science is performed in the laboratories of the Ministry of Births. Nearly everyone here has awakened to abilities that the scientists who created us never imagined."

She moved her hand over her belly. "This child isn't growing inside of me in some random way."

Aria didn't imagine it was. And yet that it was growing at all was unthinkable. "When I began to sense that you were pregnant, I did some research on the K line. It was very difficult to get access to, and I couldn't find much, but I did ascertain that not one of your sisters has become pregnant or given birth . . . until now."

In fact, her research had led her to the conclusion that K-class women were not capable of pregnancy, though most seemed to have normal menstruation. The engineers had apparently been able to separate certain emotional proclivities, such as loyalty and devotion, from the physical ability to generate a fetus, but carrying one to term was a different matter. "Are you certain you are capable of this?"

Kay's mouth turned up at the edges, and Aria was struck with the subtle beauty of the expression. It reminded her of ancient paintings of the Madonna with child.

Kay lifted the hand on her belly until it hovered a foot above the curved surface. "Have you ever journeyed to the center of a cell?" she asked, and looked down at her hand.

Aria followed her gaze. Between Kay's hand and the folds of fabric over the arc of her belly, Aria could see the leg of a small table beyond Kay, and the texture of the soft brown floor it rested on. As she stared, something pulled at her eyes, as though they were elongating, being drawn toward Kay's hand. The contour of the table leg began to lose its clean edges, becoming wavy, as if she were viewing it through heat waves rising from airport macadam on a summer day.

Over a tinny ringing in her ears, she heard Kay's voice again. "With your gifts, Aria, you may soon find that you can do just that. We know now it's possible to enter into the very structure of the DNA and effect change."

She lowered her hand again, and the effect faded.

"We're not simply a bundle of chemical processes. Those are only the structures necessary to house the greater beings that we are. There are levels of consciousness we've barely begun to explore, ranges that will make life as we have known it as obsolete as the dinosaurs."

Aria swallowed the queasiness she felt, as though the solid ground on which she had walked all her life was moving. Her mind grasped for something familiar, some-thing solid. She focused on Kay, taking in her changed physical form, feeling into the layers of her being. There was an awesome power within the woman. Kay was exqui-site, yes, and radiant and self-possessed, but . . . Aria strug-gled to name the subtle, unnerving quality she sensed in Kay's demeanor. Something about her radiance cast long shadows . . .

". . . don't have the skills to bypass the Guardians," Kay was saying. Aria realized she was talking about the security surrounding the little community. Was the little man who served as her guide to this place one of these? She remem-bered standing at the door feeling like she was being ob-served from all sides.

"In time, we'll become too powerful for any of the coun-cils to be a threat. Maybe then we may choose to move back to the surface, though we're prospering well enough here. We have no designs on their world."

Aria felt Kay's conviction in her intonation and words,

and at the same time the psychic upheaval they implied. "Do you know who the father is?"

"You don't?" Kay said, bemused.

For the briefest instant, Aria caught an image of the face of the young man whose holograph Kay had showed her before leaving for Dar es Salaam. Again she was stunned. "Parker Potemkin?"

Kay's smile was wide this time, and Aria felt her own heart leap in concert with Kay's.

"So . . . you didn't succeed in your mission at the World Games? That's good."

"Parker and I came here together the night I found him. He was much more of an opponent than I was prepared for . . . or much less of one. We're both lucky to be alive."

The energy in the room changed with the mention of the young man who was to have died at Kay's hand. It was, Aria thought, as though there was some deep blending of elements between Kay and Parker, a feeling of confluence. The word "marriage" floated through her awareness, but she had never heard the word used in any other context beyond chemistry, and it surprised her.

"We were looking for something else," Kay was saying. "Parker had a friend who warned him I was coming, and gave him the number of someone to contact if he was in trouble. They turned him away, but we happened upon this community the same night. We've been here since."

"Someone warned him?" Aria's attention grew sharper. The implications were instantly clear. If someone outside the CAO had foreknowledge of Kay's assignment, there were others involved beyond whoever had targeted the young athlete and his family. Someone who was protecting Parker. But why?

"Have you ever heard of the Nestercine Sisterhood?"

Aria recognized the name of the order from which many members of various councils had emerged. "Yes, but . . ."

"They've been involved in preserving and reviving the work of a group of scientists who lived at the turn of the last century." She paused and leveled a look at Aria. "Do you remember when you found me in the hall the day before I came here?"

If you only knew how much, Aria thought, and nodded.

"And when I told you I'd read about some people a long time ago who'd been trying to introduce a new generation of humans into the world, and that I thought I might be one of them?"

Aria was silent now, transfixed by Kay's intensity.

"I am one of them. And so is Parker. The Nestercines are behind much of this, though not all, apparently. Some people here know of their existence, but have never been in contact with them, which means this work is evolving from one or maybe several other sources."

Aria recalled standing with Kay in the utility room, looking at Parker's holograph and weeping soundlessly, moved by . . . something. Yes, she remembered and she felt Kay's words fall into place inside of her like pieces of a puzzle. It made sense now. Another flash of insight: despite holding onto the belief that she had chosen to come here, for all of the worry about whether she was making the right decision, nothing would have made any difference.

Everything was as it was supposed to be. This person she thought she was, the one who had tried to interest Barena Colter in the assassin's suspicious orders, the one who had schemed to leave North America and go in search of a woman for whom she felt an irrational concern . . . this person was not really in charge of her life.

Whoever, whatever was in charge was something that

Aria, with all her sensitivities and insights, could not begin to grasp. Something was happening to the world, and it was much larger than she had imagined. In that moment, she felt something inside let go. She was no match for fate.

"Please," she said, "tell me everything."

Chapter 35

Kay's story was mesmerizing. Against the backdrop of the white wall behind her, Kay's outline shimmered, leaving ghost images on Aria's retina when she shifted position. In her even, rich voice, Kay began with Parker meeting Mother Avalon, who'd showed him Dr. Termalaine's diary of the Tressaline colony, how Parker learned that the colony's founder was his biological father, and how she discovered that she was descended from Dr. Termalaine's daughter Leona.

Aria was dumbstruck at Kay's openness, the air of ease and confidence with which she spoke. Time melted away as Kay told her of pursuing Parker to the hotel and of the battle in the hotel room, their reconciliation, and of going in search of help, only to be turned away by the woman whose number Mother Avalon had given Parker.

"She offered no assistance at all?" Aria asked, incredulous.

"Nothing. She just hung up and refused any further calls."

"Was she a Nestercine sister like this Mother Avalon?"

Kay shrugged. "Since arriving here we've heard rumors about the Nestercines, but we haven't encountered them. Parker thinks that whatever sanctuary they may have been planning wasn't completed before Mother Avalon was killed, and that her death sent them into a protective mode."

"Mother Avalon is dead?" The news was disquieting.

Kay nodded. "Both she and Parker were placed at the top of the CAO's termination list."

Aria leaned back in her chair. "Who did this, Kay? Who got Parker and this woman put at the top of this list?" she asked, though something within her had already hinted at the answer.

"Someone you know. Desta Mardrid."

Another puzzle piece dropped in. Now Aria understood her last encounter with Mardrid the week after Aria had first gone to Barena Colter with her concerns about Kay. Mardrid had summoned her to her office for a routine report on her most recent readings. The aide had seemed distracted, barely glancing up from her desk monitor as Aria relayed her findings. When Aria had finished, Mardrid had let go a nearly imperceptible sigh and switched off the monitor. She leaned back in her chair, much as Aria was doing now, and raised her eyes to meet Aria's.

Aria was surprised by what she saw there—the usual look of superiority was gone, replaced with the furtive, troubled look of the hunted. For the first time, she had felt a something akin to sympathy for Mardrid.

"Do you know the whereabouts of K-1754?" Mardrid had asked. The knifelike edge in her voice sliced through Aria's sympathy, sending her stomach into her throat. She answered truthfully that she didn't, and was expecting an onslaught of questions about having gone out of the chain of command to Barena Colter, but they never came. The aide simply looked at her long and hard, then turned her swivel chair in the opposite direction. "You may leave."

Aria never saw her again. Three days later, Mardrid had been noticeably absent from a key council function, and again later at one of Mother Gretel's public speeches. Then, Aria was summoned to Barena Colter's office, introduced to an unfamiliar woman named Teresa Paquel, and told that henceforth she would be reporting to her. When she had asked what had happened to Mardrid, Colter simply said Mardrid had taken another assignment, and dismissed her without further explanation.

Now Aria wondered if Mardrid was still alive.

Aria heard Kay stir, and opened her eyes to see the assassin—could Aria even think of her in this way anymore?—gliding toward a small sink in the corner. There was not a trace of the ungainliness she'd seen in other pregnant women. Kay said, "Would you like some water?"

Aria thanked her, and Kay returned with two full glasses. The glass was cold in Aria's hand and she took a luxurious pull at hers, savoring its sweetness.

"Very deep wells," Kay said, before Aria could ask the question. "We've tapped the largest water table in East Africa."

Aria licked her lips and rested her elbows on her knees. "If the Nestercines were of no help, then how did you arrive here?"

Kay told her of meeting Mothusi, the cabbie, and of their first week underground, becoming more animated as she told of the welcome they received, and of discovering the high level of organization the colony had already achieved, and the many gardens in place. She spoke of feeling a bond with others for the first time in her life, of the freedom she and Parker experienced upon arriving, of the sensuality of being physically touched, something the Africans did frequently. As Kay shared her stories, Aria began to feel less intimidated. The shared intimacies were drawing her close.

Then Kay did something wholly unexpected: in vivid, candid detail, she described the night she and Parker consummated their relationship. Her eyes shone through the long story, and Aria found herself utterly drawn into it, feeling a charge in her cells as Kay described the ecstasy, the blending of her body with Parker's, the opening of new universes within, the deep awakening she experienced. Throughout the story, Aria shifted in her chair, pulling at the clothes that seemed to have begun sticking to her skin.

"I knew immediately I was pregnant," Kay said finally, "and I'm not the only one."

For a confusing moment, Aria thought she meant Parker had taken a harem. Again, she didn't ask aloud, but Kay answered anyway.

"No, seven women became pregnant on that same night, actually by their own lovers. We seem to pass through these phases where everyone is making love or the women are having their periods at the same time. And something else that might surprise you—a lot of men and women here are partnering. Maybe it's because there are more men here. The ratio of men to women is higher here than in North America . . . or on the surface, for that matter. There aren't any rules about this—there's always a lot of sex going on here—but many seem to feel like Parker and me, fulfilled with each other."

"But you said seven women all got pregnant that night, the night you arrived."

"Yes, I found out later during Kopquahe."

"Kopquahe?"

"The community's silent communion on the evening of each seventh day. Parker and I instituted it a moon after we arrived."

Aria let this piece of information sink in. "You and Parker are in leadership roles here?" Something stirred in the pit of her stomach.

Kay finished her water and rested the empty glass on her belly. "It was like they were waiting for us . . . not us specifically maybe, but for someone who could help carry the community to the next level. There are some here who've developed most of the abilities we have, but Parker and I seem to have accelerated more quickly. By our second week, we were asked to join the oversight council. Now everything happens through us."

Aria had so many questions she didn't know which to ask first. She stared at this woman who had in a matter of less than a year metamorphosed from a product of a society that raised her for only one deadly purpose into—what?—a leader? A queen? A mother? And what of this child that she carried so elegantly? What manner of being was it?

And what of Parker? She had only seen his holograph that once, but she remembered how the experience had affected her. That these two were together was staggering. And troubling. But why? She'd seen nothing to evoke anything but respect for them, and Kay was clearly reaching out in friendship. And yet . . . something dangerous lurked just under the surface of her awareness.

Kay set the glass aside and stretched cat-like in her chair. "And now," she said, getting to her feet, "you're here, and we must make some decisions." She turned and looked toward the sliding door by which Aria had entered. "I believe it's time you met Parker."

Aria stood too. "Yes, I'd like that." She hoped the twinge of fear she felt was not too obvious.

They passed through the open door, Aria following in the wake of this new Kay, this woman who was obviously at home in this womb within the earth. Aria was torn between gawking at the impossible new world around her and at Kay's shiny hair swaying between her broad shoulders as she led the way. How incredibly lovely she seemed, the torso tapering to wider hips than Aria remembered, the elegance in her step. They stopped at another small knot of men and women who turned from their work momentarily for a lighthearted exchange in Swahili.

Aria was marveling over Kay's command of the language when she realized that maybe their roles hadn't really switched at all. Maybe she had only fantasized that she was this woman's protector or friend or whatever it had been. Maybe all along Kay had been her mentor.

They came into a large room that smelled of burned herbs. Many rows of carved stone benches circled the center of the room, which rose nearly imperceptibly to a broad, flat pedestal whose sides were etched with designs that at once looked both like fractals and ancient hieroglyphs. Aria's eyes were drawn to the high ceiling where a hundred thousand pinpoints of light, the dazzling ends of fiber optic filaments that drew light from the surface somewhere above, gave the impression of the heavens sparkling through a daylit sky.

The sight made her want to spread her arms and float upward like a bubble on a warm breeze. She turned slowly in a circle and let her eyes fall back down to stone walls upon which hung huge sculptures that extended outward into three-dimensional space, so perfectly capturing a sense of kinetic movement that the reflected light from the ceiling seemed to be in motion across their graceful lines. She felt a deep thrill, like she was hearing a rich, sustained chord played by an invisible orchestra.

"Our council room," Kay said.

"It's . . . beautiful."

"Wait here, Aria. I'll get Parker."

The mention of Parker's name pulled Aria back into her

earlier discomfort. She watched as Kay strode up a row between the stone benches to an arched door at the far end of the room and disappeared.

Aria turned to the nearest bench and touched the cool, smooth surface that was contoured to fit the hips. She sat down and began to center herself with slow, deep breaths. Again she wondered again why the thought of meeting Parker was unnerving.

Chapter 36

Alone now in this strange cathedral, Aria closed her eyes, feeling the inaudible hum that imbued the atmosphere. Soothing and rich, it seemed to come from all directions at once. Gentle hues of purple and violet played behind her eyelids. She felt her muscles relax, and the thrill of what had happened to her since she had walked into the market-place this morning welled up inside. Unbelievable, and yet marvelous. A new world.

And Kay, so lovely and present, so at ease and seemingly fulfilled. So . . . delicious. How had she come to this sense of devotion toward Kay? Was it there in the beginning? Devotion was a trait that the geneticists had engineered in abundance in the K-class, but sensitives like herself and her mother were not known for it. Quite the opposite, actually. It was thought to interfere with the ability to be objective in the observation of the inner lives of others. And yet there it was.

But that wasn't all, was it? Aria had always been fond of men, the way they smelled and felt, their ruggedness, their hardness inside of her. For the two years she worked for the council, she had enjoyed the privilege of nearly unlimited access to Sexual Services. But as she thought of Kay—her hair, her face, the shape of her hips—she had to admit there was a spark . . . more than a spark. A fire. Electricity, nearly the same thing she felt when she was attracted to a man. A sort of pulling at the sensitive places of the body, the nipples, the hollow of her neck.

She squirmed a little on the bench, and felt the coolness of the stone beneath her against the dampness between her legs. The blood rose in her cheeks. Why the embarrassment, Aria? Women everywhere are attracted to each other. They form relationships, live together, make love. But not me. At least never before. What was it about the idea that was troubling? The neediness? She had always maintained a sense of independence. The sexual relationships she'd enjoyed with men had never impinged on that. Now here was this huge ball of feelings for Kay, and part of them anyway were physical.

But they mingled with other underlying feelings wandering through her like the unseen bellies of the great icebergs that had once floated free in the oceans. Purposefulness? Was that it? She remembered the feeling of release she had back in the room they'd come from, the surrender to something mysterious and too big to grasp. Destiny? The word sounded tinny, too thin to match the feeling.

Her reverie was broken by the distant sound of someone approaching. She opened her eyes and stood to bring herself to the moment. As she did the bag that had been in her lap slipped to the floor. She stooped to reach for it, but the sounds were closer now, so she let it lay and stood again to her full height. She realized she was grasping her left wrist in front of her like a nervous schoolchild. She let her arms swing free at her sides, squared her shoulders, and took a deep, calming breath.

Her eyes darted to the portal through which Kay had disappeared, tears inexplicably gathering on the rims of her eyelids and something ballooning in her chest. Kay appeared first, her loose clothing swaying as she stepped, her smile gentle. Was there a hint of mischief in the corners of that smile? Behind her loomed the huge frame of the man whose face she recognized. Seeing the two of them together, Aria felt such a surge of emotion that she wondered if her knees would hold.

Parker wore simple clothing—a beige tunic-like shirt over pants whose legs flapped like loose sails in a breeze with each long stride, and sandals that moved soundlessly over the polished stone floor. At last, Parker and Kay stood side by side in front of her.

"Hello, Aria," said the unsmiling young man, his voice like a distant rumble in the walls. His right hand was raised in a formal salute, and Aria tried to raise hers in response, but her muscles didn't seem to know what to do. "You've come a long way to be here with us."

At that moment it seemed to her very far indeed. She felt every mile and footfall in her body.

In a small voice, she said, "I'm afraid I can no longer stand," and sank slowly onto the bench, her head buzzing loudly. Kay and Parker exchanged a brief glance and sat opposite her. Parker leaned forward to touch Aria's hand, which had come to rest damply on her thigh. Immediately she felt coolness in her body, and the noise in her head receded. A sense of unnatural calm crept over her, as if she had passed into the eye of a storm.

She opened her mouth to say that she felt better now, and was surprised by what came instead—a wrenching sob, a sound filled with grief, longing, joy, loneliness, elation, relief, and a thousand more unnameable emotions.

She raised her free hand to her mouth, but it was no use. The wailing noise came and came again. She buried her face in her hands and wept uncontrollably into her lap. Someone touched the back of her head as the tears soaked her dress. The spasms came so hard at moments that she thought she wouldn't be able to take in another breath.

She remembered her experience in the little utility closet at Council Headquarters nearly a year ago as she'd stared at Parker's holograph. A teacher, she thought. He is a teacher. But it's not just Parker, it's them together. She had found something she had never known was missing.

Eventually, some modicum of control began reinstating itself, and she lifted her head. Kay and Parker gazed at her, a mixture of compassion and humor playing in their eyes. She nearly wept again, but took a trembling breath and wiped her eyes on the sleeves of her blouse, a wave of gratitude rushing over her. "Thank you for letting me find you," she said, her voice cracking. She felt like she had laid down a great burden.

They sat in a comfortable silence for a few minutes, Aria occasionally sniffling and wiping the persistent tears from her cheek. Then Parker spoke.

"You've made a strong choice in coming here to find us, Aria. I don't imagine you made it lightly, but you must know that it's not a choice you can unmake." He paused and searched her face. "We can't allow you to leave. It'd be too dangerous for the community. We're growing quickly, as you can tell, but we're still forming the core of what . . ."

Aria interrupted him, shaking her head. "I don't want to leave. I didn't come all this way just to turn back. I didn't know why I had to come. I still don't, really. But I know that I must be here. I want to be here." She looked at Kay. "I knew you were pregnant months ago, and I knew that I had to find you, to be . . . involved."

She looked from one to the other, searching for words. "I only know something very important is happening here and that I have to be part of it. There's no other explanation."

The couple remained silent, Parker peering deeply into Aria's eyes, Kay looking at her hands in her lap.

"I don't have your gifts," Aria continued, realizing that she sounded as though she was pleading, though neither of them had given her reason to. She didn't care. "But I have the desire to learn and to be of service here. I can do that."

Parker nodded. "I think you have much to offer. Now that you're here, we will find a place for you. Kay tells me that you managed to cover your trail, at least for a while. That's good, but we can't count on it. Someone will search for you eventually, and it probably won't be long before they trace you to Dar es Salaam. We're not working under the delusion that we'll remain undiscovered for long, but this could speed things up."

He stood, and with his hands clasped behind his back, began to pace slowly. "We're building something here that is going to change the world forever, Aria. It's what we're meant to do." He stopped and looked at her. "Do you know about my father?"

"Kay told me something of him, and the Tressaline Colony."

"Yes," Parker said, turning to walk again. "More than a century ago he and the others started this work right here in Dar es Salaam. Isn't it remarkable that we should find ourselves here now? Children of long dead parents and their laboratories, carrying out what I'm sure they would have built if they had not been taken out by the forces that were afraid of their power."

Aria nodded, feeling the quiet intensity in his voice.

"I never sought power," he went on. "Things happened to me when I was young that made me afraid of it. I tried to avoid even thinking about it. I focused all of my attention on perfecting my skills. Then I found that I could help others, on my team. I found that I could stretch out and help them do better in our competitions, I could . . ." he put the fingers and thumb of one hand together as if he were extracting a word from the air ". . . give myself to them, and they could stand on that to reach higher. After I met Mother Avalon, I remembered some things I'd pushed away, and I began to let them come back to me."

He paused, staring at one of the wall sculptures, forming his next thought. "It would be naïve for me, for us, to ignore the importance of power now. We weren't looking for it when we came here. We were seeking refuge. We have no desire to harm anyone or cause others to lose anything. But after being here for less than a week, we knew that by our very presence, the fact that we exist and that we have come together, we'll bring chaos to the world.

"We represent change, and nothing changes easily. It's part of human nature to resist change, especially if we can't feel like we can exercise some sort of control over it.

"And so we must become powerful if we're going to survive, if we're going to avoid the fate of the colonists who brought people like us into the realm of possibility."

He stretched out an arm and swept it in an arc around the room. "That's one of the reasons for this room. Beautiful, isn't it?"

"Yes," Aria said, "and something more."

Parker smiled. "Yes. We built this in three moons. In times gone by, it might have taken years, and even then only the most gifted of architects would have been able to conceive some of the subtle mathematics of angle and proportion that give the room that 'something more.' It's our council room. We come together here as a community for all the reasons communities must come together. But you might also think of it as a resonation chamber. In this room, we practice a sort of blending of minds, our energies. Together we reach understanding and awareness and strength far greater than that of any one of us. It's part of how we are preparing for the confrontation that we know will come. And the responsibility."

Aria's stomach tightened. "How do you see that coming?"

Parker returned to the bench in front of Aria and sat down. "It's not given to us to know how, but we're headed for a collision with the established order, with the councils. We're building a new model of how humans will live, and they won't accept it easily."

He put his hand on Kay's, atop her round belly. "Our children are likely to be even more accelerated than we are. What they'll bring to the world is unimaginable. We bear the responsibility of creating a safe environment for them to become the leaders and teachers and healers the world will need. They're the ones who'll be able to make visible the changes we can only dream of. So far, we've done all this undetected at least partly because we've been able to cloak much of our activity using the combined power that comes from Kopquahe. But we can't count on this to keep us hidden forever.

"The African Council is the weakest of all the sisters. Undoubtedly that's why we have been able to do what we've done here so far with so little interference. But we're sure the North American Council has been looking for Kay since she disappeared, maybe even more so than my brotherhood, because her very existence is a secret, and because she's violated the orders that her sisterhood hold sacred. The Guardians are our first line of defense, and they've done well, but sooner or later we will be challenged. It's inevitable."

Aria knew it was true, and hoped it would be a long time before it happened. In the meantime, she must do what she could to become a part of these people. "I'm willing to help in any way I can." She turned to Kay, who looked back at her now. "I'd be honored if I could stay close to you and learn, at least for a while. Maybe it'll become clear how I can contribute."

Kay smiled, and Aria thought it so beautiful that her heart would break. "Yes, there's much I can show you. Tonight we'll hold Kopquahe here, and introduce you to the community."

Kay put her other hand on Parker's, and Aria remembered how back in the little room at the North American Council Headquarters, she had had to screw up her courage enough to put her arms around the stiff and at first unyielding assassin. Now this little display of familiarity between her and Parker spoke of tenderness. Aria could almost see the current than ran between them. It pulled at her now, but it wasn't jealousy she felt. It was, she realized with a start, a hunger to be a part of it.

"Let's begin by getting you something to eat," Kay said, "something real."

For now, at least, Aria would have to be content with satisfying a different kind of hunger. "That'd be wonderful," she said, her stomach rumbling in agreement. "It seems like a very long time since my last meal."

Chapter 37

Aria stared at the plateful of food that the large woman had just placed in front of her, unsure whether to be pleased or dismayed. The woman was genuinely amused, her generous mouth spread widely across perfect teeth.

"You will like it," she said in heavily accented English. "It is made here. Grown here. Everything."

Aria recognized none of the oddly colored, steaming vegetables. The noodles they rested upon were somewhat similar to ones she frequently ordered up from the processor in her tiny kitchen in the North American Council Headquarters, but thicker and a deeper shade of yellow. She had not eaten a fresh vegetable since her thirteenth birthday, when her nanny had imposed upon one of her friends who had cultivated a rare garden on her balcony. Aria had detested the taste then, and refused to eat, despite her nanny's insistence and anger.

She smiled up at the woman, who seemed reluctant to leave. Did this proprietary attitude mean the woman prepared the food herself? A dozen or so people were in the room, some looking her way, that peculiar sense of lightness settling over her as they did. They nodded in her direction and Aria nodded back. She raised her fork and tentatively stabbed at one of the fleshy chunks. Her stomach growled at their pungency.

She tried a small bite, and chewed thoughtfully, smiling at the hovering woman while trying not to appear too surprised at the strong flavor. The gesture seemed to appease the woman, who left, humming. By the third bite, Aria's hunger took over and she found she enjoyed the flavors. Before she knew it, the plate was empty.

The plate was not like any she had ever seen. At first glance, it appeared to be a rather dull, earthen color, but closer examination revealed subtle colors lying deep within, almost an opalescent effect. It was beautiful, and Aria wondered how it had been made.

Or how she might get it filled up again. Moments later, the woman returned. "More?"

Aria was about to say yes, when the weight of the meal in her stomach, and her weariness, set in. She shook her head and the woman took her plate.

"Would you like to rest until Kopquahe?"

Aria was grateful for the suggestion. "How long would that be?"

"Not long, a little less than two hours."

Aria wondered how she would wake up in time, but the woman anticipated her question.

"I will come wake you," she said. "Kay asked me to look out for you."

Aria thanked her and formally introduced herself. The woman said her name was Bantwalla. Her welcoming smile made it clear to Aria that she was in good hands.

Bantwalla showed her to deserted sleeping quarters, and Aria stretched out on one of the ten or so beds there, falling quickly into a dreamless sleep.

She awoke to find Bantwalla standing in the doorway with something draped over her arm. She didn't think Bantwalla had spoken, but knew she had awakened her. Aria recognized the object Bantwalla held out to her as a gossamer robe. "For Kopquahe."

Bantwalla left and Aria removed her clothes, keenly

aware of their strong odor. Three days in the African sun will do that, she thought. There was no dry bath here, but a small sink stood in the corner. Aria bathed herself with a small cloth she found there, enjoying the rare pleasure of cool water on her skin. Returning to the bed, she picked up the robe, surprised by its weightlessness. She pressed the cool fabric to her cheek, savored its fresh smell, and slipped it over her head.

Soon Bantwalla appeared again in the doorway, dressed in an identical robe. "Time for you to meet the others."

They walked in silence through the halls, others joining them from the many doorways they passed. By the time they neared the council room, Aria could no longer count the bobbing heads in front of her. She noticed that some of the women around her were as far along in their pregnancy as Kay. Despite the presence of so many people, only the gentle swish of their robes was audible, like the sound of rain on water. Aria felt almost as if she were floating. Emotion began welling up inside. Not again, she thought, and used the sleeve of the robe to wipe a fresh tear from her cheek, swallowed the lump in her throat.

They passed through the final portal, and the others filled the empty places on the stone benches. Bantwalla continued down the aisle, leading Aria toward the center of the cavernous room and the raised platform there. At the foremost row, she stopped, and gestured to Aria. Kay and Parker were there, their eyes closed and their hands resting in their laps. Her dark eyes aglow, Bantwalla motioned toward the space between them. Aria hesitated, unsure if she could stand the intensity of sitting between these two. Bantwalla's light touch and reassuring smile helped, and so Aria moved forward, easing herself into the space, taking deep, calming breaths.

She glanced at the rich colors high in the ceiling, and the play of light along the marvelous sculptures on the walls. The faces of the men and women around the circle, row upon row of them, were beautiful, serene, and lit nearly visibly from within.

Moments later, all rustling sounds in the room ceased and Aria saw that everyone else had closed their eyes. She followed, and immediately was enveloped in a deep sense of presence. To her ears, the room was quiet, but deep inside she began to hear something else. There was the subtle vibration she had felt while awaiting Parker and Kay, like an ancient pipe organ whose bass notes were below the range of the human ear.

But there was more now, as though many voices whispered together—not cacophony but a smooth, even hiss. Something similar had happened when she first tried to read Kay. Her mind tried to wrap around the experience. It's the blood in my veins, in my brain, she thought. I'm hearing my own rivers. But she realized it could not be so, for now the sound seemed to be coming from both inside and out.

The more closely she listened, the louder it became, washing away her need for an explanation. Her body felt light, as if it was dissolving. Willingly, she surrendered it, and had a sensation like she was rising upward into the rich colors above her, a cloud in a rainbow sky. Everything familiar began falling away beneath her—words, symbols, time—carrying with it her fears and cares, the sharp outlines of her body.

Something was building deep in her core, something sweet and gentle. Momentarily, she wondered if the experience would peak, and she would fall feather-like to the earth. But it continued to rise, faster and faster, until she felt like she was being gently split open. Something inside quietly gave way, and she was flooded with a feeling of boundless intimacy, as though the infinite universe had become her very body. All her knowing was direct. She was life itself, effortlessly melding and transforming, a beautiful melody with no beginning or end, reverberating through space.

A profound sense of joy began to move through this universe, swelling, intensifying. She heard herself begin to chuckle, surprised by the sound of her physical voice, so chirpy and small, so . . . silly. She chuckled harder, unable to resist the urge, and heard it echo from distant walls. But it wasn't only her voice. There were others, high and low, and all around her.

Surprised, she opened her eyes, and saw others wiping the shining tracks of tears from their cheeks, smiles stretched tightly across their faces, their teeth brilliant against the dark skin of their faces.

Then it took her like a storm. The air in her lungs, sweet and thick, rushed out of her in a spasm of laughter. She saw others double over, hold their sides, and guffaw loudly, hair flying about their heads.

On either side of her, Kay and Parker bounced like bubbles on a brook, their beautiful voices mingling with the others, pealing from the surrounding walls. Everywhere Aria turned, bodies bobbed, faces were crystalline with tears. The sight made her laugh harder. Her facial muscles began to cramp, but she couldn't stop. She felt a momentary twinge of fear that it would never end, that they would all perish, found by some archeologist in future centuries, their mummified faces frozen in these silly expressions . . . and laughed harder.

She closed her eyes again, but the roomful of people remained in her vision, only now faint shapes were in motion in the atmosphere above their heads, indistinct configurations of angles and curves that vibrated and swirled about them like silt trails in eddying water.

Much later, the feeling began to fade, the laughter coming in short bursts as people spoke in Swahili and English, some holding hands, others slapping each other's thighs and backs.

Eventually, when quiet resumed, Parker rose and stepped onto the platform at the room's center. He was a commanding figure, Aria thought again as he turned, making a 360-degree sweep of the faces in the room, his own face tightly controlled. He cleared his throat.

"That . . ." he said, pausing—and then could no longer suppress the smile—"was a *good* one." He exploded into laughter again, bending forward, whooping, his hands on his knees, and his face glowing red. Again, pandemonium broke out.

Aria felt like her heart would burst at the glory, the beauty of everything—Parker, the room, the beaming faces. Never before had she felt so much a part of anything. She felt Kay's hand fold over hers and she glanced up, but Kay remained focused on Parker, her eyes radiant, her aura breathtaking.

Once again things calmed down. Parker wiped his eyes and took a few deep breaths, and a sense of peace slowly crept over the room. Finally he said, "We have a new pilgrim in our midst. Like Kay and me, she has come here from North America. She searched hard, and with some difficulty has found us." He fell silent, as if considering his next words.

"Her heart is good, and her gifts many," he resumed. "She would like to be welcomed into our community." He repeated the words in Swahili, but Aria thought it unnecessary. They all seemed to understand immediately.

Parker turned to where Aria sat, motioned for her to come onto the platform. She rose a little unsteadily and climbed the three stairs that were cut into the side of the circular structure. Parker directed her to the center and moved silently to a spot several feet behind her. Immediately she felt the now familiar force of expansiveness, the space between the molecules in her body.

She turned slowly and looked into the several hundred faces, her hands at her sides, palms turned outward, silent. Words could never convey the depth of her feelings. She felt open, naked from the inside out, locked in a communion with these people. Let the tears on her cheeks and her open hands express it all, she thought.

When in her turning she reached the place where she faced Kay, she stopped. Kay stood and extended a hand in her direction. Aria closed her eyes and felt nearly overwhelmed with gratitude. She put her palms together and bowed deeply to Kay, and then found her way to the steps. When she reached Kay, Kay touched her hand briefly and gestured for her to sit again.

Then the young woman who had once been an assassin ascended the platform and stood at Parker's left side. Aria felt chills as the two joined their closest hands and raised the other above their shoulders, palms down as if conferring a blessing on the assembly. There was electricity in the air.

With their eyes closed and expressions of nobility that might have been carved on the faces of a monument, Kay and Parker spoke in unison.

"As the New Seed of the New Earth, the fruit of the Bringers, the holders of the key to the True Ideal, we pledge ourselves to the fulfillment of the ancient dream, and call forth the purest waters of our being to cleanse, purify, heal, and bring rebirth to the precious body of humankind.

"All who have sacrificed that we might be here, we honor you.

"All who have gone out from the world in search of the New Family, we honor you.

"All who will come after us to create the New Earth, we honor you.

"Now is our time. Now we harvest the fruit of time's labors. Now we make manifest the hope of the ages."

At these last words, everyone in the room stood and held their right hand over their heart. Aria followed their example and listened as all in the room spoke with one voice the next words:

"For this we were born, for this we live and die. For this we were born, for this we live and die. For this we were born, for this we live and die."

The words troubled her, and she groped inside of her for the source of her discomfort, but it was like trying to catch a moth in the dark. Everyone began to leave, laughing and talking, but Aria couldn't seem to will herself to move from the spot where she stood. Kay and Parker came down the steps and turned toward her. The sight of their faces, warm and glowing, chased away her dark thoughts.

Kay touched her arm as she neared. "You did well tonight. Rest now. Tomorrow I'll show you more of what we've accomplished here."

Aria nodded and smiled. "I'll do that." Her voice sounded all right now, but inside she felt a little like a girl again, awkward and unsure of herself. She looked toward the portal where she had entered, trying to remember how to find her way back to her new sleeping quarters.

"It's the third hallway on the right after you pass through

the council gate," Kay said, perfectly interpreting Aria's indecision. "There is a bed for you in the room where you rested earlier."

"Thank you," Aria said, quietly relieved. She turned and walked up the aisle, grateful that this long day was nearly at an end. When she got to the portal, she turned to wave goodnight, but the council room was empty. They must have left through the door that Parker entered by earlier in the day, she thought, and realized it must lead to their quarters. She let her eyes wander over the room, taking in its beauty, feeling its power pulsing quietly just under her conscious awareness.

She shook her head, amazed at the enormity of changes in this single day of her life. Then she turned and headed toward what she expected would be a wonderful night's sleep.

Chapter 38

Aria stared at the numbers and figures Bantwalla pointed to on the small screen. "You see," Bantwalla said, "the potassium and iron figures are more than three times higher than the strength of the surface sample."

Aria looked now at the two strangely shaped vegetables in the tray next to them, tiny probes protruding from their greenish-yellow skin. "And you did this how?"

"One part soil treatment, one part attention. We *see* them as we work with them, let them feel us. They like it."

Aria had no doubt that the plants did, indeed, like it. She liked it. She could feel her own body respond nearly every time she became the object of that attention, almost like being caressed. "Yes, I think I understand. Are the other foods like this one?"

"All of them." Bantwalla pointed to the ceiling. "And *they* really like them."

Aria was momentarily confused. "Who?"

Bantwalla said nothing, but looked into Aria's eyes. Aria felt a subtle shift within herself, and she saw a brief flash of the marketplace where she had caught her first scent of Kay, and the woman she met at the stall. "You mean the people above, on the surface."

"Parker was right. You do have some gifts. This is good." Bantwalla gestured at the numerous diagnostic tools. "We have been supplying fresh and processed food to markets throughout most of the East African territories for nearly two years."

Aria remembered the woman she met at the stall and the many people crowded around her stall. Yes, people did seem to know the difference. A flurry of questions came to mind. Was the woman at the market a member of this community? Where did they get the soil to grow these things? How did they get the food to the surface? How did all this remain undetected? Indeed, how had they constructed this elaborate network of tunnels at all, and when?

She sighed. There was time for all these to be answered. This was only her third day here. Yesterday she had spent the day with Kay, walking seemingly endless corridors, meeting others at work. She had seen wonderfully compact machinery that processed what seemed to her enormous amounts of raw food into flours and pastes and liquids. She had seen incomprehensible technology that distributed the solar energy from the surface, converting it to heat where needed, even separating the spectrum for dozens of specialized purposes.

They had visited a small medical facility, where Aria found only a few patients being treated. Medical implements were in evidence, and vials of solutions in glass cabinets, but mostly the patients she saw were being treated in silence by the staff who touched them, or held their hands over various parts of their bodies.

Over breakfast and lunch, Aria and Kay had talked easily about many things, especially about the baby Kay was carrying (a boy, she revealed), and when it was due (two moons from now). Aria had told Kay of her desire to help care for the child when it was born. Kay had anticipated this, and she'd arranged to house Aria in the east wing of the complex, near to where she and Parker spent their evenings. Tomorrow she would move there, but today she was free to wander on her own. Bantwalla had volunteered to show her some of the work she did during the early hours of the day.

"Do you spend time above, Bantwalla?"

"Not much anymore. Every moon I leave for a week or so to gather supplies we cannot produce here. It is good to see the sky, the stars at night, but there are such riches here I don't miss them too much."

"But does anyone miss you where you came from? How did you come here?"

"East Africa is very different than your home, I think. We are less developed here than the rest of Africa and the world. Birth technology only really took hold here thirty years ago, and it is still met with suspicion in many places. So you see, the sisterhoods operate here, but are not so pervasive. I was born between these two worlds in the Katanga province, north of here.

"My mother was inseminated in laboratory at the direction of the government, but I was raised in my clan there, not in the government schools. When I began to find my gifts, I got into trouble with the elders. They mistrusted me and would not allow me to play with the other children. I became very lonely.

"When I was fourteen, I ran away to Dar es Salaam, and found work in the markets selling fruit. By that time I had learned to hide my talents, even though it was becoming more and more difficult. Eventually I found a tutor, a woman who recognized something special about me. She took me in and I learned enough from her before she died to go to university and study agriculture. One of my teachers there was a Trengala—you know of them?"

Aria shook her head.

"They were a sisterhood that was broken up long ago by the Second Council, but some who survived managed to find work in education or biogenetics and agriculture. She never told me so, but I think their ancestors were connected somehow with the Tressaline community—you know about them?"

Aria nodded.

"I think they might have been trustees of some of the Tressaline lines," Bantwalla continued. "She knew what I was, though, and she gave me the encouragement I needed to begin to unfold. When she died, I was lost. I became so despondent that I nearly killed myself."

As Bantwalla spoke, Aria was experiencing something new. In some part of her mind she was seeing flashes of the people and places in Bantwalla's life without being in the trance-like state that before had always been necessary for such vision. The figure of a large black woman emerged, wearing a colorful print dress and a beatific smile. Aria liked her instantly, and could feel the weight of sadness around Bantwalla's heart, how she missed her teacher.

"But just before she died," Bantwalla continued, "she told me there were others in Africa like me. She said I would find them if I reached out with my feelings. In my despair, I nearly forgot her words. I graduated that year, but afterwards I didn't know what to do. I went back to selling in the marketplace and mostly stayed in my room at night.

"One day, someone came to me at my stall and asked me if I would sell her vegetables for her. When she showed me what she had brought, I picked it up and knew instantly that it was special. I could feel it in my hands. It almost spoke to me. I asked her where it came from, but she would only say from her family farm. She and two others brought forty baskets of it the next day, and I sold it all in three days. The next week she returned with more, but I told her

I must see where this was grown."

Bantwalla paused and smiled at the recollection. "I didn't know what she thought of me, because I was so insistent, almost angry. I told her I was a university-trained agriculturalist and that it was not fair to keep people in the dark about this. She must have seen something in my eyes, because she took my hand and gave me such a jolt that I nearly collapsed. At that very moment, I remembered my teacher's words about finding others like me, and I wept. That night, she brought me here."

Bantwalla's smile was infectious and Aria found herself grinning too. "By the next moon, I was living here and another woman sold the vegetables," Bantwalla said, and they both laughed as if she had told a joke.

"How long ago?"

"Almost two years," Bantwalla said, "another lifetime ago."

Aria knew what she meant. She had only been here three days, and already felt this way.

They spent the next few hours in Bantwalla's work area, the black woman explaining her work, tasting the panoply of fruit and vegetables that ran through the processing station. Afterward, they wandered through the labyrinth corridors and Bantwalla showed her one of the lifts where the produce was taken to the surface.

"This one comes out in the barn of a small farm on the north outskirts of the city. There are five of us there who then take it to the markets."

"Can I ask about the other portals, where you come and go here?"

Bantwalla thought for a moment. "Yes, come. I'll take you to meet my friend Njeri. She is a Guardian."

They walked back through the council room to the east

wing, where Parker and Kay had their living quarters. At one of the open doorways, Bantwalla turned and led the way down a long hall that immediately began to climb. The lighting was dimmer than in most of the rest of the complex. A short while later they arrived at a hallway that appeared to be a dead end in both directions, and Bantwalla stopped. "Now I must ask you to turn around."

Aria knew why. Nonetheless, she was surprised by the sudden change in their easy conversation and friendship. It hurt. She had forgotten she was something of an initiate.

Bantwalla gave her a soulful look. "I was here many months before I discovered the secret of access to any of the portals. Don't be offended. We must be careful, even though you are accepted here. You are special, I think, and soon you will be free to come and go as you like."

Aria nodded, swallowed her wounded pride, and turned around.

She closed her eyes, hearing Bantwalla's footsteps recede a short distance and then the groaning sound of a heavy door opening. She opened her eyes again only when she felt the touch of Bantwalla's hand on her arm. They passed through the opening, and Aria saw that the section of rock that had pivoted on some hidden axis was about three feet thick.

It closed automatically behind them as they began ascending the first of many stairs. There must be a panel, or a light beam near the door, she thought. It was not important now, though. There was time. She was content to be here, and would be too conspicuous in the world above.

When they reached the end, they passed through several doorways and into a small room with primitive furniture and no windows. Leaning against the frame of the only other doorway to the room was a tall black woman wearing a bright, floor-length dress, beads in her hair, and a broad smile. She said something in Swahili, and Bantwalla answered jauntily. They both laughed and embraced as if they hadn't seen each other in some time.

Bantwalla turned and gestured toward Aria, who was touched by the display of love between the two black women. "Aria, this is my friend Njeri."

In two steps the tall woman vanquished the distance between them, took Aria's hand in hers, and squeezed gently. "Hello. New you are?"

"Yes, I arrived from North America only a few days ago. I am a friend of Kay and Parker."

Njeri nodded, smiled, and then looked at Bantwalla, who spoke to her in Swahili. Njeri then looked back into Aria's eyes. "Welcome."

"She speaks very little English," Bantwalla explained.

Njeri turned and gestured for the women to follow. The next room was larger, sunny and ringed with large potted plants. Several pieces of furniture surrounded a small table, all made of the thin woven branches of some reddish shrub. Njeri and Bantwalla spoke animatedly, then Njeri motioned the two women to sit, and left the room.

"She offered us something to drink," Bantwalla said.

A single arched window overlooked a street, and Aria saw only a few vehicles and a single pedestrian passing. Two walls were mostly covered with a thick, multicolored weaving. The rug beneath her feet looked like straw but felt wonderfully soft.

Njeri reappeared bearing a wooden tray with three cups and a steaming pot. With the grace possessed only by a tall woman, she placed the cups on the table while carrying on a conversation with Bantwalla, and poured the steaming brown tea into the cups. Aria smelled spice and flowers and perhaps cinnamon in it.

Njeri's long brown fingers caressed the cups, giving one first to Aria and then to Bantwalla. Softly, she said a word in Swahili that sounded like a blessing, and then looked at Aria over the rim of the cup as she took a sip. Aria fell into her deep eyes, feeling suspended in a timeless moment, the rich scent of the tea reaching deep into her, filling her with a remarkable sense of well-being and welcome.

The three women sipped their tea and Aria enjoyed the silent feeling of connection. "Bantwalla said you are a Guardian. What does that mean, really? How do you guard?"

Njeri set her cup down on the small table and waited for Bantwalla's translation. Then she smiled delicately, and appeared thoughtful before answering.

Bantwalla translated again. "She says she has the gift of knowing. She can discern people's intentions, their heart. If someone comes here who doesn't belong here, or means ill to us, she knows."

Aria nodded. This was simple enough. She remembered the little man who had ushered her in and then through the labyrinth to the community, and the feeling she had gotten when he first looked at her. "But then what can you do to turn them away if they are intent on coming in?"

Njeri began speaking before Bantwalla had a chance to translate the question.

Bantwalla said, "The Guardians are of one mind. They know together, they act together. Do you understand?"

Aria thought she might. When she was a girl in training, sometimes her sisters would enter a state of mind together to enhance someone's ability to read the patterns of a subject's being. It almost always helped, but they had not pursued the art much in the latter years of school. She began to inquire further, but Njeri spoke again.

"We make pictures, she says," Bantwalla translated, "terrible pictures that frighten. She says it has only happened twice in her time here, but the pictures made them go away . . . fast."

Aria contemplated this, a silly image coming to her of Njeri or the little man holding up a painting in front of someone at their door, and the person running away.

Njeri was shaking her head, though, and spoke again as if reading her thoughts.

"You have fears," Bantwalla translated. "Everyone does. Deep ones that dry you up inside when they come, shrivel your bones. They can even make you lose your mind, forget what you were doing, these pictures."

Aria remembered having nightmares as a child, dream images that made her awaken whimpering in the night. One of them now threatened to arise just under the surface of her awareness and she shuddered involuntarily. Njeri and Bantwalla both laughed aloud at the display, and Aria blushed. "I see," she said, smiling sheepishly at her new friends.

"So far, this talent has not been needed so much," Bantwalla said. "I think by now many people must know, or suspect we have such a place in their midst. Especially the children. I overheard once at the marketplace some children talking about The People. It was like a magical story to them, though. If the council knows of our existence, they have made no move to discover who we are. If they do, I think they will be in for a surprise. Njeri and the others are very good at what they do."

Aria hoped she was right. She wondered if the Guardians would be strong enough to work their skills on a strike force or a police group that had weapons and orders to invade. The thought disturbed her enough to make her change the subject.

"Are you lonely here?" she asked Njeri. "Do you have someone to talk with or . . ."

Bantwalla translated, and Njeri smiled broadly and spoke, pointing at the ceiling and making a little circle with a slender finger. Then she pointed to her heart, and then her lap, making another little circle. Both of the women laughed again.

"She says she is never alone. The Guardians are always here." Bantwalla repeated the motion in the air Njeri had made with her finger, and Aria understood she meant the Guardians felt one another's presence.

"And then she said she has a man who visits often. He fills her heart and other places whenever he comes to visit." She laughed as she spoke.

Aria had felt the warmth in Bantwalla's voice when she spoke of him. "Is he a Guardian, too?"

This time Bantwalla answered without translating for Njeri. "No, you probably saw him at Kopquahe. He is a member of our community, but works in Dar es Salaam driving a taxi. His name is Mothusi, but he calls himself M."

At the sound of his name, Njeri arched her thin eyebrows, placed one hand over her heart, and with the other made the little circle over her lap again. "Emmmm," she said, drawing the consonant out deliciously in the back of her throat.

Bantwalla and Aria understood, and all had a hearty laugh.

Chapter 39

A week later, Aria was ensconced in her own room not far down the hall from where Kay and Parker lived. It was smaller than her room in the North American Council Headquarters, but she didn't mind, though the cold floors took some getting used to. No matter what the ambient temperature in this place, the floors remained cool.

Aria's sleep had been peaceful and dreamless ever since she arrived. A few times in the night she had awakened momentarily disoriented, but then remembered where she was, smiled, and easily drifted off again. This morning she awoke refreshed and excited to see light filling the room from the solar collectors on the surface. As she sipped her morning tea, a knock came at the door.

"Sleep well?" Kay asked, stepping inside the room.

"It's wonderful here. Like a dream. I can't remember ever feeling happier."

Kay sat at the small table next to Aria. "Parker and I have been talking about what you can do here. Many positions need filling, but none of them are particularly suited to your expertise." She smiled. "We don't yet have much need for your . . . insights."

Aria laughed at the irony of it. She had trained her whole life to be able to read the life patterns and propensities of the people around her, and now her talents were rendered nearly obsolete. She could likely learn far more about that from these people than she could reveal to them.

"I can learn new skills. I'm not afraid of hard work.

Bantwalla has shown me a lot about the growing and processing. I think I can make a contribution there."

"Bantwalla is a good teacher, isn't she? There's much to be done to maintain and expand our systems."

Aria was pleased. Bantwalla was an amiable companion, and they had already grown close.

"There's another thing we'd like you to consider, as well," Kay said, adjusting the front of her smock. She fell silent, staring at the hand that rested on her bulging stomach. She raised her penetrating blue eyes. "I . . . we . . . would like you to become a nursemaid to our child."

Aria was not even sure she had heard correctly.

"You see," Kay said, breaking the silence, "we want him to be raised on the breast, like babies used to be, but we are almost certain now that I cannot produce milk. The doctors are rather surprised I'm pregnant at all. The K's were never intended to bear children, as you know. But . . ." she gave her stomach a little pat, "there can be little doubt we've overcome that obstacle." There was a gleam of mischief in her eye. "I might have gotten a little something special in the Ministry of Births lab, something with the Tressaline genes. But we just can't seem to get my breasts to respond."

"But I don't see how . . ."

"The doctors here say they are able to persuade your body into thinking you're pregnant through the use of certain herbs and potions. It's something the Africans have known about for a very long time. They've tried these with me, but they haven't worked. If you'd be willing to try, you may have better results."

Aria thought Kay looked more vulnerable than ever. How difficult it must have been for her to give up the idea of nursing her own child. She immediately rose, bent down, and for only the second time since she had met Kay, put her arms around the younger woman. "Yes of course I'll try. I'd be honored." She pulled back then and looked into Kay's eyes, which seemed to have softened.

"Thank you. If it goes well, I'll ask you to spend much time with me. There's a lot I can share with you, I believe, and maybe you can help me to be a mother."

"Yes!" Aria said. "Yes! That would make me very happy." Indeed, her heart felt as though it might burst at that moment. In her enthusiasm she pulled Kay out of her chair and held her close, feeling Kay's tentative response and the insistent bulge of Kay's unborn child pressing between them.

A torrent of feelings for Kay rushed up from within—sexual feelings, feelings of protectiveness, awe, and gratitude—mingled with the vitality and power of Kay's being. The bulge between them would be their meeting point, their common purpose, their destiny together. She knew again that somehow this was all ordained, woven inextricably into the fabric of the universe.

"When do I begin? With the herbs, I mean?"

"Today. Right now if you can."

"Of course. Where do I go?"

"I'll take you now. But don't you think you should dress first?"

Aria realized she was wearing only the thin robe she put on when she awoke, and laughed. "Give me a minute."

An hour later she had given various samples—blood and scrapings from inside her mouth—and had completed a full physical examination by one of the two doctors she had met since arriving. The doctor told her the tests would be ready in the morning.

Aria slept very little that night, and the next morning the doctor showed her two fabric pouches, one green, the other yellow.

"Make a tea with a spoonful of the herbs in this one," she told her, holding out the green pouch. "Drink it after you wake up, midday, and before you go to sleep." She opened the mouth of the yellow pouch, revealing a fragrant powdery substance.

"This one is different," the doctor said, and proceeded to show Aria how to mix it with water into thin paste. "This you must put . . ." she stopped, searching for the English word and failing to find it. She pointed at her lips, and then at her crotch. "Inside, not deep, just here," and she ran her pudgy finger over the inside of her lips to illustrate. Aria understood. "It burns some, but only small. Okay?"

Aria nodded.

"At night," the woman continued, "before sleep. Yes?"

"How long before we know it works?"

"Oh not long," the doctor said. "Sometimes real fast. Any change, come back. Okay?"

The next few days, Aria worked with Bantwalla in the mornings and spent the afternoons with Kay, whose work consisted mostly of scheduling the community's myriad activities, including shipments to the surface and work schedules. During this time, she discovered Kay's remarkable ability to remember every face and detail without the help of notes. During their forays into the far reaches of the tunnels, Kay greeted each person they came into contact with by name, dispensing to and collecting information from all.

They shared evening meals, discussing the history of many of The People, their skills and concerns, the plans for expanding their distribution and establishing new contacts on the surface. On occasion, Parker joined them, and at these times, Aria felt an unsettling combination of awkwardness and elation. On reflection, she wondered if she was attracted to both on so many levels that it confused her, or whether the herbs were making her unbalanced.

During Kopquahe, she again sat between the two. The poultice had irritated her labia to the point of serious discomfort, but despite that, within the first few minutes she was again transported to such heights of consciousness that she scarcely noticed.

On the fourth day, she was back at the infirmary, constipated, cranky, and worried. The doctor examined her thoroughly, told her to double the amount of tea, and sent her away again. Three days later, she had missed her period and her breasts were sore.

She returned to the doctor, feeling wary and scared, unsure she could trust the physician's skills or knowledge anymore. She had never been sick a day in her life, and now she was feeling exhausted, nauseated, and bloated. But when she related all this to the doctor, she looked at Aria with a twinkle in her eye and said, "It is working."

Instantly, Aria's fears vanished, and she felt better than she imagined possible. That evening, she grasped Kay's hands over dinner as she told her the news.

Kay sat for a long time saying nothing. "Then it will be," she said finally. "We will bring forth a new being. Together."

Chapter 40

"There's no doubt then?" Mother Gretel's gaze was steady and cold beneath thick eyebrows. One of these was arched ever so slightly, menacing despite its subtlety. Just to the right behind Mother Gretel, Barena Colter bore an expression only slightly softer than her superior's.

The woman who stood at attention before Mother Gretel's massive desk, her face a stiff mask of resolve, cleared her throat and spoke in the measured pace and even tones of someone who knew that with every word her life hung in the balance.

"I can't characterize the situation with that degree of assurance, Mother. We are certain of this: there is a community in Dar es Salaam that may have evolved apart from the seedling community the Nestercines began two years ago in Mombassa. The Nestercines don't know how it might have begun, or where the people came from. At least part of it is underground.

"We've located some of their solar collectors, and we believe we've located a portal. Mother Avalon believes that Potemkin, and possibly the assassin, are there. Other than this intuition of hers, we cannot say with any degree of . . ."

"Yes, yes," Mother Gretel hissed impatiently, her stubby finger slicing through the woman's sentence. Her voice was thick with sarcasm. "And had your plan worked, Avalon would be dead now, and we would not have this opportunity at all. May we presume you have a better plan now?"

The woman waited before answering, swallowing to

force down the bile creeping up the back of her throat. To be in this position was the most distasteful experience she could remember. Then, evenly, she said, "The Nestercines have recruited ten of the members of their Mombassa colony for this mission. Since you so graciously have released me from confinement"—she tried to make this ring with a gratitude that she nearly felt—"I will travel there with Mother Avalon and train with them for a moon. They are said to be quite advanced, though we have only her word on the extent of their abilities. Mother Avalon believes they are at the very least capable of protecting us if we gain access to the community. Once we are in, Mother Avalon will attempt the negotiation."

Mother Gretel turned to look at Barena Colter, the circled braids atop her head haloing in the light overhead. "Is Avalon going to give us any more trouble about this?"

Colter shook her head. "She's ready to do what's necessary. At core, she's committed to the Whole Body. I think she always has been. Had our predecessors shown a little more flexibility, we might never have been in the dark about these developments. So, now that we have given the Nestercines the opportunity to participate as insiders, the purity of their ideals makes them formidable allies. None of the other councils ever opened such a door to them, and it's clear we made a mistake by not reaching out to them before."

"This purity"—Mother Gretel spat the word—"could as quickly turn against us."

"I don't believe so, Mother. Her order has nurtured this idea of carrying humanity across a new threshold for nearly a century now. This in the face of numerous attempts to destroy their work, even the elimination of a number in their order. The fact that these kinds of periodic pogroms have

J. D. Townsend

never been carried out by the North American Council is perhaps our greatest reason for this new development."

"We never took them seriously enough," Mother Gretel said, sounding as if she both regretted and resented the idea.

"Perhaps," Colter replied, "but now we'll reap the rewards of our own benign indifference. It's not the first irony in history."

"Mmmm." Mother Gretel turned back to the woman still standing stiffly before her, fixing her with a baleful stare. "Do we need to remind you again that the only reason you're still breathing is because you showed enough intelligence to come forward when you did?"

"No, Mother," the woman answered quietly.

"This little clandestine activity on your part might yet prove quite damaging. I have my doubts about this plan and about giving you the opportunity to redeem yourself. Were it not for Colter's speaking on your behalf, you would not now be standing here."

The woman knew this was the moment in which she should acknowledge Colter's intervention, but she couldn't bring herself to look at the aide, much less bow in her direction. "Yes, Mother," she said, and looked at the floor.

"I will say this only once," Mother Gretel said, her authority evident in her eyes. "If this negotiation doesn't work, you will not fail in your contingency orders. There will be no second chance for you. It will be your last failure. Do you understand?"

Her mouth gone dry, the woman nodded silently.

"Say it!" Mother Gretel's voice clapped like thunder.

"Yes, Mother," the woman said immediately, her voice cracking. "I understand."

Mother Avalon glowered, the words hanging in the air

362

like poison gas. When she spoke again, her tone was again businesslike. "Are you certain Avalon is ignorant of the contingency plan?"

The contingency plan. What nonsense, the woman thought. It was a euphemism typical of Mother Gretel. The previous afternoon in this very office, Colter had revealed this plan. "If indeed Potemkin and the assassin are there," the aide had said, "and if they will not agree to return and put their talents in the service of the Whole Body, specifically through the North American Council, they must die. Mother Gretel is very clear about this. This sort of rebellion will not be permitted. It would set a very bad precedent."

Then Colter had laid a tiny weapon on the table next to her and six black objects as small as sunflower seeds. "This will happen by your hand, and yours alone. No one else must know of your instructions, especially not Avalon. Her attachment to this Potemkin is too strong to allow it. She believes in him, even more than these other . . . people . . . the Nestercines have brought into this world."

Pointing to the small black objects, she said, "If you gain access, you're to drop these along the way into this underground place. This," she said, picking up the weapon, "will activate a signal if it is fired, and these," she placed the seedlike objects in her palm, "will emit a squeal that you can follow even in the dark. They are the proverbial breadcrumbs that may provide you your only means of escape. Understood?"

The woman nodded and picked up the objects. Colter had stood then and begun pacing, her hands behind her back. "I'm not convinced of these peoples' usefulness to the Whole Body, but we have seen some of Avalon's people demonstrate some disturbing skills. If what Avalon says about them is true, they may be able to read your intentions. What will you do in such a case?"

The woman had confidence in her own skills. She had been trained by a Nestercine, had she not? More than once she had been able to put the fear of annihilation into readers who had tried to penetrate her defenses.

"I'll do what's necessary to carry out the instructions," she answered flatly. To kill Potemkin—and the assassin if she were there—would be dangerous, maybe even suicidal. No one had the slightest idea how many people they would be up against. No one knew what weapons they would be facing, or even the environment they would be in. She had a hard time believing that even Potemkin or K-1754 was capable of the feats that Avalon had ascribed to this "new breed," as Avalon had once called them. But it seemed possible that if it came to this, she could pull off the assassination without being discovered. She could shield her thoughts from others. And Avalon was so enamored of her charges that she probably would never suspect Mother Gretel might have a different sense of their value.

Desta Mardrid stood a little straighter and looked at the space above Mother Gretel's face, avoiding the gray eyes. "Avalon is so confident of her powers of persuasion over the athlete that I doubt she's even considered the chance of failure."

"You've made miscalculations before," Mother Gretel said.

Mardrid remained silent, her discomfort slowly giving way to resolve. One day, she vowed inwardly, Mother Gretel would regret this humiliation.

"You'll leave tonight then," Mother Gretel said.

Colter stood and put a map on the desk. "Tomorrow

morning they'll rendezvous here in Mombassa with the contingent from the Nestercine compound." Colter pointed to a spot near the edge of the map. "They'll train together for six weeks, review plans and so on, and then travel to Dar es Salaam." Her finger came to rest on the opposite side of the African continent.

"There are ten of these people?" Mother Gretel asked.

"Twelve, including Avalon and her," Colter replied, jerking her head offhandedly in Mardrid's direction. Had Colter looked up at that moment, she would have seen the look of contempt that passed over Mardrid's face at this off-handed, disrespectful gesture. Colter too would pay dearly for this, she vowed.

"Then let it be so." Mother Gretel waved her hand dismissively. "Dare we hope for some decent judgment this time?" she said, her tone equal parts condescension and challenge.

Mardrid knew it was meant to signal that all would be forgiven in the end, if she acted wisely. She nodded, set her jaw, and bowed with as much show of humility as she could muster. As she turned to leave the chambers, she thought, You will see, you fat sow, what kind of judgments I will make when this is done.

When the door closed behind Mardrid, Mother Gretel turned to her aide. "Is the backup plan in place?"

"Yes, Mother," Colter said. "The strike force will arrive in Dar es Salaam the day before Mardrid and Avalon. If the weapon I gave her is fired, it'll signal them through a half-dozen transponders she's been instructed to drop on her way in. It's the only way a signal can get to the surface. These tunnels they've dug apparently are quite deep."

"She knows nothing of this?"

"No. She thinks the transponders will help her escape."

365

Mother Gretel nodded. "Any trouble from the East African Council allowing this strike force in?"

"They think it's a geoscience delegation coming to do research. If this comes down to a worst-case scenario, I think they'll accept that it was in their best interest to root out this community before it became a threat to their sovereignty. It may take some diplomacy, but if we have to act, we will posit it as a favor—'Our intelligence found the matter too sensitive and dangerous to reveal,' sort of thing."

"Our intelligence," Mother Gretel said. "If we had any we would have known about these people long ago. I still can't believe I didn't see what Desta was doing right under my nose. I don't really know what to do with her after this is all over."

Colter picked up the map from Mother Gretel's desk and walked to the door of the office. "If things don't go according to Avalon's vision, we probably won't have to worry about that, Mother."

Chapter 41

"To the new world, and new life," Aria said, raising her glass.

Kay and Parker echoed the toast before all three drank deeply of the sweet nectar Kay had poured from a graceful decanter. Aria had no idea what the drink was. At first it tasted vaguely like apricots, but thin and smooth, and as it lingered on the tongue, changed to a darker flavor. Aria thought it might be the most delicious thing she'd ever had.

"Thank you for telling everyone about my nursing the baby tonight," Aria said. "It made me feel . . . like I belong here." They had just returned from dinner in the community dining hall, and Aria was still feeling the warmth of the gathering, the congratulatory hugs. Someone had baked a cake for the occasion and Parker had produced a curved knife with designs carved on its blade and a lion's head on the handle, and made an elaborate show of slicing the first piece. Bantwalla had given her a beautiful caftan. "For the streets," she had said, and winked.

"Many people told me afterward that they were pleased," Kay said. "You've made friends easily, Aria. It's good."

"Bantwalla is my favorite. She's been so wonderful. And besides, I now know more about the life cycle of squash than I ever dreamed possible."

They laughed, and Aria felt a little giddy. She was still awkward around these two, even though she had spent much time with them, especially Kay, over the last few weeks. When they were all together and alone like this, there was electricity in the air, something that quickened in her, made her feel both like a child and a woman.

She fidgeted in her chair, and felt her breasts straining at her blouse. They had grown remarkably since she had begun taking the herbs, and two nights before, she had cried for joy when she had noticed they had leaked on her dress. The next morning the doctor had told her that she would need to begin extracting the milk with a breast pump so that her body would grow used to producing it. She could barely believe how readily her body had changed.

Something else, too. As her breasts grew heavier, she began having more thoughts about sex, about how it would feel if her nipples, which had become highly sensitive, were to rub against the wiry hair on a man's chest, or how someone's hands would feel caressing them. The atmosphere in the community was so unlike anything she had experienced anywhere else, intimate and rich, so . . . juicy. Africans touched each other often during conversation, something Aria was wholly unused to, but enjoyed immensely. Combined with the many other sensations she had here, thoughts of sex were almost always present.

She glanced at the bed just steps beyond where Parker and Kay sat, and quickly looked away.

"Have you found a man . . . or a woman . . . you are interested in yet?" Kay asked.

"Well, I . . . no, not really. It's been a long time since I was with anyone. And I'm a little unsure, you know, what the . . . traditions here are about this sort of thing. I mean, I wouldn't want to offend anyone by being too . . . forward." She realized she sounded like a fumbling teenage girl, but couldn't help it.

Kay cast a sidelong glance at Parker. He raised his eyes

to look at her momentarily, and something invisible passed between them.

Kay set her glass aside and moved closer to Aria, taking her hand. "We know your feelings, Aria. They're fine. People here do pair up, like Parker and me, but The People haven't fallen back into some rigid morality about such things. The things we feel, we express. As long as there is no hurtfulness in it, there can only be healing and love to come from such expression."

Aria felt her hand tingle beneath Kay's grasp, but other parts of her were growing warm as well. "I wasn't sure what the protocol . . ." She stopped and looked into Kay's eyes. "That's not it. I suppose I ought to just say it. I can't seem to hide anything from you anyway. The truth is, I find myself . . . thinking about you and Parker. A lot."

She looked at Parker, who looked back with twinkling eyes.

"When I'm close to both of you like this, I get . . . stirred up, you know?" She drew a deep breath. "In fact, I've never had feelings this strong before."

Her heart raced as she spoke, and part of her was appalled by what was coming out of her mouth, but she couldn't stop. "I would never intrude upon your relationship, but I have to be honest and tell you that I sometimes think about being with you . . . together, you know?" Now she really felt like a tongue-tied and hormone-addled adolescent.

Parker had stood in the middle of this last sentence, set his glass on the table, picked up the chair he had been sitting on, and moved it closer. To Aria, it was as though a mountain—no, a simmering volcano—was moving toward her. A drop of sweat ran between her breasts and she realized that she was breathing rapidly. Underneath the long skirt she wore, her legs were crossed and the bottom leg began bouncing up and down in involuntary spasm. Parker sat down on her other side, opposite Kay. Aria was almost afraid to acknowledge what she thought might be happening.

Kay rested a hand on Aria's trembling legs. "Dear Aria, it's all right."

Instantly Aria's leg stopped its little dance, and she felt like crying, though from joy or grief she couldn't tell.

Kay released her hand and with a smile, lightly brushed Aria's hair away from her eyes, staring into them with a soft intensity. She pressed her palm against Aria's cheek and turned to look at Parker, who took up Kay's other hand in his. Aria thought the contrast between Kay's slender white fingers and Parker's darker round and calloused ones unspeakably beautiful. She could nearly taste the delicious energy running between them.

Parker's hand now came to rest on Aria's thigh, and he drew his face near Kay's. Slowly their mouths sought each other out, touching tenderly, lips moistening one another. Aria watched and swallowed involuntarily. A rush of heat came between her legs and she thought that unless she uncrossed them, she might explode. Her legs fell open as Kay and Parker's tongues sought each other, and Parker's hand slipped to the inside of her thigh. It felt hot enough to burn her through the skirt.

Tentatively, wary of the intensity of this naked desire she was feeling, Aria raised her free hand and lightly touched Parker's hair, fascinated by the way that curled at the ends since it had grown longer.

A moment later, Kay and Parker broke off their kiss and Kay, her hand still caressing Aria's cheek, turned Aria's face toward Parker, who met her gaze. His eyes showed only black, like deep pools, and Aria fell into them, her heart beating in her throat, her senses crackling and clear. As Parker's face inched toward hers, Aria felt Kay's hand slide beneath her dress and up her left thigh, the fingertips coming lightly to rest on her pubic hair. Everything tingled within her, and she felt herself grow wet. Parker's lips descended slowly toward hers, and suddenly Aria felt hands moving over her entire body, more hands than was possible, lightly caressing and exploring. Her skin cried out silently at the sensation, pressing back against their touch.

She groaned as Parker's mouth came the last few inches to meet with hers, her flesh seeming to turn inside out, exposing raw nerve endings to cool air and hot breath. Her fingers clutched at a handful of Parker's hair, pulling his face into hers, her mouth hungry, desperate for his.

She tasted his mouth, smelled the musky odor of his skin and breath. Her body stiffened and quivered, sliding out of control. Then Parker's tongue was in her mouth and his large hand closed on her breast. Kay's fingers stroked her softly. A dam burst inside her. Juices erupted from her in violent contractions, flooding her thighs and buttocks. She cried out against the hardness of Parker's mouth, clutched at his hair, coming again and again. Milk spurted from her swollen nipples, darkening the front of her dress. Her toes curled so hard she thought they might break. She heard a deep-throated growl, like some animal eating its felled prey, and realized that it was her own voice, summoned from eons ago, deep in her genes.

She trembled, floating in a warm, viscous current, her nerves singing for joy. Through this haze she felt strong hands lift her, lie her on her back. She thought she felt her dress being unbuttoned, and then like she was a kitten being bathed by its mother's warm tongue. She drifted dreamily between inner and outer worlds, unable to distinguish between imagination and physical sensation. Was it a warm wet mouth closing gently around a nipple, or immersion in the soft folds of pink flowers? Was it lips gently brushing her fluttering eyelids, or breezes spiced with soft rain? A flash of heat rising from between her legs and shooting from the crown of her head, or was she witnessing of a supernova as expanded outward at the speed of light but within such a great expanse that there appeared to be no movement at all?

Eventually she felt the weight of some soft fabric settling on to her, and heard Kay's soft voice in her ear. "Sleep now. It's enough for the first night."

When she awoke, she was alone. For a moment, she had no thought at all, only the pleasant sensation that she had been floating without a care on a vast sea. Then she remembered Kay and Parker, their lips meeting, Parker's mouth, the feel of their hands on her, in her.

And with a rush, it began again. As she arched her back with the first spasm, the soft blanket raked across her nipples, sending spikes of pleasure deep into her body. She cried out and covered a nipple with one hand, her genitals with the other, as if she might cap the explosion. Her touch only served to heighten the experience, and she gasped.

When finally it subsided, Aria rolled her head back and forth against the pillow, her hair a tangle and a broad smile on her face.

"Oh . . . my . . . goddess!" she said to the empty room. Her sultry voice echoed back to her from the walls, and she relaxed, relishing the deep satisfaction she heard in it. She moaned aloud just to hear herself.

Her smile remained even as she later sat up and swung

her feet onto the cold floor. She was still in Kay and Parker's room. Her clothes hung over the back of one of the chairs. She stood, a current running from her feet through up through her head, feeling the weight of her breasts as they swayed with each careful step.

The clothes had been washed, she discovered, and she held them to her face and breathed in their fresh smell. She wanted to scream for joy, just open her mouth and watch her heart fly out of her throat up through the ceiling and the earth above her head and into the bright sunlight and out into the velvet blackness of space . . . and that the universe would welcome the sound of her rich new voice.

Chapter 42

"We should be going in with overwhelming physical force, big men with weapons, machines," Mardrid whispered. It was an argument she had made and lost before.

"You have no idea what we're dealing with here," Mother Avalon said. Mardrid strained to hear her reply above the hiss of the pressurizing air in the cabin of the transport. The lights were dim, and others around either them slept or were wearing headphones. Nonetheless, it was wise to be discreet.

Avalon's condescending tone rankled her. "I am not without experience in the subtle realms."

Mother Avalon gave her the kind of smile she might have given a child. "Very few people have experienced what the Tressaline progeny are capable of. I'm not implying that you're not good at what you do, Desta, or that you have no resources." She looked Mardrid straight in the eye. "I *am* aware of your training and background."

It caught Mardrid off guard. The tutoring she had received from the old renegade Nestercine sister years ago had been a secret, she thought. How did Avalon find out? Or did she simply intuit the information? This damn woman was wilier than she had first thought. Full of surprises.

"They have demonstrated abilities ranging from perfect recall to telekinesis and healing, even foreknowledge of events," Mother Avalon continued. "Some are becoming brilliant inventors. Some have superior physical attributes, like Parker and K-1754." She looked away, into the inky atmosphere outside the window and was silent. Then she examined the back of her hand idly, and said, "I suspect that Parker has developed beyond even the best of our other seeds. Did you know that he's able to render someone senseless in a matter of seconds?" She looked now at Mardrid and arched her eyebrows. "He even revealed to me that when he was just a boy, he caused a Califas brother's death simply by willing it."

Mardrid didn't really believe this, especially the latter, but kept her skepticism to herself. Whatever Parker thought had happened was probably coincidence inflated by romantic notions of guilt. Avalon had her own romantic notions, as well. The way she lit up whenever she talked about Parker or the others reminded Mardrid of the superior who oversaw her own education and upbringing at Cartagena. There was always a sort of fierce and unreasoning pride about that woman, as if she had birthed her charges herself.

"So you really think we're going to just be able to gain access to this place using only these people's mental talents?"

Avalon gave her a weary look. "First of all, these are not just mental talents. They go far beyond that. Second, the Mombassa team is only a fail-safe for us. Any hint of hostility could work counter to our goals. It could even be our undoing. As yet, you don't fully understand the power of emotion or will, and how these could be turned against us. The real tool, the best we have, is my relationship with Parker. If he knows I have come, I'm certain we, or at least I, will be permitted to see him."

"If he's there." Mardrid still couldn't believe that they had mounted such an elaborate and costly mission based almost solely on this woman's powers of persuasion.

"He's there," Avalon said, the conviction ringing in her voice. "It's where he would have to be. He's too famous to be living anywhere else, and he would have been seen leaving Dar es Salaam otherwise. When he was rejected by my sisters—the night you tried to have us killed—no one suspected the existence of another colony. Now it appears certain there is one, though it's probably small." She tucked the pillow behind her head and folded her hands in her lap. "He's there. I can feel him. And most likely he occupies an important position."

Mardrid fell silent. Avalon's reference to her attempt to have Avalon and Potemkin assassinated was clearly meant to be a knife in her ribs. Mardrid didn't need to be reminded of her failure. Avalon seemed to harbor remarkably little hostility toward her for this. Probably, Mardrid realized with some envy, it was because that for Avalon this was the opportunity of a lifetime. Not only was her life spared, now she was spearheading a potential partnership between the North American Council and her sisterhood. This mission was the first test of that partnership. For generations, the Nestercines had been working outside the establishment to seed the world with its adopted progeny from the Tressaline Colony. If Avalon were successful in recruiting Potemkin, it would likely cement her place in history. At the very least, her sisters would celebrate her for many years after her death. Reason enough, Mardrid decided, for Avalon to focus on something other than revenge.

On the other hand, she thought bitterly, all I'm likely to get out of it is a chance to remain alive and somewhere in council circles. It was enough. The humiliations heaped upon her by Mother Gretel and Colter made her want more than ever to find her way into a position where she could eventually make them pay.

She cast a sidelong glance at the Nestercine. The diminutive woman had closed her eyes and appeared to be sleeping. Just as well, Mardrid thought. She was tired of the conversation. She dreaded the time they would be spending together, having to subject herself to the woman's attitude of superiority as they prepared to mount the attack.

Yes, attack, she argued inwardly. Despite the Nestercine's convictions, this was only a diplomatic mission if it succeeded on Avalon's terms. Still, her comment about encountering hostility bothered Mardrid. It would be a challenge to mask her emotions, her secret orders to kill Potemkin if he wouldn't agree to join forces with the North American Council. If even a portion of what Avalon said about these Tressaline people and their perceptions were true, she would have to be sharp.

Mardrid distrusted the old woman, and knew Avalon had plenty of reason to distrust her. But all that was irrelevant now, wasn't it? She smiled wryly at the irony of it. In a sense, they both were outlaws now, apprehended in disparate conspiracies and thrown together to work out their salvation. This mission was Mardrid's penance for having reached too far too soon, for wanting too much.

She still wanted it. But when the assassin disappeared, and when her subsequent attempts to reach her contact at the CAO were met with suspicion, the sinking sensation in her stomach told her she had only one avenue left open to her, one hope of surviving.

It was still galling, remembering how she'd been forced to go to Mother Gretel and admit that she'd violated policy by ordering the assassinations of Parker and Avalon. She was contrite of course, presenting it as a plan to cut short a suspected conspiracy, one for which Mother Gretel was the assumed target.

If she had waited even another hour, things may have gone much worse. When Colter walked in to report on Mardrid's violation of the separation between the council and the CAO, the confession was already on the table. Mardrid still shuddered slightly at Mother Gretel's cold anger, the way she looked at her as she dialed the Census Accounting Office that afternoon.

And Mardrid was amazed how for the first time since it was formed fifteen years ago, the CAO had rescinded an order for termination. Just like that. The action was not without repercussions, of course—a dozen meetings between high-ranking Council and Ministry members, new security and fail-safe procedures instituted, endless accusations and explanations. But in the end, Mardrid had not been remanded to a tribunal. Confined mostly to her quarters for more than six months, relieved of all her responsibilities, she was repeatedly summoned for humiliating interviews.

That had been hell, yes, but she was still alive and still had the chance to make her way back into the council's good graces. If she could succeed at this assignment.

And so she must endure this new nightmare, subjugating herself to someone whom she failed to have assassinated. There was no getting around it now. They were odd confederates in a tangled mission, and Avalon seemingly more gracefully accepting of their pairing than Mardrid. So be it.

Mardrid leaned her head back against the seat and closed her eyes, focusing on the task at hand. One step at a time. First, they must gain access to this rogue underground colony, and that meant fitting in with this team of the Nestercines' specimens. She could only guess at what training they would undergo at Avalon's direction, or the methods they would employ if they were denied access to the community.

They knew pitifully little about what they might encounter. Satellites had provided minimal intelligence—infrared tracings of anomalies in underground heat that hinted at the direction of some tunnels, but not how extensive they might be, the location of solar collectors in numerous places in and around Dar es Salaam. Since their mission was a secret, they could not call on the East African Council for technical or logistical support, although they did manage to convince them that this twelve-member team would be in Dar es Salaam in order to confirm new satellite findings of water tables.

Since water had long since been more precious than oil or minerals in Africa, key council members promised not to interfere with the team when they arrived. They actually seemed to welcome the intrusion, happy with sharing in whatever profits might come to them from the tapping of new resources.

As far as ground surveillance, practically all anyone had been able to ascertain was that more people entered the portal than left it, and that several different people were doing the admitting. There were no signs of mechanical defense, no detection devices or apparent weaponry. Hard to fathom.

And what if they did find Potemkin? Mardrid thought about the bond between the athlete and Avalon, evident whenever Avalon spoke of him. What if the negotiation failed and Mardrid was forced to kill him? Would Avalon then turn her minions on Mardrid and kill her, or reduce her to some drooling idiot? A chilling thought, but then the risk was a calculated one. She doubted that Avalon would allow her anger or feelings of revenge to jeopardize such a grand project. After all, Avalon still had the others to consider. Parker—and the assassin if she was there too—were only two of at least several hundred of these people whom the Nestercines had managed to bring into the world.

Mardrid almost hoped Parker would refuse. If he simply agreed to return with them, then she would have lost the opportunity to dramatically prove her willingness to rectify her mistakes by killing him.

Her thoughts were interrupted by a recorded voice announcing their imminent arrival at the Mombassa Airport. As Mother Avalon stirred next to her and reached under her seat for her carry-on bag, Mardrid let her right hand fall to her thigh. She fingered the seam, felt the hard shape of the weapon nestled securely there. It comforted her a little, emitting a small sense of power and control amid the sea of unknowables she faced.

If things went terribly wrong, at least she had one solid means of defense, or escape.

Chapter 43

"Excited, yes?" M drummed his wrinkled fingers on the table.

"About what?" Aria finished her breakfast and feigned disinterest in his question.

M's eyebrows lifted in surprise, then his eyes crinkled and his teeth shone with a big smile. "Ah, you almost fool M. You try to make me think you go above is no big deal, eh? Pretty good act, you."

It was Aria's turn to smile. "Actor," she corrected him. "Yes, M, I am excited. Just teasing you."

"Teasing?"

"Playing. A joke. But . . ." She hesitated, not knowing how to express her complicated feelings about the excursion to the surface she and Bantwalla planned to take in just two nights.

"But what? You take first vacation on top, smell air up there, feel wind. It is good, no?"

"Sure, it's good," Aria said. "I'm a little nervous about it, I guess. I've been here for many weeks now, and I'm comfortable with the way things are. Going back up, you know, it brings up feelings." She moved her upturned palm in an upward motion from her stomach to her heart in illustration, although it was probably unnecessary. M had a remarkable ability to understand and communicate despite his weak English. Nonetheless, Aria persisted in the sort of improvised sign language that characterized their interactions since Kay had introduced them.

"This is the man who brought Parker and me to The People," Kay had said. "He is our savior . . . and a very good cab driver, too." M had given Aria a little bow, looking rather sheepish over Kay's praise. Aria had taken an instant liking to him.

"I've heard about him already," Aria had said. "A beautiful woman up there"—she pointed upwards, thinking of Njeri, the Guardian—"thinks you're more than just a good cab driver."

Aria thought had M's skin been just a shade lighter, his cheeks would have blushed bright pink. Since then, she and M had sat together during many meals, and Aria often saw him at Njeri's side during Kopquahe. She was touched by M's obvious ardor toward the Guardian, and hoped their separate duties didn't take too much time away from their relationship.

"Did you spend a lot of time down here before going back?" she asked him.

He shook his head. "M had much work to do, and could do more help The People on top. Many friends, many helps. No time to stay here long time."

Aria puzzled over his response. "You mean you have contacts . . . uh, friends . . . who can provide things?"

M nodded vigorously. "Many friends. Get tools, some foods, chemicals, help build things. You know?"

Aria understood. M apparently had a knack for making connections, securing things that no one else could get, getting things done under the noses of the authorities. He must be a very valuable emissary to the surface.

"Well, M, I'm just so new here that I'm a little afraid of what I might feel . . . outside, I mean. And I am afraid of someone recognizing me, or reporting me. That would be very bad."

M gave her a reassuring smile. "No problem. You going at nighttime, right? Dark, no one sees Aria. You wear . . ." He made a circle around his head.

"A hood, yes. Bantwalla gave me a caftan."

"But," he said, and his face became mock serious, "you make too much light."

"Light?"

He patted her cheeks. "Light! Like the moon! Need clouds!" He jumped up just as Aria understood that he meant that her white skin stood out like the moon in the night. "Wait! M is right back!"

And he was off across the dining hall and out the door. Aria smiled after him. He was a dear man, and she had no idea what he was up to, but she always felt happy in his presence. In fact, she almost always felt happy nowadays. Except for the "darklings," her private word for the occasional feelings of dread that descended on her for seemingly no reason. When they first began, Aria had tried to dismiss them as some sort of inner thermostat that was attempting to balance her frequent feelings of ecstasy. After all, her life had changed so suddenly and so radically after she found Kay that it seemed natural that she should experience some mood swings.

Lately, though, the darklings were coming more frequently. Yesterday it had occurred to her that she might be trying to rationalize away some precognition, or bury something that was scratching its way to the surface of her consciousness. She knew she probably should spend some time with these feelings when they came, let herself sink into them and see what information they might bring, but when they came, she inevitably found some way to distract herself.

Looking over the mostly empty dining hall, the truth

struck her: she didn't want to think about what the darklings might have in store for her. She was not interested in what she suspected was their pessimism. The present was filled with feelings of love and joy and purposefulness. Why couldn't the future be even better? Had the universe a rule that every good thing must be balanced by bad?

Everything she had experienced since coming here indicated that old rules were out the window. Things were changing. The Tressaline progeny were ushering in a different kind of world, as were she and M, though maybe not as directly or powerfully. The ancient longings of human beings, the dreams of a Golden Age, a paradise, seemed closer to becoming a reality than ever, Aria thought. Such enduring visions must be rooted in the deep soil of our genes, like a blueprint for evolution. Why not trust in that? Why not continue to ignore the darklings, which might just as easily be memories of past failures, things to discard like the concepts about human capabilities that were falling away daily in this marvelous community?

M reappeared in the dining hall's doorway, his smile radiant. He held something in his right hand. He practically pranced over to where Aria waited, sat down and opened the lid on what Aria now saw was a jar of a dark liquid.

"What's this?"

M grabbed her right hand, dipped his fingers into the liquid, and smeared the back of her hand with it. Her skin now appeared just a shade lighter than M's.

"Hey," Aria said, laughing. "What's the idea?"

"Clouds!" He playfully wiped the remainder on her cheek. "No moon! Now you go upstairs with no problem."

She laughed and gave him a little punch on the arm. He really was a delight, and as usual, before his smile the darklings fled like shadows from the sun.

* * * * *

Kay was alone when it happened, walking through the narrow hallway to her quarters. A few minutes before she had been in a meeting with a dozen community members, discussing the planned opening of a new surface distribution channel. At the end of the meeting, two of the women had lingered to chat about her pregnancy, asking excitedly about Kay's expected date of delivery and how she felt. Kay had told them she felt fine, which was almost true.

Her stomach always felt like it might explode, and she was often tired, tired in a deep way that she never experienced before pregnancy. And every now and then when the baby growing inside her kicked, it hurt. A lot.

But never like this. This felt like something had grabbed hold of the tissues in her abdomen and twisted them until they ripped free, a hot, searing pain that stopped her in her tracks. Kay cried out, her voice echoing in the empty corridor, and leaned against the cool wall to keep from crumpling to the floor.

Her forehead broke out in beads of perspiration, and she held her hands beneath her belly, supporting it and breathing in short gasps. Her breath smelled sour. She tried to focus her mind and direct the energy into her arms and hands, and into the source of the pain.

Eventually it worked, the pain subsiding long enough for her to walk the final hundred feet to the entrance of their quarters. And it taught her something about herself that she had never known: when the pain was at its worst and carried on its back the black beast of fear, it was not for herself that she felt concern. It was for the child she carried.

She had known it was a boy from the moment of conception, and the doctors had later confirmed it. There were moments when she thought she knew him, that she could already feel the force of his character, the depth of his power. Although she could not envision his features, she could feel the shape of his soul. The child was like Parker, of course, who was now stepping into leadership with such mighty strides that even Kay was sometimes surprised. Parker was pulling The People together and forward as if they were all tethered to him and an invisible whip was cracking at his back. She could feel his willingness, his eagerness, to do this. She had come to think of this force as the spirit of fatherhood, something the world had not seen for many, many decades. And the child within her womb carried it.

But there was another whole layer of qualities she could sense, and Kay realized these were closer to how she thought of herself nowadays. Parker was masterful at spurring The People on to greater energy and completion of projects with his energies and speeches about reclaiming their place in the sun—something he talked increasingly about. Kay's leadership was quite different.

Kay's influence was like a thread that ran through the hearts of hundreds of community members, which with seemingly little effort she held tautly in her hand. Kay understood that it was because she had lived her life until coming to the community with such a deep sense of isolation and loneliness. And because death had been her only mission. Now that she carried life within her, she was supremely aware of what a gift it was.

There was richness in her daily interactions with the others in The People, as fertile as the loamy soil that produced the vegetables they sold on the surface. Kay's presence enhanced everyone she came into contact with. When she entered a room, faces lit up, and women would surround her, touching her hair, her stomach, sharing with her the news of their own lives. It was like they swam in a warm pool together, Kay turning this way and that, the others leaning in her direction, following her movements.

Her baby swam in these waters, too, and she sometimes felt his pull on her as she imagined others must feel in her presence.

Sitting now on the bed she and Parker shared, she reached out to Parker from that place within they had found the night they first made love in the hotel. "I need you," she said aloud, though the words were unnecessary. Parker would feel her call, and come immediately from wherever in the warren of caves he was at the moment. When he arrived, the two of them would do what was necessary to deal with the spikes of fire that lingered in her abdomen. The doctors will want to know about this, too, she thought, but that can wait. What she needed now was the reassurance that came when Parker was with her. Doctoring could not match the power of that healing, she thought.

She wondered if every pregnant woman felt this kind of pain, and the thought filled her with a new respect for mothers throughout the ages. No wonder childbearing was not something everyone chose to do nowadays. Then there was the birth process itself. That was still weeks away, but the thought made her go cold. Would it be even worse than this? The doctors had assured her that they knew of many ways to alleviate the pain of childbirth, but they weren't the ones who would be going through it.

Until today, Kay had been blithely confident about all of this. Now she felt in her body, in her aching organs and the dark places in the back of her mind, the thing that an assassin should never forget: despite all appearances of robustness and vitality, life is tenuous.

As she sat waiting for the sound of Parker's footfall beyond the entrance, a tear formed and fell from one eye, tracing a glistening trail down her pale cheek.

Chapter 44

Mardrid tried hard not to be obvious about her growing discomfort, but it was becoming clear that her ability to mask her intentions would be severely tried here. Even though the ten people with whom she and Avalon were now eating dinner only occasionally glanced at her, she could feel them probing her. From the moment two hours earlier when they had been introduced to the team by several of the Nestercine sisters who had met them at the airport, Mardrid was straining at the effort.

She chewed the tasteless food they had been served, and stole a glance at the two women directly across the long table from her. One had slightly lighter skin, but she couldn't quite distinguish one from the other. In fact, all of the six women seemed quite similar. They were roughly the same height and build, with prominent noses and dark eyes. A few had fuller lips, but Mardrid hadn't been able to link those with other facial characteristics to distinguish one from another. It hadn't helped matters that only Mother Avalon was introduced by name. The men were easier to distinguish, she thought. Two were quite large and well muscled, and one of these was white. The other two appeared fit, but probably had only been laborers rather than athletes before coming here.

She decided to name them all for herself, starting with the men. The big white one, she decided would be Floptop, for the way his blond hair fell over his forehead. The bigger black one she would call Rhesus, for the monkey he resembled that had once inhabited Africa's jungles. She could only see the profile of another, but could tell that his head was very round and his hair nappy and so short he nearly looked bald. Blackball, she decided. The last of the men spooned his food with his left hand. Lefty.

In furtive glances, she looked for something odd about the women across from her. One had a higher forehead like Mother Gretel's. Greta, she thought. It was close enough without dredging up negative feelings about her superior. The other had a tiny mole near her lip. She would become Spot.

Before she could finish the exercise, Mother Avalon, who was seated at the far end of the table, stood as if to speak. Eating ceased and everyone turned toward her.

"Thank you for volunteering to join me on this mission," she said. "As you have been told, it is a mission of peace. Our purpose is not to cause harm, but to build bridges. Something you've not been told, but probably have surmised by now. We believe some of these colonists, like you, originated at Tressaline, one or two for certain, perhaps all. We are simply not aware of what happened to some of the Tressaline lines. There has been too much upheaval since those times, and much information was lost. Likelihood is, however, that they are your family, your brothers and sisters."

She paused, taking the moment to look into each of the faces around the table. Her gaze skipped over Mardrid ever so briefly, making Mardrid even more aware of her role as an outsider.

"I have special knowledge of one of these, whose name is Parker Potemkin," Avalon continued. "We are friends. He is extremely gifted, and we wish him to be back with us in North America. In fact, we wish all of them to become an active part of the Whole Body."

Mardrid carefully stole a glance at the few faces she could see from her vantage at the table. They remained impassive, but she sensed a stirring in the air, as though the collective attention was stronger now.

"We are all at an important crossroad today," Avalon said, "one I never imagined I would see in my lifetime. Soon we will all likely be living in North America. We . . . you . . . will help usher in a new chapter of human history, one where gifts such as yours will no longer be seen as a threat, but will be yoked to the task of bringing in a new age of light, of intelligence and compassion and healing to the Whole Body. Your ancestors died in the service of this ideal, and many of my sisters. They would be most gratified to know this moment has come.

"Tomorrow morning we will begin our training. Essentially, our work is to become of one mind, one heart. We must present a unified field of acceptance and welcome. We must reach out to them with the purity of our intentions and our desire to heal the schisms of the past. I have prepared exercises to that end, but I remain open to your suggestions as we progress.

"At the same time, we must be prepared to protect ourselves if we are not welcomed, and I would not give you any illusions about how formidable such a challenge might be. Parker is a world champion athlete, and he didn't become so on physical prowess alone. If others there are anywhere near as gifted, we will be hard-pressed to find our way back here. If things don't go well, it is not inconceivable that we could lose our lives."

She let this sink in. "I believe in you, and I believe in the rightness of our mission. You, and these we will meet, are the hope of the future. I am willing to die if necessary to succeed at our task. And so I must ask: is any one of you not willing?"

She stood perfectly still waiting for a response. None came.

"Thank you," she said. "We have these six weeks together in which to prepare. Let us bring ourselves fully to the task, knowing that this is our moment to leave our mark on history. If we succeed, and succeed we must, we will have laid the foundation for your progeny to see a world so different than the present one that it will be as if the old one never existed."

Her words lingered in the air like the clear notes of a stirring musical passage, and then she extended her hands to the women on each side of her. Simultaneously the others at the table reached out and joined hands, closing their eyes. At the touch of those on either side, Mardrid broke a sweat. She felt it on her forehead and in her armpits and palms, and her stomach began quaking.

A war was going on inside of her, and she fought to maintain a single thought: I am part of you. She shouted it over and over in her mind over the ringing in her ears, keeping at bay the fear of exposure and the dark thoughts that threatened to overtake her. A wave of panic was building, and she wondered if she might lose her composure entirely.

She opened her eyes to try to ground herself in time and space. Across the table from her the woman she had moments before named Spot was staring into her face with an intense curiosity. Mardrid looked away just as she felt her now clammy hands released by those on either side.

"Goodnight, then," Avalon said. "We shall meet here in the morning and begin."

Chairs scraped on the floor and, greatly relieved,

Mardrid pushed back from the table, avoiding further eye contact.

The team began leaving the room for sleeping quarters, some in quiet conversation. Mardrid shuffled toward the door taking long, slow breaths and trying to calm her stomach. She recognized Spot over the heads of several others, and as the woman passed through the doorway, she turned and gave Mardrid the briefest of glances. It was long enough, however, for Mardrid to realize that she was more transparent than she ever thought possible.

And realize that she was losing her skepticism. These might truly be dangerous, special people.

Ten days into training, at the conclusion of what Mardrid considered a particularly intense session in which they had sat cross-legged on the floor concentrating on manifesting a ball of light in the center of their circle, Spot sat staring at her with her intense black eyes.

Mardrid was on speaking terms with several of the others—Lefty and Greta, in particular—but not this one. Spot had never ceased to look at her with suspicion.

Mardrid resisted the urge to look away, staring back defiantly. Her toes curled slightly with the effort. After a few moments, Spot turned and got Avalon's attention.

"She's incapable of holding the field," she said, her tone matter-of-fact, but with an angry edge. No one asked whom she was referring to. They knew. "She's a weak link, and she has some other agenda. Why have you allowed her to come?"

Mardrid blanched; this sucked at her pride, but even more it worried her. Had Spot uncovered her secret or just her defenses?

Avalon held the black woman's gaze, then cleared her

throat. "I'm afraid her presence is necessary. It's a concession to the North American Council. I'm sorry to have to impose such a condition on our first project together, but it was unavoidable."

She looked at Mardrid, whose knuckles showed white as she gripped her knees. "In the future, I think it is unlikely we will be subject to this kind of condition. What do you think, Desta?"

Mardrid's mind struggled between relief over not having been discovered and anger at being humiliated. She took a deep breath and let both feelings go with her exhalation. "When I make my report to Mother Gretel, it will be with a recommendation to that effect."

She looked at the faces around her, and swallowed. "I apologize for the burden my presence places on you. I will redouble my efforts to improve. Please be patient with me."

They sat silently for what seemed like a very long time. Slowly Mardrid felt the knot in her stomach begin to loosen, and she knew her words had been accepted.

"Well then," Avalon said at last, "shall we take our lunch? Let's meet back here at 13:00."

Mardrid struggled to her feet well after the others, and thought again how agile and vigorous everyone was. Everyone but her. She clenched her teeth and determined for the thousandth time to work harder at everything.

A week before the team was to make its approach, they flew into Dar es Salaam and under cover of night moved into a small, decrepit residence that someone had procured. Mardrid worried she was close to a breakdown. The strain of keeping her mental defenses up while trying to open to the subtle states of mind the team was working in had been excruciating. For days, her head had been throbbing and strange pains had been migrating from joints to organs and back again.

She had noticed other changes. Last week she had begun a period, a rather strong flow of blood. She detested periods anyway, finding them dirty and inconvenient, but this one had come two weeks early and still showed no signs of subsiding. It was like she had been rearranged, as if she was a stranger to her own body. The following morning she knew she couldn't face another day of this. After a paltry breakfast, she went to Avalon who was waiting in their meeting room for the rest of the team to arrive.

"I need a rest," Mardrid said. There was no need to elaborate on her symptoms. Her weak voice and trembling hand were testament enough to the way she felt.

Avalon looked at her long and hard. Mardrid saw both disapproval and concern in the narrowed eyes and downturned mouth, but she didn't care.

"Very well," Avalon said. "Take the morning and afternoon, but we'll expect you at dinner as usual."

Mardrid turned without a word and headed toward the door. She could feel Avalon's eyes on her back, and before she made it out the door, the Nestercine spoke again.

"You know, Desta, you don't have to come along. There is no need for us to report otherwise when we return home."

Mardrid stopped and turned to face her. "I will be fine when the moment comes. I've simply picked up a bug in this ugly place. I just need some additional rest."

Another long moment of silence passed as the two women stared at each other.

Finally, Mother Avalon said, "Suit yourself. However, the option remains open."

On the way back to the sleeping quarters, Mardrid began

to hyperventilate. By the time she got there, she was clenching and unclenching her fists. She paced between the cots, trying desperately to regain control of her body. Dark thoughts raced through her mind, including the suspicion that Avalon was working some sort of nefarious mental magic on her, trying to sabotage her chances for a successful mission.

She would be damned if the bitch would get the better of her. She grabbed a pillow and began screaming into it. When she became too hoarse to scream any more, she did calisthenics until she was drenched in sweat. Finally, exhausted, she lay down and slept fitfully.

When she awoke she felt somewhat better, but the thought of spending another week with these people pulled at her like a stone around her neck.

"I will *not* be defeated. I will *not* be defeated," she whispered over and over again through clenched teeth.

The day for their departure came. Despite all the preparation, Mardrid felt less ready for this confrontation than she had even ten days ago. Much of her confidence and determination had dissolved. The last few days of exercises had left her more often in a state of confusion than clarity.

Eventually, she thought, she might realize some benefits from all of this. Now, however, she'd rather be in hell.

They spent the morning in silence, and Mardrid wandered from room to room, seeking someplace to be alone. Always, though, she would pass through a doorway and several of the team members would be sitting there, their dark eyes boring into her. Late in the morning she found a corner and slid down into a crouch, resting her head on her knees.

At noon, Avalon called them together in the largest

room. "It's time," she said when they were gathered in a circle. "I want to thank you again for accompanying me. You are magnificent, and I'm honored we've had this time together. Now we shall see what lies in store for us."

She looked from face to face, lingering on each, a silent flow of energy passing from her. When she got to Mardrid, the aide found she could not return her gaze and looked instead at the floor.

A moment later, Avalon turned and opened the door, and they followed her into the intense daylight.

Chapter 45

They arrived in three small, nondescript vehicles, parking them on a potholed street a few blocks from the portal to the underground community. They carried nothing, walking briskly in groups of four in the brilliant sunshine, their faces impassive save for the glint of determination in the eyes. Mother Avalon's group led the way, her blue robe an echo of the pale sky. Mardrid's group trailed fifty feet behind. She was surrounded and mostly obscured by the much taller men in her group.

They encountered only a handful of people on the street—a woman hurrying from her home who glanced at them and continued to her vehicle as if she had much on her mind, a small group of supervised children on the other side of the street who stared wide-eyed at the knot of strangers in their neighborhood. Mardrid glimpsed a woman's face before it disappeared behind the curtain in a second-story window. As they neared the entrance to the home they knew to be a portal, Mardrid let her hands drop again to the seams on the pants she wore, feeling again the slender line of the weapon hidden there and the tiny discs she would drop. Her fingers trembled slightly. Her hands were damp, and not just with the heat of the day.

In one way, she was relieved to finally be here. She couldn't have taken more training. She felt stretched to the thinness of petropaper, and more fragile.

They halted in front of the dull white face of a home that was outwardly undistinguishable from the other small residences on the block. Nevertheless, it loomed ominous to Mardrid. Avalon turned, made galvanizing eye contact with each of the team members. Without a word, she climbed the three steps to the entrance and knocked. Instantly, Mardrid felt something happening to her body, almost like she was filling with air. She glanced at the faces of her teammates next to her on the walkway, but they gave no indication they felt it too. They simply stared ahead, their gazes locked on Avalon's back. She struggled to maintain her composure, feeling faint in the morning heat. From behind the door, she heard a woman's voice say something in Swahili. Mardrid eyed the entrance for some sign of a camera or even a peephole in the door, but saw none.

Avalon spoke in a steady voice to the closed door. "I am Mother Avalon of the Nestercine Sisterhood. I am here with some of your brothers and sisters. We come in peace, and wish only to speak with Parker Potemkin."

Silence. Mardrid held perfectly still, emptying her mind of all but a single picture: a dense, impenetrable cocoon of white that began at her skin and extended outward for several feet. Nothing in, nothing out. The feeling that her body was expanding remained, however, threatening to sabotage her concentration. She held firmly to her vision, almost in a trance. Eventually, the sound of a door opening snapped her back to three-dimensional space. She had no idea how long they had been waiting, but the sun felt much hotter on her shoulders, the fabric of her blouse clung to her back. She was drenched with sweat.

The long face of a black woman appeared in the shadows beyond the open door now. It held no smile, but no apparent hostility either. Avalon stepped over the threshold, disappearing momentarily in the contrasting darkness.

Several minutes later, Avalon emerged and the door

closed behind her. Without speaking, she pushed through the team and proceeded back in the direction they had come. Her face was nearly blank, but Mardrid knew by the set of her jaw that the Nestercine was not pleased.

When they arrived at the dirty, cramped quarters where they had spent the night before, Avalon gathered them together. "They are considering our request. They didn't admit that Parker was among them, but I'm more convinced of it than ever. The woman at the portal told me nothing except that my request would be passed to others. We're to return this evening for their answer."

Her expression softened. "They are Tressalines, like you. I know it, but I don't think they do. And they didn't have the benefit of my sisterhood's guidance, so they're developing along some rather questionable lines. I wouldn't call them hostile, but they are quite wary. We have trained well for this, though, and should we be granted access, I feel certain that we will overcome this reticence and find common ground."

She looked around at the faces, pausing on Mardrid's. "Let us sit silently for the rest of the afternoon, holding the image of Parker that I have shown you, and this community, in an atmosphere of acceptance and non-hostility. When it is time, we shall take ourselves again to their door."

As the group began to disperse through the several rooms of the home, Mother Avalon turned again to Mardrid and spoke in a low voice. "I would suggest you take a nap, Desta. You look exhausted, and we can't afford to compromise this meeting."

Desta felt the color rise in her cheeks, and seethed at the suggestion she was not holding up her end. She hated being singled out. But rather than tearing out the woman's throat, which is what she—somewhat irrationally, she admitted to herself—would like to do, she turned away without responding and went in search of a quiet corner. When she found one, she willed herself to stop grinding her teeth, and eventually fell into a fitful half-sleep.

When she awoke, it was to the sound of shuffling feet and the stink of her own sweat. The nightmare she had been having was lost in the realization that the team was again leaving.

Chapter 46

"But this is not our agreement!"

The man, who stood nearly a foot shorter than Parker, stabbed his finger in Parker's direction.

"No groups admitted, only single," he said. "We all agreed." There were a mere fifteen people in the room, a quorum called together hastily when news of Mother Avalon's visit was passed underground by Hazika, the Guardian at the portal where the team had arrived less than an hour before.

Parker held up a hand. "I understand your concern, Urqua, but this woman has been a mentor to me in North America. She helped me, helped awaken me. Because of me, she was nearly killed. I don't know why she's come with others, but I trust her. And I trust her reasons for bringing the others, whoever they are." He was calm amid the unusual sense of suspicion and panic that bubbled in the room. "Besides, Kay and I came not singly, as you remember, and you welcomed us."

"It was the first time, but now see what it has brought us," Urqua said. The comment silenced the room. Everyone understood that Urqua had voiced an old fear of outsiders, but the way he had said it was harsh and nearly accusatory. Such dissent had seldom surfaced in the community.

Parker felt the appearance of a crack in their solidarity like it was a small wound. He closed his eyes and bowed slightly in Urqua's direction to indicate he had received his wounding and would not respond in kind.

A moment later, Nadira, a young woman well along in her pregnancy, spoke up. "How did she know you were here?"

"We must assume that the community has been discovered, at least by the North American Council. And I doubt if they would be granted permission to travel here without the knowledge of the East African Council." He turned to Malkia, who was serving that day as the emissary to the Guardians and had called the quorum. "You say there were Africans with her?"

"There are twelve. Only three are white. Hazika said they are special people, strong minds. She could find no evil in their hearts. The woman in blue said they were our brothers and sisters."

"Some of you know," Parker said, "that this lady, Mother Avalon, told me the Nestercines have been working secretly to bring our kind into the world. When we found The People, we were hoping to get help from some Nestercines here in Africa, but they didn't help. I don't know why. But clearly they must be raising others like us here too."

"But they didn't come to us like the rain." The speaker this time was Erasto, one of the older males in the community. "It is not good."

Parker understood. The People had grown organically, each member finding his or her way to the group, led by some invisible thread to encounter a member, discover a connection. Like the rain that falls to earth, creates streams and rivers that flow to the sea, or seeps into the earth and becomes great rivers underground. The Africans were steeped in centuries of tradition around omens and portents.

"I don't think we can say it is not good, Erasto. Has it not been good since Kay and I came here? Haven't we prospered and deepened? Life has smiled on us, and we don't know that the arrival of my old friend means this has changed. Maybe it will mean good things."

But even as he tried to be reassuring, Parker could feel the mistrust, the legacy of tribal animosity and superstition underneath the thin veneer of universality The People had achieved, and it worried him. This was the first real challenge to his leadership, to the group's unity, that he had faced. He was not at all sure it was going well.

"We are strong," he said, looking from one face to another. "This woman is not an enemy. She bears me no ill will. What can be the harm in letting her and her people into our midst? If we don't, we will never know why she has come or what we must do to prepare for others who may come after them."

"Why not meet with them on the surface, alone, so that they don't see everything here?" Nadira asked.

Parker shook his head. "I am still one of the most recognizable people in the world. It's not yet been a year since I led the Califas team at the World Games, and being seen in public could bring others, people who are not such friends as Mother Avalon. This will not go away, but if we discover why she's come, then we will at least know what must be done next."

They talked for another ten minutes, Parker addressing the various fears people brought up, and came to the moment when they needed to make a decision. Only once before they had not been able to come to one mind about a problem and its solution, and then, as now, they decided to vote. Seven voted with Parker to admit Mother Avalon and her team. Erasto was clearly displeased. "I will warn others about this violation of our space. We will be ready for trouble if any comes."

Parker had tried to reach out to infuse the group with a sense of calm and unanimity, but the split was strong and the spell of unease lingered. As the group dispersed, Parker made his way back to his quarters where earlier he had left Kay, a cool wet towel on her forehead. She had awakened in the morning with cramps and a slight fever and they had done some energy work together to ease her discomfort, but it had only helped a little. On his way to the meeting of the quorum, he had asked Obarra, one of the best doctors, to look in on her.

Back in their room, he found Kay still in bed, paler than usual but otherwise calm. Obarra had come, she told him, given her some herbs and read her energy. "She doesn't know what the trouble is," Kay said, "but she doesn't think it's anything to worry about. She said that the first pregnancy is sometimes difficult. My body isn't used to these changes." A small smile. "It doesn't seem to be very happy about them at this moment."

Parker held her hand, his other resting on her swollen abdomen, and told her of Mother Avalon's visit, and how the community had split over allowing her access. "I don't feel good about how it went, but I don't see any way around letting Mother Avalon and her team in." He looked down at her hand in his. "This is all happening very quickly. I had hoped for more time to prepare."

Kay heard the bitterness in his tone and squeezed his hand. "It'll be all right, Parker. The People will find the right heart in this. Maybe Mother Avalon has come to become a part of us, like Aria did. If she is as wise as you have said she is, she'll see the beauty and potential here."

Parker looked into her eyes, and felt their deep connection. She was so beautiful, and he saw within her depths the fragility that few understood. They saw only her strength and poise. Parker saw a woman who had thrown over everything she had ever known and cast her lot with him. She was more vulnerable than anyone knew, and he knew she was in pain. It pulled at his heart and darkened his thoughts, but he set them aside.

"Of course she'll see it," he said, though he couldn't imagine Mother Avalon coming here to live with them. "And we are strong enough to deal with this situation."

He gave her hand another squeeze. "They will be here soon. I need to go prepare, and speak with some others. Where is Aria this morning?"

"Sleeping late, I suppose. She'll be along soon, I'm sure. Go on, Parker. If I feel better, I will join you and the others. They'll bring them to the hall?"

"Yes. Most everyone will be there, I'm sure. I'll bring Mother Avalon down to meet you if you don't feel up to coming."

"All right," Kay said. "I'm looking forward to it."

They sat for a moment in silence, then Parker stood and strode out the door. He didn't see Kay wince and bite her lip as he turned down the hall.

Chapter 47

Dusk seemed to mingle with the faded colors of the buildings as they trod the quiet street. Mardrid found the muddy indistinctness of the scene oppressive. The evening air was redolent with the smell of cooking cabbage and other unfamiliar smells, and the heat was even more stifling than it had been earlier. She thought longingly of the clean, well-lit hallways of the North American Council Headquarters, then caught herself and refocused on the team's field.

When they were within a few feet of where they had stood earlier, the door opened. The face of the tall black woman appeared there, and then silently moved back into the shadows.

Mother Avalon led them up the steps and into the cool interior. When the door closed, they found themselves in a foyer barely large enough to hold them all. The team bunched against one bare wall, Mardrid barely able to see over the shoulders of the two men in front of her. Mother Avalon held the black woman's hand in hers, speaking so quietly that Mardrid couldn't hear. She could feel, though, and without even seeing the woman's face, sensed the wariness there. Perhaps she had grown, after all, during these weeks of torture.

The woman disappeared into an anteroom, and Avalon turned to the team. "We are to be received." She appeared pleased, but Mardrid saw consternation there too. "However, we have been asked to honor their security tradition and allow ourselves to be blindfolded before being admitted. I agreed to this."

The woman reemerged with a fistful of brightly colored scarves and handed them to Avalon. One by one, the team tied the scarves over their eyes and clasped hands. Mardrid felt the uncomfortable but familiar jolt of energy as they did, and they began moving in single file toward the back of the foyer. They began descending rough steps. She remembered the tiny discs Barena Colter had given her, and released the hand of the person both in front and back. Trying not to focus on the task, she reached with her left hand to the seam in her pants and carefully worked the first disc out, palming it. She hoped it was small enough not to be noticed.

To occupy her thoughts as she let the first disc slide from her hand, she counted steps as they descended. On the thirtieth step, she dropped another, and another on the sixtieth. When she reached seventy-five, she nearly stumbled as she felt for another stair, only to find a flat surface. They turned left and scuffled along for a while, and Mardrid realized they were still descending, but now on a rough, ramp-like floor. She dropped another disc.

They made several more turns to the right, though Mardrid could not tell if they were right angles or had reversed direction completely. She dropped another disc, hoping that if worse came to worst, the signal would be able to bounce off the walls.

The twisting and turning continued, and the rank odor of damp earth and mildew assaulted Mardrid's nostrils. She could tell from the sound of their echoing footfalls that they were in a tight space. Soon, their guide said in accented English, "Here you must lower your head." They did, bending nearly double as they proceeded. Mardrid felt suddenly like they were in some ancient, fetid tomb. She felt the walls begin to close in on them, and feared that soon they would be trapped inside the earth, unable to move or breathe. Her breath began coming in short bursts. She had never before been in such a confined space. She felt the firm squeeze on her shoulder from whoever walked behind her, and to her relief, the panic abated.

After a while, they were told they could walk upright again, and eventually the woman's voice said, "Wait." They heard her walk a distance, then a heavy scraping sound. A rush of air ruffled Mardrid's hair and sleeves, carrying with it the thick smell of flowers and fertile soil. It so surprised her that she nearly tore off the scarf, but the group had begun already to move forward. There were distant voices ahead. As she heard the door closing behind them, she dropped the last disc and hoped they didn't have much farther to go.

The voices began dropping off one by one as the team drew nearer, as if they were struck dumb by the sight of this odd parade. The strange buoyancy Mardrid had felt in her body when they had first approached this place from the outside returned, stronger this time. Others were nearby, she thought, maybe within touching distance, peering at them as if they were some sort of exhibit. She listened harder, sure now she was hearing quiet breathing, and more footsteps than before.

Her head throbbed, and the thick smells in the air made her stomach turn over. A mental picture began forming of the team, twelve blindfolded people blithely walking along, surrounded by disfigured beings with skin the color of mushrooms, rubbing their slimy, twisted hands together in anticipation of a good meal. She swallowed dryly and tried once again to clear her mind. This was a nightmare from which she couldn't awaken, an alien planet. A wave of heat roiled her bowels, as though she might foul herself.

On and on they walked, and now Mardrid was certain they were surrounded by dozens, if not hundreds, of others. She heard some whispers in the distance, and the high-pitched whir of machinery here and there, some of it shutting down as they passed. Suddenly she knew they had entered an open room. Her scalp tingled, as if the air above her head was charged with electricity. The floor sloped downward again, and after a short time, she felt stairs that climbed upward. Three steps and again a flat surface. A hand on her shoulder gently guided her backward until she was shoulder to shoulder with others, presumably her teammates.

She waited, listening to the sounds of rustling clothes, scuffling feet, and whispers. Her stomach quivered, and adrenaline pumped through her veins. She felt as if a deep bass note was sounding, vibrating her body. Then she sensed the person on her right removing the scarf, and she followed. She had to stifle a gasp at what she saw.

There were hundreds of them staring at her, their eyes bright, nearly glowing in the gentle light. Mardrid saw now that they had entered a large room. Multicolored light was filtering in from somewhere above their heads. The team had been formed into a circle in the center of this room on a raised platform.

Avalon stood outside the circle just to her right, her blue-robed back to Mardrid. The Nestercine began a slow circumnavigation to the right, her hands pressed together in a gesture of respect, silently greeting the seated onlookers on the team's behalf.

Mardrid's heart drummed in her chest, each beat hammering the dull pain behind her eyes. She felt the eyes of their hosts and forced herself to focus her attention above their heads. An insistent urge came to her, and she realized it was emanating from her team members—a call to maintain the protective field they had been practicing for all these weeks. Like a drowning person grasping for a floating object, she took in a gasp of air and reached for the feeling inside. Slowly it insinuated itself into her thoughts, and she grew calmer and highly alert, but she felt the tension crackle in the room. So many eyes.

No one spoke, and Avalon reappeared from her left, having completed the circle around the team. Mardrid was concentrating on breathing slowly when she felt a sickening surge, as if the surface under them elevated a few inches. Her knees went a little weak, and her head felt like it was filling with air. To her left, the outline of a large man emerged from a doorway at the back of the room. He began walking down the aisle toward them. As he drew nearer, Mardrid turned her head in his direction and saw that a small smile played across his lips, but his eyes held a look of intense concentration.

She watched his approach, recognition creeping over her like the clouds of an approaching storm. The wide brow and angular jaw, the deep-set eyes. The holographs she had seen could not possibly have conveyed the power and presence she felt emanating from him now, as the blood drained from her face.

Parker Potemkin was a giant, a powerhouse, and Mardrid closed her eyes against the vision, nearly praying now that she could find the field, the inner shields, anything to help her get through what the next moments might bring.

Chapter 48

Mother Avalon broke into a smile. She rushed down the steps to greet Parker, her arms outstretched. Parker, too, was smiling broadly now. She nearly disappeared in the loose folds of his sleeves as they enveloped her in his arms. All eyes in the room were riveted on the pair, but no one else smiled.

"I *knew* I would find you here," Mother Avalon said when Parker finally held her by the shoulders at arm's length. Her face glistened with sweat and her hands trembled slightly. "You have grown wonderfully, powerfully," she said, joy and awe evident in her voice. "I can barely stand in your presence."

"It moves me to see you alive," Parker said. "We thought you had been killed."

"Destiny has seen fit to allow me more time," she said, beaming. "And a new mission. Great things are afoot, Parker, great things."

Parker looked at her silently before his gaze settled on the eleven people circled in the center of the room. He pushed his chin in their direction. "Who are they? Why have you bought them here?"

"They are your brothers and sisters, son," she said, smiling up into his face, "all descendants of the Tressaline line. I wanted you to meet them . . . and I didn't know what we might encounter here. They are from a colony we began last year in Mombassa. We have been working with them for many months now. Oh, Parker, I have so much to share with you. We both survived. This must have been an ordeal for you, but something wonderful has come from it."

"Yes, it has," Parker said, nodding, "but my life is not an ordeal, Mother Avalon. It is full and rich. This is a wonderful home. Great things are happening here."

Her smile froze on her face. "Here?" she said, and then as if seeing where she was for the first time, looked about the room, first at those who sat watching and listening to them, then at the walls and the ceiling. She turned her eyes back toward him and gathered herself together, her expression more serious now.

"I have important news. Many things have changed since you left. The North American Council is working with us now. They understand the importance of the Tressaline lines. We've been making plans, glorious plans. It's the first time anything like this has happened. We have . . ."

"Yes, I see," Parker interrupted, releasing her shoulders. There was a hint of sadness in his eyes. "Things have changed. Very much, it seems."

Mother Avalon felt a sudden distance between them. "What do you mean?"

"How did you find me?"

She searched his eyes. There was warmth there, but more. Was it a sense of responsibility? Suspicion? It was hard to hold his gaze. His features seemed a little distorted, as if she were peering at him through wavy glass. And she was quite warm. She wiped sweat from her upper lip.

"People have been looking for some time, as you might imagine—your brotherhood, the council. The assassin sent to kill you disappeared, too, and they began marshaling intelligence here to determine what happened. They assumed you hadn't left the country. Several months ago someone discovered the entrance we came through. When they told me about it, I had the sense you were alive, hiding here. They don't know the extent of this operation"—she looked around again at the room they were in—"it must be quite a bit larger than anyone imagined. But they asked me to come and find you, to talk with you."

Parker nodded. "Then we have trouble." He looked again at Mother Avalon's team in the center of the room.

"No, Parker, no," she said, touching his forearm. "No one wishes you any harm. We . . . I . . . just wanted to see you again, to let you know that I was alive and to tell you how things have changed." She waved an arm toward the people surrounding them. "Can you imagine what we can accomplish, how different things will be when the talents of the Tressaline line are brought into the service of the Whole Body? There will be unimaginable progress. We can do great good. We can revolutionize the world in a single generation. There can be . . ."

Parker's expression grew steadily harder as she spoke. He held up his hand and Mother Avalon stopped in midsentence as if he had put it around her windpipe and squeezed. "You have brought the world I left through my door again. Surely you don't expect us to think they would let you come here without backup, or without informing other authorities."

Mother Avalon had backed up a step now, the fingertips of one hand over her mouth, her head shaking slowly from side to side. Parker stared at her, his expression softening into a look of compassion.

"Then again, perhaps you do," he said. "Mother, I think you're blinded by your own desires. Let's be honest. This is not simply a visit. You have come to bring me back, to be a part of your vision, but you don't even recognize what you've come into."

He looked at the circle of strangers in the center of the room, their eyes unblinking, staring out into the faces of his community. "Can't you feel the tension here? You should have come alone."

"I couldn't, Parker," she said. "The council insisted we come together. As I said, we didn't know what we would encounter here."

Parker gestured toward the room. "Surely you see the fear and suspicion you've brought into our home."

She started to protest, but again let her eyes wander over the scene. Some in the room were focused on her and Parker, others on her team at the center of the room. A crease appeared at the center of her forehead. "But we mean you no harm." Her tone was incredulous. "We come in peace."

Her hands shook now, her chest heaved. She closed her eyes. "I . . . I'm sorry. I didn't imagine it would be like this. I thought it would be more of . . . a reunion. Can't you tell them that it's all right? Perhaps we can speak somewhere alone. There's something about this room. . . ."

Parker shook his head. "This is my community, my home. These are my people and our council room. We are bound together in ways you may not be able to imagine. Whatever concerns me concerns them. Whatever affects one of them affects me. Everything is spoken openly here."

Parker extended his hand and she took it, their eyes meeting. After a long moment, she nodded and let go. She turned, squared her shoulders, and walked slowly to the center of the room, feeling all eyes in the room on her. She climbed the steps and walked back to where she had been before Parker's entrance.

Sweat stained the collar and upper chest of her robe a midnight blue. She clasped her hands together at her breast to steady them and strained slightly to take in a full breath, her shoulders rising with the effort. She cleared her throat.

"I am Mother Avalon of the Nestercine order," she began, "an old friend of Parker's." She paused, gave Parker a long look, then resumed. "You may not know this, but my order has been working for nearly a century to preserve and further the work of a colony of scientists that began their work here in Dar es Salaam."

Chapter 49

Aria awoke with a start, all her senses on alert. Had there been a noise? Something felt odd, out of place. She looked over at the timepiece next to her small bed. It was late again. Ever since she began with the herbs, her body's clock was out of whack. She sat upright, put her bare feet on the cold floor, rubbed her eyes, and listened. Nothing. Something had awakened her. The cold was not in the floor, it was in her chest, her bones.

Her clothes were draped over a nearby chair. She rose and began pulling on the pants. The rough material of the blouse made her wince as it chafed against her sore and swollen breasts. She wondered if what she was feeling was something hormonal. It didn't matter. She needed to check on Kay anyway. She cursed at herself for not getting up sooner. She had always been an early riser, but for nearly a week now she had been staying up later and later, and awakening in the mornings groggy, her mouth pasty and her body reluctant to move.

She downed a glass of water and left her quarters, headed down the hall to Kay and Parker's doorway. Ahead, at the end of the hallway, she saw a small group pass, apparently on their way to the council room. Something in their hurried step bothered her. She quickened her own pace.

When she reached Kay's door, she knocked, but no one answered. She knocked again and thought she heard a soft voice behind it. "Kay? Are you there?" Again she heard the voice. She decided not to stand on formality and pushed open the door.

Kay sat on the edge of the bed, leaning slightly forward, her face pale and her mouth twisted in pain.

"Kay, what is it? What's wrong?" She closed the space between them in three strides.

"I don't know," Kay said, her voice strained and small. "I can't seem to stop it." She was holding her belly. "Get one of the doctors. And Parker. Hurry, please."

Aria's hands sought for a place to touch Kay, somewhere that might help, but Kay waved her off. "Please. Go."

Aria bit her lip and quickly headed for the door. "I'll be right back."

She scurried down the corridor toward the council room. Her mind raced. How could something be wrong? Kay was fine, radiant, yesterday. She was . . . perfect. Aria flashed on the first day she arrived, sitting across from Kay watching the energy flow from Kay's hand to her belly. It was not possible something was wrong. And yet, something was. Kay looked very sick. She couldn't be having her baby now, could she? It was too soon, by more than a month. A dark thought crept into her mind.

She was never engineered to bear children.

She pushed away the sinking sensation in her stomach, choosing instead to recall all the miracles she had seen here, all the wonderful confidence and remarkable accomplishments. It was simply not possible, she told herself again. These people, her people, could overcome anything.

She rounded the corner at the end of the hall and saw the backs of several of the community members headed toward the council room. She recognized one.

"Bantwalla!" she cried out. Bantwalla turned her head.

The look on her face was more serious than Aria ever remembered seeing.

"Kay!" Aria managed to say. "Something's wrong!"

Bantwalla whirled around, headed back toward Aria. "What's happened?"

"I don't know," Aria said, catching her breath. "She's sick. Where can I find a doctor?"

"Everyone is going to the council room. Someone has come, found us. There is a feeling of danger."

"Kay needs a doctor," Aria said.

"I will go to her. Go to the council room. Get someone. Go!"

Aria watched as Bantwalla hurried around the corner toward Kay's quarters. Then she spun and ran toward the council room.

As she passed through the arched doorway, she looked to the center of the room. A sliver of ice pierced her heart. In the aisle ahead of her stood Parker. Beyond him at the center of the crowded room, a small woman in a blue robe stood speaking before the assembled. Behind her was a circle of men and women she had never seen.

Except for one.

It was the face of a woman she had hoped never to see again. Desta Mardrid was not looking in her direction, and Aria quickly moved to the side, crouching behind others in the room. The atmosphere was electric, dark, threatening. Aria could barely hear what was being said for the rushing blood in her ears. She scanned the room for a face of one of the doctors she had met.

She was amazed at how few people she recognized. And none were doctors.

Chapter 50

The speaker's words floated through the dense atmosphere. ". . . have had a breakthrough with the North American Council. They have agreed to form an alliance with the Nestercines, to give us . . . all of us . . . the opportunity to work with them in science and agriculture, in medicine, even in government if we can demonstrate our willingness to give of ourselves for the sake of the Whole Body."

This was a nightmare, Aria thought. Hearing the words "Whole Body" made her shudder. They had been discovered. The world she tried to leave behind had breached the sacred boundaries of her new community.

"Until recently," the woman went on, "we had no knowledge of your existence, and until today we didn't know there were so many of you. I am certain that the council will offer you the same invitation it has given the Nestercine colony. I ask you to consider the benefits for all of humanity if you will work with us. I'm not certain if there would be any objection to you remaining here in this place you have created, but I am willing to speak to those in charge about you, on your behalf . . ."

Indecision ripped at Aria's insides. If she approached Parker now, Mardrid surely would see her. What was the aide doing here? If she was recognized, what then? For certain, it would mean that she was no longer just missing from her post in North America, that she had deceived her superiors about where she had gone. Would they demand she return? Would she bring down the weight of the North

American Council on The People because of her presence? What about Parker? Did they care enough about his being here to come anyway? Or Kay? She looked again at the woman speaking, and suddenly understood this was Mother Avalon, the one Kay and Parker said had tried to save Parker. But why then was Mardrid with her? Nothing made sense.

The image of Kay, pale and scared back in their quarters, slammed back into her mind. She must do something—get Parker, get a doctor. She closed her eyes, shut out the strange scene in front of her, and tried to focus.

There was no time to think. She must act, and act now. Go quickly to Parker and tell him Kay was ill. She opened her eyes again and willed herself to stand. But Parker was now ascending the stairs, moving next to Mother Avalon. Mardrid disappeared behind his broad back. Aria felt paralyzed and helpless as Parker began speaking.

"My family, Mother Avalon was my friend before I ever knew you. That is why I gave permission for her to come here. I'm glad to see her alive, but she's also brought something into our lives now that I had hoped would not come, and certainly not this soon.

"We are now exposed. Our safety and seclusion have been compromised."

Mother Avalon shook her head and started to interrupt, but Parker raised his hand slightly in her direction, and she remained silent, her face twisting through a rapid succession of emotions—frustration, fear, sadness.

"It's not her fault," he continued, "but we now have some difficult decisions to make." He turned slightly and looked over his shoulder at the outsiders behind him. None of them returned his gaze but remained still, looking out into the gathering. His eyes paused for a brief moment on the one standing nearly directly behind him, a white woman whose eyes were closed and whose upper lip was wet with perspiration. She looked as though she might pass out.

He turned back to face the community. "These people have come into our world. There is no changing that now. Mother Avalon says that they mean us no harm. That may be so, but that is not the whole truth. You can feel it, just as I do, can't you? She says they are our brothers and sisters. This may be so also, at least by the cells that make up our bodies. I can feel their strength, as you can. There is no doubt they share some of our gifts.

"But they also have an agenda, something that they believe is right. And they don't have our experience, the feelings that have grown up here with us. They don't have our trust, nor we theirs. They don't have Kopquahe, or the hope of children about to be born. They don't know us."

He took Mother Avalon's hand in his. "We have several options, then. We can have them stay with us here, absorb them into our lives, or we can send them away. Either way, trouble is coming, for they represent not just themselves, but those who sent them, and these are many and they control much in the world above."

He looked at Mother Avalon. "There is another option, but it would mean we turn our abilities to the dark and destroy them, or harm their minds." He paused momentarily, letting this sink in. "But the results likely will be the same. Sooner than any of us would want, there will be others who will come, and they will either try to control or destroy us.

"I am sorry I have brought us to this difficult passage. Had I not allowed them in, we may have had more time to decide on a course of action—not much, perhaps, but a little more.

"I hold this woman in high esteem, and I wish no harm

to come to her . . . but I surrender my will to yours. We must be of one mind, more now than ever. The test has now come. How shall we meet it? What shall we do?"

Mother Avalon paled at these words, and Aria saw that she understood that Parker's commitment to The People was unequivocal, and that her life and the lives of her charges were in their hands.

The tension in the room was nearly unbearable. Aria knew then she could not take Parker from this critical moment. But neither could she wait any longer. She leaned down and put her hands on the shoulders of the two women directly in front of her. They turned, surprised, and stared into her face. "Please, Kay is very sick," she whispered. "She needs help immediately. Where is a doctor?"

They stared at her uncomprehendingly, as if mentally they had to travel a long distance to speak. Then one turned and scanned the faces of those on either side of her, settling on someone to her right. She pointed and whispered, "There, in red." Aria followed the gesture and vaguely recognized a black woman wearing a red scarf around her neck. Aria nodded to the women in appreciation, and moved quickly down the row. She got the woman's attention, motioned to her to come. At the end of the aisle she took the woman's arm, hustling her out as she explained what was happening.

As they entered the hallway that led to Kay's quarters, Aria heard the first responses to Parker's question, and shivered. It was the only time she had ever heard anger expressed here.

Chapter 51

Mardrid desperately wanted the ringing in her ears to stop. And the pressure in her chest. Avalon's speech was doing nothing to relieve the intensity of the onslaught Mardrid felt.

Her connection with the rest of the team was faltering, and she knew it. It was as though they stood in an invisible sandstorm being eroded away one molecule at a time by microscopic, razor-like bits of flying detritus. Parker faced her a short distance from the platform, his outline shimmering in the subdued light in this terrible room. He was like a small mountain, his dark eyes expectant, roaming over their team, Mother Avalon, and the rest of the room, searching, probing. Each time that gaze came her way, Mardrid closed her eyes, took a deep breath, and refocused on the team's field.

What folly it had been to walk blindly into this situation, she thought. She rued her own weakness and wondered if she would ever see sunlight again. She seethed with bitterness toward Gretel and Colter for putting her in this situation.

Avalon was talking to the crowd now, something about what they could bring to the world if they worked together. It was an impassioned speech, vintage Avalon, but even to Mardrid it sounded thin, like the foolish idealism of a child, a pretty picture that skipped over all the dark nuance of the thing portrayed. Nothing in Potemkin's demeanor, or for that matter the attitude of anyone in the room, suggested that Avalon was winning any hearts.

Potemkin was moving now, powerful and graceful despite his size, toward the stage. In a moment, he was standing directly in front of Mardrid, his broad back blocking her view.

Through her tangled thoughts, Mardrid could barely make sense of the words he spoke. Something about them—the team—staying here. She didn't want to stay here. She wanted to be far away. Now. The impulse to break free of the circle, to run as fast as she could for one of the portals in the back of the room, was growing. She felt the others inwardly reaching for her, calling for her to maintain the field, to stay calm.

She heard Potemkin say ". . . harm their minds . . ." and the words sent a spasm of fear through her. They are going to twist us, she thought. They'll take the terrible force in this room and squeeze my mind until I'm an imbecile. A great weight pressed on her, as if a wall had fallen on her. She sucked in air through her open mouth, but there didn't seem to be enough oxygen in it. It's this place, she thought. No air underneath the ground.

A hand gripped her arm—was it Spot?—and she flinched away from it. Her head spun with the barrage of thoughts. They want me to stand here like a statue, to stand here and be turned into mush. Isn't anyone going do something? Maybe the team wanted to stay here . . . among their own. Where would that leave me? Alone, surrounded by alien beings, freaks. Maybe we're going be killed, or worse, and no one is doing anything about it. Maybe the rest of the team wants to die, she thought. Maybe they're tired of being different.

The hand squeezed her arm until it hurt. For a brief moment, her head cleared. She opened her eyes and saw that some of the people out there were standing and talking, gesturing at Parker and Avalon. They spoke loudly, sometimes several at once. She heard the anger in their voices. They're going to kill us, she thought again. She jerked her arm away from the constricting hand, and as she did, her knuckle rapped against something hard in her clothing. Reflexively she looked down at her hand. A memory stirred in her mind. In a flash she knew what she had felt, nestled in the seam of her pants. She remembered its slim shape, the deadly dart it housed, the tiny mechanism on its side that released the safety, and the trigger.

An idea seized her, gripped her heart and flushed her face. Only one way to end this. She looked up at Parker Potemkin's broad back. One chance to break the awful spell of this place, one chance to escape. In the back of the room the open archways loomed. She imagined herself leaping from the pedestal and sprinting for the dark hope they offered. She hated Potemkin and his massive back before her, hated him for being the reason she was now here in this hideous hole in the ground. With him gone there would be chaos, confusion. A chance.

Her fingers caressed the cylindrical casing, easing it toward the slit at the narrow top of the seam. The tip emerged from its hiding place like the slender ray of hope rising in her heart.

Chapter 52

Aria hurried down the long, empty corridor to Kay's quarters, the doctor at her heels. The darkness she had felt in the council room pursued them like a shadow.

Questions raced through her mind. How did they find this place? What entrance had they come through? Were there others outside waiting to come in? Was this an invasion? Had they followed her here?

This last thought brought another rush of anguish. In her clumsy search for Kay had she been the unwitting breach of security?

One thing was certain: something terrible was going on in the council room. It was as though the very walls had changed. Since her first night here and being introduced to the community at Kopquahe, the council room had been her favorite place. Being in there always had brought back the deep feelings of wonder and joy she experienced that first night. This time it had been like stepping through a mirror. Everything looked the same, but the atmosphere was violent and threatening, supercharged with negativity. She shuddered again.

They passed the corridor that led to Njeri's portal and Aria imagined herself running up the many carved stairs, fleeing this place. Don't panic, she told herself. Kay needs you. At that moment pain shot through her abdomen. She cried out, fear bearing down on her. She broke into a run.

Just as they made the turn into the last hallway, an agonized scream hammered her eardrums. Tears blurred her vision as she ran toward Kay's door. She held her hand over her mouth to keep herself from echoing the cry, and burst through the open door.

The first thing she saw was blood.

It was on Bantwalla's hands. At Bantwalla's feet, the deathly white form of Kay, her smock pulled up to her breasts, her legs splayed. Something stretched from between them to Bantwalla's hands.

Bantwalla's eyes met Aria's.

"Help," Bantwalla whispered. Bantwalla held something glistening, something impossibly small in her hands.

With a cry, Aria sprang to Kay's side, her hands fluttering over her friend's cold face as if they were afraid to alight. "Kay! Kay!"

Kay was silent. The ghastly color of her skin made Aria's heart sink. The doctor appeared at her side, felt quickly for a pulse, and began pressing rhythmically on Kay's chest.

Bantwalla's voice came again from behind her. "Help me. Aria, help me."

She looked up. It was what she feared. The tiny form in Bantwalla's hand was still. Perfectly formed, but still. Bantwalla placed her mouth over the mouth and nose of the infant, and the little chest rose with her outbreath. As if in a dream, Aria saw her repeat this once, twice. Then her mouth came away from the infant's face and spoke.

"Cut the cord, Aria."

Aria looked down again at Kay's ashen face and the doctor working over her, and a sob arose in her throat. She bit down hard on the back of her hand.

"Now, Aria." Bantwalla's voice was sharp now. "Cut the cord."

The voice worked like a slap in the face. Aria jerked her head up, looked around the room. Something sharp. She leapt to her feet and scanned all the surfaces in the room. Nothing. She ran to a stack of drawers and flung the first open. Clothes. She grabbed at them, throwing them onto the floor. Nothing. She pulled on the next and it flew out of its place and clattered to the floor. She upended it, spilling more clothes and small boxes onto the floor.

Sobbing, she turned and saw a chest against a wall. She ran to it, fell to her knees, and flung the lid open. She plunged her hands in the cavity there, feeling against the bottom for something familiar. Something cold and hard brushed her knuckles, clattered away. She grabbed at it and felt it bite into her fingers. She ignored the pain, held the object tightly, and withdrew her hand. In her white fingers, she saw the curved and etched blade of the ceremonial knife she had seen Parker use on the cake the night they had celebrated her becoming a wet nurse to the child. Drops of blood seeped through her fingers. She eased her grip, grabbed the carved handle with her other hand, turned, and struggled to her feet.

Bantwalla's mouth remained over the infant's, but her eyes were on Aria, who hurried to where she stood. Aria tried to remember what she had read in the old midwifery texts. She seized the slippery cord with her bleeding left hand, and with her right, made a clean slice just above the infant's navel. Milky fluid oozed from the dangling cord.

Tie it. It must be tied.

She dropped the knife and it clattered to the floor. She twisted the slimy cord, guiding the end back through the loop, but it slipped out of her hands before she could knot it. She tried again, this time bending her head to the infant's stomach. She gripped the loose end with her teeth, and pulled it tight, leaving a neat knot against the stomach. Just then a ratcheting noise issued from the infant's throat, followed by a long, piercing cry, an achingly beautiful sound.

Bantwalla hurried to the bed, grabbed a small pitcher of water from the nightstand. Dazed, Aria watched Bantwalla tear the spread from the bed, dip an edge into the water, and begin wiping the mewling infant's body. Then Aria whirled and bent to the figures of Kay and the doctor at her side.

"Help me get her to the bed," the doctor said. With some difficulty, Aria forced one arm under Kay's torso and the other beneath her bloody legs. Kay was unimaginably heavy. The doctor tried to lift from the other side, but was a good deal shorter than Aria and her effort was ineffectual. Aria felt a surge of will and with a cry lifted Kay's limp body from the floor and lurched toward the bed. She heard a splash at her feet and looked down to see a stream of blood and placental slime trailing down the front of her pants onto the floor.

She ran the rest of the way, wailing.

She lowered the body to the bed, and fell forward, off balance, her torso pressing deeply into Kay's chest. Over the cries of the infant behind her, she heard air rush from Kay's lungs. When she yanked her arms out from underneath, she heard the almost miraculous sound of an inbreath. She clasped Kay's face between her palms. A tear fell from the end of her nose onto Kay's parted lips.

"Kay! Kay! I'm here! Please!" The doctor worked at Kay's chest beneath her.

Kay's eyelids moved ever so slightly, as if searching for sight. They opened slightly, then wider, until Aria saw the blue irises. But they were not the eyes Aria had known. Drained of their iridescence now, they sputtered like a candle in the wind.

Aria commanded her heart, her soul, all the vital forces of her being to pour into her hands as she held Kay's narrow face.

"Live!" she shouted, squeezing her own eyes shut, willing away the cold fog that had found its way into Kay's eyes and body.

She heard her name.

"Aria."

She opened her eyes again. Kay was looking at her, but they were both falling dreamlike through space, the distance between them slowly widening. Kay's face and eyes grew smaller in her vision, until she could no longer clearly see their glimmer, or if Kay's mouth even moved when she spoke. But Aria heard Kay's words. "Love him," she said. "Love him."

Then everything stopped.

Time and space ceased to exist. Kay's face remained between Aria's hands, but everything became flat, a mere picture of reality, as still and lifeless as a painting. Kay's eyes were indistinguishable from and of no more consequence than the rest of her lifeless features. Aria felt a yawning stillness, as if the core of her body had become so dense that not even light could escape it. Beyond her range of sight, the baby howled, but deep beneath its cries Aria was aware of a vast silence that so utterly dwarfed the noise as to render it meaningless.

She knew not how long she sat enveloped in this nothingness, only that it lay against her, through her, unfathomable, impenetrable, endless. Her hands fell to the pillow on either side of Kay's face, but even then she felt no movement, no sensation in her fingers. There was only the cold knowledge of the shadow side of the universe, the vast unmoving, unmanifested, silent void holding her in its deathly embrace.

Then, somewhere down through the layers of her being, a flicker of warmth. Ever so slowly, she became aware of a pressure at her shoulder, and the soft, urgent sound of her name. It was Bantwalla's voice, and Aria turned to see the anguished, tear-streaked face of her friend, and that of the doctor. Beneath Bantwalla's hand, she felt energy pouring into her shoulder.

"We must go," Bantwalla said. The tiny bundle squirmed in the crook of her right arm. "We are needed." She looked in the direction of the door. "Now."

With this, she gently bent down and placed the infant in Aria's arms. Beneath the sheet, the nearly weightless form jerked, fighting furiously to be free of the constraining sheet. Aria looked at the tiny red face protruding from beneath the folds, at its mouth opening and closing, hearing the frustration in its throat. The energy and vital force she felt from this being, however, was anything but small. Like a wave breaking on a shore, the force of its will to live jolted Aria upright. A stab of pain shot through her breasts, and she watched in amazement as two dark stains began spreading at their peaks.

Just before disappearing down the hall, Bantwalla turned and looked at Aria with haunted eyes. Then she was gone.

Aria gazed at the wriggling form in her arms. She unbuttoned the front of her blouse, freed her left breast, and touched it to the infant's mouth. He seized it with his lips and sucked it deep and hard into his mouth. Aria heard herself draw in a sharp breath, and felt her vagina contract spasmodically. Both breasts squirted at once, soaking her blouse on one side and filling the infant's mouth to overflowing. He coughed once, spewing the milk and spattering Aria's face, but immediately and greedily pulled again at the nipple.

Aria closed her eyes and moaned from the rush of pain and pleasure, her grip going limp. The child was taking something from her body, but she could feel too that it was filling and revitalizing her, crowding out the all-encompassing emptiness that had engulfed her moments ago. Against her hip, she felt the weight of Kay's lifeless form and she wished with all her might that she could take this sensation and send it into the cold flesh that lay beside her.

She turned and stared at the dull pallor, the empty eyes that once animated Kay's face. The mouth hung open now, a blue tip of tongue protruding from the blackness. Aria reached out and gently closed it.

She stood, weak-kneed but determined. The infant made throaty little noises as he sucked, and Aria paced around the room staring into his face, marveling at the miracle in her arms. Soon, his mouth grew slack and he drifted into sleep. Aria covered herself again and for the first time since the child had been laid in her arms, remembered what was happening outside this little room.

She must find Parker, now, she realized. He must hold this miraculous being in his arms. Whatever was going on in the council room was not as important as this. She pressed the sleeping infant to her breast and hurried through the door, not looking back.

At the end of the first corridor she stopped, alarmed by what she heard. Shrieks and shouts, voices contorted with anger and confusion echoed off the stone walls. She cradled the head of the infant, covering the tiny ear that was not pressed against her breast. She felt caught between the urge to flee, and her mission to place the child in Parker's arms. The sounds emanating from the council room sent shivers through her, but she set her mouth in a tight line and pressed on. She almost broke into a jostling run, but resisted the urge for the sake of the sleeping infant in her arms.

At the end of the hall, she stepped through the archway, and into hell.

Chapter 53

When Potemkin pitched face-first over the edge of the podium, it was like a great tree falling in a forest. His body slammed against the stone floor with a sickening thud. A collective gasp arose from the community and the members sprang to their feet like leaves bouncing from the impact.

To Mardrid, however, it was like watching him sink slowly through a clear pool of water to settle on the floor. Voices were distorted beyond recognition, nothing more than distant moans carried on a warm wind.

She smelled smoke, although she couldn't imagine that the weapon in her hand emitted the odor.

A word rattled around in her head: escape. It urged her legs to move. The doors in the back of the room beckoned. She wanted to fly toward them, sailing over the dark, bobbing heads of the people in the room.

But her feet remained glued to the floor. She looked to her right, as if the answer to this dilemma might lie there. She saw what she thought was Spot's face, but the woman's fingers were curled into the shape of claws and were raking the flesh of her cheeks into red strips. Her mouth was open and her eyes rolled up in their sockets.

The sight seemed almost comic to her, but she couldn't laugh because the smoke was nearly choking now, though she could see no sign of it in the air. She looked again to the openings in the back of the room, and beneath them the hundreds of dark eyes pulling at her, sucking her into their depths.

But they wouldn't have her. She knew where she wanted to go. Through those holes at the back of the room. Into sunlight. Back to the surface. Back to North America. Back to her life.

She had done what was required. Now she wanted her reward.

She managed to lift her left leg.

That's good. Now bend your right knee. That's right. It must bend in order to spring, to propel you off the stage.

Toward the door.

The smoke was now so thick she began to retch.

Ignore it. Smoke doesn't matter. The door matters. And what lies beyond it. She felt her thigh muscles contract, and the familiar feeling of forward momentum. She was at the edge of the stage now. A swarm of people were below her, their backs hunched over the hulking form of the athlete. Had she been able to breathe, she would have cried out in triumph.

Now. Now she would leap onto those backs. She would skip across them like a piece of paper blowing down a bumpy street, and right out the door at the top of the aisle. It was easy.

If she could just get a breath. But her jaw was clamped so tightly she could not open her mouth to suck in air. A great weight pressed on her chest. And the smell. So thick. A tooth cracked on the right side of her mouth. Her jaw muscles tore as if they had been jabbed with a knife.

No matter. Just take that step. Now.

Her foot extended beyond the edge of the stage, and she felt weightless, certain now that she could fly. She raised her arms at her sides, the weapon still clenched in her right hand, and focused with all her might on the doors in the back of the room.

Forward now.

436

But the doors flew upward in her line of sight. Instead, she saw the back of the athlete and the backs of the heads of those around him. They rushed up to meet her. She was falling, falling.

And she knew she would never be going home again.

Chapter 54

From where Aria stood in the arched doorway of the council room, she saw clearly the fragility of her dreams. Once she had stood on the circular platform, filled to bursting with joy and hope and a feeling of belonging she had never imagined.

What unfolded before her now was a scene more grisly than her worst nightmare, a tormented artist's depiction of the darkest ages of mankind. The very same people who had welcomed her into their midst were now destroying these visitors with unimaginable cruelty.

On the platform, the invaders jerked about in a macabre dance, their tortured screams echoing from the walls. Blood poured from self-inflicted wounds. Some held fistfuls of hair they had yanked from their bloody scalps. Mother Avalon, recognizable only by her blue robe, lay twitching on the floor, a bilious fluid oozing from the dark gash that was her mouth. The eye of one of the women, who knelt in the spot where Parker stood the last time Aria had seen him, hung from its socket, framed by the bloody hands that raked into strips what was left of her face.

Mardrid and Parker were nowhere to be seen.

Aria held the infant tightly to her breast, her body quaking with silent sobs, her heart breaking beneath her ribs. For a brief moment, the aisle in front of her cleared and she saw a huddled crowd of The People grab the clothing on a woman's limp body and fling her onto the stage like a sack of garbage. Beneath where the woman had lain was another, a large body, and in a sickening moment of recognition, she knew she was too late, that her reason for coming here was gone.

Then, from a layer of her soul that had never before been uncovered, the howl of a wounded animal arose and found its way into her throat, out into that chamber of death and rage and terror, adding its song of pain to the cacophony that resonated in its darkest corners.

The infant stirred in Aria's arms, whimpering at the mournful sound.

Aria gasped, startled. She relaxed her grip at once, fearing she had crushed the boy. She looked into the tiny red face that twisted into a succession of emotions, as if unsure which to settle into. The sounds of the room faded into the background and Aria saw not the face of a newborn, but a moving tableau of a thousand generations—old faces and young, men and women, moving across the tiny features like wind shaping and reshaping the face of the ocean. An unearthly calm settled over her, muting the chaos around her.

Understanding seeped into her soul. There was nothing left for her here, and nothing in her past she could turn back to. There was only this child, and the yawning chasm of the unknown before her, which would unfold second by second with only her intuition to guide her.

And in this moment, there was only escape.

She turned, taking one brief look at the room in which a dream had lived and died, and then fled back toward her quarters. She passed the room that had been Kay and Parker's, not stopping to look through the open door at the form she knew lay on the bed there. Once inside her own room, she eased the infant, who had become silent, onto the bed and placed her ear close to its face. Assured that he breathed, she hurriedly found the caftan that had been Bantwalla's gift to her only days before, the costume she was to wear on her first visit to the surface. She slipped it on over her clothes.

Panic overridden by resolve, she moved through the room with remarkable speed and agility. She grabbed the large cloth bag she had arrived with and began stuffing it with as many items as she could find in the room that might be of value to a woman on the run in a strange land. From a small chest at the foot of her bed, she dug out the money belt she had worn on her trip from North America, the one she had thought she never again would have use for, and strapped it on. From a cabinet, she gathered the few containers of processed food she had eaten only a small portion of, and a flask of water, and dropped them in the bag. She stuffed the small cloth bags of herbs from which she had made the tea that tricked her body into producing milk into the caftan's large pocket.

For a moment, she stood motionless in the center of the room concentrating, and then her eyes widened with a realization: diapers. She lifted the sleeping infant from the bed, and set it gently on the table. Whirling again to the small bed, she pulled the sheets off and began ripping them into squares, stuffing them into the bag.

Satisfied at last she had everything she could afford to take, she slung the bag over her shoulder, gathered the infant in her left arm, and fled down the hall away from the council room and toward the entrance that would lead her to Njeri's portal. Floating in the corridor, the muted sounds of screams and shouts. They tugged at her emotions, threatening to pull her off course, but she severed them as if they had been the hands of drowning people pulling at an overcrowded lifeboat. There was nothing she could do for anyone here. They were lost to her now. One day they might awaken to what they'd become in an instant of revenge and retribution, find their way back to sanity, but Aria knew she could never again live among them. Not after what she'd seen and felt in the council room.

She paused at the entrance to Kay's room. On impulse, she flung open the door and went to where she had cut the umbilical cord. The ceremonial knife lay on the floor where she had dropped it, its curved blade streaked with blood and umbilical fluid. She stooped, swept it up and into the bag, and left again.

As she climbed the ramps and stairs that led to the world of sunlight, her rational mind tried desperately to conjure a plan. It shouted fearfully at her about the dangerous and insurmountable obstacles that lay ahead. She ignored it. It was not the logical part of herself that she must rely on now. Rather, she reached for the birthplace of vision, of inner sight, calling to it wordlessly with her heart, melting away the layers that separated her from the resources with which she knew she was gifted.

Eventually, she came to the seemingly solid wall where Bantwalla had told her to close her eyes and turn around on their visits to Njeri's portal. Tears filled her eyes at the memory of the friendship she had felt for the woman. She wiped them away with the back of her free hand and faced the wall she knew held the hidden stone door. She surveyed its craggy surface for a trace of the device that would trigger its opening.

There was nothing. She ran her hand over every centimeter of the wall she could reach again and again. She divided the wall into sections and pressed lightly, then harder, leaving no surface untouched.

The wall remained inert and gray.

Tendrils of panic crept upward from her stomach, and she took slow, deep breaths to drive them back down.

Reach, she told herself again. Reach now for your gifts. She closed her eyes and melted the time between this moment and when she and Bantwalla had come this way. In her mind's eye she saw Bantwalla's round face, heard her asking Aria to turn around and close her eyes, saw the woman's ample figure behind her turn and walk to the wall, reach for it . . . the vision ended.

Aria gritted her teeth in frustration, but forced herself to find the calm, clear place within. Once again she brought forward the image of Bantwalla's face, the tone of her skin, the sound of her voice, the tilt of her head, the rhythm of her being. She felt herself drop into a deeper level of consciousness, as if the ground beneath her had dissolved and she was suspended, weightless. Bantwalla's dark eyes beckoned her forward, and in a shift so subtle Aria barely noticed, she was now looking out from them, feeling the heavy bones and thick tissues of Bantwalla's body as her own.

She saw Bantwalla's hand, her hand now, float now toward the wall behind them and reach for a smooth spot in the wall, one that Aria had already tried, and nestle the palm gently into it. In the next moment, the grating sound of stone against stone made Aria open her eyes. To her surprise, she was no longer standing where she had been when she went into her reverie, but now stood next to the opening door, her hand on the wall.

She drew in a quick breath, stunned to realize that she had crossed a barrier she had not even known existed. She had not simply imagined herself to be Bantwalla. Impossibly, for an instant, she actually had become Bantwalla, in some form. The door's triggering device had to be programmed to recognize a biofeedback or DNA signature, or some other physical attribute, and her own had not been recognized.

Aria stood before the now-open door in awe of the implications. Reality as she had known it was falling away like the walls of some long dead city.

She took a moment to feel her feet beneath her and stepped through the door, heard it close behind her. Her skin tingled as she climbed the final stairs to Njeri's portal. She passed into the brightly lit room where she, Bantwalla, and Njeri had taken tea and laughed together, but she saw no sign of the Guardian. The infant made a mewling sound and stirred in her arms. His eyes fluttered and his lips smacked. First things first, Aria thought. She would look for Njeri later.

She laid the boy on the wicker chair from where she had once heard Njeri's story, and worked the caftan up above her swollen breasts. For a few minutes, the little boy pulled at her milk as Aria gently rocked back and forth, as much to comfort herself as him. She listened intently to the noises he made at her breast, marveling again at how all the nerve endings in her body seemed to stand at attention as he suckled and how tiny beads of sweat formed on her brow, as though her body was marshaling all its energy to pour into him.

Soon his little mouth fell away again. She wiped it with the coarse fabric of the caftan and cooed over him until he drifted again into slumber. The noise of traffic outside the room intruded on her hearing now. She sat still, staring at the tiny particles of dust floating through the shafts of late afternoon sun that streamed through the window. She knew she must go out into that street, but she had no idea what way to turn when she was there. Fear threatened to return, but Aria took strength in remembering what had happened at the stone door below.

Time to go. Beyond the arched doorway on the opposite wall was another that led to the street. She gathered the infant and her bag again, and stepped into a small room with a heating plate and a few dishes stacked neatly on a counter. Another doorway opened into a bare, narrow foyer. Light poured from above through a single skylight in the roof. The furthest edge of the light illumined the back of an ornately carved, high-backed chair that sat facing a heavy closed door. Through the haze of light, Aria saw the rounded top of a head protruding above the chair's back. The hair showed the fine ridges of braiding.

It was Njeri, she knew, who sat there, motionless and silent.

She swallowed hard, her mouth dry. "Njeri?" she whispered.

No response. She edged toward the chair, its stark outlines ominous in the contrasting light and dark of the room. She came around the side and saw Njeri's beautiful profile—the full lips, the aquiline nose—but the eyelids, with their full lashes, were quivering.

Aria knelt directly in front of the seated woman. Njeri's eyes were rolled up so that the only part visible was the whites below the iris. Beads of sweat stood out on her broad forehead, and her hands gripped the arms of the chair as if it were careening wildly through space.

"Njeri," Aria whispered, and reached for the long fingers that curled over the end of chair's arm, but her hand paused in mid-air. The Guardian was in trance, she realized. This was not the time to jolt her back to this reality. Aria stared at the glistening black skin stretched over the high cheekbones and broad forehead. Then with the force of a blow, she realized what such a trance meant: the Guardians were linked. They were doing battle, creating their nightmares

444

for someone. Was it for those unfortunate souls in the council room, or were there others? Were The People under attack from without, as well?

Aria stood and looked at the door that led to the street, her heart pounding. There was a small panel at eye level, and she summoned her courage to inch it to the side and peer out.

No marauding hordes, uniforms, or menacing faces, only the occasional vehicle passing by on the street. She slid the panel back in place and turned again to gaze upon Njeri's face.

Goodbye, my friend. A wave of sadness and affection passed over her heart. You are a fine warrior. May you and I survive this ordeal, and find better circumstances.

She let the warmth swell in her chest and imagined it reaching out, surrounding the seated woman, strengthening and nourishing her. Then she turned, covered the infant's eyes against the bright light, pulled the caftan's hood over her own head, opened the door, and stepped into the street.

She searched the street and sidewalk for some sign of danger, but saw none. She turned and walked away from the door at an unhurried pace. Halfway up the block, something inside made her stop. She looked ahead and behind, at the dark windows in the buildings across the potholed road, but saw nothing unusual.

A small set of steps next to her led up to someone's front door. She nearly climbed them and knocked on the door, but hesitated. Slowly, she sat on the steps and began quietly rocking the bundle in her arms, opening her senses, reaching for whatever it was that halted her escape.

Minutes later, a small green cab lurched around the corner to her right and sped by where she sat, coming to a sudden, noisy stop across the street from Njeri's portal. The cab's door flew open and Aria saw the burly figure of Mothusi emerge, his face etched with anxiety. As he slammed the door and sprinted across the street, Aria leapt to her feet and headed back to intercept him. "M," she cried, "M."

The cab driver heard her just as he made the sidewalk and was about spring to Njeri's door. He turned and looked uncomprehendingly at the woman with an infant in her arms.

"Mothusi, wait," Aria said, and she motioned with her hand for him to come to her. Mothusi shielded his eyes from the sun's glare, and peered at her. Then his jaw dropped in a look of astonishment. He looked apprehensively at the door again, but he turned from it and ran to Aria.

"What's happen?" he asked, winded. "Why are you here, and what . . ."

Perplexed, he saw the child in Aria's arms.

Aria gripped his thick forearm. "We're under attack. I had to flee."

Mothusi's eyes widened, and Aria saw that he was about to turn and run back for the door.

"No!" she said, pulling at him. "No, you mustn't. Njeri's in trance. The Guardians are battling someone. You can't disturb her. It could be very dangerous."

M's face twisted in consternation. Aria felt his agony and desire to protect Njeri, to do something for his beloved community. "M, you cannot help anyone in there right now. There is nothing you can do. There were intruders, people who knew Parker was there. I don't know how or why. Something went wrong. They're all dead. I saw them. And I think someone else is trying to force their way in. The Guardians . . ."

She didn't have to say any more. She could see he understood the gravity of the situation. Unspilled tears rimmed the bottom of his eyes, and he looked down again at the infant, the question forming on his lips.

"Kay and Parker's child," she said. "They're . . . gone. Dead." Her throat closed around the words and she choked back a sob.

Mothusi's eyes closed, squeezing tears onto his cheeks. He moaned.

Aria gripped his arm tighter. "I need your help, M. We need you," she said, thinking of the boy in her arms. "Can you help us? Now?"

The pain in his eyes tore at Aria's heart, but he nodded silently.

"I must flee this city," she said. "I must go somewhere far away, north perhaps, hide this child. Protect it. I have some money. Help me, please."

His eyes were on her face, but it was as though he looked through her. Aria thought she had lost him. Then he shot a look over his shoulder again at the door behind which his beloved sat, and turned back to her. "M knows people who can help. Come, hurry."

They scurried across the street into the green cab. They sped away from the curb and M turned down a street darkened by the lengthening afternoon shadows.

They had traveled only half a kilometer when M slowed and turned into a side street, pulled over, and stopped. He pointed ahead, but Aria had already seen the group of what she guessed to be thirty men and women in the street halfway up the block. From their clothing and weapons, she knew they were a fighting unit, but they appeared to be fighting one another. In some cases, they fought nothing at all, swinging their arms wildly and aiming weapons at open air. Aria could see a half dozen lying still on the ground.

"They try to come in here," Mothusi said. Aria understood they must be near one of the portals.

Suddenly one of the men broke free of the group and ran toward them. Aria stiffened, but Mothusi put his hand on her knee, and she remained still. The man ran at remarkable speed, and when he was almost parallel with the cab, he turned to look back over his shoulder. The look of utter terror in his eyes made Aria shudder.

"Njeri does well," Mothusi said, the trace of a smile softening his grimace.

When the man had disappeared around a corner, M gripped the wheel and whipped the vehicle in the opposite direction. Twenty minutes later, they pulled up outside a small brown building in the far north sector of town. He told her to wait, and slipped inside the entrance. Aria lifted the sheet from the infant's face. Satisfied he was sleeping, she leaned her head against the seat back and closed her eyes.

A small feeling of gratitude rose inside her then, and along with the warmth of the sun shining through the window, she let it seep into her tense muscles, feeling their grip on her joints begin to relax. This felt right, she thought. Everything else might be going wrong, but this was right. M was a good and capable man. He would find a way for her out of the country. She sighed and felt her shoulders ease down to their normal position, her breath become steady and deep.

Where will we go? she wondered. In her mind, an aerial view of the African continent slowly took shape. She floated above it like the moon, appreciating the white peaks of the mountain ranges, the tiny islands amidst busy oceans, the pockets of valleys, some still impossibly fertile in the remote regions of the continents. A simple place. Somewhere we can live without the eyes of authority on us. Somewhere a boy can run free in bare feet and laugh and grow tall and find his soul.

She floated northward, above the deserts, across the blue ocean waters, tiny islands swimming into her vision. The Mediterranean Ocean and the ancient isle of Crete drifted beneath her. She remembered spending two days on a small island near Crete with the sisters when she was just a girl on tour: how isolated it seemed from the rest of the world, how the people there had lived uncomplicated lives, farming and raising animals, going to market. They had managed to avoid the attention of the Europa Council. At the time, the place struck her as stifling, deadly boring, and she could not imagine herself in such a place. Now, though, she felt the unmistakable inner pull it exerted on her. Yes, this could be a place to begin. A place to make a quiet stand and raise this boy.

M would help her get there. Wily and wise Mothusi. He would know people who could spirit her out of Africa, build her a new identity. She felt certain of it.

And if she used all her gifts, honored Kay's last request and poured all her love into this boy, maybe, if destiny held, he would become a light for others. The boy stirred in her arms, and Aria knew deep within herself this was true, despite the twisting, troubled path that might lie ahead. She felt it in his very presence, in the vitality and will coming from him. The world was hungry for this being, and he for it. They would meet fully someday and the world would be better for it.

The thought comforted her, and she caught the briefest of glimpses of the two faces she loved the most, Parker's and Kay's. She thought of their dream of a world of healers and harmony. They had missed it, but perhaps they had done just enough to make it come true.

Meanwhile, she thought, there was this moment, this sunlight warming us both, and someone we can trust coming soon to help us start our new life.

"We'll be fine," Aria said aloud to the babe in her arms, "you'll see."

As she drifted toward sleep, she imagined the words taking shape and rising through the open window, floating like seeds on an invisible air current, searching for a cool, damp place to fall to earth, a place out of harm's way, where they might sink their tender roots.

Epilogue

Barena Colter closed the door to her office, sat in the chair behind her desk, and rubbed her eyes. The strain of three eighteen-hour days was getting to her. She didn't think it would go on much longer, but at least until the hearings were over next week, she didn't expect to get a full night's sleep.

She sighed and thumbed her monitor to life. Several messages awaited. The first was a secure communiqué from the consulate in East Africa:

> Final attempt at council negotiations failed. Last remaining staff will be leaving tomorrow at 08:00. All records are either secure or destroyed. Sorry about this, Barena, but they just won't have us here for now. See you on Thursday.

Colter toyed with the thumbpad, watching the cursor skip around the screen from word to word, her eyes focused on nothing in particular. She felt like swearing, but she was too tired and it would do no good. This was a long time in the making, ever since the strike team had gone berserk in Dar es Salaam last year.

She couldn't really blame the East African Council for its hostility. After all, seventeen of their citizens had been killed in the streets during this sorry affair. How many had died underground was still an open question. Getting information had been nearly impossible. Still, this latest development was more bad news after a string of diplomatic missteps and expensive reparations. Among the first things to go after that incident were the potential water and uranium leases that were being negotiated at the time. Quite a few people had been burned in that one, a lot of plans changed. Indeed, it was a deciding factor in Mother Gretel being forced out of office. Colter hadn't seen or heard from her since. At least Mother Theodora, whom Colter now served, was an easier taskmaster.

Colter was still intrigued over the affair, especially Parker Potemkin's role in it. She hadn't been in favor of the mission to recruit him in the first place. Since then, however, she had learned more about him from the Nestercines, who were, for the moment, cooperating fully with the council. It was probably better that he had not returned, Colter thought. It seemed unlikely he was the sort who would easily have given himself over to the council's directives, and that would have meant more problems than benefits. Some of the other Tressaline progeny were showing leadership capability and proclivity for independent thinking. Time would tell if they manifested the potential that Parker was rumored to have had.

But was he dead? It was evident that Mardrid had at least attempted to carry out her assignment; otherwise, the outside team would not have been signaled by the discharge of her weapon, and subsequently tried to go in. Neither Avalon nor the assassin had surfaced either. The East African Council had shared none of their intelligence since the incident, and now with the North American Embassy closing down, there would be even less.

In her guts, Colter knew it was not the last they would hear from this affair. Since the incident, she had learned of a number of pitched battles in various sectors of Dar es Salaam. Whoever had occupied that underground community had been, and perhaps still was, a force with which to reckon. Maybe when the West African Council finally fell apart. She was nearly certain it would. Just last year three members had split off and formed their own alliance. War clouds were gathering.

She tilted her chair back and laid her head against the rest, unconsciously twisting a laser writer in her fingers as she stared at the ceiling. What did she care about all of this? She was approaching retirement. She didn't have to think about this anymore.

It was an argument she'd grown tired of having with herself. She could let almost everything go, but one thing kept coming back to gnaw at the bottom of her conscious mind: What about Aria Helsing? The fact that she'd gone missing before Mother Avalon and Mardrid had departed for Africa had almost gotten lost in the melee. But Colter remembered the last time she had called Helsing in to tell her to back off the K-1754 thing. Helsing's words of acquiescence were at odds with the glint of defiance in her eyes.

Investigators had established that Helsing had probably flown to Dar es Salaam, not New York as she had said. At first, the information led nowhere, and didn't appear important. Then, just last month, some low-ranking person in Intelligence had happened across Helsing's holograph and the old files of the case, and recalled reading some obscure reference to a woman matching her description—light skin, obvious North American roots, suspicious papers—having been seen in the Mediterranean region a year ago.

Colter had awakened the morning after receiving the report with a curious conviction that finding Helsing could be important. Some good investigators were on the project now. Maybe Helsing would turn up someday, maybe before

Barena was forced to retire.

It seemed important, but Goddess only knew why.

Thousands of miles away, Aria watched the seagulls atop the foam of the blue waves that eased their way onto the shore where she sat, the sun warming her back. The boy shouldn't be out in it much longer, but he was having such a good time, squealing as he outran the incoming waves, throwing pieces of torn kelp at the crying birds, digging for the little crabs that buried themselves in the sand with the tip of the big knife. Aria had tried many times to refuse him the use of the knife. In another child's hand, it would be dangerous. But the boy was inconsolable every time she took it from him, and was deft in his handling of the ceremonial blade. Besides, Aria found she could refuse him nearly nothing, so strong was his will and his power. After all, it was a gift from a father he would never know.

She could not look at it without vividly remembering severing the cord between mother and infant. She had named him Leon, in honor both of his grandfather, whom they had nicknamed "The Lion," and his grandmother Leona, about whom Kay had told her.

She smiled as she watched him now, all enthusiasm and vigor, his dark curls whipping in the steady onshore breeze and his limbs a constant flow of motion. She loved him so much sometimes she thought her heart would break into pieces. Now was one of those times, and as he waved at her, jumping up and down with his smile bright and his wet trunks clinging to his stocky little legs, she felt the old lump come up in her throat. He had Parker's brown eyes and strong chin, and Kay's fluid movements. And all their inner gifts. He was a handful.

Their lives here were a struggle. This was a primitive

place, far removed from the civilization on the mainland and the larger islands—and their prying eyes. Only rarely did she leave it. She managed to find work from time to time in the village, doing mostly manual labor—cooking for others, sewing clothes, cleaning toilets, tilling soil. When the villagers understood that Aria was no threat to their livelihood, and that she had unusual abilities to interpret dreams, the women with whom she worked befriended her and her sparkling child, if somewhat cautiously.

Last year Aria had begun to grow vegetables in a small plot of ground her adopted family had bargained with the neighbors for. It was all very primitive by the standards she'd learned under Bantwalla's tutelage, but she had learned well and her vegetables were becoming popular in the marketplace. Aria figured that next year, she and Leon would have their own place, and she could begin his schooling in earnest, although it was unclear who would be the teacher and who the student. Most of Aria's efforts were now spent in teaching the boy to mask and control his abilities in order to live among others.

Far offshore she watched the swell of ocean waves as they moved to unseen forces beneath and above, capturing the glitter of the sunlight in their dark mass. Her eyes teared in the bright light.

Or was it that the scene reminded her of Kay's dream? Aria marveled at the symmetry of it all, how she, and not the dreamer, now stood watching the horizon. No threatening wave loomed out there, no ominous roar as Kay had heard it again and again in her nocturnal wanderings. Aria wondered if Kay knew long before she that this moment would come, this shimmering moment in which her child would know life without fear, would live in the safe embrace of Aria's love.

The vapor trail of an SST scarred the face of the blue sky many miles above the horizon. This safety would not last forever, Aria reminded herself. Painful as it was to imagine, this tiny island would never be able to contain Leon's destiny.

But for now, there was his brilliant smile, and the fecund smell of the place where earth meets water, and the promise. Always the promise.

About the Author

James Townsend is a veteran of journalism, a musician and a student of the mysteries of consciousness. He lives in Boulder, Colorado, where he writes, plays music and enjoys the humbling presence of the Rocky Mountains.